I0831266

GABRIEL'S CREEK

Alan Livingston

Three Nineteens Publishing

COPYRIGHT

Gabriel's Creek

http://www.alanlivingston.com

Published by Three Nineteens Publishing,

Las Vegas, NV 89123

ISBN: 0-9915605-2-3

ISBN-13: 978-0-9915605-2-3

DEDICATION

With love and thanks to my wife, Mary, and the fine people that are both her children and my step kids; Eric, Chad, and Deanna Fischer.

You all deserved better.

TABLE OF CONTENTS

CHAPTER 1

"Sir? Excuse me, sir? Mr. Collins?"

I shook my head to come back to the present. I heard a young man behind the golf shop register trying to get my attention. He suspected my mind was somewhere else. "I'm sorry, yes?"

"You're welcome to hit away whenever you'd like to, sir." He paused as I looked up and smiled at him. "Of course, if you've changed your mind and would like to join the next group, they're wrapping up on the range right now." This kid was so accommodating to me this morning in the short time since we met. He could see that there was something odd about me today, and he was trying his best to help me without the attitude you might expect these days.

"Thanks very much, I think I'll go ahead. I appreciate your help." He returned my smile as I walked out of the shop. He was the first one there this morning; at least he was the one who unlocked the door to let me in just before dawn. He struggled to turn the key with a puzzled look on his face that said it was a rare day that golfers were already there before he opened. How different that look was, his look of excitement, not the annoyed ho-hum you might see at shops that always expect a crowd when they open their doors. I could tell that here they were used to having their second cup of coffee - or in The Kid's case, his second Red Bull – before someone rousted them. The expression on his face said he thought it was cool that someone would be waiting, waiting for him.

Earlier, I was sitting on the bench outside the golf shop ready for the one that turned out to be The Kid to open up. The beauty of the morning was astounding. The air was crisp and clear, and the rays of the morning sun reached across the sky as if stretching to wake up. Birds chirped with the sound that announced they were just awakening as well. I savored the scent, that wonderful morning golf course smell of fresh cut grass. In one direction, there was the sound of a distant greens mower humming. In the other direction but just as far away, I heard the distinctive and different sound of a tractor cutting the fairway. Between those two, the staccato *psst-psst-psst* of sprinklers spitting water in rhythm. As a day wears on at a golf course, you don't hear those sounds, and you don't smell these smells. I was so glad to be here this morning to enjoy them, today more than ever.

You see, I want to tell you about a big day for me, even though I was just another guy hanging around at a golf course waiting for it to open on this day. I was just a guy as happy to be there on that bench as anywhere, because I am one that always wished he could play every day, or at least somehow spend a majority of his time on a golf course. I've done neither. The truth is I don't play much anymore, and maybe I shouldn't say I play anymore at all. The fact is that it has been a few years since I've even been on a course. I have been away from golf for long stretches of time before, but this has been my lengthiest. It has been time through which both body and budget have begun to fail. Backs and shoulders and joints and money have conspired to keep me away from what I've loved for so long. Like being away from an object of your affection except for that lucky once-in-awhile visit, like the child moved far away that you seldom get a chance to see while they travel through adulthood. It has been as if a piece of my heart has been missing. "A piece of my heart missing": what a profound analogy.

You see, today is the last round of golf I'll ever play. I will be dying soon.

It has only been a couple of days – seems more like hours – since I learned I have precious little time remaining to live. I've been faced with how to use what little time might be left before I go on to whatever comes next; been compelled to spend some of that time here, alone at a golf course I never heard of until this morning. That's why every wonderful thing about the morning this day was magnified, every sense attuned to a keen level.

In many ways, my feelings are not unlike any other golfer at any other course on any other day. Every player is eager in anticipating a coming round. It goes beyond enjoying the beauty of Nature, with whom you'll spend your next few hours. It's the itching to make perfect contact, to shape a 4-iron around a tree limb on its way to the green, to drain the long bending putt, to feel the perfect flop shot nestle near the pin, knowing "today could be the day" on the tee of every par-3. All the senses are ticking, in overdrive. I'd love to play alone, but if I got paired up with someone, that's fine. I just hope I don't have to explain to anyone the real reason that I'm here.

All these, the sounds, the smells, the feelings – perhaps they mean nothing to the non-golfer. To them, it's just another day. Maybe the person uninterested in golf doesn't associate these sensory experiences with the game, but I do. To the person who loves golf, they are everything. I love golf, and have since I was a child. I've missed golf. I want these sounds, these smells, these feelings again, even if it is one last time.

The pre-dawn light this morning took me back to the events that brought me here. The subdued glow reminded me of lying awake in the hotel room near the hospital, the steady and rhythmic thumping of the window air conditioning unit's fan seeming louder every hour I remained awake. Struggling to get to sleep while running over and over the things on my mind was nothing new for me. What *was* new was trying to sleep just hours after being told I had only days to live. Glances at my sleeping wife turned into affectionate stares, but I succeeded in not waking her. I stared at her not so much because she was as beautiful as ever, but out of reluctance that I would be leaving her alone so soon.

It was a scramble to plan the trip to Houston for the battery of tests set up by my cardiologist back home in New Mexico. I didn't quite know how to plan our return trip so I left it open. The hotel that the hospital recommended felt like a college dorm room. It was small, but it had the essentials. Fighting insomnia, I had already tried the Murphy bed, the floor, and the couch. I got up to watch TV, laid down again, and repeated. Then, I would get up to read a magazine or a newspaper, have a cold sip of water, lie down again, and repeat. Unable to keep my eyes closed, I stared at the walls and the ceiling as the night moved on and on.

After travelling hundreds of miles for two days of tests, when your doctor looks at the floor and starts by saying, "This is never easy to tell a patient," you know it can't be good. My doctor began with just those words and my mind bristled, preparing for the new diet and exercise program, maybe even the surgery, the recovery process, all those things I expected he was about to tell me. He began to review my tests and their results one by one. Attempting to process what he was telling me, I was becoming more lost with every word of medical jargon. I was still focused on his opening words. If it was not "easy", why did he seem so comfortable going over the details of the tests now? I realized it was because he was in his professional comfort zone, but I wanted some comfort, too. I wanted to know what the hell the deal was. I couldn't keep myself from cutting him off.

"Doctor Crosland, I'm thinking this all comes to a particular punch line. Shall we cut right to the chase and revisit these details another time?" His face became washed with a look of resignation. Drawing a deep breath, he stood from his desk chair and walked around to sit on its edge in front of me. He was in a purposeful pause but I continued, "You've got a lot more experience at this than I do, but if you don't mind?"

"Chris, it's pretty simple: cutting to the chase means that there's nothing you or anyone else can do. You have days, maybe even hours. It is *not* weeks or months." Now my mouth hung open, silent, and unsure of what to say. My blood pressure accelerated, and my body swooned. He went on, "I can tell you with all the certainty that I have that it would be a waste for us to spend any of the little time you have left discussing alternatives. I can tell you that when this disease is found early, options exist. There is a history of some success with various treatments and therapy for this. It's unfortunate, but for you, we are just too late." The sound of his voice said the shock on my face wasn't unfamiliar to him. "My experience level does not make it any easier to tell anyone news like this, believe me. I can't tell you how sorry I am to have to do it. But you want me to *cut to the chase*?" In a tranquil and soothing voice now, he paused for affect after each word that came next: "You – are – done." His eyes steeled and fixed on mine, looking for all the different ways I might react. I sat staring at him in stunned silence. "Before you ask, I've reviewed your case with your home doctor, with others I trust, and with the hospital board, everyone, looking for someone to tell me that I am wrong. I just can't find anyone to tell me that." He paused. "Do you understand me? Chris?" I looked away, then back at him. He could tell that this was certainly not what I was expecting.

"Yeah. Yeah, I got it." I tried to let him know with my eyes if nothing else that I had heard and understood him. I didn't know what else to say, but he waited for me to find it. There was silence for what seemed like a long time, but may have been only a few seconds. He reached over and put his hand on my shoulder.

"I'm going to suggest you look at this like I do: you are very blessed, very lucky to know what I've just told you. You're so much more fortunate than the patients and families that I deal with every day." He leaned back. "I've known your doctor in Albuquerque since we were both fresh out of medical school. He's told me a lot about you. Often, I refer patients to a certain psychiatrist who could give you some guidance. I'll save you that trip because to be quite honest, there's no time. I want you to prioritize how you spend your time left like it *is* hours. Spend all the time you can with the people you love. Beyond that, if there's something you want to get done, forget it unless it's of deep importance to you. If you knew – and now you *do* know – that you only had time to finish one task, or to do one more thing, one more time, do it, and do it now. Right now."

Part of me wanted to go back into the tests, go over their results and try to understand the medical details that led to what he was telling me. The other part tried to pay attention to his advice to not waste another minute. I wanted to be with my wife. I should have caved in when she begged to come with me to Crosland's office. She was waiting back at the hotel, waiting for the news I would bring back to her. How would I tell her what I just learned? Of all the possible outcomes of this trip, this was the last thing we expected. How do you tell the woman you love, the partner that you both expected to spend many more years together, that you may die before you finish the sentence?

My mind raced to our two adult kids and a granddaughter about to have her first birthday. I ached to hold that grandchild in my hands. I began to envision not seeing any of them again. Both of our children appeared in my mind. How would I tell them, or should we tell them at all? My mind roared ahead, thinking of all the things that I wanted to say to my wife, my kids, those things you always wanted to say but did not. My thoughts went beyond that, beyond my family, to the need of mending all the potholes that life creates. Flashing past my eyes like the countryside does from the seat of a fast moving train, the face of every person I ever heard say that we should treat every day of life as a gift. How I wished that I would have heeded that advice long ago. Now, each *hour* would be a gift.

I could still hear the sound of the doctor talking. A quick look at him confirmed that he was making conversation, but I wasn't hearing him; my mental rocket was thrusting onward, the rushing and roaring sound in my head going with it. I have always been so focused on having everything prepared for the day I die, so that my wife and kids have as little to do as necessary. Now, all of a sudden, I felt completely unprepared. I began a mental audit, a run through the file cabinet at home, hoping everything was in order so whoever needed something could find it. My God, the guy I worked all the details out with at our local funeral home, I hadn't spoken with him in so long. Was he even still working there? What if he was not? What about all the insurance papers? Should we call the bank? What about our neighbors, our friends? I wanted to see my pastor back home. What would he advise me?

"Hey. Hey, Chris, are you in there?" Crosland snapped his fingers in front of my face, bringing me back to the moment, quieting the thundering sound in my head. I could hear what the doctor was saying now, and he was glaring at me hard. "Hey, you with me?"

"Yeah, yes. Sorry, I'm sorry. I've got to tell you I'm not sure what you were just saying." His expression told that he had seen this reaction before, too.

"It wasn't important anyway. Look, your time is valuable; I'll not monopolize another minute of it." I'd sure never heard *that* from a doctor before. He reiterated how lucky I was to know this news. He told me to be careful, because nothing meant I could not die first in an elevator accident or get hit by a car crossing the street. He said I should pick a day within the next few to be my last time to drive a car. "Don't want an accident to hurt someone else, you know."

"You said it might be hours?"

"OK, maybe that was a stretch, but yeah, it could be. Definitely think in terms of days, though." His fixed eyes were stern. "Days, I said. Weeks could happen, too, but think days."

"I guess there's not much else to say, then." His nod said the same in return. "I've got a lot to do, starting with telling my wife."

"That's a job I don't envy," he said with a warm smile, continuing, "But realize how fortunate you are to have the knowledge, and use it wisely. It's a challenge to decide how to use that time the best you can."

I looked around his office at the abundance of golf-related paraphernalia around the room. Framed posters titled "Challenge" and "Integrity", tee photos of the doctor with celebrities and friends, nick-knacks from pen and pencil sets to paperweights, all spoke to a love for golf. I recalled how my doctor back home told me so much about Crosland's reputation, emphasizing that his love for golf was one reason I could trust him. I felt his eyes follow mine before we met together in a stare that meant we understood each other. "You think I've got at least four hours?" A hesitant smile beamed across our faces together.

"Funny," he said, "Golf is a four-hour game, isn't it?" The doctor stood up and extended his hand, "Hit 'em good, Chris." My knees were weak as I stood. I could feel my arms quivering as I took his hand, "Hit 'em good," he echoed.

Walking out of the office, I knew I had to come to grips with how – or perhaps *if* – to share the news. Should I tell anybody anything? First and foremost was how to deal with my wife. It would not be fair to even consider not telling her. I had to. She might even be expecting the worst outcome of the tests while I was expecting the best. Cameron was most often right on health matters and I was most often wrong. What a bummer it turned out she was right this time. When I agreed to the Houston trip for my tests, it was not because I believed something might actually be wrong with me. I went neither because of my doctor's urging nor my wife's insistence, but just as an excuse to "get away" for a couple of days. I thought we might even go to an Astros game.

What should I tell friends? There were not many anymore, most of them people at church with plenty of others to pray for already, I thought. The few friends I had now, I was not close enough to share this with them. Old friends I was close to once, I didn't know how to find them anymore, much less whether or not they were still alive.

What should I tell our kids? I was convinced for years that neither of them could care less whether I was dead or alive. Now I wondered both if it was fair to believe that, and if it was really true. I felt that they loved me, but their lives had taken paths in such opposition to what any of us had wanted, and I felt responsible for that. Sure, I wanted to be a good provider, but as our kids became adults, I wanted to be involved in making life easier for them than it was for me. Like any parent, I wanted them to have the things that I never did. I wanted them to experience the good things that I did, too. Riding down in the building's elevator, I had the feeling I failed both of them in all those efforts. In reality there was nothing they could do about my situation anyway. The main reason to consider telling them what was happening was something very important to me: I wanted them to be there, to be supportive for their mother.

I made it from the medical office building out to the parking lot. I fumbled with the rental car keys. My still trembling hands had trouble unlocking the door. I finally got it open, sat inside, and pulled it shut. I sat motionless, staring straight ahead. Glaring at the steering wheel, I knew none of these things would get repaired right now. It was time to focus on getting our kids together with their mother, my wife Cameron.

CHAPTER 2

Our daughter Shannon lives in Huntsville, Alabama with her husband of three years, Dan, and their daughter, A'Dell. Shannon graduated from Auburn an engineer and soon found a job there where her boyfriend lived. They were married not much later. Our granddaughter's first birthday was just three weeks away. Our first and still our sole grandchild, we of course see her as perfect in every way. We were there for her birth and again a few months later. We've wished we could see her every day.

Shannon was an active child but never got into golf, maybe because she grew up in houses around golf courses. I could still see her playing on and around the golf holes bordering our back yards when she was young. Back then, if I had laughed with her more than I scolded her, or tried to be her Daddy more than her coach, maybe her feelings for me now might be different. As she got older and my career changed, life seemed to draw her and her brother farther away from me. Nothing seemed able to rescue those relationships, certainly not golf.

Dan is an office supplies salesman for a large business furniture and equipment company. He's not athletic-looking, but he pretty much excels in any sport he tries. His sole interest in golf is business related. For Dan, spending time on a golf course is just a means to an end, a way to close a deal. Maybe that was where Dan and I got off track at the beginning of our relationship – we didn't like each other on a golf course. I loved nature and being with the course. He enjoyed drinking, doing business, and playing to win in any sporting competition, no matter what that meant. As a result, Dan and I never enjoyed playing together. Our minds are as polarized on golf as almost any issue. Politics, religion, sports, you name it, we see eye-to-eye on just one thing: we both have intense love for my daughter. As far as I can tell, Dan is a good husband and a good father. Back when they were dating, my wife convinced me that I would never admit *any* man was "good enough" for my daughter. I woke up to the fact that this is true for any father, and accepted Shannon's maturity as being a better judge to identify who she would spend the rest of her life with. After that I was OK.

Years ago, my first meeting with my prospective father-in-law was on a golf course. It was the perfect situation for me at the time. In those days it was the forum that made me the most comfortable. I knew how much you learn about someone during your first round of golf together, and I wanted to make a good initial impression. I saw myself beyond acceptable as a prospective son-in-law in every way that should matter: I came from what I thought was "good stock", I was healthy, and I had a good job with a great future ahead. Most important to him, though, his daughter Cameron loved me. He and I enjoyed each other that day, we felt good about each other, and therefore I knew we would have a great relationship.

I drew a deep breath as I put the car key in the ignition. I hesitated, waiting another second before starting the rental's engine. I thought about how every parent faces decisions of whether or not to tell their children potentially disturbing news and if so, how. This was one of those times. Even if I didn't tell them about my situation, I had to find a way to get them together with their mother. If I were to come up with a quick reason to fly them to New Mexico, we couldn't afford to do that anyway.

I thought of how we could at least go spend a few days at our daughter's house. I gulped realizing how assuming the thought of "days" was for me. Whether we would have any time with our younger son Austin was a looming question. He lives pretty close to his sister, in Nashville, Tennessee. He would be happy to drive the 120 miles down to Shannon's because he'd love to see his Mother and sister, but he could care less about me. Maybe I could just get Cameron to call Austin and say she was going to visit Shannon. If we told him we were going up to Nashville to see him, he "wouldn't be able to get off work", the excuse he used on other trips we took there.

After a couple of years at Vanderbilt, Austin left school and started his own business, a limousine service catering to the music industry. I knew now that I had handled hearing his decision all wrong. I told him how stupid I thought it was to blow off the chance he had at such a great university, much less the investment we made for him already. For the sheer business opportunity it was, I thought he had a great idea. I wanted to support him beyond just the money, but his impatience to finish two more years at Vandy took me by surprise. I feared how he would look back at that decision 20 years later. Austin didn't see it that way. To him, I was being nothing more than a pain in his ass once again. Words a father and son should not say to each other were said, and couldn't be taken back. I was able to forget, but held out hope that the reality of his hatred for me would end. Up to now, it had not.

I was tough on Austin growing up, harder than on his sister, because I felt he needed it. If there was a silver lining to our relationship it was that his dislike for me was driving him to become successful. An unmarried workaholic, he was determined to shove his ability to do so well in my face, for spite if nothing else. I just wanted him to be happy. If being disgusted with his father led him to that, so be it. I knew the fruits of his labor would bring success that would give him great pride. I hoped that as years went by, he would grow to see my pride in him, and to know how much I loved him. My news seemed to make the chances of that impossible. I so wanted to mend our fences before the end came, but that didn't seem possible. I would have loved to play my last round of golf with Austin, to spend the day walking and talking with him: Father and Son one last time. He was a good athlete and a good golfer, much better than me. But he hated spending four minutes with me, much less half of a day.

The moment Doctor Crosland gave me the news I was so anxious to see A'Dell and our kids I just wanted to get to Shannon's as soon as possible – I didn't want to wait any longer. We took the next available flight out of Houston.

Back in that pre-dawn light now, I heard the key push into the lock from the other side of the golf shop door. I looked up to see The Kid and that pleasant, surprised look on his face when he spotted me on the bench.

“Good Morning!” He was split between excited and scared to see a player before he was ready. He stepped to the side, propping the door open with a small sand-filled bucket, which doubled as both a makeshift ashtray and a door stop. He was a very thin young man, about 5’6” tall. Soaking wet, he might have weighed 140 pounds. His do-it-yourself haircut and tiny wedding band said he was part of a young married couple watching their budget.

“Well, good morning yourself,” I said, still sitting on the bench. “I’m in no hurry. Please, take your time and just let me know when you’re ready.”

“Uh, well, OK, thanks! It will just be a few minutes, sir.” The Kid cracked me up, but I respected his good intentions. I drifted back into my thoughts, remembering the morning and how it brought me there to the bench. Those beams of the morning’s sunlight above me tried to wash away my anxiety. So many emotions swirled through me regarding my decision to play golf this morning, anxiety that had kept me awake much of the night.

In Shannon’s spare bedroom just hours before, my wife slept beside me. Her tossing and turning meant she shared many of the mixed feelings that I did about my decision to spend this morning on a golf course. Time was so short, we wanted all of it together, and we had come to Huntsville to be with the kids. What if something happened to me while I was on the course? What if this, why that.

Going to bed that night, my plan was to leave around dawn, giving myself time to drive to the Robert Trent Jones course half an hour outside of town. Dan said he would be getting up for work about the time I planned to leave, so he offered the use of his clubs. He would get them for me when we both grabbed coffee before heading out. Insomnia got the best of me, though. I didn't feel like I'd slept, but maybe I did at least a little anyway. When I saw "4:00" on the nightstand clock I threw the covers off and got up. So what if I arrived at the course too early? I would just wait until they opened up and let me go. Being as quiet as I could, I washed my face and shaved, ran a brush through my thin grey hair and threw on the clothes I'd readied before going to bed. I took my shoes in hand, and maintained my old ritual, leaning down to kiss my wife goodbye.

"You leaving already?" She was still more asleep than awake.

"Yeah, honey. I'll see you later." I kissed her again on the forehead. "I love you."

"Love you, too," she said, rolling over, back to sleep.

Dan wasn't up yet, so I decided to skip coffee. I could get that at the course. Besides, I didn't need his clubs anyway. He was less concerned about helping me have equipment to play with than he was being a pompous ass. He just wanted to make sure I knew that he owned the top of the line in everything golf-related. It was all in a huge bag that would make anybody but him groan to pick it up and carry for even the shortest distance. I looked forward to telling him later in the evening that I decided I would rather just rent a set for the day when I got to the course. I grinned as I premeditated my rude comment, knowing I would be wrong to say it just the same.

The night before, I studied a map well enough and I talked to Dan about how to get to the Hampton Cove course. I felt good about where I was going and how to get there. It was still pitch dark when I pulled away from the house around 4:20. I found my way to Governor's Drive, headed east and then southeast away from the urban sprawl of the city on U.S. 431. The sparse amount of traffic was still in that night-creatures-only mode, which was turning into farmers-only the farther out of town I drove. I found my left turn to the northeast and knew I was getting closer. The natural anguish of finding and playing a new course, a tough course unknown to me, playing with people I did not know, all of it began to intensify when I realized I was within a couple of miles from the entrance to my destination.

I drove the two-lane road with the worn-out center stripe through the Northern Alabama hills. There was just enough light from the moon and the pre-dawn creeping over the horizon that I could see the serene countryside. I looked around at forested slopes fronted with lush pastures and occasional farmland. From a distance my headlights caught a short series of six-foot planks on sticks no more than five feet above the ground, just the other side of the barbed wire fence along the right-of-way of the road. With a nostalgic smile, I bet myself that they were old "Burma Shave" signs, and wondered how any of those could still be around. Drawing closer, I saw that these signs were peddling something else.

"Good Golf" – "Near By" – "Gabriel's Creek". The hand-painted signs were weathered but readable. They were spaced apart so that you were digesting one just as you saw the next. "Past Golf Trail" – "7 more miles" – "Come see us!" The apparent age of the signs made me wonder if such a golf course could still be there. Each sign's wood was cracked and dry, and they were mounted on posts that both time and wind had crocked askew. Some letters in the old water-based paint were barely legible, looking like they were drawn on with the ball of a shoe polish applicator. Driving away, they were behind me when I wondered why I never heard of another golf course out this way. Dan hadn't mentioned it, but perhaps it just wasn't pretentious enough to suit him.

I remembered looking online while we flew from Houston to Huntsville, looking at the golf course listings for the area, thinking ahead to the possibility of doing precisely what I was now. I didn't remember seeing anything about Gabriel's Creek, but maybe it was because I was so focused on the Golf Trail course. The state of Alabama has every right to brag about The Trail. It includes courses I played years ago in Mobile and Greenville with other locations around the state. Thinking ahead to my mission of getting in a round while we visited Shannon, maybe on the plane I just wanted to play the Trail course so much I'd ignored any others I saw – yes that had to be the reason I didn't recall it. This part of the world seemed so perfect for great golf with its lush vegetation, warm days and cool nights, cutting the terrain through the hills. Maybe there were several golf courses in the Huntsville area my subconscious ignored.

Now, just ahead around the bend of the road, I saw the entrance to the Trail Course. It was marked with a heavy expensive brass sign that swung from a huge flagstone pedestal the height of a large tree reading, "Hampton Cove Golf Course". I slowed down and put on my turn signal for the right turn I was about to make. Thoughts flashed through my head, starting with those old wooden advertising signs again. Like magic, I felt them reaching for me from behind as if they were beams from a lighthouse. Then, all my earlier apprehensions about Hampton Cove returned. I realized that I didn't have a tee time anywhere anyway, did I? Cameron would be pissed that I didn't go where I told her I'd be, but she was still sleeping. I had a cell phone to tell her later, and I knew my wife would understand. Besides, if this "Creek" place turned out to be a goat ranch I still had plenty of time to come back here, right?

I turned off my blinker and resumed speed, passing the turn off with a newfound wonder of what might be seven miles ahead. Dawn's early light grew as I passed a light pole, whose bulb turned off just as I passed under it. I drove on with an eye ready to find the forthcoming turn into Gabriel's Creek.

"Yes, sir, we're ready for you now, sir," the voice of The Kid just inside the door he'd just opened brought me back.

"Thanks," I said, and got up off the bench to walk inside. I immediately felt at ease in this small, modest shop with its dated furnishings. It was a very long way from the country clubs and multi-star resort golf shops I'd become accustomed to as a young traveling professional. But, it was so close to the kind of shops I hung out in as an adolescent learning the game many, many years ago.

The store fixtures looked like they came from a retail store's closing sale. There were two glass cases forming a cashier's cubicle with a cheap office mega-store register on top. Large, almost blank tee sheets were spread out next to the cash drawer. Behind the counter, a doorway led to a back room. Above that open door, the circa-1975 plastic Pepsi clock felt perfect, in touch with the dark paneling on the walls. Planks fashioned into shelving using a few L-shaped braces and screws made room to display a variety of boxed balls. In one corner, a floor display with a sparse selection of shoes was there just in case somebody needed a pair. Four circular shirt racks had a similar low number of items hanging on dollar-store hangers. A homemade wooden rack with rough notches in it ran along a wall at the height of a chair rail. Against it, several putters and a few wedges stood at attention, hoping to be sold.

The staining of the ceiling tiles suggested this building had its share of roof leaks during heavy rains. Bathroom entrances were at the back of the shop where a separating glass wall's door led to a small grill. Eight round cocktail tables with four empty chairs each and eight empty stools at a dining counter stood ready for any impending breakfast orders. Beer taps faced the stools and clean liquor bottles lined up along the mirrored wall behind the counter. It was obvious that the bar and grill's stock turns over faster than the golf shop's. Two guys leaning against the opposite end of the counter were course maintenance employees. One had a cup cutter in his hand and a tool belt was on the waist of the other. They were engaged in a smiling contest with a flirtatious young woman who was the grill employee. Their laughter in the background said she wasn't busy making breakfast for anyone at the moment.

"I'll be right with you, sir", said The Kid, straightening the large manual tee sheets and other desk items as if preparing for a morning rush. Out of the door behind the counter came a tall, sturdy man, wearing a wrinkled PGA polo shirt, khaki pants, and spikeless two-tone golf shoes. The attire said he was the Professional, even though his ruffled hair and unshaven face suggested he just woke up from sleeping in his car. He nodded "Good Morning" toward me with a smile as he walked to a storage closet near the bathrooms.

Now ready, like he was following a training script, The Kid asked, “So, what can we do for you today, sir?”

“Thought I’d chase a little white ball around for a while, say 18 holes?”

He shuffled the tee sheets, saying, “OK, let me see”, studying them, even though I could see they were pretty blank. Out of the corner of my eye, I saw the Pro come out of the storage closet and lean against the door jamb. I could see his sigh more than I could hear it while he listened to The Kid’s routine.

“For Heaven’s sake, Doug, ring the man up and let him go, would you?” They exchanged a look that said this was not the first time this now-named Kid had been told that. Doug just wanted to be in a position where he had to achieve squeezing somebody in.

“Uh, OK, how many in your group, sir”, Doug asked me. The Pro just looked to me with a grin.

“I’m just a single, but if you need to pair me with somebody, I don’t mind”, I told him. Doug looked up at me, then to the Pro, as if excited at the prospect of proving he could manage his tee sheet today.

Startling me, outside behind the building a dog’s loud bark stole everyone’s attention, most of all Doug. It was easy to see that he both knew the dog and had been unsure where it was. “There he is! Mr. Skip could you –.”

“I got it, Doug, go ahead.” The Pro motioned toward the door just as his young assistant leapt over the counter and ran out the door like he was on fire. He zoomed around the corner, back to where the dog’s sound came from.

The Pro chuckled, "I've never figured out what I did to deserve either the boy or the dog, but somehow this place seems to need 'em both." I laughed with him.

I was happy with myself that I didn't show the affect a dog's bark still had on me. It was a little over two years ago now that I lost the second of my two animals within a year, two dog-friends that meant the world to me, both as individuals and as a collective team. They were at home anywhere I was, which meant they loved being around anything golf-oriented. For years and years, as they ripened into "a couple of old dudes", I always hoped they would outlive me, because I never wanted to deal with their deaths. Now, I was so glad that they would not have to deal with mine. I flashed on how anxious I was to see them both again, and soon.

I looked away from the Pro to hide any visible emotion that might well up in my eyes. Turning my head, I could see through the glass wall and into the grill. Large, panel-size windows opened up the room on the two exterior walls. Another door split the nearest wall and opened to the front of the building. There, a gravel parking lot that never filled with cars had railroad cross ties as stops to mark the parking spots. Along the far wall, windows starting at the corner of the building ran back to where the counter ended with a lift-up staff opening. The view outside was a panorama down into a valley and back up a distant gentle slope. The thick forest that started to the right behind the building bordered a green that was just a gentle grade down from the corner of the clubhouse. A flag flapped on a pole in the center of the green below the windows, the number "18" showing when it furled out. The long 18th hole flowed down to a creek that crossed it. Just past there the ground rose to a flattened tee where those same woods became the horizon.

The vista from the grill lacked the definition one would see from the clubhouse of many other golf courses, those where the different shades of green shift from the deeper forest color of the denser rough, first to the second cut, and then lighter to the tightness of the mowed fairways. No, it was not Augusta National, but it neither pretended to be nor wanted to be. As I stood looking out there, I could feel it telling me it wanted to be nothing other than Gabriel's Creek. It reminded me more of looking out across a farm. Often over the years I labeled what I pre-judged to be substandard courses as a ranch, a pasture, or a farm, but this was so different. I hoped this was nothing I would ever label as negative. It was simple, and it was peaceful. It put a warm smile on my face. I felt like I was glowing inside. At that moment I knew I could stand there and gaze out at the beautiful view from the grill for hours.

"You a coffee drinker?" The Pro's question startled me.

"How'd you guess?" He started toward the grill and I followed him. He grabbed two small white foam cups and set them on the counter, turning to take the fuller of two commercial coffee pots off the double hot pad. After pouring the first one, he pushed it towards me, and then he filled the second cup for himself.

CHAPTER 3

He stuck his hand out across the counter and we exchanged a firm handshake when he introduced himself. "The name's Arnie. Arnie Bartlett. I'm the Golf Professional here." He paused with anticipation, waiting for me to return the introduction.

"Chris, Chris Collins. Nice to meet you, Arnie." I looked around the room, adding, "Nice place you have here."

"Yeah, it's practically the Pebble Beach of Northern Alabama," he said with a chuckle.

"Eye of the Beholder, wouldn't you say?" It was an honest feeling; to *my* eyes, the place was great. He grabbed two spoons and placed them near us on the counter, shoving together a small container of sugar and sweeteners, along with a small bowl holding five small packaged creamers inside. He nodded to the condiments, indicating I should help myself.

"Where you from, Chris?"

"New Mexico now, but I'm originally from Texas."

“No kidding? I’m from Texas, too. Whereabouts?” He looked excited that we were both Texans, but there’s a lot of room in Texas to be from.

“Weatherford.” The furrowed brow said he was not quite sure where that was. “Little town about half an hour west of Fort Worth.”

“Gotcha. I was a lot further west than that. Grew up down in Marfa, then moved to the bright lights and big city of San Angelo after college.” I knew both of the West Texas towns well. “You been out of Texas long?”

“About a hundred years,” I joked. “I went to school at TCU, and then left after I graduated 40 years ago. Never got back much after all my kin were gone.”

“TCU – a Horny Toad!” People always had a remark if they knew the Horned Frogs.

“Yeah, yeah,” I groaned, proud though I am of my alma mater. “What about you?”

“I stayed at home for college up the road at Sul Ross in Alpine. Got my degree and went into the oil business, first in San Angelo, then up in Sweetwater,” he spoke of another West Texas place I was familiar with. “Got married a few times, divorced a few times, made enough money to support the ex-wives and realized I needed to get back to golf for my own mental health.” I was envious of the decision he made before I knew anything else about it. He sipped his coffee and continued, “Somebody knew someone who knew a man who owned a little golf course in a pretty little part of the world with lots of trees and lots of good people. His name was Gabriel, ‘Mister Gabe’ to us. He didn’t mind owning the place, but wanted somebody else to run it. He was looking for a golf man who wasn’t looking to make a ton of money. This part of Alabama seemed to be the perfect distance away from wife number four in Arizona, so it sounded good to me. I needed money a lot less than I needed a place like this. Been here going on 20 years." I was impressed.

"You don't look old enough to have done all that and been here that long," I noted. His eyes and his skin had a weathered look about them, the signature of someone who was outside a lot, befitting a golfer. It was more than that, though. He had a healthy, almost nautical look. If I tried to guess his age, I could be wrong in a range from 15 years older than me to 15 years younger.

I followed those eyes as they looked out the grill windows, out over the course. The fondness in his eyes was both pride and wonder together. "There's something magical about this place." He turned a piercing stare into my eyes in a way that made me think he'd been waiting for me to get here so he could tell me what followed: "These hills will do things to you that you'll never forget."

I wasn't sure just what he meant, but the comment was strange enough to make me a little uncomfortable. I sought a change in subject, and glanced behind him. "So, is the grill open?"

"Sure, you hungry?" He asked the question but didn't wait for an answer, spinning around to spread some oil across the grill.

I took a drag of coffee, wondering how to get out of a big breakfast that I really didn't want. "Maybe just something quick to walk with, just to tide me over. I got started a little early this morning."

The words were leaving my lips when The Pro cracked two eggs on the grill, and then threw four slices of bacon next to that. The reaction of the others in the room meant a special event was getting underway. The other employees moved over to create an audience and my discomfort grew. I wondered what I'd gotten into. I could feel a couple of golfers over in the shop leaning our way, looking to see what the commotion was. The maintenance man on my side of the counter saw their curiosity. He took a couple of steps toward the passage between rooms and raised his voice so they could hear. With genuine excitement, he said to them, "Skip's making his Special!"

Arnie noticed my expression, wondering who Skip was. "Skip, that's what they call me. It's a long story." He smiled and grabbed an empty, almost flat, square stainless steel container in one hand, and a gallon jug of Red Hot sauce in the other. "You *did* say you're from Texas, didn't you?" He asked while he poured an inch or so of the fiery red liquid into the vessel.

The girl behind the grill wore a name tag that said she was "Claire". She jumped into expediter mode, tossing an almost new loaf of Texas Toast into the prep area. She grabbed two chilled glass mugs from a cooler under the beer taps and set them on the counter near our coffees. The Pro continued cooking while she grabbed two small sandwich plates.

"For you, we'll just call it Skip's Welcoming Gift," he said, drawing a cackle from everyone watching. While he spoke, the girl took a few slices of processed Pepper Jack cheese out of the cooler. Arnie grabbed four slices of bread from the loaf. Like anybody would make French toast by dunking the bread into egg, he soaked first one side and then the other in the vessel of hot sauce, and then slapped each down onto the grill: one, two, three, four slices, like he was on autopilot. My eyebrows rose a little more with every sizzle of the toast hitting the hot grill. All eyes in the place were beginning to burn with mine when the sauce cooked into the bread. He moved fast with a spatula to flip the bacon and stir the eggs. Claire put two slices of cheese on a plate in his prep area. "How's your heart?" he joked as the audience chuckled.

"Hungry!" I said, aware that he couldn't know the truth of how bad my heart was. I knew whatever concoction he was making for me was not going to make any difference to my health at this point. Watching him create, I was more concerned about my stomach.

"Mr. Skip! Mr. Skip, I found him, I found him!" Doug came running into the golf shop carrying an excited black and white dog who struggled to lick his face while the boy carried him. Everyone looked up to see him and smiled at the sight of the dog, suggesting he was the course mascot. The Kid stopped in his tracks near the register when he saw Arnie working at the grill, and put the dog down. The Border Collie ran into the Grill and in two leaps, used a table's chair to launch himself to a quick halt on top of the counter stool that was right next to mine, tail wagging and panting fast, with a smile of readiness to eat on his face. No one but me followed his action with a look of surprise. It was obvious that to all other onlookers, this was a normal occurrence.

Doug stood still since putting the dog down. He seemed torn between following the dog into the Grill and darting back behind his register, lest he miss a big sale. There was, after all, a crowd of two people in the shop. He smelled the cooking in the air and knew what was in production. The Pro didn't hesitate to put more eggs and bacon on the grill, finishing ours while he began making more. "Don't worry, Doug, I've got you covered," The Pro yelled out of the grill.

"Thanks, Mr. Skip!" Doug smiled with excitement as he moved behind the counter, ready at the register. "But, uh, Mr. Skip could you –."

"Yes, Doug, I've already got one going for Ralphie, too," Skip said over his shoulder. He turned and looked at me, where I sat at the counter taking in all the action. He saw I wondered who Ralphie was. "Chris, meet Ralphie." He nodded at the dog on the stool next to me. This looked like one happy, healthy, and clean dog, his coat shiny with rich, contrasting black and white fur. His moist black nose and bright white teeth highlighted his face with brilliant blue eyes, perky ears, and a wet red tongue that darted in and out of his smile when he panted.

The dog and I turned to look at each other at the same time and our eyes met. In that non-verbal communication that exists between people who like dogs and dogs who like people, we said, "Nice to meet you," to each other. His eyes suggested we would both feel even better if I scratched him on top of the head between the ears, and I did so with pleasure. "Good dog," I said to him, thinking of my departed canines.

Back on the grill, Skip was finishing the first two of what might best be called breakfast sandwiches. Two pieces of grilled hot-sauce-soaked thick toast were married with scrambled egg, a slice of cheese, and two slices of bacon. Skip cross-cut each one into halves with the spatula while Claire poured the two mugs to the top with ice cold milk. Onto the plates he tossed the first two completed sandwiches, the ones he made for the two of us. His motion at the grill continued. He chopped two pieces of bacon and mixed them with more scrambled egg, scooping it all into a small bowl that Claire had already placed in front of him. Skip went back to finish the sandwich he started for Doug. Claire tore up a slice of cheese and garnished the bowl. Ralphie was thrilled when she set the bowl on the counter in front him.

Without looking over his shoulder, Skip said, "I don't give Ralphie the toast anymore – the hot sauce gives him the farts." Claire and the maintenance man nodded their heads in animated agreement. The dog just smiled.

We all laughed watching a cheerful Ralphie inhale his breakfast bowl reminiscent of how my two dogs enjoyed their treats for so many years. Skip displayed the skill of an experienced waiter when he grabbed three small plates containing one Special each in one hand and his coffee in the other. "Chris, how about you snag the milks and your coffee, and follow me, please sir?"

I did so, not knowing why we weren't going to eat in the Grill. He walked toward the counter of the golf shop and set The Kid's plate down on top of the tee sheet. Doug grabbed it and placed it out of sight behind him. "Thanks, Mr. Skip!" Doug's appreciation implied not much cooking like this happened at home, maybe the reason he looked almost anemic.

I followed Skip around the counter and back through the door under the Pepsi clock into a small room. The original building must have used it as a storeroom. Now, it was Skip's office. A small desk looked like one you might see on a curb the day of trash pickup. Someone beat the garbage collector to it and placed it in here. The pitiful desk was distinguished with what I knew to be an official Professional Golfers' Association pen and pencil set, with a fine nameplate proclaiming it with pride the desk of "Arnold 'Skip' Bartlett", along with the PGA seal. An old, beige push-button telephone was on the desk, the kind that had a few clear buttons across the bottom of the face for multiple lines. I hadn't seen a phone handset like that in years.

One end of the desk was pushed up against the large pane window that took up most of the exterior wall. Through its value-priced, self-applied tint, Skip had a good view of the cart barn, the practice range, and the putting practice green outside the clubhouse. Traffic to each of those, by foot and by cart, moved not far outside the window. The opposite wall was crowded, covered with many small inexpensive frames containing photographs covering his life. In a range of ages from high school to today, he was shown with many different people. There were a variety of attractive women enjoying happy times, and there were several tee photos with men, some of whom I recognized as professional golfers and celebrities. A few pictures showed men holding shovels standing in front of oil rigs at different locations. Another was of a younger Skip and an older man in front of what looked like the building we were now sitting in. There must have been 50 small frames covering this small wall.

Skip walked around to his desk chair, motioning for me to pull up a small side seat to the front of it. He placed one of the two plates he carried on my side of the desk. "Take a load off, Chris." In the open closet behind his desk, a terrific PGA Professional staff golf bag leaned into the corner. I didn't have to see the side facing away from me to know it was embroidered with Arnie's name. Having the bag so handy at his fingertips but still out of the way said that while Skip was quite proud of being a PGA Professional, he was too busy to play except on occasion. I knew I was right without asking him.

"Thanks," I said, setting my coffee down with the two milk glasses, one in front of him. "So, what's the long story about the name 'Skip'?" He snickered while we both got comfortable. He reached to a small pile of napkins on a file cabinet behind him and placed a few in front of each of us. I expected something about boats, ships, the Navy – something of a maritime nature. Just before we both took our first crunchy bite of the sandwich at almost the same time, the story began:

"I was on the golf team in high school. There was this one jackass on the team that was giving me constant crap about a girl he asked out to the Prom that day. Seems it was the same girl I told him a week before that I was going to ask." He saw my eyes light up when I chewed my first taste of the Special. Pausing his story when he saw me trying to breathe, he chuckled and asked me, "You OK?"

This may have been the best tasting thing I'd ever eaten, but yes, it was hot. A just-right-for-a-Texan hot, my mouth was on fire but at the same time very pleased with the egg, bacon, and cheese crunching with the toast. "Yeah, see, you can tell it's perfect: my eyes are tearing up and my nose is running already. Man, this is delicious!" I was being quite honest.

"Glad you like it," he said. "Somehow, I knew you would." Whether his omniscience was another indication that this place was indeed magical, or he was just noting that any Texan should enjoy his creation, I was unsure.

"Now I know why the cold milk comes with it." We both took a swig to chill the heat of the toast.

"Anyway, this little son of a bitch was getting on my nerves," his story continued. "He only asked her 'cause I hadn't yet. I should have made the date with her before he did. I snoozed, I lost, and he wasn't going to let me hear the end of it." We continued eating as the story went on. Putting his food down, he used his hands to help describe the next scene of the story while he told it. "We're on the 18th hole, this long par 5 that has a wide lake across the front of the whole green. There are some trees just into the rough on either side of the fairway, too. I push my second shot over to the right, short of the lake but right smack dab next to a tree. The trunk is blocking my stance, and the limbs are restricting my swing. I've shoved my ball into this spot where I've got an impossible third shot, so he just gets louder."

I follow his descriptions with a vivid vision. While he talks and I eat, out of the corner of my eye I see a black and white dog, moving stealthily, almost tip toeing into the room. He sits next to me with quiet and patient anticipation while I continue eating. Ralphie reminds me of the two dogs that would do pretty much the same thing anytime I ate in front of them.

"He's jacking his jaw because he's sitting up there real nice in two, just 10 yards left of the green after clearing the lake with his second shot." We're finishing up our sandwiches but I feel Ralphie wanting me to make sure I save a little for him, which I do as The Pro keeps going. "Now, since it's the 18th, the rest of the team is up behind the hole waiting for us to come in, the coach with his clipboard and everybody else. A couple of guys even had their girlfriends there waiting with them. It's like a real gallery out there, and he's standing on the green yelling at me about this girl and telling me how much my game sucks. I'm just trying to figure out what to do with my shot."

My attention is divided between anticipating the end of the story and Ralphie. He is peeking up at me with a premeditated sad look on his face, his ears up. I try to focus on Skip's tale while I try to remember the importance of *not* slipping the dog anything with hot sauce when the time comes.

"Anyway, I figure out what I'm gonna do, so I yell back at him. I say, 'Hold it! Here's the deal: I'm going to get my third shot on the green, and you're going to shut the hell up.' He stops, not knowing what I mean. I yell, 'If my third doesn't end up on the green, I'll pay for your dinner on Prom night.' He stood still as a stone while this smile grew from one of his ears to the other. I yell again, 'But if I get it on the green, you shut up about all this, and I mean you shut up forever'". I wondered if I was about to hear there was more to the bet. "He yells back, 'Is that all?', and I say 'Yep, that's it'. He says, 'I got expensive dinner tastes, and so does your – oh, I'm sorry, I mean *my* date!' What a smart ass."

I wiped my mouth with the napkin, listening while Ralphie's stare got stronger. The dog licked his lips. "I set myself up, hooded a 7-iron and put it way up, way in front of my feet." He stood up now, becoming more animated to demonstrate the shot, "I whipped up and through it, keeping my hands way ahead of the ball. I avoided all the tree's parts with a follow through that made me look like I was fencing. I put as much topspin on it as I could." I knew what he was talking about, because most golfers have tried this at one time or another.

"The ball took off and flew like a fast knuckleball. It skipped *five times* on the lake, you know, like how a flat rock does when you throw it. It hit the bank on the other side just as perfect as you could imagine." He sat down to continue, "My ball hopped up, landed in a slow roll, crawled across the green and stopped about six feet from the pin. Our teammates stood up and cheered while the smart ass didn't say a word. I walked around the lake and up to the green with my putter while everybody was waving towels, clapping and chanting, 'Skip! Skip! Skip!'" We laughed together. "You could say the name stuck." His expression indicated that was the end. "I *told* you it was a long story."

"It's a long one but a great one. Thanks for sharing it."

"It's a longer one to explain how the girl heard the story from everybody, and dumped him. She went to the Prom with me anyway, and we got married right after graduation." I didn't expect that conclusion. "That was my first wife – the first of four." He pointed up to the wall that was filled with pictures. I took that to mean she was up there somewhere.

"Four?" I asked, wondering which of the several pictured women on the wall had been wives, and which one was that first wife.

"Well, yeah. Practice, practice, practice, you know. That fourth one, though, she was a good one. I shouldn't have messed that one up." A grin of fondness crossed his lips. "God, she was hot."

"What happened?"

"She thought it would be better if we were saving the money I was spending on drinking," we both chuckled as he paused for effect. "I disagreed." We chuckled louder.

I wanted to change the subject again. "I've got a friend down here looking for a handout." I nodded down at Ralphie, who was still patient and waiting.

"He's famous for that," he said as he noticed the small bite I kept on my plate. "Sure, go ahead." I handed the scrap to a happy dog. Skip continued, "You could give that dog a full turkey dinner on Thanksgiving, and he'd still be at your feet wanting your leftovers."

I scratched the happy animal in the similar spot between the ears as I did before. "Seems like an awful good dog."

"He just showed up out of nowhere one day as a pup. We put up notices on phone poles; put an ad in the paper and everything." He now spoke as if a proud father, "But it got to where we just didn't want anyone to come claim him, because he became a part of the course. Doug still freaks out anytime he runs off, but that dog isn't going anywhere – he loves us almost as much as we love him." He leaned over, gave Ralphie a wink and a smile, and said, "Don't you, dog?" Ralphie replied with one sharp bark. "Yeah, he's a good dog. Part of the place more than you can imagine."

"You gotta love a good dog," I chimed again.

"Matter of fact, Ralphie and Doug are an awful lot alike." Arnie muted the volume in his voice a bit as he switched the conversation to his shop attendant. "Doug dated his girlfriend, Martha, all the way through High School." He looked out of the office door to make sure Doug was on station at the counter and out of hearing distance as he continued. "End of the summer after they graduated, Doug goes off to school at Calhoun Community College down the road in Decatur." His voice grew softer while the story developed, "Came home for a football game one Friday night. Lo and behold a few weeks later, Martha's pregnant. Doug's Dad comes to me – Bubba used to play out here a lot – comes to me and asks if I've got a job for a kid that's going to be a daddy way sooner than he should be." Arnie leaned back in his chair, arms outstretched. "How could I *not* find something for him?"

We both looked out at Doug now. I said, "He sure seems like a good kid."

"That's what I mean," Arnie said, pointing first at Ralphie, then out at Doug, "Good dog, good kid." We both nodded, agreeing to the analogy. "That kid is the salt of the earth, always here and always on time. He loves that baby and takes care of that girl." He continued with the sad by-products, "But he left school and hasn't gone back. You know how that goes – he never will, he just can't admit it yet. I talk to him once and awhile about getting in the PGA Apprentice program, maybe even over at Hampton Cove. If he doesn't go for that, I'd like to see him get a real job, like out at Redstone Arsenal or something, but," he realized it was time to end the story, "You know how kids are."

"Yes, I sure do."

CHAPTER 4

The line button on Skip's desk phone began blinking when the telephone rang out front at Doug's counter. The light changed to steady when Doug answered it as Skip asked me a question: "So, Chris, just what kind of golfer are you, anyway?" Just then, Doug poked his head in the door.

"Excuse me Mister Skip, its Larry out in the shop on Line 1. Can you talk to him a minute?"

"Sure." Arnie picked up the handset and pushed the lit button. He looked at me and said, "This should just take a second." He looked out the window toward the cart barn and spoke into the phone. "What can I do for you out there, Larry?"

I stared out the large pane window and processed the question. I wanted to come up with a short answer because it could be a very long one. The Pro knew that what a person is on a golf course tells so much of their story – what you are on a golf course is a reflection of what you are in life. He was asking about *me*, not about my golf.

"Well, you've got to get those bed knives sharpened, Larry," Skip said into the phone. His authoritative-manager voice was pretty much the same as his shooting-the-breeze voice. I rose up a little in my chair and motioned to Skip, checking to see if he wanted me to leave the room while they talked. He shook his head and pointed for me to stay seated. "Keep your seat, I'll just be a minute," he whispered. Only a few seconds passed while the call continued. I tuned out his conversation to think about my answer.

I love golf for so many reasons. Years ago I would say I was just someone that played golf who wanted to be a golfer when they grew up. It was a little late for that now. It's easier to describe the kind of golfer I am *not* than to explain the kind I *am*. I have always enjoyed practicing the game, but not in order to pursue greatness. No, I just get a kick out of hitting balls on a range. I am not a high handicapper or a low handicapper, but I have been both. I don't play every day and haven't for years, but there sure were times that I did. As a player I never used a caddie, but a few times I've caddied for players. My game strategy and course management skills are sound. Technically, I pretty much know what I am doing. Like any amateur in any sport, just knowing what to do does not mean you can execute it with consistency and accuracy. Still, I feel I can play with almost anyone without embarrassing myself or annoying them.

Unless I play alone, I prefer playing the game *with* somebody as opposed to *against* somebody. That has nothing to with a lack of competitive instincts – I can show plenty of fiery competitive nature when playing with friends or with good people. Golf can be even more fun when each hole is worth something. Whether a buck a hole, lunch or drinks later, it doesn't matter when you are playing with friends. For some reason though, bets with strangers are just not as entertaining for me.

True personalities surface on a golf course. In golf just like in everyday life, once in a while you run into people that are way too impressed with themselves. There aren't many things I don't like about golf, but I don't care for jackasses on a golf course any more than I care for them anywhere else. I like the fact that golf is called a "gentleman's game". Being a gentleman by no means excludes being competitive, though some jerks excuse their childish behavior that way.

Maybe most of all, I enjoy being able to use all my senses on a golf course. I like the sights, the sounds, the smells. Fresh-cut grass, fresh air; scents I love so much I would bottle them up and keep it if I could. Birds, the breeze blowing through the trees. The variety and contrast of colors: grass, lakes, sky, sand in the bunkers, flowers, all kinds of plants and trees, even the mulch and rocks. Azaleas and olive trees. Magnolias and gardenias. Water spraying from the ocean or in a still pond covered with lilies. Sounds that range from cleats walking across a cart path to the simple and joyous sound of silence. A well-kept course is a beautiful thing, but that doesn't mean it should be easy, either. I agree with what the Scottish say – rough should *be* rough, hazards should *be* hazardous.

I like the feeling of doing something better than the last time I tried it. That defined my professional career and lots of day-to-day things in life, but it was magnified in golf. Things like making perfect contact, better than before. Shaping the ball around or under a tree. A lobbed wedge that flew higher and stopped quicker on the green, closer to the pin. Reading a green and then hearing the ball rattle the bottom of the cup after holing a long and difficult putt.

I've told many a golf professional over the years that I am their model customer. As a player, I'm not so good, but not so bad. I need a place to buy golf's "things", those things not needed so much as wanted, from shirts and shoes to balls and gloves to the putters and wedges and towels and hats, all those things that fill a golfer's garage over time. I'm the customer who wants a practice range, a place where I should be taking lessons but rarely do, where I wished I was beating buckets of balls every day, but probably was not. I'm a spoiled enough customer to believe when a course has amenities, they should be taken care of or taken out. There should be no ball washer without soap or water in it, never a full trash can or an empty water cooler. At the same time, I acknowledge that the creators of the game neither had nor may have wanted any of these things that so spoil us.

And, like so many customers of so many businesses, I enjoy feeling a kinship with the place. I like a place where everybody knows you and you know them. Places where when they see you coming in the grill, they know what you want before you ask. A place where you can be as comfortable talking to the shop attendant about their game as you can the guy driving the fairway mower about how his kids are doing.

I never knew anyone who enjoys watching golf on television as much as I do. Maybe I got that way by attending so many PGA tournaments as a spectator. Like the football fan that develops a hatred for dealing with the crowds and the weather, TV is a good way to avoid those problems in the comfort of your home. At the same time I believe televised golf ruins the game for a lot of us amateurs. The professional's constant paralyzing analysis of each and every component of each and every shot is almost understandable for those making their living at this, but none of what they do has a place for amateurs on the courses we play. Public golf has crept to a crawl thanks in large part to televised golf. Keeping things moving by grabbing a stick and hitting your ball can and should be a lot more fun than trying to emulate the stressful play of the pros.

Still, I find joy and happiness in the Golf Channel.

In general, I'm more interested in watching the televised course than the individuals, even though I have had my favorite players over the years. I enjoyed some for their character: Lee Trevino, Gary Player; some for their swing: Payne Stewart, Fred Couples; some for their competitive tenacity: Raymond Floyd and Lanny Wadkins; some for their skilled precision: Billy Casper and Tiger Woods; and some because they seemed like they would be fun to spend the day with: Julius Boros, Arnold Palmer. As a young man, I counted the days and hours, looking forward to Shell's Wonderful World of Golf. I'd huddle around that portable black and white television, anxious while I awaited the day's match. I couldn't wait to see what players it would feature and where they'd play. I'd watch with wide eyes, feeling like I was right there, walking with them in awe not only of their ability, but of where they had a chance to be. To transport myself to wherever they were on that day was as thrilling as their play itself.

"Well, maybe Bert can handle that for you," I heard Skip's conversation with Larry continuing. "Oh, wait, he's off today because his wife had that doctor's appointment, that's right." I went back into my thoughts.

I decided I should think of Skip's question in terms of how I see the game. Unlike some people I see golf as a game for everyone, for any and everybody. Golf is not just for the elite or the affluent. To me, golf is for anyone who loves being outdoors, and who enjoys a mental challenge as much as a physical one.

It is a game that invites players of a wide range of skill level to play with each other. This is a sport that men and women, boys and girls can play and enjoy together. I love that couples can play side by side through the end of their days, and always wished my wife Cameron felt the same way. She does not. She always accepted and accommodated my love for golf but would not participate with me. That always made me sad. I know how funny that sounds to husbands who play with the main purpose of getting *away* from his wife.

To me, golf is beyond a "sport". So many things we call sport are played on a common-sized field or court. Not golf, where every hole is a hurdle unlike every other on its course. Beyond that, each course is different from every other one. Golf is a challenge that resembles real life – a constant variety of challenges are difficult for unique reasons, in unique ways. In golf, athletic prowess is less important than mental toughness. When one belittles this game by saying golf is "not a real sport", it shows they know nothing about it.

Golf is a walking game. The Scottish who defined the purity of the game centuries ago had no carts. Powered carts exist to make more money for course owners by both speeding up play and catering to our comfort. They provide nice shade and a place to sit. I disagree with one of the most well-known maxims about golf: Mark Twain's remark that "golf is a good walk spoiled". Walking a golf course and playing alone was common for me through my adolescence. I am often more comfortable alone than not, whether that means I should be labeled an introvert, or a loner, or something else. Maybe this day was a good example. Psychoanalysis would probably say that's what caused me to pass the turn off to the Alabama Golf Trail course in favor of the Burma Shave sign course where I sat now in the Pro's office. Such an expert might say that I made my choice favoring the prospect of playing solo on the unknown, out-of-the-way layout instead of facing the likelihood of playing with strangers. I suppose they might also say I was too cheap to play at the upscale course.

I've always been able to understand people disliking golf. I never had an interest in many things that many people immersed themselves into with the same feelings I had for golf: fly fishing, tennis, scuba diving, weight lifting. I could never share their love of diversions of dedication like those, so I understand why someone might not share my interest in golf. I even get why some find golf a boring waste of time. It's not boring to me, though.

I heard the click of the phone being placed back into the cradle of the desk set, but my mind still drifted a few more seconds. "Chris, are you in there?" Like the doctor a couple of days before, the Pro's voice brought me blinking back to reality. "Sorry to take so long on that call, but you looked like you were a million miles away anyway." He peered into my eyes to see if I was all the way back from wherever I was. "I didn't realize I asked you such a tough question," he smiled.

I came back to our conversation from my stare out the window. My eyes met his and I gave my condensed answer: "I'm just a guy that likes to be outside, and prefers to be on a golf course when I'm there. As a player, I pretty much stink, but I don't slow too many people down behind me, or rush anybody ahead of me." He paused, waiting for more. I decided I didn't want to get into everything else. "That's about it."

"Fair enough. You sound like our kind of guy, alright."

It was time to get going. "Well, thanks so much for the breakfast. It was great." I stood up and stuck my hand out across the desk. "Sure nice to meet you, Arnie."

He stood up with me, grabbing my hand to return the shake, looking like he enjoyed our chat as much as I did. I felt him wishing I would stay and talk some more, knowing I'd like the time for that, too. Instead, he deferred to my desire to get outside and get started. "Hey, Chris, it's a pleasure to have you here. Glad you liked the sandwich – most people do," he said with a proud grin.

"What do I owe you for that?" I asked as I reached into my pocket.

He waved me to stop reaching, "No, nothing at all, my pleasure. Like I said, call it a welcoming gift." I began collecting my dishes and trash. "Oh, just leave all that. It'll give Doug something to do." He stepped into his closet behind him and rustled around while he kept talking. "You could do me one favor, if you don't mind."

"Sure, what's that?"

"Get rid of this box of balls for me, will you?" He handed me a fresh box of brand new top-of-the-line golf balls from behind his desk. He knew I didn't arrive with any. "I get so many freebies from vendors I don't know what to do with them." He saw me preparing to decline the gift. "You'd be helping me clean this closet up if you would get these out of here."

"That's awfully nice of you." I missed the kind of southern hospitality that I was feeling here. With the box in my hand I turned to walk out of the office door. Arnie came around his desk to follow me.

"Hey, if you want to return the favor, next time you come, bring me some of those New Mexico chilies!" I didn't choose to tell him that my visit was a one-shot deal, nor why it was. "By the way, where in New Mexico do you live?"

"Just outside of Albuquerque."

"I hear that's a nice place. Sometime I'd like to get up there, up to Santa Fe, too. Maybe I'll look you up." He was the kind of guy I always enjoyed playing golf with. He was a good guy, one I would like Cameron and me to entertain in our home. I wished I would be there when he came. I knew I would not.

"Sure, you do that. We'll get you all the peppers you want when you come." I knew I needed to go.

We walked back into the shop. Skip gave instructions to Doug before I could ask The Kid anything. "Doug, set up Mister Chris here with everything he needs. He'll need a rental set – give him the nice Wilsons with the Callaway woods. And make sure there are tees in the bag." It sounded good to me. After all, I was not here today to conquer the course, not to set a new personal low score, not to avoid being beaten by a buddy. No, I was here to enjoy one of my final days, that's all. Skip could have given me a set of tree limbs to play with, and I would be just as happy. Doug scrambled from behind his counter and headed to the storage area near the bathroom while Arnie continued. His voice grew louder when Doug dove into the closet out of sight. "He's got plenty of new balls, but he'll be walking today – get him that nice pull cart we've got. It should be back there next to the rentals." In his office moments before, I thought of, but did not mention my preference to walk. How did he know that? "Throw a couple of bottles of cold water in the bag, too," he added. Arnie looked back at me, and then down at my feet. "Our hills mean you'll need shoes. About a 12, am I right?"

"Yes, great guess, a 12," I was impressed, but since that's what he does for a living, I supposed he should know. "Nothing fancy at all, just for the day, you know." Skip walked to the stack of boxed shoes, going straight to pull a box as if he knew right where the ones I needed were in the large stack of sale items. Doug flew by us, awkward as he carried a nice compact bag of clubs on one shoulder and a folded aluminum cart with two big wheels under the other. He stepped out the front door, unfolded the cart, and began rigging the bag up onto it.

"Here you go," Skip said, opening the shoe box. He handed it to me and motioned to a tiny bench inside the shop, there just for the purpose of trying new shoes on. I sat down and put them on, noting there were metal spikes screwed into the soles. I thought all golf shoes now were spikeless, using the short, rubber styled spikes.

"Wow, are these spikes OK on your course?"

"Yeah, you might notice, we're kind of *old school* around here," he laughed, stating the obvious.

The shoes could not have fit better, and they almost felt broken in already. I was almost afraid to ask, but I did anyway. "So, what do I owe you?"

"Let's worry about that later, Chris," Skip said, and then he winked at me. When somebody winks at you like that, you always wonder if it means there is a catch attached. "After you play, come back in and we'll talk."

"Are you sure? I think I'm into you for quite a bit here," and I should have been, "The clubs, the cart, the shoes, breakfast." I was getting more embarrassed each time something else was added.

"We'll have a cold Nehi when you're done and get to calculating," Skip said with a smile and a hand on my shoulder, "We'll take care of everything soon enough. Just make sure you don't lose too many bets while you're out there," and he patted my shoulder now. How I could lose bets when I was playing alone? Of course, I thought, he was just joking.

"OK, Skip. Grape, Orange, Red, I don't care, but a cold Nehi sounds good. Ice 'em down, and I'll take you up on that when I get done." I shook his hand again, and headed out the door.

"Hit 'em good, Chris," Skip said the same words the doctor had said. It was eerie. "Hit 'em good."

I stepped outside where Doug had me set up. The cart was lightweight, but heavy-duty, the kind I knew would be handy on a course with lots of hills. On the handle just below the rubber hand grip was a small clipboard. A fresh pencil and a scorecard were attached.

The card was unlike any I had ever seen. It was nothing more than a bunch of blank squares. It read "Gabriel's Creek Golf Course" and was numbered 1 through 9 on the side facing up. I trusted hole numbers 10 through 18 were on the reverse. The odd thing about it was that under the hole number, it showed the par for each hole, but no distances or other information. No handicap for each hole, no diagram of the layout, nothing but hole numbers and par for that hole. I never saw a card like that in my life. I looked up to ask Doug about it, but before I could say anything, there was Skip in the open doorway to the shop.

"Call it part of the magic," Skip said, with a twinkle in his eye. He was answering my question without hearing it, a bit strange, I thought.

"Excuse me?"

"I told you this place is magical, didn't I?" I nodded my recollection. "The scorecard is just part of it." We just stared at each other a few seconds. "You'll see what I mean." He pointed around the left corner of the building, just past the door he stood in. "Right around this corner and you'll be on your way to Number One. I've got to go into the grill and get a food order ready to send in. You're welcome to wait inside, do some shopping or just hang out a minute. Doug will let you know when to head out." He lowered his voice a little again as I started back toward the door into the shop. "I like to let him feel like he's in control, like he's a real Starter, you see." He winked again and said, "It won't be long."

With that, he headed for the grill, and I stepped back into the golf shop, alone again with my thoughts as I waited for The Kid to send me on my way.

CHAPTER 5

I began walking around the side of the clubhouse pulling the two-wheeled cart, following a sign pointing to the first tee just around the nearest corner. On my right, two players taking their time putting on the practice green returned my nod when I passed. Beyond them, four players on the driving range seemed in no hurry to go anywhere. I wanted to stay ahead of them, keeping plenty of space between us since they were next to follow me off of hole Number One.

Past Skip's office window, the path to the first tee turned left around the back of the building. The tiny almost hidden parking area there must have been for employees. When I saw the mint yellow 1967 Buick LeSabre convertible in the lot, I was confident it belonged to Skip. The only other cars parked back there must have belonged to Claire or Doug or the maintenance guys. The yellow classic had to be his. I knew it was a '67 because a Mr. Engberg, a neighbor of ours across the street in Weatherford, had a big red one he bought brand new. I moved away to start my career after graduation and thought of that car for years. On a visit home once I begged him to arrange a way for me to buy it, but I never followed up with him after he first turned me down. One day I heard he passed away, and the car vanished when the family took care of his effects. Now, here was a new-looking one that I stared at with envy as I kept walking. How odd, that Arnie would drive a vehicle so much like one I salivated over for so long.

The first hole was nowhere in sight yet. Starting the day with a long walk was nice on such a morning. Again and again I stared back over my shoulder at that car, wishing the convertible top was down so I could see inside better. Maybe when I got done I could get Arnie to show it off to me.

The aged asphalt cart path curved around to the right. I followed it into the forest, away from the old Buick and its companions. A tunnel cut through the trees, taking the golfer looking for the first tee into woods so thick that within a few paces I all of a sudden felt isolated, miles away from anyone. The path became damp with dew yet to evaporate in the softened light. There was a wonderful, fresh smell to the forest that I breathed it in deep to savor. I walked ahead to a short bridge over a cascading brook below. Crossed wooden timbers supported a belt-high railing the length of the bridge. Stepping onto the span, my cleats and pull cart made a much different sound than the gas powered two-passenger rental carts do, but this old bridge had heard more cleats than carts on its wood through the years.

The smell of the dense pines and the wood planks of the bridge mixed with the freshness of the stream. Maybe it was the years of rubber wheels and oil dripping from the carts that had seeped into its boards, but the smell was like that of a railroad along the river. A bird's elaborate mid-morning refrain echoed through the thicket as I stopped a moment on the bridge, enjoying the sound of the water rippling over the stones of the stream. How peaceful, how tranquil it was. Since getting my news from the doctor, this was the first occasion of being alone with my thoughts about was happening to me. I had a whole round of golf ahead of me for my reflections; I didn't need to digest everything here on the bridge. I just wanted to stop and enjoy the scene, like you do when you're walking in a park and find just the right moment. I leaned against the railing, looking out over the creek. My mind was clear, and all my senses loved this spot.

I heard a familiar pitter-patter on the path behind and approaching me. I hoped it would be Ralphie, and turned to see it was. He was just stepping onto the bridge, walking like he didn't want to disturb me.

"Hey there, Mister Ralphie," I said as he came up and sat next to me, his head high, wearing a broad smile as he panted. I asked him, "What's up?" It was always a source of entertainment for anyone who knew me that I would have conversations with my dogs. At least I never claimed the animals talked back to me, although I never doubted that communication was there with a dog that looked like it was listening. After all, who could be sure that dogs can't understand us? Looking into their eyes, I felt we could comprehend each other.

"So, are you going out cruising this morning?" I waited for an answer while the dog just panted. "Going to chase a few squirrels or go fishing in the creek?" The dog sat, receiving my quick pat on the head, and gave me a concerned look that said, *'I'm not sure yet what I'll do today, but how are YOU doing? Are you OK?'*

I shrugged and hoped nobody saw me answering my imaginary question from a dog. "Why don't you grab your sticks and join me? You live on a golf course so you *must* have your own clubs, right?" Ralphie shot me a look like I was nuts. He stayed calm while he walked around behind me and sat on my other side, facing me. His grin gave me a look that said, *'No, you idiot, I'm a DOG!'*

We stood there on the bridge together in silence for a nice but short time that felt much longer than it was. Then, his head spun around when something in the distance caught Ralphie's attention. He sprinted off the bridge a few paces ahead of me. He stopped and stared a moment, then gave me a glance back over his shoulder. The look said, *'Sorry, mister, gotta go! I'll see you later!'* and he was off. Like dogs tend to do, he sprinted faster than I imagined he could. I watched him, never identifying what or who he was after. He dashed out of sight along the path and into the woods.

Standing there alone on the bridge again, I was unable to suppress any further thinking of my dogs. It was a common problem for me. Houston and Tyler were "The Boys", who anyone could argue were as close to me as – maybe even closer than – my own children. Without a doubt, millions of people have had this same kinship with their dogs. The older they live, the more they still need you. They are unlike the child that grows into their own independence and ability to function just fine without you. The dog goes from child to elderly as if a train passing you by, but all the while continues to love you and need you. They tell you with their eyes they just cannot live without your love in return. My two boys embodied that, men that became old dudes as I aged myself. I gazed down into the stream, thinking of them.

Houston was the product of running out of excuses for telling our kids why they couldn't have a dog. A new home with a large, fenced yard and lots of trees eliminated all my remaining reasons. Their mother felt they should have a pure-bred dog and the kids agreed, but I resisted them all and convinced them that we should adopt our new family pet. Off we went to the County Pound, where the cutest Basset Hound I ever saw captured us all. On the way home, each of us reached to pet the happy pup, but a name eluded us. Their mother suggested "Houston", a favorite boy's name of ours. We'd named our son Austin years before, so we continued the trend with our new doggie.

Tyler came two years later, a mutt sold from a cardboard box by neighborhood kids going door-to-door. Lying in that box on our front porch, his face said we needed him as much as he needed us. The dirty blonde color in the box that day would transform with a bath to a brilliant rich gold color. The happy-faced puppy was a Golden Retriever with a few other breeds mixed in. Like his predecessor and now older brother, Houston, he was a puppy with as warm a smile as you could imagine. Our kids took to him the second they laid eyes on the new pup, loving him just as much as they did Houston. The Texas theme continued when we named him Tyler before that first bath was over. In just a few weeks, the cute little critter curled up on the towel that night would turn into something quite different: a dog twice the size and ten times the energy of his brother the hound.

In their youth, we lived in a golfing community outside Denver called Antelope Run, where a challenging course went winding through the large subdivision. It was a course that was easy to hop on for a few holes late in the day. I would sneak out on summer evenings to get in a few holes just because I could. The Boys would come with me when I went out for those late afternoon holes after work. Houston would cruise along the out-of-bounds markers, oblivious to me but visiting every resident he could find in their yards or on their decks. He knew no one could resist a Basset Hound, and would squeeze a snack out of whomever he met in reward for his cute wide-footed, floppy eared disposition. While Houston shopped, his brother Tyler would zip from one side of the fairway to the other, running, bounding along until Papa had a shot. Then he would dutifully gallop to my side and sit silently until the ball was away, after which he could resume his run.

Houston was always cool and calm in any situation. He craved attention, knew he could get it from anyone, and would go looking for it. Tyler was the opposite. The sole attention he craved getting was that of the kids, their mother, and me. Unlike a true Golden Retriever, Tyler would always avoid strangers at all cost. The only times that both of them were as calm as a cucumber was when they were with me, their Papa, and when the three of us were around golf.

In particular, I loved taking them both with me to the driving range. Whether it was late in the evening under the lights, or first thing in the morning when they opened, no leash was needed for either dog. Both would hop out of the car and wait for me to put on shoes and grab my clubs. Then they would escort me like bodyguards, walking on either side of me until I set my sticks down on the range. They would wait right there, relaxed but vigilant, while I walked away to fetch my bucket of balls and return. They watched each swing of my practice. Both of them would follow my ball through the air to its finish whether I struck it well or not. We would "discuss" my needs and my improvement plans with that same communication of my voice and their eyes. They were both my harshest critics and my biggest fans.

As time moved on, one could argue that I included them far too much in my life. They got older, and like ornery old men, they belched, passed gas, and snored more often and louder, and became less active every day. My wife didn't share my view that their mellowing made them even more loveable. They aged as I did. The times came when I faced the tough choices that many pet owners do when a series of ailments slowed them, and eventually took them away. I lost Tyler first at age 14, when no more surgeries could help make his life better. After that, Houston just seemed to age much faster without his brother around, perhaps wilting away from day-to-day loneliness. For almost his entire life, he had a sidekick with him when we were all at work or school. Now, without Tyler, he had no one. The sad day came when I found him on his favorite blanket, sleeping to awaken no more. They both lived long and full lives, a fact we used to console us when they passed. It was a difficult time for me, as tough as the passing of anyone in my life. Both dogs' ashes were prominent in our house in urns befitting their meaning to us, or at least what they meant to me.

My deep grief seemed foolish to family and friends, the fact I would mourn so for two animals. The loss of my boys was no different than the passing of my dearest family members. When we bereave those closest to us, over time we're able to hide from others the grief we feel, but the depth and pain of that sorrow in our hearts never leaves. So it was with The Boys. After they were gone I felt an emptiness I never experienced before. It was in my faith that I found comfort. I always felt God put me in charge of making both their lives better. They more than made mine so much richer in return. I was responsible for doing whatever was needed to make their lives better. In some cases that meant to make them happy, in others it was to ease their pain. In Tyler's case, I felt that it was my duty to keep him from suffering any longer. That day, I held his paw and gazed into his eyes while the euthanizing equipment was attached to him. I mustered all the faith I had to focus not on losing him, but instead to celebrate his life and send him on ahead of me. When our veterinarian left us alone, I tried hard to look strong for my boy, but I failed. With his last breaths, his eyes and that trademark smile were instead consoling *me*. The tears flowed down my face while he told Papa that everything would be OK. Then, he was gone.

Much the same as I was after the passing of my parents years ago, not a day went by after my dogs' deaths that I didn't think of them. Cameron kept the loneliness from swallowing me the way it had Houston. I missed my parents, I missed my dogs, and I missed everyone that was gone. Now, since "my news", I was coming to grips with the fact I would soon be able to be with them all. My faith was strong enough not to question that, and just thinking about it made me smile.

It seemed the songbird was encouraging the water to move downhill just a little faster, and I used that to get myself moving as well. I crossed the rest of the bridge back onto the cart path pavement and continued walking through the forest. I rounded a curve and went over a rise. Several yards ahead, there was an opening out of the trees. I grew closer to it and then broke out into the daylight. Exiting the forest's passageway I felt like I was stepping into another land. The warmth of the sun hit and a wave of emotions rolled through me. I stopped when the hair on the back of my neck stood up as if electrified. Seeing the fresh-mown green grass in the bright morning sunshine, I felt energized.

Back when golf was part of my everyday life, never had this feeling been so strong in me. I'd never appreciated this moment for what it was. Right there and then, it hit me how often and for how long I took for granted so many things that were part of my normal day-to-day life. In that instant I saw that so many people all over the world would be thrilled to have any of my life's experiences. Golf was the subject on this day as I neared the first tee, but the things I had to be thankful for today went far beyond golf. It was beyond that blessing, the chance to just once be standing where I was at that second. It was the ability to drive through the countryside, the opportunity to enjoy the day's dawn, the breakfast sandwich and coffee with Skip. It was the two bottles of water Doug placed in my bag. It was the gift of the knowledge that I was about to die. Just to have any of those things, so many people would get a similar sensation of excitement to what I was experiencing while standing there. These people would value the chance to do what I was about to. It took my entire life to get in sync with them, to share their emotions as I stood there soaking up my first glimpse of the first hole at Gabriel's Creek.

Stepping onto the first tees of the many golf courses of my life, I always saw that moment as nothing more than the first of 18 holes. It was the beginning of a round, the start of a recreational endeavor, the onset of a walk in the park. Now more than ever before, I sensed golf was telling me something about myself. It had to be the golf course telling me, showing me a lesson of life I should have learned already. I was being slapped in the face with the realization that I should have treated every moment on earth as the unique opportunity it was. I should have always seen how lucky I was to be walking, to be breathing, to be witnessing what was laid out in front of me.

At this very instant there were hundreds, thousands of people treating their moment in golf the very same way I had, not being grateful for what it is. Until the chat with my doctor led me to that very spot, to this very revelation, I did the same. No matter how subtle they seem, golf can give us substantive lessons about life if we allow ourselves to pay enough attention to learn them. Right now, around the world, golf is touching so many:

A young French businessman new to the game sinks his first 45-foot birdie putt. He wants that feeling again, so he immerses himself in his newfound love for golf. He is so desperate in wanting to break 100 that he plays as often as he can afford it, but still lacks the commitment to make him want to practice. Excusing himself out of working to improve his game is routine – he says he just doesn't have the time. He can't see this irony as he slices another 5-iron into a water hazard.

A college golf team's #7 player hits balls on a range in Arizona, trying hard to move up to the top competitive group. He practices with diligence, less because he wants to lead his team, but more because he's tired of hearing his Dad tell neighbors that his kid is wasting study time on golf, because he'll never be very good anyway.

In Kansas, a young man struggles with his continuing status as a PGA Apprentice. He works hard, but can't advance through tests and playing obstacles to become the Golf Professional he wants to be.

Another man goes through the drudgery of heading to work as a mechanic in a golf course maintenance shop in Spain. A leaf blower is spitting oil, a tractor engine will not start and its seat is broken anyway. He doesn't feel good, partly because he was up all night with his sick wife, pregnant again. He is here, though. He's the breadwinner. It's his job.

A retiree trods into the pro shop at his club in Florida, knowing he will hook up with somebody and play today – like he does every day – not so much because he wants to as that he has nothing else to do.

At a similar community miles away, the Ladies Club has the course, one foursome playing together for the third time this week, updating each other between shots on what has happened with their grandkids the past two days.

A father in England slips his well-worn Royal & Ancient Rule Book into his daughter's golf bag while she packs her car to move away to university.

A woman in California just got a new sand wedge for her birthday, so she takes out her smart phone and pulls up the Rules of Golf on the USGS website to check the number of clubs she can carry in her bag.

A professional golfer in Dubai asks a marshal for a ruling in a tournament, while half a world away in Wisconsin, a debate rages in a club's 19th hole bar over what rule applies when Dave's ball hit Ernie's while it was on the green and bumped it four feet away.

A young man lies awake in Australia, remembering his actions earlier that day in a fairway bunker. He used his club to rake the sand and build a makeshift tee, carving around his ball so he could get a clean strike at it. Doing so, he looked around, hopeful his playing partners wouldn't catch him. He's still not sure if anyone saw him. His insomnia is the same as the 20-handicapper in Japan, recalling his play in a tight Calcutta where he kicked his ball in the rough a few feet nearer the fairway so that he could avoid having to work a shot around a tree limb. While these two fret about if anyone saw them cheating, a man in South Africa tells his playing partners how he stepped on his ball by accident while he was looking for his ball in the woods. No one saw it but him. He explains what happened so that together they can discuss the correct way he should penalize himself.

These events are all happening at once, just as a man walks down a cobbled street in Scotland. He is bundled up against the chill of the damp afternoon, the brim of his woolen Tam o'Shanter cap pulled down low to his brow. He heads to the market, looking over and beyond the short, old stone wall bordering the road, looking onto the first golf course we know. To many, it is a Holy Grail of the game. To him, this is just part of the scenery; a pasture he passes that is no warmer than the pavement where he walks. No big deal to him, this simply is where he lives. It is merely a field he sees every day, day after day, without knowledge of or concern for how sacred that ground could be to a man half a world away in Alabama, USA. A man walking alone to a first tee box, pulling a bag on a two-wheeled cart, about to tee off as a single, about to play the last round of his life.

How natural that I'd think of Scotland today. It was on a long list of places I always wanted to go, but never did. Now, I never would. As a young businessman, I dreamed of travelling there to play where golf began, on the oldest courses in the world. I wanted to walk with caddies and follow the footsteps of golf's legends by touring the courses that Great Britain uses to define golf to the world. My uncle went there a few times to play, his tales helping to fuel my aspirations. Many times I looked ahead on my schedule, looking for the several week block of time I thought I both needed and deserved in order to complete a golf addict's pilgrimage to the Mecca of the game. I never found that block of time. Now I never would.

Over my life I invested a great deal of time and money in this game only to miss what its whole point should have meant to me. At last I could see, at the literal end of my life, its point is to take nothing for granted. The thing that makes golf a metaphor for life is that each moment on a golf course is different from each and every other moment there. Each and every experience is unique. It may be gone in an instant, never for you to see again. Golf was showing me this today, right now. I was brought here by a decision to spend some of my final earthly hours on a golf course. Looking at the first hole, I wished I had learned much earlier to not take my life for granted. I wanted to have seen it more than 50 years before now. I wanted to have seen it in the eyes of our newborn children. I wanted to have seen it before I approached the first tee at Gabriel's Creek, when it was too late.

I looked skyward, knowing there was a reason I made that decision, knowing there was a reason why I was here, a reason why I was having these thoughts.

CHAPTER 6

It was time to get focused again on the last round of golf I'd ever play, to get my mind back to Alabama, back to the first tee at Gabriel's Creek. There was no special tee marker here, no artsy etched and polished boulder with a colorful planter around it. The sign looked like it was made at the same time, in the same place, by the same person as those along the road that led me here to begin with. It was just a post anchored in the ground by a vegetable can-sized pour of ready-mix concrete, with five planks nailed one below the other onto it: Hole 1, Par 4, 460 yards (painted in blue), 435 yards (in white), and 370 yards (in red).

The elevated tee box looked downhill into a shallow valley where bright green fairway grass ran the length of the hole that was lined with trees on both sides. A forgiving bank slanted a little to the left, leading to a wide landing area. A creek crossed the bottom from left to right before a steep climb went back up to the elevated green on the right. That creek was Mister Gabe's, I assumed. I could just see the fluttering flag through the double bend of the hole at about my elevation on the other end of the small basin.

Long ago I might play from the long blue Championship tees, but as I got older I'd play from the shorter white ones. There was no reason to change now. The teeing area was marked by two white painted pieces of wood that were no more than a foot long. What looked like railroad spikes pinned them into the ground at the width of the flat mowed area that defined the tee box.

Taking a deep breath of anticipation, tee and ball in hand, I bent over and stuck the little wooden pedestal into the ground like I've done thousands of times before. I stretched my back a little, and my pre-shot routine began. Sometimes my pre-shot visualization would translate into the actual result, but most often it didn't. I kept going through it anyway, since the most basic golf instruction involves conditioning the mind to help the body perform with a brief repetitive routine before each shot.

I took two leisurely, loosening practice swings before I stepped forward to stand behind the ball. I looked up and away from the tee to follow its imagined flight from the level teeing ground. I visualized its powerful takeoff into the air, the ball sailing above the right side of the fairway, then beginning to take a slight right-to-left draw. My mind saw it taking a perfect gentle bounce angling to the left with the downhill tilt of the hole, running down to stop just short of the creek in an ideal spot for my second shot. I placed the club head behind my teed ball and squared its face to my intended ball flight. I put my feet together and stood a comfortable distance away from the ball. I peered down my mind's image of the dotted line that went from the ball into my flight plan. I spread my feet, and then looked back down at the ball, positioned off my left heel, my left toe open ever so little. I double checked that my feet were spread apart the width of my shoulders, then flexed my knees and told myself to *sit down* just a bit.

That morning sun was up enough now that I felt its gentle warmth on my arms. I set up for that right-to-left draw by pulling my right foot back a tad, ever so slightly closing my stance. I looked one more time down the fairway to my target. I took in a deep breath and filled my lungs with the pine-scented air, releasing it while stilling myself in preparation to swing.

Just as I pulled the head of my driver straight back and low to the ground to start my backswing, I had a startling thought: this was the very last First Tee of my life, the last I'd ever be on, the last time I'd experience that promise of the round's first shot. Sure, there were plenty more holes today, more tees on which a golfer always thinks "this could be the day": for a hole-in-one, for an eagle from the fairway, a chip in from the deep rough, a sand shot finding the bottom of the cup. But every golfer on every first tee of every round knows they *may* hit every shot perfectly today, that they *may* be starting the *best* round of their life today. Like a snap of fingers, that thought distracted me. This was the last time I would feel that prospect of joy the first tee of the first hole gives a golfer. My distraction proved why concentration is so important to the golf swing. The anticipation of the perfect round filled with my striking nothing but crisp shots ended when my driver's head hit the ball near the toe, on the bottom of the face. The ball was not shooting up and away like a fighter plane from the runway, but darting ahead low in front of me, and heading to the right. Only a hole shaped just like this could accommodate and forgive such a lousy shot as I'd hit. The ball bounced often, piddling down the right side. The left-leaning slope held it in play, letting it go farther down the fairway until it stopped. It finished with the illusion that I had hit it well. Yes, I am a lucky man.

"Well, nobody took a picture of it," I said aloud to myself, shaking my head in disbelief. I remembered how my Uncle Clyde would say that when we played together so many years ago. He would smile and laugh with an arm around my shoulders, explaining he just meant that the result of the shot was more important than how it got there. It was the golf equivalent of the baseball proverb "that's a line drive in the box score". It was encouragement to concentrate on the result, not how it was achieved. It was an appropriate memory here.

I grabbed my cart handle and began walking down off the tee. The old steel cleats were helpful going down the grade, gentle at first going past the juniors' and ladies' tees, then steep down the next 20 feet or so until the hill slowed to a comfortable downslope. Walking down that first fairway, I wondered how long it had been since I was on a golf course alone, playing by myself. Many years before, walking was reserved for those hot summer days when I was too young to care, on municipal courses where I wasn't slowing anyone down. From grade school through high school and into college, we walked first because we didn't know any better and later because we couldn't afford powered carts on a student's budget. Later as a young businessman, the opposite became true – we could afford to play the courses that required driving in carts, so we did. Seeing a golf course again from a perspective other than driving on the cart path was nice. Walking allows the player to see golf as it was meant to be seen. I wished that many years ago I would have prioritized the enjoyment and exercise factors of walking golf over riding in carts so often.

It impressed me how *easy* this walk was. Yes, I was walking downhill, but in my condition I should be tiring already. I was not. It was only the first hole, but I could swear I was feeling stronger with every stride. The air was so clean, so crisp. I felt younger each time I filled my lungs. I looked up at a sky that was such a beautiful, deep royal blue, like the brilliant blue of Lake Tahoe. Was I already in heaven? I had my answer when I looked down to find my ball, twenty yards ahead. If this were heaven, I would have hit it another eighty yards further.

The ball ended up much better than I deserved, even as short as it was. The grass was a beautiful green, but there was very little difference in the mowed height of the rough compared to the fairway. It was already easy to see that an influx of money could make Gabriel's Creek as lush and challenging as you could find. The view I had toward the green confirmed that the course architecture was already there. I was making too many value judgments about an entire course by walking its first 220 yards. I had other things to worry about.

I was fortunate that the slope had given me more roll than I deserved. The ball stopped short of the blue post along the trees, the marker that indicated 200 yards to the hole. No sprinkler heads marked with the exact yardage, no GPS system, no yardage book, none of the bells and whistles many courses now give the player to tell a precise, measured distance. I liked the ambiguity of this golf course. It was being true to the game because it was willing to make me think. The golfing gods in Scotland were able to figure out what club to hit for hundreds of years on their own. So, even though artificial help like rangefinders was cool, that didn't mean I needed it. I played so few times the past many years that an eyeballing approximation was just as good as if I were to step the exact yardage off from my ball to the 200-yard marker. I could not expect this day's play to benefit from detailed information.

I concentrated on looking at the 215 yards (or so) remaining to the pin. It was quite a photogenic view. It would have looked even better if I was closer to the hole. Sloping down another 100 yards yet, the fairway cut through the thickening trees. The creek came into the hole from my left before crossing the fairway at a diagonal towards the mesa-like green to the right. The opposite bank of the creek was retained by a very old rock and mud wall that was five stones at its highest. Two small cart bridges crossed the creek, one at either side of the fairway. From the far bank of the brook, the hole went up and right, quite steep at first, then flattening out the last 30 yards in front of the green. It was a sign of good design: for a player who hit their ball just a little short, the hole avoided too severe a penalty because it would not make that ball roll all the way back down the slope and into the creek. The trees were tall and thick up around the green, turning that part of the hole into what seemed like a sanctuary, made even calmer by the sound of water running in the creek. That gentle trickling would be magnified as I got nearer to the green.

The tallest tree close to the playing area was where the right corner of the fairway met the creek. It stood in the exact line between my ball and the center of the green. A small bunker left of the putting surface kept me from thinking of bailing out that way. The shot would play much longer than the distance because the ball would have to carry all the way to the target above me. My lousy drive meant I had to either lay up in front of the creek or go for the green, a shot that would require me to bend a left-to-right fade around the corner. The right club for the shot was my trusted old five-wood, back at home in New Mexico, dusty from lack of use. These rentals had a similar club, though, so I pulled it from the bag. I opened my stance and turned my right hand just a hair on the grip. I chose just one swing thought: make an easy swing and let the club do the work.

The contact was perfect and the ball flew high. It started toward the bunker left of the green before shading to the right, going around the corner. I watched the ball fly as close to what my mind had drawn up as I could hope. I was thrilled when it bounced the first time 20 yards in front of the green, bounding as it slowed to rolling, and then going up onto the putting surface. The forward tilt of the green allowed me to see it from the fairway, still moving, about 10 feet left of the pin. Now I hoped the ball would not go through the green, afraid these Tennessee River Valley hills would spell trouble if the ball went out of my sight. I could see where it stopped, just off the back collar. I wasn't playing this hole the way it was drawn up, but I was quite happy to have pulled off the shot, and to know my ball was laying 2 just off the back of the green.

I walked up the left side of the hole, wanting to cross the creek using the bridge on the left for no other reason than to see the view up the hill to the green that was tucked back into the trees. Pulling the two-wheeled cart was made easier by staying on the paved cart path. The trees pinched in where the fairway neared the creek. Looking off into the woods when I grew closer, I could see pretty far. The forest floor was covered with leaves, branches, and fallen logs. It was passable, but you sure didn't want to be searching for your ball in there. The depth and density of the woods was what I imagined most of Northern Alabama looks like.

The terrain leveled out when I approached the green. I loved the serenity of the scene. Across the putting surface, the hill dove deep into the woods. The cart path came to a parking point above the green from which golfers would have a nice look back over the hole when they walked down the slope to the short-mown grass. I parked my cart and walked behind the green, down to the flattened area behind the hole. The rough was much thicker in the shadows. My ball was just five feet past the last cut of the green, sitting up nice on the lush grass. It was thick but not too tall, just about half-shoe height. This green was a long one. About 2/3 of the surface was between me and the flag, and it was gradual but downhill all the way. A negative thought flashed through my mind: I saw myself hitting the ball past the hole, running it back down the hill and into the water. I tried to erase that mental image.

Through a couple of practice strokes with a 7-iron I focused on taking the back of my left hand straight toward the pin. I just wanted to hop the ball those few feet to the green, getting it rolling along the putting surface to my imagined 3-foot circle with the pin at its center. I hoped to read the slight right-to-left break well enough to get close. My stroke was similar to a putt, straight back and through. I addressed the ball and was ready to hit.

"Don't let the creek bother you", said a familiar voice, startling me, making me flinch. I was alone, but it sounded so near. I wondered if it came from someone hiding in the trees. I *knew* this voice. Back at the shop I had seen no one but strangers, but this wasn't the kind of thing strangers would say to each other anyway. It

reminded me of good natured needling exchanges with golfing friends of my past. Unnerved, I restarted my shot routine, nervous while looking all around me. The downward slope of the green and the sheer drop beyond now taunted me. I addressed the ball again, bending my knees toward my target a little. I looked at a target spot just onto the green, and stroked. As soon as I made contact I knew I had a problem. The slope got into my head and I hadn't hit the ball hard enough. The ball hopped onto the green short of my target and was creeping, rolling, but well short of the pin. I left myself what looked like a very long 10-foot downhill putt.

Just as I dropped my 7-iron into my bag, as I was reaching for my putter, the voice shook me again: *"Maybe next time, get your sister to hit it!"*

"Who is that?!" I yelled, way too loud for someone on a golf course. I heard nothing but the gentle returning echo of my own voice and the breeze swirling the fallen leaves along the path behind me. There was no other sound. There was no voice, no cart, no spikes, nothing. I was unable to concentrate while I surveyed my next putt in silence. I took my stance and stroked it anyway. My conviction to not leave *this* one short gave the long par putt too much speed to break. It cruised by the hole until stopping three feet past the cup.

Walking across the green to my ball, I heard, *"You didn't lose your turn"*. Not just the voice, but the banter itself was more than familiar. Then and there I decided that I would focus on why I was here, have fun with it, and not allow who or whatever this was to bother me. This was either all in my mind or somebody was just being a real jerk. Maybe the doctor forgot to tell me I'd be losing my mind along the way these last few days.

I stood relaxed over the three-footer for bogey. I gave it a firm stroke uphill, playing for the break. The ball turned as predicted, arrived at the hole on its left side, dove in and rattled the metallic bottom of the cup. I stood up erect and still, looking up and around while I spread my arms as if inviting adulation. Almost shouting, I asked, "How was that?" There was no response, just the tranquil quiet of the woods and the babbling brook below. I bent over to retrieve my ball with a grin, and strode off the green. I put my putter into the bag, and marked a "5" on the scorecard attached to the clipboard on the pull cart handle. I searched my memory for who that voice reminded me of. I knew it was a voice from my past, my distant past, but I just couldn't quite place who it belonged to. There had to be another explanation, but this was *my* last round of golf. I was not to be distracted by some games my mind decided to play on me.

I looked all around, turning 360 degrees with a remaining hint of trepidation. I pulled the cart back onto the path and followed it away from the green on its way to the next, the second hole.

CHAPTER 7

Walking up the grade away from the first hole, the path entered the forest again. On the way to Number Two, I kept looking around, still hunting the source of that voice I heard behind the green. I found no one.

Through the trees and into the open again, there was the second hole. It was long and a little uphill all the way from tee to green, with a gentle dogleg to the left. There was a large, long fairway bunker on the right side that only a poor, pushed tee shot would find. A slight left tilt to the fairway would take balls away from that bunker and help them turn with the dog leg. Nearing the tee box, the scent of gardenias grew stronger. It came from a row of mature shrubs that ran along the opposite side where many spent blooms were on the ground. It was a wonderful smell, a signature of the South to greet arriving players. The sign showed this par 5 was 500 yards at its longest, 480 yards for me, and 390 from the ladies' tee way up there on the right. A ball washer next to the hole sign was full of clean soapy water. I used it and polished my ball dry with the large, fresh towel hanging from it. A small empty trash can sat next to the ball washer. I thought of Skip and his attention to the little things.

I hoped I would hit a better tee shot with my driver than I did on the first hole. In my pre-shot routine, I focused on positive thoughts: relaxing, making good contact, and having a good time. That fairway sand trap looked distant enough and it was uphill anyway. I lined up aiming straight at that bunker and swung away. My contact was nice and solid so I held my follow-through like I was posing for a portrait. A hint of a right-to-left draw on the ball flew it back toward the center of the fairway. It felt good to smack a crisp, solid drive. A golfer can hit a hundred bad shots, but it only takes one just like that to make us pay to play over and over again. Watching it roll, I was afraid that I underestimated the degree of the slope. Too far left and the trees would block my second shot. I urged my ball to hang on with a mumble through gritted teeth, but it still stopped more to the left of where I'd hoped. I put my driver back into the bag and started walking up the right side of the fairway. I wanted a better look around the corner of the dogleg at what my second shot would involve.

I could see the flag, elevated above me enough that I couldn't see the green's surface. On an upslope behind it, there was the small but brilliant blaze of orange color from a clump of azalea bushes. A large sand trap gaped diagonally from the far right side of the putting surface around and across the front. Thickening woods on either side of the fairway came closer to the playing area as it got closer to the green. I angled left across the fairway toward my ball.

Walking up this second fairway, my mind drifted back to what brought me here. I began to think of how often through my life I'd wondered how brave would I be – could I be – if I ever knew I was about to die. I marveled at the strength of people who learned they had a terminal disease, knowing I could never be as courageous as them. I always thought I would be more scared than anything else if I found out I was dying. And yes, I was scared, but I was more pissed than anything else, mad at myself much more than at God or fate or anyone else. I was pissed at myself for not being "finished" with so many things I wanted to do, places I wanted to go, things I wanted to say, burned bridges I wanted to mend. I was already starting to look back on life, beating myself up for opportunities wasted, over roads not taken versus the ones I *did* take. *"Why me?"* was in none of my thoughts at all, though. To a great degree, I was glad it was me instead of anyone else, as if I was taking the place of someone I thought was more deserving of a longer life: a scientist, an educator, a philanthropist, or a mother. After all, I know how very fortunate I am to have lived as long as I have, so blessed to have lived much longer than so many people better than me. There were also hundreds, thousands, no more like millions of people dealing with situations like mine and so much worse every day.

I needed to reconcile how I thought my faith was so strong when at the same time I saw myself as weak in the face of death. I thought a belief in the highest being of any religion means we have confidence in their ability to facilitate their grander plan for us. A person of faith should fear nothing; or, is being scared part of what God wants us to learn from the experience? It doesn't seem sensible that I could profess I am a believer and also be so apprehensive to have my God's will be done.

I arrived at my tee shot just inside the left side of the fairway. Another 220 yards uphill remained to the green. A direct shot was blocked by the woods at the corner where the fairway turned left ahead. I couldn't see my target landing area around the bend. If I tried to reach the green and failed, I would never see my ball again. It was smarter to just hit something that would leave me with a full wedge shot in front of the green inside around 100 yards. Drawing a nice middle iron around the corner was an easy shot that would give me a better chance at a par anyway. I took a 6-iron from my bag, picked a tall tree straight ahead as my starting point, and got ready to curve the ball left into the center of the fairway. I set up for the draw with confidence, and with what felt like a velvet swing, hit the ball.

"Oops," I said, finishing the swing. The ball was struck well but it flew straight as a string. The ball began coming down, headed for the woods. I heard the loud crack of the ball making solid contact when it hit a tree trunk about halfway up. The ball bounced and rattled its way down, down, down to the leaves on the ground below, careening off a couple of neighboring trees along the way.

Almost immediately upon hearing the report of my ball smacking the tree, I heard a loud chorus of laughter. It was almost like a gallery standing around the green of an adjacent hole had been told a joke I couldn't hear. The difference was the sound *surrounded* me – it wasn't from one place, but came at me from all directions. It was not a crowd, just a handful of voices. But like when you're with a group of friends or family for lunch and someone tells a joke, you could almost close your eyes and know which belonged to whom: each laugh, cackle, and snicker. As individual sounds they were familiar, but just like that voice on the first green, I couldn't put my finger on who they were. Maybe whoever that was minutes before had brought more friends with him to torment me now.

The best explanation again was that I was imagining things. It must have just been other golfers on the course having a good time. There was the possibility that they were laughing at *me*, at *my* shot. Back when I was a young guy, maybe that would have made me mad. Now, I had to agree: the fact I set up for a superb golf shot only to drill it into the boonies actually *was* pretty funny. Forgetting the voice and those that now seemed to have joined him, I headed toward the woods across the fairway. I didn't expect to be able to find my ball once I got there. Good thing Skip gave me that box of balls. It looked like I was going to need them.

I tuned out both the errant shot and the laughter to think again about what brought me here today. It sure wasn't to agonize over every rotten golf shot I might hit. My purpose was to experience a last thrill of something I loved, the good and the bad. It was to spend the day out in nature just one more time before death came. I wanted to reflect, to be retrospective, to flash on the wonderful memories golf has given me – which *life* has given me. There was no better place to do that than while playing golf. My reason for being here was not to drag myself through the figurative mud of anything, not of experiences, not of my poor play. I was here to enjoy, and not to look over my shoulder with an expectation of the Grim Reaper walking toward me, darkly cloaked and carrying that long-handled sickle.

It would be wrong to say I lived my life being obsessed with death, but I always wondered what it was going to be like. Not so much the religious aspect of what happens next; no, that was a different question altogether, one that I felt I resolved long ago. Millions of people have wondered the same things as I, and had the same questions through the annals of time. For something that happened to every person who had ever lived, for every living thing as far as that goes, how could we still not know ahead of time what death's arrival holds? My lifelong natural curiosity craves to know more about the process of the transition from this life to what comes next. I can't believe it possible that I'm the only one who wonders about these things.

A lifetime of preachings and teachings told me that passing from the short-term earthly to eternal heavenly life was something to look forward to. As strong as my faith had ever become, I could never convince myself that I should *prefer* to leave life on earth behind. I feel strong enough in my faith that my issue was not meeting my maker and getting into heaven, nor what I would find there. My question is how we pass, what it feels like, what it looks like, what it tastes like, what our senses are, what the experience itself is like. Are there bright lights and an accompaniment of angels like we hear about, or is there nothing but darkness, an anticlimactic end? Doctor Crosland's advice to remember that something else could kill me first meant that it could happen while walking this golf course. The broken club head of another golfer could fly over the trees to impale me. Or maybe a stray golf shot's ball might embed into my skull without warning. What would either of those be like? Would either be the same as I will experience if I pass from my disease as the doctor predicts?

With the impending inevitability of my passing at hand, I seemed more confused than ever. I was resigned to the acceptance that this phase of life – its end – was here, but for some reason I was concerned most about what my feelings, my senses, would be. It felt like the anxious anticipation of a first date: it may or may *not* be all I hoped it would. As calming as was the knowledge that I will experience death within days if not hours, not knowing the details of what sensations are involved is disquieting at best. We always say that we hope the end is painless, but don't know how realistic that is. We hope that those dying will pass "peacefully", but don't know what that means. There must be a sensation the dying body feels. Whatever "peace" is, it must come at some point, regardless of how death comes.

Getting closer to the edge of the woods, I was shocked to see my ball. It sat in a little opening a few yards back in the thicket, as if it were peeking out of the cave. I parked the pull cart and walked in to see if I had a shot. A lot of golfers would kick it out into a playable area and move along, but I was never was one of those. At least, if I was ever going to do it, I wouldn't do it today. The area the ball lay in was open enough to accommodate the arc of my club. There was a clear enough path toward the hole to think about going that direction, but a treacherous route it was, a mesh of tree limbs only a professional should try to shoot through. "Don't do anything stupid," I thought aloud with a whisper, convincing myself that I should just pop the ball out into the fairway and back into play.

I confess to being conscious of the possibility that I really *was* being watched, and didn't want to hit consecutive lousy shots in front of whoever it was. I could hit a low shot out of the woods toward the hole, keeping my ball just under the branches. That would leave me a short third shot to the green. I grabbed a 3-iron, looked down at the ball, and hit it with an abbreviated, punching swing. Leaves flew from a hanging branch when the ball came up a bit higher than I wanted, clipping the limb when it went straight through. I ran out of the woods past my bag to see the ball bouncing into the short fairway grass. The result was exactly what I wanted. It was sitting right where I hoped it would before I hit that second shot – it just took me an extra stroke to get there. I cupped a hand to my ear like I was waiting for applause, but it didn't come.

Dropping the club back into my bag, I thought again of Uncle Clyde. He taught me many of those get-out-of-trouble shots, long, long ago. "If you're going to play golf, you're going to get into trouble, so you've gotta know how to get out of it," he would tell me. As I got older, I knew that was another of many pieces of golf advice applicable to everyday life. A successful man in a small Texas town a few hours' drive away from our home, he fueled my interest in golf at a very young age. It was his passion. He was always happy to help me once I started playing the game regularly with childhood friends.

No one could have had any control over how my uncle passed, but I knew more today than ever how important family support could be when you are dying. Back then, I excused my inability to visit him while he was sick as due to my "business responsibilities". I said I was just too busy and it was too far away. I told myself that he'd be OK, that Uncle Clyde was tougher than any disease, but I still wished and prayed for his recovery and for his suffering to stop. Instead, his condition deteriorated. A long and painful illness preceded his passing, the kind that at least I'm told I'll not go through – for that I am thankful. It seems unfair that he had to endure that, and I will not; he was such a better man than I. I wasn't there for his family, or for him, when he died. How I want to see him, to apologize to him. I supposed I'll be seeing him soon enough. I kept walking up the grade.

I needed to push all these peripheral things in my head aside, at least while I prepared for and hit each shot. Walking golf alone is as good a time as any to be thinking about things, but I didn't want to let my mind screw up an enjoyable game. I reached my ball, about 90 yards from the green. The lie was good and I could just see the top of the flag. It seemed about as easy a shot as I could have, even though it would be my fourth. I grabbed a pitching wedge, went through my routine, and hit the ball. Every well-hit shot in golf is a pleasure, and this pitch shot sure was. The ball flew high and straight, just the right distance to clear the protective bunker in front and land on the unseen surface. The bounce of the ball I watched gave me confidence it would stop in good shape.

I got back on the cart path to climb left of the green. Over the final ridge the path flattened out to a parking area. I was admiring the orange azaleas until I saw the sand trap at the back of the small putting surface. That's when I noticed my ball was not on the green ready for a putt, like I expected. I walked across the green to the flagstick. I muttered aloud what I asked myself, "Who knows? Always check in the hole first, right?" I saw the mark of my ball where it hit the green a few feet in front of the cup and had a moment of hope. I leaned over to look in the hole before repairing my mark. I wasn't surprised to see the cup empty. Hesitant, I walked to the back of the green. The small bunker I couldn't see from the fairway below was surrounded by thick and heavy grass. There, I saw my bright white ball lying atop the sand like it was sunbathing.

Logic says that a shot out of the sand is a much easier shot than out of rough. I hate sand anyway. Always have. I sighed as I walked back to the bag to get the sand wedge and putter, ready to go back and face the music that awaited me in the greenside trap. I pulled the putter first, but when my hand found the sand wedge, I abruptly stopped in shock. Now in my own little trance, I flashed on Skip and his "magic" comment.

There is no way I would not have noticed this club until now. The engraving into the once bright silver finish of a new club head was worn down a lot, much like the rest of the rental set. It was still readable, though. So, when I saw "Ben Hogan Sand Wedge", I took a step back. This was *my* club. This has been my club for 40 years. I knew this club better than almost anything I owned, just as I knew that this club was back home in New Mexico. I was deliberate as I drew it up and out of the bag, inspecting it for any explanation of how it could be here, expecting to see *something* that would confirm my mind was playing tricks on me, that this could *not* be my sand wedge. *This* old wedge had seen years and years of use in every situation a lofted club was useful, just like mine. Perhaps a different grip, a different shaft, something, anything would show that this was *not* the club I bought in high school and carried ever since. My mind flashed through the yards I mowed and the chores I did to make enough money to buy it at Phillips' Sporting Goods store a few blocks from my childhood home. I thought of all the times I wanted to throw it in a lake or into the woods as far as I could, just to get it out of my sight, hoping it would absorb the blame for my last shot. I dropped the putter to my side. I held the wedge in both hands, rolling it around, still looking for something that would tell me I was crazy, to tell me that this was just a coincidence. It was no coincidence: this *was* my club.

Just its *feel* confirmed my suspicions. It was the club I hit well and hit poorly, used the right way and wrong way, used as a putter for fun, used in so many situations with so many outcomes for so many years. It was the club that taught me there were many uses for it other than *in* sand. This was the club I never sold, discarded, or gave away. I always kept it in my bag with every new set, every new bag, and every equipment change I ever made. It was not because I was so good with it; it was just because it was that Hogan wedge I worked so hard to get. It was the one I was so proud of on the golf team in high school that I had it and you did not. It bore the name of the fellow Texan who was one of the greatest golfers who ever lived. I was not even sure when the last time I held it in my hands was. This club was not there before now. There is no way I would not have seen it before.

The loud crow of a nearby blackbird brought me out of my daze. I took my wedge and the putter across the green. I walked over and stepped into the soft sand. I decided that whatever caused this club to mysteriously be in my hands did not intend for me to simply think of just getting the ball out. Why not try to hole it? I took my stance knowing I could do it, and tried to relax as I made a couple of half practice swings down toward the surface. I shuffled my feet to anchor myself into the sand. A couple of looks up at my target, and I was ready.

My swing threw the club down and the Hogan wedge made a loud *thump* pounding into the sand an inch behind the ball. I powered the club through the sand and the ball floated out in a cloud of powder. It dropped onto the short grass of the putting surface and began a slow roll, straight at the pin, rolling true. My eyes widened as it crept closer and closer to the cup. Could it really happen? Could it really go in? When it reached the edge of the hole, the speed was just a bit too much.

I watched it go around the full edge of the cup in slow-motion. It rolled around the pin and back toward me, making the dreaded 180-degree "horseshoe", stopping just two inches away.

I wore a broad smile as I grabbed the rake and smoothed over the trap, then stepped out and knocked the sand off my shoes with the Hogan wedge. I stared at the club again in wonder and walked to the hole, still beaming. I wouldn't need my putter for this one. With one hand still holding the wedge, I tapped the ball into the hole with the blade and picked the ball out of the cup. "That's a pretty good six," I said, gazing at that wedge.

Turning to walk off the green, I was surprised to see Ralphie laying there quiet, watching me, his head resting on his front paws. "Well, hey Dude," I said. His head came up and he looked at me, his tongue coming out with his pant. "That was a pretty good bogey, huh? Bet you didn't think I could hit a sand shot like that, did you?" He gave me a single bark and a grin. "Yeah, me neither," I replied.

He sat up on his hind legs, smiling and panting. I placed the clubs into the bag and wrote a "6" on my card. I began thinking how comfortable I was with him around when something caught his eye off in the woods again. He stood up, looked back at me, and I could swear that he winked at me. He took off at break neck speed, bounding through the thicket.

"See you later," I yelled behind the running dog. I turned to look back once again at the scene that was the second hole. It was both odd and entertaining, I thought. It was fun, despite good shots and bad, despite my morbid thoughts, and in spite of the curious laughter. It made me see again a connection to the contrasts within my life, but I hoped "looking back" was not becoming the theme of this day. It made me feel I should have spent the past half century and more as if that airborne broken club head would be spinning over the trees at any moment inexorably headed for me as its target. If I had learned before now to enjoy every minute as if it could be my last, maybe I would have fewer reasons to begin looking back now. Maybe I wouldn't be wishing I'd made different decisions, wishing I'd lived my life so differently. Then again, maybe I would just play golf and have a good time on a nice day.

I looked at the Hogan wedge that had given me such a memorable shot, no matter how it got here. I looked ahead up the path where a winking dog departed after it appeared from nowhere. Off I walked again, following the path into the tunnel through the forest on my way to Number Three.

CHAPTER 8

Sunlight streaked with sharp contrast into the shady forest from openings in the treetops while I walked the path from the second green. These calming transitions between holes were proving to be just what I needed. They were so calming and comforting I hoped they'd continue the rest of the day.

The ground flattened out again, and I could see through the opening in the woods to the third hole ahead. A powered cart sat parked at the tee box. There was no way I could have caught up to another group already. When playing solo, it's only natural that you move quick enough to catch anybody ahead of you because you don't have to wait on your companion players. I thought I'd been taking my time so far, though, just so I'd avoid doing that. It was just one golf cart by itself, not the two you'd expect to be carrying a group of four. This single parked cart had only one bag on it. How could a single golfer walking like me catch up with a single golfer driving a powered cart? What, was he playing four balls by himself?

There was no one standing on the tee. A man sitting in the cart was relaxed, feet up with hands interlocked behind his head. He was a tall, thin man wearing shorts with a polo shirt and an off-white visor. "Great," I muttered to myself, "I caught up with a guy because he's taking naps on the tee." This hole was short, a 375 yard par 4 from the white tees; you could see the flag from the tee box. The hole was almost as wide to the tall bordering trees as it was long to the green, and there was a small pond in front of the slightly elevated putting surface. The pool was almost begging players on the tee to try and drive the green. Two small fairway bunkers sat on opposite sides of the fairway at about the 100-yard post. A mound in the middle of the fairway about halfway to the hole looked like bouncing on its sides might kick your tee shot into one sand trap or the other.

I looked ahead of the reclining person to see that there was no one on the hole anywhere, all the way to the green. I wondered if there was a group of golfers way off in the woods somewhere that this guy got stacked up behind. I looked back to the waiting player. I wanted to scream it, but silent and to myself, I wondered: what is this guy waiting on?

"*You,*" said the loud voice in the cart without turning around. *That* was The Voice. Without a doubt, this was the same voice I heard back on the first green. I kept walking toward him but still couldn't see any features other than his graying blonde hair under the visor.

"Pardon me?" I asked as I walked closer to him.

"I've been waiting for *you.*" He straightened his seated body in the cart. I noticed the cart he was driving was different from the fleet I saw back around Skip's clubhouse. This was a brand new bright green one, not like the dingy aged white cars back around the practice areas. Turning to step out, he kept the brim of his visor down. He mumbled to himself, "Gotta stay short of that pond – better not hit the driver," while he pulled a fairway wood from his bag. He continued his original thought in a normal voice, saying to me, "Not that waiting on you is anything unusual, I've done it so often." He turned his face up to me for the first time, grinning while buttoning his glove and walking onto the tee box. I was about 30 feet away from him. I recognized him and stopped cold in my tracks. Stunned, my legs quit moving and my jaw hung open. He stared into my eyes and said, "But I have to admit, that last sand shot was just about the best I ever saw you hit."

"Pretty good bogey, that's for sure," my mouth moved in a shocked response. He ignored my bewildered reaction and stepped between the tee markers, looking ready to tee up and play. "Scott?!" I wouldn't say I screeched, but I sounded just as surprised as I was. Even after 30 years, I knew it was him. The familiar sweat-soiled Oregon State visor he wore said it was my once closest of friends that I hadn't seen in so many years, it seemed like forever.

"See, that's what happens," still smirking, he bent over to tee his ball, "First you stop calling, and then you don't even send me a Christmas card anymore." He walked to a point behind his ball and looked down the third fairway. He swung his club to warm up a couple of times, laughing while he continued, "You just forget about me like a penny that dropped behind your dresser."

Scott Hancock was my dear friend for several years when we both were pursuing our post-collegiate, young professional careers. My arms were tingling while I started walking again, staring at him in disbelief as I grew closer. I was delighted to see him; I just couldn't understand *how* he could be right in front of me. He was still grinning when he started his swing. He brought his club back in a signature awkward fashion, making a little loop at the top where he paused to begin his down swing. He came through the ball with what was still about the ugliest swing I have ever seen. Seeing his patented swing erased any remaining doubt I might have – I watched that swing thousands of times back when we played together regularly. I was even more shocked when his ball left the tee straight, strong and long. How uncharacteristic of him.

“You’ve been practicing,” I said, needling him while watching his ball land in the ideal spot and keep rolling. I left my carted bag just off the tee box and walked to join him on the tee. “Man, you *still* have a swing only a mother could love.”

He looked away from his stopping ball to see me getting closer to him. “Oh, no, you’re not going to try to *hug* me, are you?” Despite never being a hugging kind of guy, it was true that I was planning to do just that. He walked around and away from me in a trot toward his cart. I was motionless now on the tee box, remaining transfixed by seeing him here, seeing him now.

“No, I don’t need to hug you, but I thought I might shake your hand,” I said while he sat down behind the wheel in the car. He crossed his legs again to await my tee shot.

“Maybe after you’re done freaking out.” I continued to stand frozen on the tee, and Scott just stared at me. “So, are you going to hit? Are you waiting for the light to turn green, or what?”

Numb with confusion I walked back to my bag and fastened my glove. Also concerned about that pond in front of the green, I pulled out a 3-wood. I walked to the area between the two white sticks, teed my ball low and went into my routine. I still didn't know what to say. I was dumbfounded, but I wanted *some* kind of answer. "Scott, what in God's green earth are you doing here?" There was still silence. "How did you find me?" For several more seconds, we just gazed at each other.

"So full of questions, Chris," his statement accompanied by another moment of smirking. "We'll get into what I'm doing here later. For now, just try to keep up with me, would you?"

"Try to keep up," I said, mocking him in a grumble from behind my ball. I was ready to fire back some smart remark about how he would be the one having trouble keeping up. That's when I looked up and saw Scott's ball. His drive split the fairway between the two fairway bunkers and just kept rolling to the perfect position. I couldn't help but compliment him: "Nice shot", I said.

Scott always had a distinctive, cackle kind of laugh, and he spoke through it, saying, "Thanks. Too bad you were so busy being all dramatic before, or else we could have made a bet on the hole."

"It's never too late – how about five bucks?"

"Do I need to make you show me the five dollars first? I mean, I'm in pretty good shape up there."

"Just like a damn banker," I played with him and got ready to take my shot. "Go against your nature and trust me."

I stepped up to the ball and looked at my target area. The short hole's only worries were the lake in front of the green and the two sand traps astride the fairway. Scott's drive was so long it had flown the mound in the center with no problem. I felt I could get past it, too. I looked over at Scott. He'd aged very little since I last saw him. We were within a few months of being the same age. In general, he'd kept in better shape than me back then, but why did he look so much younger than me now? I mean, sure, I was sick, but he looked like he was around 40, maybe even younger. While I wondered, he spoke for the first time with a tone of sincerity in his voice.

"You look pretty good, too – for your age, I mean." He paused to let me swing before adding, "All things considered," when I held my follow-through. How did he again know what I was thinking? I'd hit the ball well, a fine shot to just left of the center of the fairway. It stopped between the 150- and 100-yard posts, still about 30 yards back from Scott's ball. "Good ball," he said. I picked up my tee and was about to ask where this mind-reading trick came from when he stepped on his golf car's pedal and headed down the cart path. Moving away, over his shoulder he smiled, "Even though *your* ball *is* a little short."

Walking at a slow pace off the tee, I watched him drive into the fairway, on the way to his ball without looking back at me again. So far, this Scott was a little different from the one I knew. We were two guys far from being "touchy" back when we were closest friends, but now it was almost like he was annoyed with me. I never knew him to dodge a handshake. I mean, he was a banker, for crying out loud. The Scott from back in the day was about the nicest guy I ever met. We messed with each other constantly, whether on a golf course, in a business meeting, or out together with and without dates. People often asked if we were brothers. We would say we were even closer than brothers, because we never *really* fought.

When I walked into the fairway, I saw Scott slowing to a stop near my ball ahead, parking to wait for me. While I walked, I thought back to when he was a young bank Vice President and I was a young airline Operations Director. We met when I moved to Denver on a new assignment just a few years out of college. Part of my cleaning up and revamping the Denver station's financial discipline included changing local banks. Scott was one of several representatives from different banks I met with to see who wanted our business the most. There was no contest – he worked his butt off to earn our account, and he succeeded. Once we got started our account was so large his bank tried to assign someone else to be their point person with my office. That precipitated my meeting their CEO in San Francisco to let them know I would move our accounts again and leave their bank if Scott was not our guy.

After he got a stout promotion, Scott and I were joined at the hip professionally, and our outside-of-work friendship began. For a while we were even dating two women who were best friends. We went out to dinner as a foursome a few nights a week. Even though we both spent more money on "playing" than we should have, he did a much better job of saving for the future than I did. It was common for us to go to San Diego for the weekend, using my flight passes, playing a variety of local golf courses, and staying in hotels one or the other of us had connections at. If we could get away during the week, we would play golf at Torrey Pines, then play the horses and drink too much beer at Del Mar's racetrack.

Once our Denver station became more stabilized and our airline expanded, I began travelling more often to our other airport locations, and Scott grew closer to one of those dinner dates, a gorgeous woman named April. On one of my trips to Phoenix, I met Cameron, and we began a relationship that grew fast. We both really liked the woman the other had found, and we were happy for each other's relationships. We vowed that neither women nor families nor new job locations would interfere with our friendship. *Nothing* was going to keep us from playing golf together whenever and wherever we wanted to. April and Scott were married in a wonderful ceremony overlooking Monterey Bay in California. On the trip there to serve as my buddy's Best Man, Cameron and I became inseparable and were married two years later.

When I reached my ball, Scott stayed seated in his golf cart 15 feet parallel to where it lay. I noticed another thing different about my friend: Scott had always been a chain smoker, so I was a bit surprised to see he wasn't puffing a cigarette now. Come to think of it, the last time we played together, we *both* were smokers. I quit almost 20 years ago.

"You quit smoking, huh?" I asked, still trying to get some conversation going.

He chuckled, "Yeah, in a matter of speaking." I wondered what that meant. Seemed like a pretty simple yes-or-no to me. "You would know that if you had kept in touch." If he was still trying to make me feel bad, it was working. I just sighed in response and turned to attend to the shot at hand. It was just a little uphill to the green, and that pesky pond was in front of it. I pulled a 9-iron from the bag. Before hitting, I wanted to respond to his comment first, and stopped my routine to do so.

"Hey, you two started making babies – *you're* the one that didn't have time for *me*." There was fun in my tone, but the point was accurate, and he knew it. "*Lots* of babies, as I recall." They had five children, last I heard.

"True, but it wasn't long until you and Cameron started, too, you know." He paused to let me hit.

"Yeah, but we stopped after we had two." I swung down onto the ball, taking a good solid divot. I'd put good spin on it, showing off a little with my twirl of the club at the top of my follow-through. It was close enough to the pin and on the green. The ball danced as it hopped and stopped.

Scott and I looked at each other, his face showing feigned disgust, mine smirking. We always acted like we were very competitive with each other, but we really just wanted to bring out our best. Scott chuckled and drove away toward his ball. I replaced my divot, stuck my club back into my bag and took my glove off, my first step in getting ready to putt. Scott stopped next to his ball, pulled a wedge out of his bag and stepped up to play "ready golf", not wasting any time. He hit a full wedge, also taking some good turf with his swing. His ball flew higher, and looked like it would end up better than mine.

"Be as good as you look," Scott pleaded, hoping to direct the ball. It bounced within a couple of feet from the pin, hopped once and stopped. He turned toward me, and smiled. "In your eye," he chided with a chuckle.

I kept walking, pulling my cart past him. “That’s a great shot, buddy,” I smiled as I complimented him. “Guess I’ll be putting first.”

“Too soon to tell,” he said. He bagged his club, got in the cart, and pulled it alongside and just ahead of me to my left as I strode. He stopped and said, “Let’s go see.” I paused, looking at him, not sure what to do. “Get in,” said with a smile. Holding my pull cart with my right hand I sat on the passenger side. He pulled away and headed slowly for the cart path where it approached the green. I pulled my 2-wheeler from where I sat as we sped up, praying Skip wouldn’t see me doing it.

Scott spoke first. “I can remember driving up to the green together when we’d both just be hoping either of us could find our balls at all. We’d hope to find them somewhere – in the rough, in the weeds – just find them anywhere.”

“Yeah, maybe in the woods, or on the beach,” I finished the thought he started. We nodded in unison, agreeing as we reminisced.

“Of course, you always look for it in the hole, just to make sure,” Scott smiled. “I saw you do that on the second hole, when your ball ended up being in that back bunker.”

“Hey, I was just checking,” I chuckled with him. I glared at him, a bit irritated at myself for not recognizing back then that the voice had been his. I didn’t know why he would have been hiding. Scott read my mind again.

“Sorry man, just part of the plan.” What plan, I wondered?

Getting closer to the green, Scott began stretching his neck to see the putting surface better, hoping to see our locations relative to the pin. We both knew how often the actual spot of the ball on the green is distorted when you see it from the fairway. Sometimes what appeared to be a shot tight to the pin would prove otherwise by the time you got there. Not this time. Coming around the pond, we saw my ball about 10 feet away from the pin. I would have an almost flat putt that would turn just a little left-to-right. Scott could not have been four feet away, straight and uphill. We were giddy enough we grinned at each other while he pulled up and parked. We got out and walked onto the green with our putters in hand. Repairing our ball marks in the green, we noted how each imprint was closer to the hole than where the ball finished. Scott's mark was less than a foot from the hole.

"You almost flew it in there, Pods," I said, because he almost had.

"Well, I haven't been called *that* in a long time." He referred to our once-common and much overused abbreviated term for "Partner", or in Texan, "Podnah". He looked back at our two putts and said, "You want to go ahead and pay me now?"

"No, let's just putt them first, before we do that. Maybe you still putt the way you used to."

I took a quick look at my putt, stood over it, and stroked it. As my ball rolled toward the cup, Scott said, "You don't waste time analyzing putts like you used to". The ball stopped just outside to the right, stopping two inches away. Scott knelt behind his ball for a quick look at his line as I walked up to tap the finisher into the cup.

"I've noticed as I get older things that I used to take a long time to do, I now do real quick, and vice versa." He laughed and I tapped in my par. Although I was joking, it was pretty much an accurate statement.

"What do you think of my putt?" he asked.

"I think if you miss it, I'll have to leave this five dollar bill in my pocket. Knock it in so I can pay you, Pods." Despite all the grief we always exchanged, we were always encouraging each other when a situation warranted it. He smiled, and with a confident stroke, holed it. "Atta boy, good hole," I added. He picked his ball from the cup and I replaced the pin. I handed him the five dollars.

"That was a good par yourself," Scott smiled back at me.

We walked off the green together, both feeling good, not just about both playing the hole well, but about overcoming our initial tension with each other. I still wanted to know what he was doing here. I wanted to know why and how he appeared out of nowhere the way he did. We reached our carts and with no fanfare, he extended his hand toward me. We were quiet as we exchanged a firm handshake, brief, but with feeling. Letting go, I felt so much better now about being with my friend. I forgot how much I missed him. I still had hundreds of questions, wrestling with myself about how to ask them while we put our putters away. We sat in the cart and took a brief, uncomfortable glance at each other before turning to look ahead, up the path. Then, Scott pulled away.

CHAPTER 9

The cart path went into the woods again leaving the third green on the way to Number Four. I struggled to hold onto the rolling hand cart I was pulling abreast of the powered cart while Scott drove. My wheels bounced over the roots, twigs, and leaves alongside the paved path even though he wasn't driving very fast through the cool forested tunnel. We laughed as I almost lost it a couple of times, nearly dumping my bag. I had a quick and negative vision of Skip coming out on the course and catching me doing something this stupid and immature.

We came out of the trees and an elevated tee box was right there, looking down onto a 540-yard par 5. The familiar creek crossed the hole again about halfway to the pin. Below the tee, the hole flattened out the rest of the way to the green, although there was a bit of a left-to-right slant in the fairway the length of the hole. The tree line was much closer than on the previous hole on both sides, making the playing area feel much tighter.

"Two par 5's in the first four holes is kind of interesting," Scott said, and I nodded in agreement. Scott skidded to a stop next to the tee sign. I felt like I wanted to kiss the ground after surviving the ride. We both sighed with relief and then laughed together, visualizing ourselves for a moment as stoned 25-year-olds, acting crazy again. We stepped out of the cart and both pulled the drivers from our bags.

"Your birdie has the tee, sir," I said, acknowledging his previous hole. He tipped the brim of his visor and nodded his acceptance in return. He bent over to tee his ball between the white markers.

"Let's see if I can hit my driver as well as I did that fairway wood on the last tee," he said, and went into his routine.

While he prepared to hit, I wanted to start getting somewhere with Scott, getting some kind of information out of him about what was happening. "By the way, just so you're aware, I'm having a really weird day today." He kept staring at the hole in front of him while I continued, "And you're a big part of it being weird."

He chuckled, "What's the matter, not happy to see me?"

"Quite the contrary, Scott. I can't tell you how delighted I am for fear of inflating your ego too much. I sure don't want to compliment you on how young you're looking, that's for sure." He took a couple of practice swings. "I'm just anxious for you to explain to me what's going on here."

"Well, Chris, the truth be told, you're in for an interesting day. It's just getting started, in fact." He set up for his drive, both of us staying quiet a moment while that wild, loopy swing connected. He made good contact, but pushed it to the right. He grimaced while holding his follow-through. The slant of the hole kept it moving right. His ball was short of the trees, bouncing a few times in the rough to a safe stop. "I *hate* doing that, blocking it, pushing it right like that," he complained as he walked off the tee. Then, in an odd gesture, he looked skyward and said, "I know, 'hate' is a strong word. Sorry."

"So, what does that mean?"

"What?" He leaned down to pick up his tee.

"What you said about how I'm just getting started."

"Pretty simple what it means – it means you're up." His retort was stern. I was trying to avoid becoming even more confused, when he followed with a cold, "Your shot." How abruptly the brotherly love we enjoyed while walking off the last green seemed to have vanished.

I thought about refusing to do anything else until he gave me an explanation, but then I realized maybe I was imagining the whole thing anyway. Besides, for all I knew, Cameron was showing her clandestine streak and had arranged our meeting anyway. It was just the kind of surprise she might take pride in organizing. I decided to go ahead with my drive even though it was hard to relax. I was keyed up, stressing because I wanted an answer about what Scott meant with his comment about *just getting started.* Following through the ball with my swing, I made the opposite mistake that Scott did – I got ahead of the ball and pulled it left. It wasn't a duck hook; it just started left and kept going, in a way even the right slant of the fairway couldn't help. My ball had finished in the rough about the same as his, just on the opposite side of the fairway, at about the same distance. "Well, we're both off to a good start here," I said, and picked up my tee. I was going to keep pursuing elucidation from Scott, whether he liked it or not.

When we were ready to pull away from the tee's parking area I told Scott, "If I keep pulling my cart while I'm riding in yours, something is going to break – like my arm." Figuratively, the ice broke and we shared a nervous laugh. "I'd better go back to walking." I got out.

"Well, it *is* a nice day," he said, and stepped out with me. He walked to the back of his cart to unstrap his bag. When he did, he looked down at my feet and said, "Your shoes are untied." I looked down and saw he was right. Funny, since I didn't notice it in the cart just seconds ago. I put one foot up on the wheel of my pull cart and retied my shoe. When I looked back up, he was pulling taut the strap holding his bag onto a 2-wheeled cart of his own. He walked to the driver's side of the powered green golf car, gathering his belongings and zipping them into his bag.

"And just where did *that* come from?" I asked.

"I had it in my back pocket," he snorted, feigning irritation at my question before he just chuckled. I stood a few more seconds staring at him. "Look, Chris, a lot of things will be confusing today," he said, more serious now, grabbing the new pull cart handle and walking away from the tee before pausing to wait for me to join him. "Come on, man," his face said he wanted me to quit worrying about everything that I felt was out-of-order. "Let's go. Time is short, you know." Brother, how I knew. We walked away from the tee together.

"Time *is* short, yes, I *do* know," I said. I could feel him grinning and wondered if there was more to his comment. Maybe Cameron tipped him off. I asked, "So what do you know about time being short, Scott?"

"More than you can imagine." He glared at me. "I've got all the time in the world, but *you* have none to waste, Chris." We walked a few silent paces. "Confusing, isn't it?"

"Confusing, you mean like the group of laughing hyenas back on the second hole?"

"Oh, yeah, don't worry about that. Besides, it *was* a pretty funny shot, wasn't it?" He knew I had to agree.

"So, where are all your laughing buddies?"

"Who said they're *with* me?" Neither of us said anything, then after a few paces, Scott continued. He changed to a tone as serious as I ever heard him. "I need you to listen to me, Chris, and listen to me close. A lot of things will not make sense today, but this can be the most interesting day of your life if you follow one simple direction: whatever you do today, you've got to keep going, keep moving. Don't stop playing. Just keep telling yourself to keep moving, keep moving." He paused when he saw the curiosity in my furrowed brow. "Quitting is easy, you know? I mean, people do it every day, it's the easy way out, isn't it?" His head turned toward me. "After all, you've done it."

"Done what, quit? What are you talking about?" He didn't answer, he just stared at me. "Besides, why would I want to quit on what you claim is supposed to be the most interesting day of my life?"

"You quit on the airline."

"Wait a minute that was because of Cameron – "

"You quit on your friends, you quit on me." He had me there. "As far as that goes, you quit on your family, too. And what was your first major at TCU? You quit on that, too, didn't you?"

"Yes, but I graduated and had a good career – well, for many years anyway, I – "

"Don't avoid admitting that you quit on Theology." Not many knew that was my original major. "You have to find out for yourself if that means you quit on God." I didn't know what to say or how to respond. To accuse me of quitting on God sure seemed like a personal assault. I never thought of myself as a quitter, so I wondered why Scott was trying to make me feel like one now.

"What about today, though? I mean, I think I understand your point, that there are some things in my past that can be argued. But let's get back to today: I tell you I'm having a weird day, and it seems you know why. You've been reading my mind since I bumped into you back there. You start explaining to me and then we go off on a tangent. Next thing I know you equate changing my major to quitting on God, which is a little strong, don't you think?" Now I looked straight at him. "I want to know about *today.*"

Scott was calm, but direct. "What I can tell you about today is this: do not for any reason, hesitate, linger, hang out, or do anything that amounts to slowing down your round. Keep moving. Play at a normal, relaxing pace. You should enjoy the day. But, whatever you do, don't hold up play, and most of all, don't quit. Keep moving. Finish the round." He looked deep into my eyes. "Keep moving."

"What happens if I ignore you?"

"I don't think you want the consequence that comes with that. Look, just don't do it, don't give up today." Then, his tone became more positive. "Hey, enjoy the day! Not many get a chance to have the experiences you'll have today." He smiled. "Humor me, OK? Appreciate the day, just make sure you don't quit." His face lent gravity to his point, punctuated with, "No matter what happens. You hear me? No matter *what* happens."

He changed the subject, first to our tee shots, then the natural beauty of the area and this course. I looked back a couple of times to the tee behind us, to where Scott left the powered cart parked. I was trying to think as we walked and talked about what I would tell Skip back at the clubhouse to explain why we just left a cart sitting right there at the tee box. The third time I looked back, that green golf cart was gone – simply vanished. Scott returned my puzzled gaze, reached over and just gave me a pat on the shoulder and said, "Stop worrying about it."

We began asking each other not about families, but of old friends and acquaintances, just making small talk now that we were back to being comfortable with each other again. Each person we spoke of began with one of us asking, "Hey, do you remember...?" Most of them I never heard from again after a certain point, but Scott filled in what I didn't know. He was current on everyone and everything, omniscient about whoever we discussed, including where they were now and what their life was like since last I heard.

We continued chatting through hacking at our second shots, both of us catching too much grass when we hit out of rough that was more punishing than it looked. The crossing creek was intended to challenge a long drive. We both flirted with it as we flew our second shots just over it. We walked toward our third shots, finishing up talking about our old friends. I was about to ask Scott about his family. Again, he knew what I was about to ask, and he began.

"April's doing great," he said, "She moved back to Orange County to live with Bob and his wife." He saw the puzzled look on my face. "Bob – Robert – our second child, remember? There's Karen, Robert, Amy, Tracy, and Kelley." I remembered they had several kids, more girls than boys, but the details eluded me. He went on to describe in detail how they each had grown and what they were doing, and we drifted away into old memories again.

To his single friends, Scott and April were one of those boyfriend-girlfriend couples that were great at nothing more than occupying each other's time. As his buddies, we couldn't see it lasting, never turning into anything. I was the most surprised to hear they planned to marry. With Cameron as my date to their summer wedding, I almost expected one or the other to not show up at the altar. Soon, she was pregnant with what became Karen. That was pretty much the end of our socializing, so often is the case with young couples. Years later it would be the same with my wife and me.

Scott was still talking about them through hitting his next ball. He hit an 8-iron that finished just short and right of the green, leaving an easy chip remaining. We kept talking about his family. I recalled the time after they moved to Seattle, we visited them once after a few kids were running around their house. Cameron and I were soon to be married, and I wanted Scott to return the favor of being my Best Man. Once I saw the natural chaos of their young household, I knew he wouldn't be able to get away to oblige me. I remember seeing how much the two of them had changed, had matured. I saw what parenting did not so much *to* them as *for* them. Our kids were still a couple of years away, so I didn't yet have first-hand knowledge about the many benefits of parenting. That day we visited Scott's home, if anyone told me that he and I would not see nor hear from each other again for this many years, I would have said they were crazy.

When we crossed the creek and reached my ball, we were talking about his son Robert. You could hear his pride swell, telling how his only son was a decorated Marine, stationed at El Toro, California. We spoke often long ago of how we both regretted not serving our country in the military, so I knew how genuine his feelings were. He told me a little about his son's career and how he met the woman that became his daughter-in-law while I pulled a fat 8-iron left of the green into some deep grass behind a greenside bunker. Scott wasn't saying why his wife April was living with his Bob and his family. I wondered if they were divorced, but I was waiting for him to tell me.

Walking toward the green, Scott told me how his parents passed away in Oregon within a couple of years of each other. I'd met them a few times when they came to visit Scott in Denver years ago. I could still see his Dad's broad smile, telling me, "My bride here is Martha, and you can call me Jimbo," while giving my hand a vigorous shake. I could visualize the happy aging couple while Scott detailed what they went through with the illnesses that led to their deaths. They always treated me with warmth, which told me Scott's conversations with them about me had been positive. I knew they were good parents for him. They were a wonderful and charming couple, and I was sorry to hear they were gone.

"I'm sure that was a tough time for you," I said.

"It was a lot tougher on them." He voice softened. "Before they died, they had to deal with surviving their child. Nobody should have to do that." I was unsure what I missed. Did I forget about a brother or a sister of Scott's that something happened to? My buddy was an only child, I was *sure* of it.

I was sheepish as I asked, "What do you mean, Scott?"

"I mean, we all believe our children will outlive us, that's what we all want, right? Kids are just not supposed to go before parents." He looked at me, and I still didn't know how to respond. "But, life doesn't always work out the way you think it will, does it?"

"You're talking in riddles to me, man," I said, sympathetic but frustrated.

"It's just part of your day today, Chris," he stared into my eyes again when he said my name. I felt like he was reaching in and grabbing my soul, but I still didn't understand why. "There's your ball," he said, before his eyes followed the nod of his head toward where my third shot lay, cozy where it sat in the deep grass. He walked over toward the other side of the green, where his ball lay.

I stood next to my ball, able to see nothing but a gaping sand trap in front of me. There was plenty of putting surface on the other side of it, though. I closed my eyes as I reached into my bag, knowing this was another perfect situation for that magical Hogan wedge.

What I pulled out was just the rental set wedge this time. A hopeful look into the bag confirmed the Hogan was gone. I didn't need to wonder if I left it on the ground behind me on the last hole. I knew it was gone as mysteriously as it had first appeared. This rented club would have to do. Scott kept walking while I took a couple of practice swings through the rough, focused on just getting the ball onto the green. I always had a lot of confidence in this shot, but it had been a very long time since I'd hit one. Scott stopped and parked his pull cart while I prepared to hit.

"Tough shot," he said across the front of the green to me. "Get it close."

An almost full swing took the ball very, very high. I hoped it would just clear the bunker and get onto the green. It seemed to come straight down, and landed just beyond the trap's far lip. From where I stood, I couldn't see it, but I knew it would be good.

"Very nice," he said, and he added a few simple golf claps with his hands before he reached into his bag for a club. "You're going to like that one." It looked like an 8-iron he pulled out, which seemed smart for his uphill chip. He was just a few feet from the green, but there was another 30 feet to the cup.

I pulled my cart to the left of the green. Now that I could see my ball just twelve feet away from the cup, I was pleased indeed. It would be a tough but makeable putt for par, an accomplishment to be happy with whether I made it or not. I stopped as Scott made a nice chip with his ball from his spot on the other side. It rolled toward the pin and got inside mine, about 8 feet away. "Nice up, Pods," I said.

He pulled his cart up on the opposite right side of the green, and we both removed our gloves, walking with our putters to look at the putts we had remaining. I would be hitting first.

“You have to hit that putt a lot harder than it looks.” He was speaking like he had course knowledge, like a caddie giving me direction. He had come nowhere near my ball to look at it. “It’s slower than you’d think.”

“How do you know that?” I asked, standing up from reviewing my line. “I didn’t know you played here before.”

“I didn’t say I have,” his response came with that spooky stare again, “But I didn’t say I haven’t. It’s your choice whether or not to trust me.” We glared at each other a few seconds, then he grinned and continued, “Just remember, Chris, nothing has to make sense today.”

I got ready to stroke my putt. The 12-footer looked like about a two-ball outside-left putt, a left-to-right breaker into the cup. My mind calculated the speed my putt would need. I believed that if I listened to Scott and hit it as hard as he suggested, I would zoom the ball past the hole on the high side and have a tougher putt coming back. I glanced up at him again, and his face said *suit yourself*. His voice said, “Get it close!”

“Smart ass,” I mumbled with a smile. I knew the worst thing that could happen here was I would prove myself right. That might be even better than making the putt. I pulled the putter head back and hit through the ball. I hit it much harder than I felt I should. It took off as if shot out of a cannon. For a second I visualized it going off the other side of the green, when the grain, the wind, the moon, something slowed like it was being grabbed. My ball turned hard to the right and dropped into the metal bottom of the target.

Without moving from my putting stance yet, I looked up at Scott in stunned silence. After a few seconds, he smiled that big grin and said, "See what trust can do? Well done – nice par."

I was impressed. I stood and walked over to retrieve my ball while Scott got ready for his par putt. I picked up the flag, waiting for him to finish up. He was staring down at the cup as he prepared to stroke. He said, "Before this day is over," he paused to putt the ball and watched it with confidence until it dropped for his par. He continued, "You'll understand a lot more than you do now." He picked his ball out of the cup, and looked at me, "You'll believe there is a reason for you being here, for me being here – a reason for everything. You've been given a beautiful day, and a wonderful place to enjoy this day. You can question it, destroy it by stopping it, or," his stare had a twinkle in it now as he fixed it into my eyes, "You can *seize* it."

That was the most profound I ever heard my friend. He walked off the right side of the green and I walked off the left, both of us carrying our putters back to our pull carts. I wrote down a proud "5" for the fourth hole, grabbed my cart handle, and headed for the path. I thought of how delicate I should be when asking what he meant by his parents losing their child. I looked over for Scott, expecting him to join me on the path where it headed for Number Five. He was gone, nowhere to be seen. I stopped in my tracks once again. I wanted to yell his name, to call him, to find him. I drew a breath to yell – and stopped. Trust him. Don't question it, but seize the day. I regretted that I let pass yet another opportunity to say so many unsaid things to him. I moved again, walking up the path on the way to the next hole. It was great to spend some time with Scott after all these years. I hoped I would see my friend again.

CHAPTER 10

I was still thinking about Scott when I came out of the dense trees to a long and wide tee box several yards ahead. At the level I walked the surrounding trees were near their tops, showing the tee was well elevated above what was in front of it. The sound of showering water grew louder as I approached. The sign said the par 3 Fifth hole staggered down from the blues at 215 yards to my whites measuring 185 yards, then a few more paces to the red tee at 155. When the path reached the teeing area, I looked down just a little at the nearby green not too far below the tee. It seemed suspended in air. Radiant floral color in bright red, yellow, and white circled behind the green on a slope that looked down on the flag and back toward me, like it covered the walls inside of a cup with the putting surface as its bottom. I walked onto the flat tee among the many divots to the front of the white tees. A deep and narrow valley below made up the rest of the hole. This would be a tough one.

Right in front of the ladies' tee, a sharp drop went down to a pond that started at the middle of the ravine before covering its right side. A beautiful tall and broad fountain sprayed from its center in an arching fan that reached to just inside the round shore line. The tallest pines of the day so far completely engulfed the hole. The cart path along the left side had to move in a serpentine descent to negotiate the precipitous hill. At the bottom, the path crossed a small wooden bridge that was just a few paces long and arched over the creek flowing out of the lake. The crisscrossing timber sides were treated but unpainted natural wood. Going up to the green, two more long switchbacks were needed to get the path up to a small parking area. The far slope between the water and the flag was faced with natural stone from the lake's edge up to the collar of the green. Pronounced undulations in the green made it look like closely mowed hills. The bright banner attached to the pin flapped with a pop, helping the eye distinguish it from the flora on the slope above it.

"What an awesome hole," I uttered while enjoying the view. I wished Scott had stayed around to see this. I knew he'd appreciate it even as I wondered if being with him the last two holes was just my imagination. The challenging tee shot would have to carry every inch of the yardage. There was only one place to miss – you could be a little long if you could keep it out of the shrubs behind the green. There, the grass was short enough that a ball too long would probably dive under the hedge and stay there.

Birds cawing in the very tops of the tall trees echoed to punctuate the quiet of the woodsy setting. A gentle breeze ruffled those tree tops, giving my feathered friends a gentle sway while they sang. After a moment of debate, I pulled a 4-iron from the bag hoping I could hit it well enough to find the green. I teed my ball and stood behind it to visualize its flight. I remembered playing a similar par 3 in Georgia with my brother-in-law, Ryan. His sister Cameron rode with us that day. Looking out at the hole made me think of my wife now.

She loved the natural beauty in golf, like someone appreciates botanical gardens, but she never developed more than a passing interest in the game itself. If this were one of those rare occasions when she played with me, she would skip this breathtaking hole because it looked too hard. There was also the fact that she loved seeing a course from the passenger side of a powered golf cart – Cameron would never walk a course.

Standing over the ball, I took a relaxing breath, flexed my knees to sit down a bit, and on my backswing I thought *smooth and easy*. My solid contact flew the ball as well as I could have. It was straight at the pin at first, but then began leaking a little to the right. "Hang on, hang on," I pleaded. Going too far right would shoot the ball deep into the woods never to be seen again. It landed on my side of one of the green's large mounds and bounced high twice before rolling over the next mogul. I held my breath while it rolled. Just before taking one suicidal turn too many to go over the edge, my ball stopped. It was safe, and I exhaled. I bagged my club, walked onto the path and started down the grade. It was steeper than I thought, and I had to catch myself before tipping the pull cart over a couple of times as I snaked downward. Walking carefully down the hill I remembered how I met Cameron.

It was 32 years ago, on a Mountain View Air flight from Denver to Phoenix. I saw her before the flight in the boarding area and was instantly attracted to her, not so much because she was drop-dead gorgeous – which she *was* – but just because of the way she carried herself. I saw both self-confidence and a longing for something missing in her life when I watched the way she stood, the way she sat, the way she read her book. By sheer coincidence my aisle seat was next to hers by a window in First Class. It was as if a magnet drew us together.

After takeoff, she looked sad while she stared outside. The glass of the window reflected a tear going down her cheek which she wiped away. I used her blank glare as my opening to start a conversation. I made some crack about how, since I was with the airline, I would be burdened with a lot of paperwork if she were to jump out the window. I was determined to make her smile, and although reluctant to do so, she obliged. Embarrassed at first for being caught in her depression, she explained that our plane was taking her home to Phoenix after visiting a friend in Boulder. I was going to Arizona on business for the week, I told her. We chatted until peanuts and sparkling waters made her more comfortable with me and she opened up. Around the end of our first bag of nuts, she began describing a man and their relationship. She told me how she tried to make it work for many years. She spent the past week learning that it never would. A shuttle took her to the airport that morning before he was awake. She left a note telling him she was "moving on" even though she didn't really know what that meant yet. She wanted to be with someone stable, someone who didn't travel or relocate much, someone who focused on her more than on his job. As she continued describing her dream mate, the further away I was from fitting the profile. She was intriguing.

I reached the foot bridge spanning the creek and stopped. I looked back up at the tees, then the other way, up toward the green. Deep in this lush little canyon, the showering sound of the fountain splashing in the pond echoed tranquility. The water leaving the pond rippled over rounded stones and became a stream again where it moved under the bridge and off. In the creek below my feet, a leaping frog helped me realize my need to follow Scott's direction and keep moving. I looked up again at the green, believing I could trust Arnie's magical air to help me climb the steep path and make it in good shape. I walked off the bridge, onward and upward.

The talk Cameron and I enjoyed that day ended much quicker than either of us wanted when the nonstop flight landed at Sky Harbor Airport. When the jet way connected, I asked if she would like to go to dinner one night. I knew it was too soon to be pushy, so I let her avoid answering. I gave her my business card and shook her hand. She left the plane to claim her baggage, and I headed for the station office. I never expected to hear from her again, so I was surprised when she called the next afternoon.

That first night out together for dinner in Phoenix, we couldn't have imagined the road ahead for the two of us. Like any first date, we danced around how to order, what to order, what to say, what not to say, exploring first whether or not we even liked each other. Our tones indicated how at ease we were with each other through what we both expected to be a simple, casual meal. Both of us detailed our lives more and more, and dinner turned into several hours at the restaurant. Neither of us noticed we were their last customers until our server said everyone was waiting for us to leave so they could go home. Night turned into morning. We both dealt with the awkwardness of wondering if we did the right thing by sleeping together that night. That week went on and we dined together each evening. Our relationship developed and became deeper each night. I remained hesitant, wondering if there were signals of a rough future ahead for us. She was on a rebound, and I was seeing my friends start their own married lives. I thought I was successful but I had no one to share my successes with. Maybe we were both just too anxious for a relationship, I worried. My future was bright and I considered myself quite a catch. Maybe I was too conscious that someone might seize the chance to take advantage of those successes. I was defensive against that. I didn't want to wind up with a trophy wife who was willing to put up with me long enough to claim a big divorce settlement that would financially bury me for years.

Looking back at it later, I knew Cameron was the one for me before we finished the appetizer that first night. We laughed at each other's stories those first several dates, and my concerns that she was "gold digging" were diffused. She made me feel content that I wasn't just something different for a woman coming out of a relationship. Months later my family members were surprised that I was ready to marry her even though I admitted I didn't know if I was in love with her yet. I told them the key was that I *liked her* so much. I liked her a lot. I felt she would be a lifelong friend and I believed she would be a good mother. It was clear that I wanted to spend the rest of my life with her. Something told me it wouldn't be long until I *was* in love with her, but I didn't feel like I needed to wait for it to happen before I married her. For that matter, maybe I was just tired of living alone, of being alone, while everyone I knew was either married, divorced, or widowed. I was interested in marrying once, and only once. This would either work or not. If it didn't, trying again until it *did* work with multiple marriages was of no appeal to me. Maybe it was a combination of all these factors that determined I could accept no woman as the right one until Cameron.

Our first week, she convinced me she appreciated my work ethic. That was important, because I believed that trait was what made me as successful as I thought I was. We had long conversations about how she understood a man working very long hours, many days in a row, and travelling a bit, all of which I was accustomed to doing. In the weeks and months through which our relationship was forged, she always accepted with a smile what I was, and what I would always be.

Her frustrations began to show only after we got engaged, and they increased soon after we married. It was real life now, not just those planned weekends away together. Her description of the ideal husband on that first memorable trip was proving to be in radical conflict to what my professional behavior was, confirming my fears. That same work ethic I was so proud of was showing itself more as a curse than a positive peculiarity. Every day began with me leaving for work before she got up. Her work day ended and brought her home to an empty house with an unknown agenda until I ended my day and got there late. Day after day, brief talks were more like scheduling meetings, even arranging when we would "work on" getting pregnant. Somehow, children were born, but I still didn't change my work habits. The children's formative years were with their mother, and a grandmother that flew in to stay for first weeks and later months at a time. I was too stupid to see until it was too late that I was ignoring my wife and family. The state of Cameron's discontent built when the kids got into grade school and I would miss an event, or be unable to help when they had to be at different places at the same time. Through this all, houses were bought and moves made, babysitters were paid, and homework was helped. There were soccer and football and volleyball and baseball practices, sleepovers, all the things of busy home life were achieved. Through those frustrations of hers, I discovered later, my problem was that I never *heard* her complain. During the time when I was falling in love with her, we should have talked more, I should have worked less, and I should have been paying more attention to her.

Maybe I shouldn't have been so shocked when I learned she was having a passionate affair with another man. She emphasized my listening deficiencies were a primary cause. My workaholic tendencies left her empty, wanting the companionship she thought we would have once we were married. When she made her confession, I saw the fear of a cheater in her eyes: she figured I would either leave her or kill her. Only after she believed she was going to die at my hand anyway did she provide more details. There were important details, like how they avoided being caught, like how she kept the kids from finding out. Details like how she did not do it *for* sex, but it did lead to, and there *was* sex. She confirmed it happened because I prioritized my job over her and my family. It was true that at the time I felt I was working the long hours, doing the travel, immersing myself into my job, all *for* my family. She disagreed. The 90-hour weeks and the travel didn't go well with her 9-to-5 boredom-preventing job. She had to deal with kids and animals and plumbers and yard men alone, she said. The little daylight time I *was* home, I was thinking only of golf, she said. Back then, these were the reasons she gave me for why she needed to "go out with the girls". That was why we needed babysitters more and more often once I agreed that she needed some fun time. One night I came home early and tried to contact her through the girlfriend she was supposed to be with. When that girlfriend botched the lie, I learned what a sucker I was. Cameron's instructions to Brenda were to not answer if I called her. She *did* answer by accident, though, and her awkwardness couldn't cover the story she tried to concoct on the fly.

I trusted Cameron. I believed she was being faithful, so I was, too. I resisted the temptations of after-hours trysts with suggestive women who couldn't care less if I was married or not. I worked hard, like I always did. Early in our relationship the importance of golf in my life was covered. When we were dating, I wanted clear as conditions of developing our relationship things like the work, the golf, the trust and faithfulness. I wanted all these cards on the table before we ended up getting married. Back then, she agreed to it all. When we dealt with her infidelity, I brought up the fact that she had accepted everything. Despite all that, for some reason, I took the blame. I said I did *not* want to kill her and her companion (which was not so true but that's what I told her). I was not going to leave, and that we were *not* going to get a divorce. Once she felt safe, she agreed what I said was true; it *was* my fault, that I drove her to do it. Don't push it, I told her. I was making it my responsibility to change without her blaming me for what she did. I knew it might destroy us fiscally, but I said I'd do whatever it took for our marriage to survive, and I meant it. All I asked in return was for her intimate relationships with others to stop forever. She was shocked that I would even consider staying. I still believe it was this day that she fell hopelessly in love with me. At least that's what it looked like.

The cart path wiggled uphill toward the green while I reflected on how our lives turned uphill as well the night of that telltale conversation. By the end of that week, I resigned the job in which I planned to spend my entire working life. In a heartbeat, we were forced to adjust to a much lower income, but we felt secure in an investment opportunity with a close and long-time friend of mine, Nick. I convinced Cameron that we should pour all our savings, and all our trust, into Nick's prospective golf travel booking business. Later we learned that he literally gambled every penny away, without ever even saying he was sorry before vanishing forever. We were broke, my career was in ruins, and my best friend had swindled us, but we salvaged our marriage. Whoop-te-do.

All this happened because I focused my faith on my wedding vows and our kids. It was simple: when the day would come, I felt I could not face God if I hadn't done everything I could to fight for my marriage, and to be a better husband. I was never quite sure whether it was the right choice or not. Couples get divorced every day. People commit to their careers knowing what it will do for their future, choosing how happy they may be later by sacrificing today. I wondered if she would leave me because of the life I threw away for us by quitting the airline, but I couldn't control that. I believed my faith told me what I had to do.

I reached the cart parking area next to the green, and saw my ball just off the mounded putting surface. The route from my ball to the cup looked like the Smoky Mountains. Peering back at what I just climbed, I knew I'd better be *very* careful with my next shot. I grabbed a pitching wedge and a putter from the rental bag and walked to my ball.

I wondered why I was having these reflections today: of Cameron, of how we came together, of how I drove her to cheating, of how I sacrificed a career to avoid a divorce. There were positives, too, like how we came back together as two loving parents to raise our kids. It was all part of the what-if-this, what-if-that process my mind was going through more and more since I got the news from the doctor. I wondered if Scott was involved in this.

I knelt behind my ball and saw so many ways I could screw this shot up, it wasn't funny. I could hit it too hard and go off the front of the green down into the pond or the creek. Or I could hit it too easy, and then catch a mogul and roll away to the left or right, perhaps even off the green and into the woods. I was able to visualize almost any circumstance except holing the shot.

Visualizing circumstances: maybe that's what these flashbacks were all about. What if Cameron and I didn't meet on that flight to Phoenix? What if I divorced Cameron for her infidelity or done something even worse, like turning to murder? What if I'd cheated with one of those women at the office or on the road when I was with the airline? What if I stayed with Mountain View Air through retirement? What if I had given Nick's proposal the due diligence I would have given any other business decision I ever made? What if I never strayed from the faith I was brought up in, that I went to college to cultivate? What if my close friends and I were still in each other's lives and we could be there for each other when needed? What if, what if, what if?

I was a couple of yards off the green, about halfway between the collar and the nearest hedge. There were two different mounds on the green in the 50 feet between the pin and where I lay. If I could chip onto the green and *just barely* roll over the crest of the first hump, maybe I had a chance. I needed to quit thinking and just take the shot.

I swung the wedge too easy, caught too much grass and didn't carry the ball past the collar. It struggled to reach the putting surface, where it began rolling aimlessly. Gravity carried it, creeping to places I kept hoping it would stop. A little up the mound, a little right as it came back, then tracking right this way, then left that way. I dropped the wedge and picked up the putter, watching while the ball wobbled at a teasing pace, making me guess where it would give up. It finally stopped with still another 30 feet to go. I got down on one knee behind the ball to look at the new line. I could see at least two dramatic breaks that made this par putt seem impossible. I was irritated that I had given myself almost no chance to make it.

I picked a spot on the crest of the nearest hill. I visualized how it would roll through that first mark and then on to a secondary point along my imagined line. My mind saw the ball rolling from the head of my putter all the way to the hole over and over again. Through practice swings, I focused on that first mark. I stared at it and pulled the club head back. I hit the ball with just the amount of firmness I wanted. The ball rolled to my first mark with perfect pace. The ball paused, looking for where it should go next before it picked up speed, as if now it was behind schedule. The lay of the land and its forces took over to roll the ball a little different from what I hoped before it crept to a stop about three feet left of the cup.

"How appropriate," I chuckled aloud to myself, seeing the irony of a three-footer remaining. It is said that life is a series of three-foot putts. The problem with three-foot putts is the same as with the challenges of life – we expect to achieve them, but often we cannot. The remaining putt was just uphill enough, just right-to-left enough, that I strode to take my stance with confidence. One practice swing before a firm stroke, and the ball rattled the bottom of the cup as it disappeared.

I walked off the green to my cart, bagged the clubs, and wrote down the bogey score that could have been worse. I took a fond glance back at the difficult hole once again before marching off up the path. I breathed in the fresh forest air walking to the next hole, hoping it would clear my head and I could return to enjoying the day.

CHAPTER 11

The cart path approached Number 6, where the tee was a grassy, rampart-like rise that forced the asphalt road over to the right into a tight space against shading trees. Directing golfers up some stairs was a split log nailed to a post with a point chopped into its left side. The flat side of the log facing me had "6th tee" hand painted on it. The directional sign looked like it was erected with haste. I imagined one too many groups failed to stop and drove past the tee box above only to have to turn around to come back. I couldn't see farther ahead than where the path curved and ducked down to disappear past the front of the teeing area. Along the bend of the path, vines of honeysuckle were winding around the trunks of the trees and across the ground where the woods began again. A wisp of wind blew just the slightest scent of the honeysuckle toward me, just enough to make me want more.

Standing next to my bag at the bottom of the steps I wasn't able to see any of this hole. The scorecard described it just as a par 4. I grabbed a driver, a 5-wood, and a 4-iron hoping that my tee shot would need one of them. A ball washer next to the sign had a clean towel hanging from it, which I used after cleaning the two golf balls I had in my pocket. I left the small parking area and headed up the steps with the three clubs.

I reached the top of the eight flagstone steps onto the tee where the long, beautiful par 4 opened up in front of me. The tee sign said it was 440 yards from the white tees. A long lake ran down the left side and held beautiful, clear blue water. The breeze put little ripples in the water that were trying to become waves. A serpentine coastline crept into the fairway at strategic spots on the left before angling away to meet the thick woods about two thirds of the way to the green. Lots of mounding starting near the lake gave the hole a cool, colorful moonscape look, where bright green contrasted against the blue water. The rest of the fairway was flat from its center over to the woods that bordered the length of the hole on the right. In the distance, the bright flag waved in the center of an elevated green with no protective bunkers. I dropped the unneeded clubs to my side, teed my ball, and got ready to hit the driver. I tried to focus my practice swings on making a good turn. I wanted to let the club do its job and hit with my body, not just my arms.

The ball flew away straight, but reached its apex and began to drift a little to the left. When it started down in that direction, I knew I would either be lucky or wet. Bouncing and ricocheting here and there on the tops and sides of mounds, moguls and humps kept where it would finish a mystery. It ended up taking a net positive right kick into the fairway, but the stifling of any forward roll made it end up shorter than it should have. At least it was dry. That alone made me happy as I took the steps back down to the cart and bagged the three clubs.

I grabbed my cart handle and headed down the path again where the scent of honeysuckle returned, the aroma growing stronger with each step. It reached a wonderful crescendo where the path dipped away from the tee and into the open fairway. I've loved the smell of honeysuckle since I was a kid. How often I took it for granted as an adult, passing by without appreciating it. I stood there a few seconds with my bag, taking in deep breaths, enjoying the flowers just once more. I admonished myself again to keep moving along down the path. The woods covered it with a cool shade, creating a nice contrast with the bright sunshine bathing the hole ahead. I stepped out into the warm, bright daylight leaving the path to walk into the fairway on the way to my ball.

Walking up the middle of the fairway, my time remaining and the lack thereof crept into my mind. Like the walk of a child on his way to the Principal's office, I realized that I was coming to a point of "facing the music", when after death I'd have to deal with my significant sins. I wondered if I still had time to right a wrong, if there were any wrongs that *could* be righted. I wanted to find someone whose feelings I hurt, someone I was insensitive to, and find out if I had time to do something about it. In a flash, that honeysuckle connected me to someone that would be perfect for what I was looking for, except that she was long dead and gone. I wondered how many years it had been since I last thought of Mrs. Creel.

An elderly lady living alone seven houses down from us on Wilson Street, Mrs. Creel was a neighbor of ours when I was growing up in Weatherford. As kids, we all knew she was the Devil. Her immaculate yard was highlighted by mature honeysuckle vines all across the front of the house, at their thickest around her porch.

That yard was not just off limits to everyone, she wanted nobody any closer to her property line than the middle of the street. Like children will do, I joined my friends riding our bikes up and down the street, darting in and out of her driveway for no other reason than to torture her. Hearing her screams from behind the cracked-open front door would confirm our success. A few times a month, a Checker Cab picked her up to take her somewhere. While she was gone, we'd ride up and down her driveway, in and out, just because we could get away with it. We'd stop at the honeysuckle bushes around her porch, pulling the blooms, getting that one little drop of "honey" on our tongue to savor it. It tasted good, and they smelled terrific. One of us would watch for that taxi to return, and he'd warn the rest of us to get away before the cab came around the bend and into sight.

Halloween was the worst for her, when sundown would bring what seemed like the entire community's children to flood the street, many heading for her door. She would sit on her porch and bark a long soliloquy about how what rotten kids we all were and why. Growing into my teens, I began feeling bad for having been so rude to her. At the same time I refused to be intimidated by her any longer. I made money doing odd jobs for every other house on our street – why should she be any different? I summoned up the necessary courage, dressed up nice, and walked down the street to her house, calm as a cucumber. My best friend Jack laughed at me when I walked past his house, two doors before hers. I knocked on her front door jamb and heard her quick but raspy remark from behind the locked door. She demanded that I leave at once or she would call the police. I responded in a gentle voice, telling her I was visiting to see if she needed any yard work done. She hesitated before unlocking the door. After staring me down for what seemed like minutes she invited me in. We sat in silence across from each other on the two couches in her living room while she inspected me with curiosity, deciding if I was trustworthy or just another rotten punk with a rotten trick up his sleeve.

Mrs. Creel got where she felt comfortable enough to ask if I would like some iced tea. After my smile and "Yes, Ma'am," she went off to the kitchen while I sat and waited. Her musty home welcomed the light and fresh air coming through the front screen door. I heard her open the back door from her kitchen, and a nice breeze swept through the house with a whoosh, like air filling the vacuum when you open a new jar. While the room looked spotless and clean, it had the smell of being closed up tight, the victim of its frightened old occupant. The fragrance of those honeysuckle bushes around her front yard rushed into the sitting room while I sat there. There were many framed photos on the walls, and even more stood on lace doilies that lined bookshelves and end tables. The old woman returned with a tray holding a pitcher of tea and two tall glasses of ice which she sat on the coffee table that separated us. She was as cordial to me as an aunt or a grandmother. I commented on the many pictures while she poured the two glasses full. I said I'd like to hear the stories behind them "sometime". She told me how they were all of her late husband and her children, ending her quick description with a comment that the pictures were "all I have anymore". She said she visited their gravesites whenever her Social Security checks afforded her taxi fare to the cemetery. Then she changed the subject to ask how I was doing in school. She smiled when I told her I was an honor student, and we got to know each other a little more while we drank the tea.

She agreed to let me work on her yard, with a firm caution that her late husband was very particular about how the outside was kept. Before working in any neighbor's yard, I would always ask them to show me their particular concerns, and I did so with her. She had trouble getting around, so I suggested she stand on the front porch while I walked the yard, asking her this or that. I walked through the back yard while she stood outside the screen door of her kitchen on a small concrete pad with a short handrail. It was as beautifully landscaped as the front, lined around its perimeter with an amazing garden of rose bushes. There was a wonderful array of colors and fragrances and I complemented her. She told of the painstaking work of her loving husband, how he built up the beds, meticulous and careful in planting, mulching, and cultivating their development with tender loving care. She got misty telling me how he did it all for her, just because she so loved roses.

I knew I could do a better job than whoever was doing the yard work after her husband passed away. Trained by my father's demanding perfectionism, I felt I could take the harshest critical eye Mrs. Creel or anyone else could muster. We agreed that I would come by to work in the afternoons after school at least two days a week. I would begin each day whenever I wanted without checking in with her, and I would use my own tools. She suggested that after seeing me work the first couple of days, she would pay me each month on the same day. I told her the price other neighbors paid me, but she could decide what my work was worth to her; whatever she wanted to pay was fine. I was proud of myself and felt good about growing up a lot that day, maturing from being her bicycle-riding tormentor into being her hired hand. I would start the next afternoon.

I reached my ball sitting in a nice spot in the center of the fairway about 190 yards out and parked the cart. The gentlest of breezes quartered from ahead to my right, and it was the same at the treetops, too. The slight elevation of the hardhat-shaped green meant that if I missed it, surrounding slopes would kick the ball far away to leave me a difficult chip. The flag on the stick flapped with the breeze in my line of sight, but it was pretty much in the middle of the green. A nice easy swing with a 3-iron still caught a little more grass than I wanted to, but the ball flew low and straight toward the pin. I hit my shot just fat enough that the ball stopped short of the green. It bounced and bounced and bounced to a halt just 20 yards on my side of the rising putting surface. "A chip and a putt," I told myself in preparation for my third shot and began walking again. "Just a chip and a putt."

Returning to Mrs. Creel's yard the next day after our agreement, I pushed my dad's lawnmower down the street and cut the grass, starting in the front. When I took the mower near the driveway, she came onto her porch and waved with a smile. She was pensive watching me, saying nothing to me when I edged the grass by hand everywhere from the curb to the driveway to the flowerbeds. I rolled the mower to the back yard and guessed she was still watching while I avoided looking to see if she was. I took everything home when it got dark before I finished. A couple of days later, I returned to work on those flowerbeds, tilling and mulching, handling each plant with the tender loving care my father taught me to use in our own yard. That day, she peeked through the blinds at me several times. A couple of times I let her know I saw her watching, giving her a smile and a wave, and she returned them. Some of the rose blooms were ready to cut, so I made a small arrangement for her by putting them in water in a mason jar I found sitting on a bench. I sat the jar on her back porch, motioning to her at the window that they were for her. Through the blinds, she beamed a broad smile at me when she saw them, and it made me feel good.

Then, just a few weeks into my routine, our new relationship crumbled. I was ready to trim some of the trees she had in her back yard and carried my ladder through her gate. She stormed out her back door, yelling at the top of her lungs that I was a thief taking advantage of her. I was so dumbfounded I dropped the ladder. She screamed that she knew I was no different than all the other scum in the neighborhood, those other punks I hung out with, blah, blah, blah. I picked up my ladder and ran home, hearing her holler almost all the way back to my house, embarrassed at what neighbors at other houses would think, most of all Jack and his family.

When I told my parents, they said something must have happened to make her snap, so they decided to visit her and smooth things over. I was surprised they came back so fast, and they were both so stern I knew something was wrong. I was confused when they demanded I sit down and "tell them the truth", because I already had. When I began retelling my story, they stopped me. It seemed Mrs. Creel told them she turned down my offer for work that day I knocked on her door, and asked me on more than one occasion since to stop. It was my refusal to quit that caused her to blow up at me, she claimed. She told them I was scaring the daylights out of her on purpose every time I went to her house. They told me she said I made a move at her like I was going to assault her, stopping only because she threatened to call the cops.

It turned out my parents knew me well enough to know her story could not be true. They knew my story *was* the truth, and everything did go just as I described. We concluded that I should go back to leaving her alone, and just let her be the crotchety old lady she always was. They told me to not go anywhere close to her house again, and to not bother trying to collect the money she owed me. I always minded my parents, but this case demanded my satisfaction. Everyone in the neighborhood I worked for always paid me a fair price, whether it was for washing cars, mowing yards, running errands, whatever. On top of that, I could just imagine the grief I would hear from Jack and my other friends. I was not accustomed to being stiffed. I was one mad teenager, and I intended to get even with the old bag.

"A chip and a putt," I repeated when I stopped the cart next to my ball in front of the green. I pulled the pitching wedge and thought of how this is the kind of shot that over-thinking can turn into a disaster. I stepped up to the ball, looked from my ball to the target and back again, then swung the club with relaxed hands. The ball flew the short distance onto the front of the green, rolling uphill not too far to a stop about eight feet left of the pin. I put the wedge back in the bag and headed to the cart path that started again near the right side of the green. A few steps later, I stopped at the parking area, pulled the putter out, and unsnapped my glove. I put the glove in my back right pocket and looked at my forthcoming putt. It would be a left-to-right slider, just long enough to make it scary.

I told no one of my clandestine plan for Mrs. Creel that day back then, not siblings or friends, not even Jack. I was ready for the moment and waited for the day the Checker Cab came again. When it took her away, I went around the block to come at her house from a different direction. I wore a hat that came down low to hide my face, and a ripped shirt and a pair of gloves I had reclaimed out of our family's Goodwill donation sack. I wanted to hurt her – not physically, that just wasn't my nature. I wanted her to be sorry for her own wrong, for what she did to me. I had not yet grown into knowing that "two wrongs don't make a right". I planned to act fast, without being seen from neighboring houses. I carried a pair of pruners in my pocket, and entered her back yard stealthily. With planned precision, I destroyed almost all of her prized rose bushes. Grabbing, pulling, and snipping fast, I yanked them out of the ground, then cut them above the bulb before I chopped up the roots. When I got to the last one, I froze. I decided to leave her just one still planted in the ground, just to be mean. The others I vandalized were now trash. It would take a minor miracle and a lot of work to return them to life. Many months if not years would be needed before they could produce blooms again. I darted out of the yard over her back fence. I sped through yards and around houses of neighbors I didn't know, going the opposite direction of my house in case I was seen. I was breathing heavy, much more scared of being caught and disciplined by my Dad than anything Mrs. Creel could ever do. Over a mile away, I stopped running when I got to Eagle Park and stripped off my disguise. I found a trash can and buried the hat, shirt, gloves, and shears deep inside. I collapsed at the base of a large pecan tree. For a moment I relished in the pride of my success, but it was only a moment. Then, I began to cry.

I knelt behind my ball to see the line of the putt with my mind still sitting under that tree at Eagle Park. I stood over the ball and stroked it. It was not a bad putt, but stopped about 6 inches left of and just past the cup. Walking up to tap the ball in, I remembered how I wept uncontrollably for a few minutes that day under the tree, feeling like a teenage murderer. In the deed's planning ahead of time, it never occurred to me that I would feel so horrible. My actions were the same as if I cut Mrs. Creel's heart out, threw it on the ground, and stomped on it. I knew nothing could justify what I had done, just as I knew no one could ever find out. I never told a soul, not anyone.

In those moments back at the park, bawling behind the tree trunk, I learned the truth of an adage I heard often as a child but never understood until that moment: "Character is what you do when no one is looking". I'd tried to remember and practice that every day since then until today. I felt that all of the good I did as an adult never made up for my childish behavior that day.

Without bothering to pull the pin out of the hole, I rapped the ball with my putter, swinging it with one hand. I picked the ball out of the hole without reflecting on the just-completed bogey 5. Walking off the 6th green my actions against Mrs. Creel bothered me. I knew the old lady was far too heartbroken to do anything about what happened, whether or not she had any idea if I was involved or not. I never heard from her or saw her again. I would walk or ride my bike down the street never farther than Jack's house. Before long, I was driving, and I could look away if I drove by. Soon, a For Sale sign was in her yard a short time, and then a moving van appeared to deliver the couple who bought the place. I never knew what became of Mrs. Creel, whether she died before or after her house was sold, but I was certain she must have been dead by the time I graduated from college.

In the years when I grew into adulthood, when Cameron and I began our family, roses were a big part of our yard. I bought many more than I could keep up with, and always delighted in my wife's love for the cut bunches I brought into the house for her. Every time I planted a bush, each time I mulched and pruned, treated for pests or fertilized, I knew my love for roses were caused by that day of hateful destruction. Each rose I enjoyed until today, I felt the pain of my act. I always knew I couldn't take back what I did, but now I wanted to right this wrong as much as any other.

I told myself to keep moving, and shook my head to avoid reliving awful deeds like this on a day designed for having fun. I pulled the cart toward the path's entry into the woods on my way to Number 7.

CHAPTER 12

On the path I tried to finish thinking about Mrs. Creel. I needed to find some way to ease my mind about what I'd done to her, but there was nothing I could do about it now, there in the forest. Even though my whimpering in the park that day is what I believed triggered my toughening up in the years that followed, it wasn't enough to balance the scale. Besides, if I was being truthful that I was looking for a wrong to right, maybe I could find a better subject. For instance, there was that situation in Denver worth considering. I came out of the trees and decided I was done occupying my mind with these things any more. It was time to get back to the business of golf.

Hole number 7 was a simple-looking par 3, 175 yards. Flat as a pancake, it had a small tee box, a lake instead of a fairway, and a large square green. All of it was surrounded by a thin ring of sparse trees. It looked like a simple, fun hole. I teed up my ball and finished a casual practice swing with my 6-iron when there was a sudden pickup in the breeze. Within seconds, it went from a gentle whisper to a deafening roar. Leaves flew and the surrounding trees swayed hard. After only a few seconds, as quick as the wind came up so strong, it subsided again.

The wind blew my ball off its tee. I bent over to re-tee it, with my habit of lining up the maker's name and logo with my intended line of flight. I stepped behind the ball to look at my target, then moved to address the ball, ready to hit. I looked down again at my ball, and my eyes froze large as saucers when I saw something I hadn't seen since the 1960's – there was a little sombrero logo imprinted on my ball. I bent down to pick it up, handling it like it might be a live hand grenade. It was a Lee Trevino Spalding golf ball, just like the ones I "had to have" as a kid, when I was a huge Lee Trevino fan. It was a ball that was last manufactured over 30 years before. Maybe it was in the bottom of the bag when Skip gave me the rental set. There was no other way in the world this ball could be here. Scott's words earlier echoed in my head: *don't hold up play, no matter what happens.*

I replaced the changed ball on my tee again. When I did, the shade and color of the grass beneath it changed, in an instant turning a much lighter green, almost brownish. Now it was bare, perhaps from a combination of a lot of play and precious little maintenance. The temperature rose several degrees, and my peripheral vision felt things open up around me, like the sky got bigger. I looked up and the trees around the lake said this was *not* Alabama. *These* trees were sycamores and mesquites. The forest I left through the tunnel behind me was gone. The land all around me was a rolling prairie.

"You going to hit today, or what?" A familiar voice behind me made me jump. "'Cause I'm ready to hit, yep, put this ball right on the green --,"

The fact that I hadn't seen Jack Harrison in over 30 years wasn't the main reason I lost my breath and almost my breakfast the second I saw him. It was the fact he had been dead for at least 25 years.

"I might even make a hole-in-one here. I'm not worried about the lake, no. Why should I? I'm not trying to hit it in the lake." His lifelong trademark staccato vocal delivery hadn't changed, nor had the big belly that belied the strong body it was attached to. His head held his wide, excited eyes and was topped by a red-haired crew cut. He almost ran me over when he teed his ball up next to mine and moved into position over it. He looked like I imagined he must have just before he died. In life he was the same age as I, so he looked much younger than me now. "You don't mind if I go ahead, do you, Chris? Thanks!" There was no pause for my reply when he took his stance, still talking.

"I'm hittin' a 5-iron, that's what I'm hittin'." He turned toward me and gave an inquisitive look down at my club. "What are you hittin'?" He gripped his club like a baseball bat. "OK, here we go. By the way, how ya been, Chris?" His flat swing had an uptick at the end that made him top the ball and drill it straight into the center of the lake. Before the splash was finished, he was teeing up another one. "I wasn't ready, so I'm taking a mulligan. Everybody OK with that?" The announcement of his intention to hit another ball was loud, like he was telling someone else up on the green. Again there was no pause for a response. "Good, thanks guys. I appreciate it." Which guys? What did he mean?

Laughter came from the left of the lake, a high pitched cackle I haven't heard since high school. I looked over to see a short fire plug of a guy with bushy, blonde but graying hair, carrying a discount store stand bag with a few clubs in it and a big towel dragging the ground behind him as he walked. It could only be Terry Travis.

He yelled, "Wait!" He dashed over behind a tree, then peeked out from behind it. It *was* Terry. He glanced at me and waved, "Hey, Chris!" I looked back at Jack for his second swing. He topped it again. At least this time it flew high enough that it had a chance to get over the water. We all watched, wondering if this one would make it.

The hole was so familiar I could play it, walk it, and even draw it in my sleep. This was *not* the hole in Alabama I was on moments ago. It was Number 7 at Higdon Park Municipal Golf Course in Texas, about a mile from where I grew up, and a couple of miles from Pat Neff High School, where we all graduated together. A tee box almost absent of definition looked north across a stagnant pond to a large flat green. The ditch that came into the water from left of the tee and departed right of the green could be called a creek only after a heavy rain.

The smattering of a few trees around the pond and one behind the green were the densest concentration of foliage on this otherwise barren, wide open field of a public golf course. The rolling rectangle-shaped course had a tiny clubhouse at its high point halfway on one side of the parcel. You could see almost every hole on the course from one end to the other. Crooked pins rising from the ground like needles in a pin cushion were the signs that a hole ended here or there. A busy boulevard bordered one side; quieter residential streets edged two others. Along the remaining long side rode the railroad spur, frequented by trains carrying materials to a nearby industrial area. The tee of our par 3 backed up to those tracks, therefore providing the launching point of many a too-used-to-play-anymore or found-in-the-weeds golf ball. During the hundreds of rounds we played here together from when we were pre-teens through High School, we longed for a train to come along when we got to this hole. Waiting to turn around toward it the moment the engineers passed us, we'd stand around trying to look disinterested, as if they might care what we were doing. Once they had gone by, we'd hit balls in rapid succession to either bounce off and away from the steel cars or sail away into the surrounding right of way. The goal of an ideal shot with a beaten, smiled-up ball was to shoot it though the moving, open doors of a freight car. If the ball had a big enough cut in it, its flight would swirl with a whistling sound like Fourth-of-July fireworks. We meant no harm, and we really did no harm. Most of all, we had a lot of fun doing it.

Jack's ball hopped mere inches beyond the lake's opposite bank and rolled up onto the green. Dodging a ball already laying there, his shot stopped about 20 feet in front of the pin. The three of us were roaring our amazement when a fourth voice joined us, the loudest of all. A deep and guttural, almost Santa Clause-like but goofier "Ho, ho, ho", the raucous laugh drew my attention to just off the right side of the green. In an out of place Rolls Royce replica personal powered golf cart sat a giant man that I last saw when he was a giant teenager.

"Ned?" I said when I recognized him. Jack was already trotting off the tee around the right side of the lake, headed to the green.

"You can go ahead and hit. See, my clubs are on Ned's cart," Jack said with a shout over his shoulder. I just stood there with my mouth hanging open. Across the lake Ned struggled to get his huge frame out of the parked cart so he could walk onto the green.

"Don't worry, Chris," Terry's high-pitched voice came from his spot on the left bank of the lake. "If you hit Jack, you can't kill him *again*!" The other three howled again, and I joined them without knowing why. Maybe I was losing my mind. I thought of how the current scene would play at a Country Club or some other prim and proper golf setting. Here we are, adults but not acting like it, all on one hole. One is about to tee off while one walks onto the green, and another nears the green as he jogs along the right side. The fourth of the group is about to hit his pitching wedge from an adjacent fairway across a pond on the left, all oblivious to each other. It was just like the old days, except one of us was a dead guy.

I took a step back away from the ball for Terry to swing. He looked like a munchkin chopping wood, but the wedge was graceful, sending his ball over the trees and water to a soft landing in the center of the green. He glanced over at me on the tee and put the club in his bag. Like he was Ferris Buhler, he boasted, "Never had one lesson!" We both laughed hard.

From the green, Ned whined, "Jeez, come on already – I don't have all day!" I thought about Scott. This reunion would certainly fall under his admonishment to keep moving *no matter what happens*. I hit my ball and caught it flush. The instant I struck it, I worried it would be too long. All three of my old friends followed the flight of the Trevino along with me. The aged ball hit with no dance at all on the large green past the pin. It rolled until it stopped just off the back on the collar. I would be the last to the green, and my ball was the furthest from the hole. These guys were never too worried about golf “honors”, though. I moved fast, pulling my bag around the right side of the lake while I watched them all survey their next shots. The way things were going, I expected they would all hit their putts at the same time.

I’d played what must have been hundreds of rounds of golf with these guys. I met Terry and Ned our first year at Pat Neff when we were on the high school golf team together. We became good friends when we played together almost every day through those years, because we were about the same relative strength on the team – we sucked. Jack and I grew up on the same street only a few houses apart. His family lived between Mrs. Creel and our home. He was my best and closest friend from before kindergarten until we were in high school. We played every sport together, including golf. He excelled at football and baseball. In high school, the right cheerleaders started going out with him, and he became more and more popular. I left football and basketball to make golf my main sport. I got great grades while Jack was included in more and more of the higher profile cliques of our school. It was simple: many of us long-time pals just became the wrong kids for Jack to hang out with. I could never fault him for enjoying the limelight. Small town high school sports star in Texas was a good thing to be. So what if he ran with another crowd for a few years? He never belittled nor looked down on us like some of his newfound friends did. And hey, the girls were prettier, the parties more fun, and something about him got his picture in our senior year high school yearbook on 38 different pages. We all thought we would stay friends the rest of our lives and grow old together. Instead, we drifted apart.

Our senior class experienced a bad sports year at Pat Neff, limiting the interests of the bigger colleges and thus, Jack's exposure. He accepted a baseball scholarship that took him away to a small college in Missouri, where a blown out knee as a junior ended many of his dreams. Our paths rarely crossed when we left our respective university lives. I entered business, and he went home to teach and coach. The last time we saw each other was at my mother's funeral. A phone call from his sisters a few years later told me about his sudden and unexpected death. I remember how glad I was to hear, "He didn't suffer." I apologized that my job would keep me from being at his service. I sent a large spray of flowers, and forever regretted not being there for his parents and siblings on that occasion. I always hoped I could summon the courage to apologize to them for that. So far, I had not.

On the green, Ned putted out and was waddling back to his cart. I think he hit it at least three times while I walked, but it was hard to tell. I wondered what became of Ned, because I last thought of him many, many years ago. Ned was always the kind of friend that never quite made you feel like one. He was a perpetual sour-puss, but all of us together were responsible for making him that way. It was horrible the way we treated Ned. Back then, Ned had some sort of mental affliction, although I was never sure what it was. He was not a poor student, but compared to the rest of us he struggled with his classes. He had a huge frame, yes, and he was beyond a half a foot taller than I, almost seven feet tall. He was heavy back then in school, but nothing like now. Today, he had to be well over 300 pounds.

The main thing about Ned though, his head was *enormous*. There wasn't a hat on earth that would fit him. Calling him names once in a while would have been bad enough, but when we were kids we called him

"Ned the Head" all the time. "Hey, Head," or "Head's on the tee," or "Nice shot, Head," all the time. In adulthood, I often thought how awful it was for us to make fun of something he had no control over. A cliché in golf says, "Golf is played in the space between the ears." This is such a mental game; I hated to think how often we made it so much harder for him to play. I grew to appreciate what it took for him to play physically, and how tough he had to be mentally. It took even more strength for him to endure all the other rude kids that were *not* his friends. Everyone experiences mental illnesses, if not our own, then in someone close to us. The older I got, I often thought of this guy. The Rolls Royce cart he squeezed himself back into as I reached the green made me realize I must have missed something through these years.

"Wait for me, Head," Jack barked to Ned from the green just as he hit his putt. It was a miss well to the right, and it was still rolling as he ran up to it, stepping through Terry's line to redirect it into the cup. "Yeah, that's a par, good par for me, don't you think, guys? Yeah, never saw a bad three, nope, never have." None of us were going to say anything about the mulligan, about hitting out of turn, stepping in a line, hitting it while rolling, none of that. We wouldn't say anything, because we never did. It was fruitless, and it didn't matter to any of us anyway. We always just played together for fun, forgiving any etiquette shortcomings because we all loved each other like brothers. As far as I knew, Jack was a ghost. If not, he was at best an illusion. Jack trotted off to bag his flat stick on Ned's cart and hopped in. The two of them prioritized little over grabbing the beer they had in their cup holder and taking a big swig. I couldn't help but think how improbable the two of them bonding together would have seemed back when Jack was "Mr. Pat Neff High

School", and Ned was hacking around this goat ranch every day with Terry and me.

My sudden arrival didn't make much of an impression on my three old friends. It was like we'd been together as often as back in the day. Just then, Terry walked over to me and stuck out his hand for a quick handshake, almost without breaking his stride toward his ball. We traded smiles and a quick greeting, "Hey, Man."

Ned's vehicle was beyond out of place here, and as much as I was confused about Jack's presence, I just couldn't understand this cart. Quiet enough to not be heard by the other two, I asked Terry, "What's the deal with the Rolls?"

Terry started his answer with a question. "It's been a long time since you knew what Ned was doing, right?" I nodded in confirmation. "That thing belongs to Ned. He bought it, and takes it everywhere. Pulls it on a cart behind his Hummer just to thumb his nose at anyone he plays with." That was a statement he knew would puzzle me. "And I'm still pretty much the only one that will play with him," Terry said, trying to keep his trademark snicker quiet.

"His Hummer? His Rolls Royce golf cart?" I was trying to imagine how Ned's life could lead to toys like that. "Did he hit the lottery or something?"

"Oh yeah, you haven't seen him since graduation," Terry had a gleam in his eye, proud of the story to come. "Ned's a doctor. Doesn't practice anymore, just plays golf and drinks beer, far as I know. He wanted to be a pediatrician and help kids that were like him. But even when he was in pre-Med at college, he couldn't go anywhere without people making fun of him. You know, like we all did back then. Kids would be scared as hell when he would walk in. Parents would freak out. Call him a doctor or not, it didn't matter. But old Ned, he was determined, and he redirected himself. He went the research route, became more of a medical laboratory scientist kind of guy." Was he talking about the same dork, my friend who had trouble passing Chemistry in high school?

Ned and Jack chatted like old buddies in the fancy cart with their beers while Terry and I went about our unceremonious finish of the hole. Terry looked over his putt while I chipped a 7-iron onto the green to stop within four feet. Terry waited until my ball rolled past him to take his stance. I picked up my putter and tossed the chipping club near my bag.

"You can pick that up or finish it, your choice," he said, taking a casual practice stroke.

I always prefer to hole out everything, so I said, "Thanks." I took a contorting stance to avoid Terry's line, stepping up for a quick tap in – and missed it. We both laughed. "Bad decision, huh?" I said, and I picked from the cup the result of the final two-inch putt, kicking myself for rushing the four-footer that got there. "Make yours, buddy," I encouraged him and Terry stroked. His ball went in with authority, dead center.

Smiling, Terry walked to the cup while I waited to replace the flagstick. "Anyway, back to Ned. He got interested in Down syndrome to help kids. Not sure exactly what he did, but he won some huge scientific discovery award, got a zillion dollars for it, worked a few more years, and retired in his early 40's. That's pretty much it."

"Wow. Who would have thought, huh?"

"Yeah. But lots of things have happened that none of us would have believed, isn't that right, Chris?" Sounded like Terry was shooting me a loaded question.

"Yes, that's true. But hey," I thought I should change the subject. "It's good to see you, old friend." Terry nodded and we both smiled. He collapsed the portable stand on his bag to pick it up onto his shoulder. I wrote a "4" on my scorecard under Hole #7 with a sigh and grabbed my cart handle. Off we went to join the other two. I had so many questions, for and about all three of these partners, but Jack most of all. Walking away from the green, I lowered my voice and said to Terry, "You've got to tell me about Jack."

He snickered as he tried to keep the other two from hearing us. "What's the matter, Chris, never played golf with a ghost?"

CHAPTER 13

"A what?"

"A ghost. I mean, that's what you're asking me, isn't it?"

"Well, I don't know. He doesn't *look* like a ghost, he looks –,"

"Oh yeah? Just what does a ghost look like, Chris?"

"No, I mean, I know he's dead. I don't know anything about ghosts, Terry. I'm just wondering if I've been hit in the head or something. I don't know how I can be here, or how *you* can be here, and I sure as hell don't know how *Ned* can be here. But most of all, how on Earth can *Jack* be here?"

"Well, let's see," he said. "Starting a couple of years after his funeral, we came out here to play, and here he is. Shows up on the second hole, tells us some story about how he skipped the first hole, so he'll just card a par so we don't have to go back. You remember Jack. He never stops long enough for you to ask him anything, anyway," we both chuckled and nodded. This was the Jack we always knew. Terry continued, "Then, everything is as you would expect until he leaves the 17th green and just disappears."

The next tee was a flat bare spot just a few steps away with the shot back in our direction. Number 8 at Higdon Park wrapped around behind our previous hole in a dogleg right, a long-playing 400 yard par 4 that turned sharply uphill once it got past the level first 200 yards. At Higdon Park, yardages were a pretty general thing, more a guesstimate than precise. Hole layouts were more a product of where a tee or green would fit rather than a product of thoughtful golf course architecture. We would pick a spot on each unmarked tee, figuring that was about where we were supposed to hit from, then we'd let it rip. Ned and Jack were standing there, impatient as they waited for us to get out of their way so they could tee off.

Each hole at Higdon Park had a wide area of short grass and bare dirt you could call a fairway if you liked, and the eighth was no different. It was bordered by very sparse but often waist-high weeds that began where you strayed too far away from where you should be. The fairway slanted away from a tall old tree about two thirds of the way to the green marking the turn of the dogleg. The flat and nondescript green was up high, above and behind that corner tree another 140 yards or so. In front of the green on the right, there was a rare bunker guarding it. One hesitates to describe this as a sand trap. I remembered it always contained pretty much whatever it had collected over time: sand, gravel, mud, leaves, you name it. A large pecan tree beyond the green near the next tee had grown to be huge since the last time I was here. Nuts and husks would roll from that tree down into the trap. You could say the bunker lacked routine maintenance.

A *WHACK* at the tee preceded Ned yelling, "Aw, hell!" Unlike any golfer I've ever been around, Ned could hit his driver only one of two ways: either a huge, pulling duck hook, or the opposite, a slice that made almost a right angle. This time his ball was turning left before bouncing down that right-to-left slope, heading through the brush on the way to the 12th hole. It was a *long* way away from the green we were shooting for. We all watched and shared Ned's agony, but then Jack shoved him aside to tee his own ball, getting that baseball grip ready to swing away.

We could hear Jack barking away at Ned on the tee. "If I was you, I would have taken a mulligan, that's what I'd do, yep." The rapid-fire rhythm just didn't stop. "Course, I would have never hit it over there, nope, never do, just don't do that. All you guys know I don't do that 'cause I hit my driver so much better than you guys do, yep." I had forgotten how old his shtick could get. Before you knew it, he was ready, and swung away. *WHACK.* "Noooo, noooo," Jack cried. Ned busted out laughing. Jack's ball was headed way left just like Ned's, a screaming dead pull straight in the direction of Ned's ball. Before it bounced twice he was teeing up another ball. "Hey, that one don't count 'cause you guys were talking. No problem, I forgive y'all, I'll just take a Mulligan. This one's going right down the middle, yep, 'cause I can hit a good one, you'll see." We tried not to laugh too loud while he hit another one. It went down the middle but maybe never made it more than two feet off the ground, "burning worms" as we say. It skimmed the dirt fairway, bouncing every five yards or so before stopping about halfway to the hole from being tired if nothing else. The two plugged themselves back into the cart, grabbing beer cans with a sigh in unison before Ned drove them away to find his ball. They zoomed away past us, Ned scowling while Jack rambled on about having seen the exact point where their tee shots went into the tall stuff. Neither showed the least bit of concern about Terry and I being next on the tee to hit.

I motioned Terry to take the honor and hit his first. Little fanfare accompanied Terry teeing up. He used that hacking swing to send his drive up the right side. It started out at the tree, then bounced along to stop at a nice spot left of the center of the fairway. He beamed a smile at me like it was the best shot he ever hit. I remembered that smile as one that came after almost every shot of his. I knew that smile came every time he made his mother happy, every time he was able to help one of his siblings, every time he did anything for anybody. Terry was a very positive guy, but always happiest to be on a golf course. I returned his smile, because I was just glad to be able to be around such an unselfish person like Terry again. I was also sorry I pretty much had forgotten about him until he showed up here with me on the last hole.

"Great shot, partner," I said. Now that I knew a little about Ned and Jack, I hoped to find out more about Terry's life as we walked. When we were young friends, Terry and Ned were almost inseparable buddies. A midget and a giant, together they were comedic just to look at them. Terry's mother was an invalid, and he made it his job to take care of her. His dad died long before I knew him, when he was a baby. His mother's illness was too complicated for young boys to understand. Terry was the oldest of four kids. He took charge of managing the family and caring for her, starting before we got into high school. Even way back then it seemed he never thought of himself.

When we got to high school, the golf team met every afternoon on the golf course. We played a minimum of three days per week. The other two days, if we weren't playing golf, we were inside, working out or doing something active. The golf coach, Mr. Atwater, was strict about his schedule no matter what your rating, your place on the team. Terry's parents encouraged him to adhere to those rules. If he wasn't involved in golf or other school-related activities, Terry was always there for his family. When I was in college I only saw Terry a couple of times when I seldom made the short drive home from TCU. He put off going to college, hoping his mother's condition would improve. It never did.

I teed up my ball, trying to ignore the sound of those other two arguing. Jack was blaming Ned for making him yank his ball into the weeds, and Ned was accusing Jack of cheating and telling him how much he sucked. They were driving around in tight, fast circles. Ned was looking for his ball while Jack was hunting for any free ones he could throw into his bag. My driver made good contact with the Trevino ball, which felt like hitting a rock. It flew over Terry's ball before bouncing the first time in the fairway, ending maybe 40 yards ahead but 20 yards left of his. It would be a long uphill second shot for me. We walked off the tee satisfied enough, happy we weren't over there with those other two. We began walking and talking with an eye on the escapades of our partners. Jack was walking around in the tall grass, bending over to pick up a ball he found every several feet. At the same time, Ned would get out and hack at a ball that would dribble several yards at most. An expletive would be shouted, the cart would drive the short distance over to it, and the cycle would repeat. With each swing, Ned inched ever closer to being on the right hole.

I prompted Terry to begin telling me how his mother's illness worsened before her ultimate death. He grew familiar with more and more elderly people that needed an affordable way to get to doctors or hospitals in Fort Worth or Dallas, some even as far as Wichita Falls or Waco. He researched the transportation options for patients in major cities, wondering why their methods couldn't work in smaller towns. With government funding for capital, he created a not-for-profit company that contracted with the county to give rides to home-bound people who needed them. He got his siblings involved, orchestrating management of the company in concert with the care of his mother.

"I felt good about what I was doing, and I was making enough to get by, so everything was fine." He punctuated the story with his characteristic smile. After his mother died, a little time was required to deal with all that comes with a mother's passing. An old friend from high school, Tammy, was there to help him through it. They realized they were quite a team while they became even closer. Before long they were married. "We both wanted kids, but I wasn't making enough to afford them," he told me. The desire to add to their household was what prompted him to start another business, only this time, one for profit. Weatherford had no trophy shop, so schools and businesses needing awards would either order by mail or drive a long way to get them. It helped the two make a better living, and they were providing a needed service to his old friends and their kids. His family continued to operate the transportation company, all while Tammy got pregnant once, twice, and more. "More kids brought bigger bills. Our little shop was helping us just keep our head above water. But then the internet came along and our sales exploded worldwide. We got all the business we wanted, at our own pace."

At last Ned's ball limped into the fairway ahead of mine. Ned drove away to meet it, leaving Jack still looking in the weeds while the ball he needed to play was about 20 yards ahead of where we walked. Terry knew we needed to roust Jack back to playing with us. In a parental voice, Terry shouted, "Jack, if you don't come hit this ball, we're picking it up!" As if Terry shot a starter's pistol, Jack sprinted our way, and then realized his clubs were on Ned's cart. He stopped for a second, long enough to see another option. Then he started running toward us again.

Jack yelled, "I'll just use your clubs, OK Terry?" Terry laughed and stood his bag next to Jack's ball. We waited the few seconds until he arrived huffing and puffing. Jack never stopped and yanked Terry's 3-wood out of the bag, even though his distance to the hole was less than 200 yards. He jumped into a stance in front of his ball, fiddling with his grip. Always in motion, he had everything moving before and after his swing. He never learned that he couldn't play this game like baseball. He could never succeed in applying to golf his same grip, his same open stance, and most of all that powerful home run swing.

KA-THUNK, the combination of Jack's big swing with Terry's short club brought the base of the fairway wood down on top of the ball. He topped it so bad it bounced higher in front of us than it advanced forward, back-spinning to a stop only a few feet ahead of him. Before the ball stopped moving, Jack already dropped another ball from his pocket on the ground. "Yeah, see, that just happened because Terry's clubs are too short for me, so I gotta hit another one, yep." He was still talking when he swung again, catching more of the ball, but still topping it. It was a bullet with all topspin, sailing five feet off the ground before slamming into the slope leading to the green. Like a rifle shot the ball hit and bounced high and forward, picking up speed with every hop until the steeper slope began to slow it down. It reached the green but still whizzed past the pin. The ball rolled off the back of the green and up the embankment near the next tee. Before it stopped, Jack was trotting, already halfway to the cart parked by Ned's ball.

Terry and I walked toward our second shots. "I'd sure like to talk to him," I said.

"Who?"

"Well, both of them, but most of all Jack."

"What do you want to talk to him about?" Terry's tone sounded like a combination between a shrink and an agent.

I chuckled, "Well, what do you think, Terry? A friend I haven't been with since we were kids has been dead for how long? Add the fact that one minute I'm playing alone in Alabama, the next I'm back home here with all of you guys?"

"Alabama?" Terry now looked as confused as I was.

"It's a long story," I paused. "Terry, did I not just show up out of nowhere on the last hole?" We arrived at Terry's ball. He stood his bag and looked at the 160 yards he had left uphill to the hole. "Don't you think that's a little weird, too?" He pulled a club and gave it a couple of practice swings.

"I play here with a dead guy that pops in and out of here like a hummingbird at a feeder, and I'm supposed to be surprised by *you*?" For a few seconds we chuckled nervously before Terry addressed his ball. That woodchopper swing sent his ball flying straight and long, destined to be just off the green at worst. Terry bagged his club, finishing his thought, "All I know is that we're not *all* dead. See, this can't be heaven. If it was, we'd be playing at some fancy country club, not this dump." He had a point. "Anyway, Ned and I don't talk about Jack much. He never lets me ride in the cart because I don't drink, which is fine, because I like to walk anyway." Terry then pointed toward Ned's partner, "And Jack, you know, he's always been like that. It doesn't seem like death has changed him a bit. I don't know whether to call him a ghost, or a figment of my imagination, or what."

We reached my ball, a very long 130 yards out. I would need to add a full club or two to reach the green. I decided to hit an 8-iron. There was a sound of resignation in Terry's voice, "I don't get many chances to get out here anymore. Once in a while I'll call Ned and we'll meet here, maybe Jack joins us, maybe not." Sadness crept into his tone, "I'm always working or taking care of *somebody*. All that travel I was going to do when I grew up never panned out. I'll play the round by myself if Ned doesn't show up." His eyes looked out to nowhere in particular. "Lots of times we've wished you were here to play with us, but we didn't know where you were." I wanted to tell Terry more about how I was playing alone in the lush, forested hills of North Alabama before I popped in here. I was still confident I'd return to Gabriel's Creek soon. Maybe they were destined to go back there with me. I hoped they would, at least Terry.

Keeping track of Ned and Jack's escapades was hopeless. If I didn't hit my ball soon I'd have to deal with them walking on the green, ignoring us back down here in the fairway. I gave quick consideration to the steep uphill shot ahead, and swung. Maybe because I had my mind on avoiding them on my left, my ball was flying short and right. I hoped to catch the sand trap, because too far right would be a real problem. That's exactly where it came down. Instead of a cushiony landing the ball made a loud shallow-sounding *thunk* when it hit the hard pan inside that junk bunker, like it was bouncing off the pavement in a parking lot. The ball shot almost straight up in a skyward bounce twice the height of a telephone pole. It scared both of my friends near the green. We all watched it come back a little left to land in the short grass just in front of the green on the left side. We all busted out laughing again.

"What the hell was that?" Ned yelled down at me with a scowl, like he felt he was supposed to be mad at me for some reason. I just smiled big and waved to him. Terry and I climbed up the left side of the hole toward Ned's cart. I stopped short of the green where my ball was, took a pitching wedge and popped the ball up onto the green, where it stopped about six feet right of the cup. Moments later, Terry chipped up close enough to tap his in for par.

I pulled my putter and walked across the green. I looked down into that trap, where by all rights I should have been laying in two strokes. I saw the assortment of things in its bottom. It was no wonder my ball bounced so high out of it. There was no sand at all, just leaves and rocks, sticks and acorns, pecan nuts and husks, even something that looked like an old tuna can, all atop a hard, cracked dirt bottom. Jack and Ned were arguing over which of them was away. Terry laughed while I marked my ball. He stood back with me to watch the comedy in action. Ned had to be lying about eight. It was impossible for anyone to know Jack's true count with the mulligans and all.

Once they finished, and Terry tapped his in, I readied my six-footer for par. In the background, Ned was saying he had a five, but Jack protested it was really a six. I knew they were both wrong because I saw that many attempts by both just while Terry and I were talking in the fairway. I took a quick look at my flat straight putt on the bumpy, ill-kept green, and just stroked it. It bounced along to wind up five inches right of the hole. I stepped up and tapped it in for my five.

I picked up my ball and turned to look back at the hole with the nostalgia of a man looking back at his childhood playground. Back then this place was as good as St. Andrews to me. I remembered how often we imagined playing the U.S. Open, the PGA Championship or the Colonial National Invitational here. We pretended that huge galleries of fans stuffed this land to overflowing, following us up the 18th, tied in a battle for the trophy. It was the same as when we would play the NFL Championship in the street with designated driveways as goal lines and gutters for sideline markers. It was this group of then boys and now men that played for the Stanley Cup in the dead winter grass of Jack's back yard with golf clubs for sticks and pecans for pucks and rolled up newspapers as the goals. With our other childhood friends we played the World Series at our grade school's recess field, always featuring our favorite teams. Yes, this parcel of land deserved to be called a golf course, because it meant so much to this group of kids that could walk to it from home so they could imagine so many wonderful things that life would never bring them. It may have been a goat ranch then, and it may be a goat ranch now, but it was forever *our* goat ranch. The years gone by made me forget how much I so dearly loved it. My three friends moved to the next tee nearby while I finished soaking up the images and memories of the layout in front of me.

"Hey, who's this?" Terry said. I turned around, and laying on the ground, patiently waiting with the happiest of panting smiles, was a friend to which I wondered aloud my thoughts with a big smile of my own.

"Ralphie, what the heck are *you* doing here?"

"You know this mutt?" Ned grumbled.

Jack sounded off: "Yeah, he's a mutt, just a crazy dog. What's he doing here? Don't he know this ain't no place for a dog to be running around, much less laying on the tee box? You know we gotta hit, it's our tee, we gotta get moving," He was, as we used to say, 'talking to hear his head rattle'.

"Cool it, Jack, that's no mutt – that's my pal, Ralphie!" As soon as I said it, Ralphie jumped up and ran to me. "He's the pride of Huntsville, Alabama!" I bent over to both enjoy his greeting and to return it. He jumped up and down with a 'glad to see you' yelp, licking whatever part of me he could, just as I petted and rubbed whatever part of him I could. "What are you doing here, boy?"

As I spoke, the ground below us rapidly changed and the wind whipped up. Tall, swirling trees appeared, and just as suddenly as the change happened two holes ago to bring me to Higdon Park, it happened again now in reverse. This time, though, it transported the two of us. The dog and I were back in Alabama, and my friends were not.

I looked deep into the eyes of the dog with sadness, and he returned my glance with the comforting eyes of a wise old sage, as if to say, *'Don't worry, Chris – everything is alright. I'm your buddy. I'm with you, and you're OK.'*

CHAPTER 14

I stared at the ground while I walked with Ralphie, pushing myself to *keep going* toward the ninth hole. The grass was green and the scent of pine and magnolia was in the air, confirming that I was back in Alabama again. Something made me want to look up again to see if my friends were still there, but I knew they were gone. I felt lucky that I had a chance to be with my buddies again, but empty that I didn't get to say goodbye. At least I was confident I would see Jack soon enough.

The design of the tee marker I approached was further proof I was back at Skip's course. Number 9 was a par 4, 425 yards from the white tees, and downhill all the way. There was a sharp dogleg to the right beginning less than 200 yards from the tee, where taller trees thickened and the fairway pinched to a narrow neck. For the moment, it was just Ralphie and I again. He looked up at me with that calming smile.

"Hey, Ralphie, maybe we'll play this one together, just you and me." I nodded up the fairway. The dog looked at the hole with me, and then turned his eyes back to mine as if to say, '*Well maybe we will*'.

I could see the 200 yard distance post at the farthest point of the dogleg, leaving only 175 yards or so from the tee to the nearest corner's landing area. I thought about how many times when I was younger I watched an older playing partner take a smarter two-shot route to the green by starting with a shorter iron off the tee. Now, I was that older player, and this was my play. I took out a 5-iron and teed the ball a little higher than normal for an iron shot. Ralphie was calm as he sat down a respectful distance straight back behind me, able to look down my intended line. He reminded me of a golf pro during a lesson, preparing to give my swing a close look. I took a couple of casual practice swings while I flashed back to two special dogs, back to those late afternoons when my boys ran the course with me. "Have I told you about my dogs yet, boy?" He cocked his head and perked his ears inquisitively. "They both used to sit back there, just like that, Ralphie," I said, reflecting. "They're both in heaven now, and they'd sure be glad to see you here with me." Ralphie gave me a single soft bark, and I took my stance.

I looked down the fairway at my target and then back at the ball. Through an easy swing, I followed the smooth flight of the ball to see my tee shot roll to a perfect place. It stopped left of the center of the fairway, visible just past the near edge of the dogleg. Ralphie stood up with a broad smile, his tail wagging fast. It felt like he was applauding me. I reached down and scratched him atop his head, between his ears. We both felt good when I did. I walked off the tee to put my club in the bag, and Ralphie was walking with me. I expected him to dart off into the woods again, but he seemed content to stick around for a few minutes.

The dog, the pull cart, and I walked down the grade on the way to my second shot. I caught myself beginning to think of the friends I'd encountered today. I thought about my errors in days gone by, when I was wrong to let my life's to-do list minimize the priority that I should have placed on my friends. I wondered how all our lives may have been different if I would have treated my relationships with those friends by honoring the values I was raised with. The question made me think of my parents, and the principles they tried so hard to instill in me with arguable success. The traits in a person that were important to them were worth thinking about.

My parents were good people. Each developed the roots of their standards in their Depression-era upbringing. Working hard was their expectation of themselves, of others, and of their children. My Dad was one of a large family that broke apart and scattered to various relatives in his adolescence. My Mother was part of a small family who lived in a one-room farmhouse on the rolling plains between Cleburne and Granbury. As the world approached war, both were in college on scholarships they earned. War came, and both sacrificed completing their education to join the war effort. A bad ear and the balance problems that came with it pigeonholed my Dad as "4F" when he went to enlist. To get involved, he looked for a job where he could do his part, looking for a war-related job wherever he had relatives to live with. The railroad in Fort Worth wouldn't hire him, so he hitched a ride 30 miles west to Weatherford and found a job in a machine shop that built automotive parts. Double shifts started the first day he went to work and continued through the war. He moved into a small apartment with a cousin who needed a roommate that worked on a ranch outside of town.

Meanwhile, by coincidence my mother had kinfolk in Weatherford. She moved there and began working in the music shop her uncle owned downtown on the courthouse square. Her contribution to the war effort was moonlighting with a small oil company whose only customer was the United States Government. She took care of the company's bookkeeping at night after the music store was closed. The oil man leased land on the ranch where my Dad's cousin worked. Somehow, some way, an introduction happened that put two people on a course to a courtship. When the war ended on V-J Day, marriage was proposed. Their meeting led to my conception, to my future, to this day.

Not long after my Dad began working at the parts plant, the company studied how they could propose supplying vehicle parts to the Army. My Dad had a vision of starting his own plant similar to the one he was working in. Minimal re-tooling of such a small plant could make tools and parts for building aircraft instead of cars. The nearby cities of Fort Worth and Dallas had several large aircraft manufacturers. To service them he could move there and cut his prospective new company's shipping costs. But, he had already met the musician/bookkeeper, and he didn't want to move. Instead of turning his idea into his own new business, he took the ideas to his boss. Oddly enough, aircraft tools and parts became their new main product. Over a short time it grew from a small parts plant into a big factory, one of the larger businesses in town. My Dad got a small raise and an occasional "thanks" from the people that by all rights should have made him a major shareholder or Vice President, or something important. He stayed there the rest of his working days, through several wars and the government contracts that came with those conflicts. This man I saw as a visionary engineer lived the life of a dutiful line employee for over 40 years. They gave him a plaque and a tie bar engraved with their logo when he retired. The amount of money made by others on his original idea that turned the company into one of the area's main employers was never quantified. To be sure, little of it was seen by my hard-working Dad.

Still, he never complained, and he was proud of the work he did. We talked about that at his retirement party. When I asked him why he did not do this or that, or asked them to give him this or give him that, I was almost egging him on to bitch and moan about something, like the young know-it-all I was. He just looked deep into my eyes with a smile and told me, "I have no regrets, not a single one. I've lived an honest life, I've done good things, and I've been able to provide for my wife and kids. That's all I wanted to do. I have nothing to be ashamed of when I meet my maker. I have no regrets." I never forgot those words he said. How I wished that now I could say the same.

My Mother's dream before the war of becoming a concert musician turned into hoping a customer would come into the music shop. She asked her uncle if she could teach lessons after hours inside the store since she was skilled in a variety of instruments. Her request was denied but he liked the idea, and changed her job to include being a music teacher for *his* customers. The store advertised that they had music lessons available, and kids began coming after school. Instead of starting her own music teaching business, she allowed her uncle to use her as his store's attraction. There was a war on, after all, and the uncle provided her a place to live and one of two jobs. On top of that, she had already met her future husband. After the war ended her moonlighting job, the music store was changing. Local public schools got their teachers back, and students went back to learning there. The sheet music and instrument business of a small store in downtown Weatherford just couldn't compete with mail order houses and the bigger stores that were springing back to life in Fort Worth. One day, my Mom's ageing uncle and boss laid her off by attaching a pink slip to her time card, not even mentioning it over breakfast at home before they left for work. Then, he sold the store within a month. He never shared the profits of my Mom's suggestion, nor commissioned her lessons, nor her sales in the store. Not once did the old man offer to sell the store to my Mom. In those days, it may have been unusual for him to offer it to a woman, but it would have been reasonable to think he might offer to sell the business to his niece's new husband.

Visiting home from college one weekend, I mildly berated my mother for not demanding this or that, not pushing back at the uncle's unfairness. "You have to understand," she told me, "He gave me a place to live where I could participate in the war effort. I was lucky to have a job and a home with family during those times, and I met your father, too. I have no regrets – none at all."

Ralphie and I cruised up the fairway, walking together. On the tee he made me think of Tyler, and now he was acting just like Houston. He was in and out of the rough on one side, across in front of me to the trees on the other. We didn't walk side-by-side, but I sure appreciated that he was *with* me. Walking along with my wandering thoughts of days gone by I feared I was ignoring him, but the rambling dog sure didn't seem to care. How I wished The Boys were here now with him, together with us.

Both my parents were proud of being long-term employees. They were both contributors to their employers' successes, with little benefit other than having a job. They never looked back at what may have happened to them if they finished their academic years, if the war had not changed all that. They always refused to get bogged down in the useless "what if -ing" that I was doing so much all day. Beyond the fact they knew their patriotic work made a difference, they thought that just *having* a job was great. Go to work, go to church, pay your bills, and provide for the family you raise. Everybody be nice, and don't rock the boat – that was the kind of life that they, as a couple, thought was great. "No regrets."

My Dad grumbled when I decided to accept the TCU scholarship and start college as a theology student. Like so many freshman, I wasn't sure what I wanted my future to be when all of a sudden I was attending a prestigious university with a free ride. A natural major at something called Texas *Christian* University seemed it should involve religion, even though I couldn't say I ever dreamed of ministering. My Dad respected what he called "pastors" and "preachers", but he somehow didn't see the clergy as a productive, hard-working living. He ignored what I knew to be fact from my teenage involvement at our church: it seemed like these people worked 24 hours a day, 7 days a week, 365 days a year.

After my freshman year, I began to believe I couldn't be a good enough listener to be an effective leader in a church. I changed my major to Business and kept the scholarship intact. "Business" could lead to many things, so I could remain ambiguous about what I wanted to do after college. My Dad seemed to feel better. A job fair my senior year introduced me to Mountain View Airways. I liked them and they liked me, and my career began two weeks after graduation. I became what I believed was successful, and I did it quick enough I felt it proved that the change of my major had been warranted.

In the short-mowed grass of the fairway, there was a drastic change in my view of the hole the closer I got to my ball. I couldn't have placed a better shot off the tee. My ball was sitting on a nice patch of grass with about 180 yards to the pin. Around the dogleg to the right, the area that had been hidden before by the trees at the corner revealed a majestic view uphill to the green. The tall trees enclosed an alcove that contained the green and cast long shadows in contrast with the bright sunlight above it. Beautiful terraced outcroppings of flagstone enhanced the face of the hill that moved up from the corner. Two large sand traps guarded either side of the front of the green, filled with deep golden powder. The tip of a waving flag said the cup was there, just beyond sight.

"Hey, Pods, what do you think?" I had to speak up because Ralphie was investigating something 40 yards from me at the edge of the woods. He stood with his ears perked up, then darted over to my side while I fumbled in my bag, still deciding what club to pull. I swear he looked at my ball first, and then up at the green before raising his eyebrows, growling just a bit, and finishing with a *woof*.

"You think so? It's all carry, you know," I offered back to him when he looked up at me. "Besides, I don't know what's behind the green. What if I go over?" I don't claim to have been in a dialogue with the dog, but I decided he meant, *'It's uphill, hit a 4-iron'*. I pulled that club from the bag. With a couple of gentle practice swings brushing the grass, I looked back down to him.

He cocked his head again, as if to say, *'Trust me!'* He sat, dutiful while awaiting my shot, again just like Tyler would have. Unsure whether I was more worried about being too short or too long, I decided to trust my friend, and hit the ball.

A perfect divot of turf flew away from me, trailing the departing ball like the spent stage of a rocket booster falling away, having done its job already. Ralphie watched the flight of the ball with me. He gave a quick *arf* like he was saying, *'I told you so'*. I was confident I'd be safe on the green. The dog walked up the fairway ahead of me, beginning to trot as the grade increased. I saw the ball bounce once after it cleared the crest right between the two sand traps, straight at that tip of a flag. "I think that's as well as I can do it, buddy," I said to the departing wagging tail of the dog. I told myself he was running up to see where I had landed on the green when he went out of sight over the apex. I bagged my iron and followed him up the left side of the hole, leaving my glove on until I knew for sure I was going to be putting next.

"No regrets" – I heard my parents' words repeating over and over. What a wonderful notion it was. I had *so many* regrets, *so many* different things I wish I had done; there were *so many* people I wish I'd treated otherwise, Ned among the many. There were *so many* places I wanted to go but never made it. I wondered what it would be like to be happy with how you lived your life, like my parents. To dream of worldly travel as a teenager and then never make it out of the state like Terry, but to be so perfectly happy and content. Like Terry, it would be great to know you would one day leave a legacy of help and service to those less fortunate. Or like Ned, to do important work, to help people with a perspective of what their experiences were. Like Jack, to teach children, to help them grow, to develop both their bodies and their minds. To have risked your life for others, to protect their freedom with your own life, like Scott's son and so many thousands and thousands of military service people, like those high school friends, like neighbors on the block in Weatherford and so many other towns across the country.

If my faith was as strong as either I wanted it to be or I thought it was I could harbor no regrets. Strength of faith means having confidence that everything happens in our life just as our God intended. That should mean that there *are* no regrets, because life follows a larger plan, God's plan. Given that I had *so many* regrets, given that I truly wanted to live, that I truly did not want to die, given that I still wanted to do so many things, to correct so many wrongs, go so many places – did all that mean that my faith was weak? I kept coming back to that, coming back to challenge the depth of my own belief.

I topped the pinnacle of the hill and looked with eager anticipation onto the green, hoping my ball was resting there. When I came to the crown of the cart path, the first thing I saw was Ralphie, smiling, panting, and sitting just off the putting surface. He looked from my eyes over toward the pin and back at me. I looked at the green, too, as a few feet more of it came into view with each step I took. I saw no ball, no ball, no ball, and then – oh, yes! How I got a long iron to stop within five feet of the cup was beyond me. "Ralphie, like I said when I hit it, that's about as good as I can do it." We exchanged broad smiles. "Are you sure you didn't go fetch it and drop it right there for me?" I asked my partner. His replying *woof* had a *you'll never know* sound to it.

I fixed my half-inch-deep mark at the very front of the green, where my ball's first bounce would have been just out of my line of sight. It must have caught just the right amount of slope to spin it to a slow stop near the then unseen pin. There remained just the slightest break, just under a full ball outside the cup's edge. "We can make this, buddy," I said to the dog. The closer I got to it, the break and its corresponding speed looked more difficult.

I marked the spot of the ball with a coin, then picked it up and cleaned it. I gave the ball a quick look from kneeling behind it so that I didn't over-analyze it. "No paralysis from analysis," I muttered. It was just a bit downhill, left-to-right, five feet in length. Ralphie gave me a loud encouraging *BARK*. I looked at him and winked, took my stance, stroked the putt with conviction, and it rattled the bottom of the cup. A birdie on a tough hole was wonderful.

I looked over to share my joy with Ralphie. In an instant, he was gone again. The figurative wind came out of my sails when I looked up the path, over the next ridge into the woods, all around the green and back down the hole. Spending this hole with him had been such a joy, but now I felt more alone than I had all day. I returned the putter to my bag, and carded my score. I told myself that my buddy Ralphie would be back again soon. I hoped he stayed long enough to see me make the putt.

A quick adding up of my score on the front nine brought the pleasant surprise that I had a 41 so far. "Hey, that's pretty good for an old guy who hasn't played in a while," I said. "Now, if I can just keep from turning it into a 100 before it's done." I'd hit some lousy shots so far but some good shots, too. Considering the encounters and the time-warp travelling I was experiencing, I had to be pleased. I thought of how often over the years that any time I finished nine holes with a score under 45 I would be delirious. Off I headed, onward up the path toward the back nine.

CHAPTER 15

I expected nothing after the first nine because I knew this course didn't return to the clubhouse until the final 18th hole. I hoped there might be an outhouse or something though. Ahead, in a clearing in the woods, there sat an aged building, a frame shack whose last paint job had been peeling a long time. It was an abandoned Halfway House that long ago served its last hot dog. Its size befit a course that was very busy, while its condition said those days were forever gone. The side was about 40 feet long and supported an awning, erected to give golfers shelter while accessing the now padlocked restroom doors on each side at the rear of the building. The end of the structure facing me was boarded up. About 20 feet wide, it was once a service counter for the refreshment stop. The awning wrapped around in front to cover the spot where you could walk up to the counter. A weathered menu was hand painted on its own planks of wood above the window, perhaps made by the same person who did the tee signs. Prices were still visible, and a reflection of how long the snacks stand had been closed: Cheeseburger $0.75, Hot Dog .25, Fries .15, Candy Bar .10. It looked like an old burger joint, or a concession counter at a high school football game. I knew exactly what it reminded me of. I stopped to stare at it and reminisce.

The large deserted snack stand looked just like the one that was bustling every summer back when we were kids hanging out at Misty Lake, a popular private recreational area between Weatherford and Mineral Wells. A family outside of town had a nice round freshwater lake surrounded by trees and hills that was easier to get to than the huge reservoirs in our part of Texas.

To a kid it was an enormous inland sea. Thinking back now, it may have just been an oversized lagoon to adults. The people that owned it charged each carload a dollar to get in, which is why so many station wagons were always there. They wanted a family crowd so they kept alcohol out the best they could. Jack's parents took him and his sisters every Saturday in the hot Texas months when school was out. They asked me to come with them each weekend, and most times I did.

The Misty Lake concession stand got lots of my yard-mowing and car-washing money. I was one of what seemed like hundreds of sunburned kids in swimming suits running back and forth the several yards between the man-made beach and the sandy-fronted service counter facing the lake. It was always busy, open on three sides. Ten-cent refreshments were snow cones, popsicles, and soft-serve ice cream. There was no grill because most people brought their own picnics. Dotted around the perimeter of the beach were several cast iron barbecue pits. Just thinking about it, I could almost taste that mix of summer smells you got every day in the fresh air at Misty Lake – the smoke from the grills, the sweetness of the cool treats, the suntan lotion and the sweat. I could almost hear the kids playing, the mom's shouting, the water splashing.

Near the entrance sprawled what once was a pasture but was now our makeshift baseball diamond. Jack was always more anxious to be out there with a bat and ball than on the beach. The owner mowed the meadow once a month or so with their big bush hog. Enough play over time wore dirt base paths out of the grass in semi-straight lines between the spots we laid the towels used for bases. Jack's passion for baseball was strong from a very young age, but we never played very long. We were, after all, there for the water, the sand, the food, and the snacks. Besides, it was hot out there.

I thought again of Scott's admonishment to *keep moving, don't stop*. "Let's get going," I told myself. I continued walking the path on my way to Number 10. The path sloped downward, winding through the woods. The walk seemed a little long, but it was a natural way to break up the front nine from the back. I enjoyed it and kept going.

I recalled one time Jack put his junior golf bag in the back of his Dad's station wagon when we left for the lake. We brought a few balls we found playing the previous few weeks at Higdon Park. We took them to the "outfield" to hit, to "shag" balls. It had been a few weeks since the field was mowed, so while hitting them wasn't so bad, finding them to hit again was. We would find a couple less each time we hit from a different spot. We would get so tired of the hunt we would tee them up one more time and hit them into the adjacent forest as far as we could before we put the clubs back in the car. I remembered walking around the field on that day. Jack talked in such detail about the definitive plans he had for years later when he would grow up. He would be a Major League Baseball player with a long career. Somewhere along the way, he'd marry a rich, good-looking girl. When he retired, he'd go be a baseball coach at a high school, then a college, and then maybe even manage in the Big Leagues. He held those dreams for so many years. Those pages in our high school yearbook listed his certain recipe for a life of success. I was sad thinking of how much he wanted his dreams to come true, and that they did not. First the injury, and later his death; they combined to end a life filled with the joy of a storybook future.

Jack was so loony when we played those two holes together just a few minutes earlier. (A dead man playing golf with a dying man – maybe it really *was* a dream.) He was always like that, and I envied the zeal with which he lived his life. I marveled at his focus on running toward the finish line through the years he was with us. I wished I could say now that I ever felt any such vigor for anything.

I thought of so many other childhood friends that I grew up with, other kids from the neighborhood that would come to Misty Lake, too. All week I looked forward to seeing everyone. We swam, we played, and we acted like kids do. Walking the cart path, I could see all their forms, I could see some of their faces, but I couldn't remember but a couple of their names. I must not have been much of a "friend" if years later I couldn't remember them; it couldn't be just "old age". My parents tried to teach me that treasuring friendships was as important as anything else. I felt now that I'd failed those lessons. I remembered once our family met with Jack's and others of my Dad's co-workers for a big cookout at Misty Lake. My Dad looked down at me with a warm smile to say, "Cherish nothing greater than friendship". I wished I would have gone on to treat the friends I met earlier this day the way my Dad tried to teach me.

From a distance there grew a sound of cleats on pavement. At first I thought it was the echo of my own in the woods since the clicks and clacks were in unison with my steps. Through the trees to my right I saw the source of the sound, another golfer walking on another path. He walked with his head down and wore a navy blue cap. He was pulling an identical rental bag on a cart that looked exactly like mine. I wondered why a path intersection would be here, thinking maybe it was the crossing of a couple of holes on the back nine. Within a few paces, I realized that these paths were not crossing, but merging. I sighed at the prospect of playing the back nine with a new, unknown player at this point, and wondered if this meant my reminiscent encounters were over for the day. Like him, I turned my head toward the ground, looking in front of me while I walked to avoid any eye contact. Now we were much closer together and I looked up at the figure. His head was still fixed facing down, still ignoring me. As we drew even closer together, his head came up and turned toward me. Our eyes met.

"Eric?" We stopped at the same instant.

"Chris? Chris Collins?" He was as stunned as I was. We moved toward each other with hands extended.

We both mumbled our disbelief, almost in harmony. Our hands gripped each other in firm, genuine handshakes, the honest kind that meant we were glad to see each other. His grip was weaker than it should be, I thought. Eric's face was expressionless, but that was normal. He always had a wonderful dry sense of humor, the deadpan kind that always made you wonder if he was joking or not when he was pulling your leg about something.

"I sure didn't expect to see you here, Chris. How in the world? Oh boy," he stammered, unable to hide that he was shaken. Our hands stayed together a few seconds while we stared at each other, not knowing what to do or what to say to each other. I glanced up at his cap and chuckled at his well-worn trademark Chicago Bears hat.

"If I had any doubt it was you, that hat would clear it up," I noted. Through the years, on the job or off, I almost never saw him without one. Eric broke the silence first, with words that foreshadowed what was to come.

"Chris, I'm having a really strange day today, and I've got orders to keep going," he had my attention now. "How about we talk and walk?"

"That sounds good to me. Let's go." I let go of his hand and patted him on the shoulder. We resumed pulling our carts up the path.

Eric Stafford was one of our employees at Mountain View Airways in Denver. I knew him well at the airport, but not so well away from work. Small talk between us always included an exchange of pleasantries about home interests. We were cordial at work but we didn't socialize. The professional side of me concentrated on the fact he was, after all, my employee. Eric was in charge of the ramp, responsible for all the people who worked outside in the elements in Denver when I was the station manager he reported to. His Chicago toughness was just what we needed to orchestrate that outside concert of luggage handling, food trucks, and cleaning crews in and around moving aircraft. He guided his crew to get it all done with clockwork precision, despite the impatience of terminal gate teams.

The two of us came to Denver via very different routes. I joined the airline straight from college and got the job in Denver with one of my several quick promotions. Eric spent a couple of years at Robert Morris University before leaving to pursue a dream of playing professional hockey. He abandoned that after several tries, winding up in Denver with a mechanic's job at an auto dealer's garage. He earned a rapid move up to a salesman's position before punching a customer who rubbed him the wrong way. That led him to our airline's employment office. When Eric was hired, management may not have realized they were giving a chance to a man who would take charge of a troublesome department and stay with the company until they gave him a gold watch at retirement. I left the airline long before he did, but I knew he was responsible for a lot of the recognition we got for timeliness and customer satisfaction at the Denver location. The way he nailed down that aspect of the operation let me focus on other inner workings, cleaning up the messes that were accounting and administration when I moved into my job there. He was the reason for many of the successes that were attributed to me.

We kept walking, exchanging small talk while ignoring our surroundings. We joked about how we both looked, now in our older ages. "I don't know about you, Eric, but I sure never thought I would end up looking like *this*," I said, and we laughed together. We joked that we were both experiencing the melting process of ageing, and what melted was collecting in that same place around our waists.

“I’ve found growing old, fat, and ugly has saved me a fortune on social expenses.” Eric’s comment made us laugh together. Back in the day, Eric was known around the airport as a sharp-looking ladies’ man. Whether or not that was connected to his two marriages I knew of that ended in divorce, I was unsure. Eric couldn’t be more than a couple of years older than I. He was athletic back then, but he carried a middle-age gut now. Back then, he was stocky and built strong like a linebacker, like the tough hockey player he was. It was striking what a different figure he was now. He looked very tired. There was an ashen, almost jaundiced look about him. A black man with thin grey hair curling from under the cap, he looked like he was withering away. He struggled to move, fighting to make every step we took. Eric was Chicago through and through, born and raised there. He was all about the Bears, the Blackhawks, and the Bulls. He had lived several places all around the country, but returned home in his retirement. He mentioned the house he bought in Schaumburg, where he said he now lived alone.

I decided to get the subject off our health for a minute. I nodded to the bag he pulled. “Skip gave us both the same setup, I see.”

“Who?” Eric looked down at our equipment. He stopped, and then looked back up at me like I was from Mars.

“Skip. You know, the dude back at the clubhouse,” I said. He remained motionless, frozen like a statue. He looked even worse when I added, “You know, Gabriel’s Creek? Huntsville, Alabama?” I could see his lips quiver, the confusion returning to his face. “What brings you down South here, anyway?”

"Yeah, I rented them at the golf shop alright. But Chris, I don't know anybody named Skip." His speech was slow and deliberate. A look of near terror enveloped his face. "I don't know about any *creek*, and, down *South?*" Then came the bombshell: "Chris, I've never been in Huntsville, Alabama in my life." We both stood hushed a second, eyes fixed on each other. "I just came down to Champaign today to see my brother, and thought I would get in 18 while he was at work."

"Champaign? C'mon man, what are you talking about? You're not in Illinois. Look!" I turned and stretched out my arm in a sweeping motion. I wanted to show him that *this* was Gabriel's Creek, and that we were enjoying this bright warm day among these beautiful hills of Northern Alabama. I stopped before I could get the words out. Eric saw my face, turned his head with me, and then reflected my expression. All of a sudden we felt a crisp chill in the air. Neither of us spoke for a moment.

"I don't think this is Alabama, mister," Eric said, and I knew he was right. Like Skip's course, we were in a place cut out of the woods, and the sunshine was bright, the air clear. But there wasn't a hill or a rocky outcropping to be seen. Before us was a long, stunning golf hole. The grass in its fairway was two shades of green in a gorgeous cross-cut mowing pattern like what you would see at a major golf tournament. On either side was a third shade, a deep forest green indicating the rough was deep and punishing. We were standing on a long tee box. The ground rolled away ahead of us, uneven to a deep valley below our sight. From there, it flowed up again to an elevated plateau. The hole streamed down and back up, not doglegging but rolling a little one way and then the other. A cold breeze in our face freshened.

Almost at the same time we said together, “I know this hole.”

I looked at Eric, “And this ain’t Champaign, Illinois, either.”

“No sir, it ain’t,” he answered. “We're farther north, and east.”

Together, again as if we were flying in formation, our heads turned to look at the tee sign: Par 5, the yardage was 611 yards from the tips, 585 from the whites. We looked at each other first, then together back up the fairway. Yes, I knew this hole.

“Eric, you ever been in Cleveland?” I asked.

“Yeah, I’ve got a cousin there.” His look turned nostalgic. “I took a bus there to go with him to see the U.S. Amateur a long time ago.” He turned back to me.

“I’m guessing they played it at Canterbury Golf Club that year. That’s in Cleveland, isn’t it?”

“Yeah,” he nodded. “Canterbury. They played the Western Open there for long time, too.”

I stared another moment before adding, “If this isn’t Canterbury, it sure as hell looks just like it.”

“Yeah.” He nodded back toward the tee marker. “Says this is the 16th hole.”

“At Canterbury, I think it is.” After a moment, I added, “I’ve got a brother-in-law that worked in Cleveland. He got me on the course for a charity scramble once when we went to visit.” I just stared toward the green in the distance. “I know this hole. I’ve played this hole.”

"Kick your butt?"

"Yep, kicked my butt." The entire course did, that was certain.

"You already played 15 holes today, Chris?"

"Nope, this is my 10th today. You?"

"My 12th." Eric pulled his driver out of his bag, his movements stiff, like a mummy walking in an old movie. "Chris, I don't really know how to say this, but like I said, I've got to keep going." He took a ball and tee out of his pocket. "You want the tee, or you want me to go first?"

"No, go ahead, please." I tried to focus on joining him. I drew my driver out and put on my glove, wishing I had a sweater while Eric teed his ball. We'd only played together a couple of times at company events long ago so I didn't know what to expect from him as a golfer. We were both still dazed when he looked up the fairway and took his stance, ready to hit. This was a demanding tee shot, hard to pull off on any day, but even more so given how stunned we both were.

"Chris, you ever have one of those days when you feel like you don't know what the hell is going on?" He came still after his question, ready to swing. I waited for his shot before answering. Eric's short backswing preceded his strong downward club speed and solid contact. His ball was straight and long, bounding down the right side of the uneven fairway before disappearing with the slope. We were sure it rolled down the embankment to finish in the center of the unseen driving area.

"Nice ball, Eric," I said when he picked up his tee. "And yeah, I know the kind of days you're talking about." We were trading positions on the tee, Eric walking off to await my shot. I teed my ball and went into my routine. "In fact, funny you should mention it, because," I paused to look him right in the eye to say, "I'm having one of those days today myself."

"Is that right?" Eric asked. I felt his blood pressure escalate with the volume of his words. Those three words sounded incredulous, with a *yeah, sure, you have no idea what I'm talking about* tone. He held his tongue and waited for me to hit. I remembered to aim up the right side from my visit here many years ago. My subconscious must have wanted to match Eric's powerful swing because I got ahead of the ball and pulled it straight to the left on take-off. When the ball went out of sight, I knew it would end up in the heavy grass of the troublesome rough.

I put the driver back into my bag and we stood next to each other. We gazed into one another's eyes like we both had a confession to make. We started walking off the tee box, both of us noiseless. I noticed Eric seemed like me, less surprised than confused by what was going on. I wanted to know why he would say he was having an unusual day. Why did he seem to have the same directions as I, to "keep moving"? Why was our equipment matching? I could bet I knew what subject was our common ground.

"We have to keep moving, keep playing, Eric."

"Yes, Chris, we do." His voice sounded irritated. "I told you that already."

"Yes, but there's another reason I know that. You see, we've both got the same marching orders." He looked at me like he missed something, perplexed by my statement. "I think we should discuss our health. Don't you?" We walked and looked at each other, both knowing we were about to share things we didn't want to. "How about you go first?"

"Why me first?"

"'Cause I asked you first."

"You sure you're not just trying to boss me around again?" We walked in awkward silence before he sighed and started talking.

CHAPTER 16

The disease was much different than mine, but the projected outcome and the expected timing of his result was the same. He stared at the ground while we walked, as apathetic in telling his story as I was attentive. Within the past week Eric received his diagnosis of pancreatic cancer after a barrage of tests at the University of Chicago Hospital. Surgery wasn't an option – the disease was just too far advanced. He drove to Champaign to see his brother, to share *his* news. He asked the brother to take off work for an "important chat", but the brother refused. He told Eric he couldn't miss work "just to visit", and added that he didn't want to miss his bowling league later tonight, either. Maybe another time, the brother suggested.

I concentrated on listening to Eric, never interrupting nor talking over him. He was telling me in detail what symptoms he had for how long, and what tests had been run. He described how after each round of exams they told him what they suspected his problem was, once, twice, and a third time, changing their conclusion on each progressing occasion. I became a bit ashamed of how much I wanted to jump in and share my story with Eric. Our situations were so similar, but if there was ever a time for me to become a good listener, it was now. Somehow I felt I owed it to Eric to hold my story until I learned if I could help him in some way. There would be plenty of time to tell my story later. I spent a few steps realizing the fallacy of that thought: "plenty of time". My goodness, neither one of us had that.

Eric walked with me down the left side of the hill. We could see his ball in the center of the fairway. I knew mine would be in the rough, but finding a ball that disappeared out of sight in *this* depth would be a miracle. We wandered into the thick, damp grass that was well above our ankles. The anxiety of spending time searching for a ball was on both our minds; we were both conscious of our need to keep moving.

"Might be the only way we're going to find that ball is if we step on it," Eric said. He was right. The woods were close by, thick and dark with oak and locust trees. There was a good 20 yards of the deep grass from the first cut of the rough to the edge of those woods. I was looking hard when I stepped on a small piece of a tree limb. I looked down, and an inch away from my feet was a bright glimmer of white. It was my ball nestled deep down in the thick blades of the high rough.

"Got it," I shouted. Eric walked the few paces over my way to see.

"Ooh," he grunted when he saw my ball. "Better you than me, Chris. Good luck." He headed back toward the shorter grass, to his own ball in the fairway.

My ball was buried so deep I'd be lucky to get any club on it at all, much less hit it out. It would be easy to wind up with a 10 or worse on this long par-five hole if I was foolish and got too aggressive in attacking it. I needed to hack it out to the playing area without screaming the ball across the fairway and into the rough again. I pulled an 8-iron out of my bag, looking down deep where my ball was encapsulated by grass.

"Coming your way, Eric," I shouted in warning, and he acknowledged with a wave back. I chopped down hard onto the ball, swinging hard, trying to coax the ball out. It came out like I hit a foam coffee cup, flying just a few feet before dropping into the rough again. I sighed before I saw how much better my new lie was. It was now sitting atop the grass instead of enveloping itself back down into its warmth. Eric gave me a sympathetic shrug when I looked up at him. I walked the few steps to my new spot and took my stance again. A smoother, more normal swing this time flew the ball out well, where it bounced about 15 yards ahead of Eric.

My partner took a 3-wood out of his bag while I pulled my cart out of the rough. His swing caught the ball on the sweet spot, sending a perfect straight shot sailing out of the valley to disappear past our line of sight to what I was sure would be a good position in the fairway ahead. I also pulled out a 3-wood and used his line as my target, striking my ball with a solid swing. It was a little fat, kicking up a divot just large enough to tell us my ball wouldn't travel as far as I'd hoped. We followed its flight, on the same line as Eric's ball. Then we talked as we walked about our expectation that the two golf balls would be close together when we crested the grade that dissected the fairway. We came over the rise and saw two balls in the fairway ahead, together just as we thought.

"Just remember, I am there in two, and you are laying four," Eric was fast to point out, and he was right. The nearest ball was mine, about 130 yards out from the flag. Eric's ball was about 20 yards ahead of me. We kept walking and he finished describing his medical problem. He didn't ask about my situation, so we just talked about his. I wondered if maybe my true purpose was to give *him* some comfort.

"So, this morning you're in Champaign, Illinois?"

"Yep," he replied.

"And you went to play golf today?"

"Yep. Just wanted to get 18 in, kind of a one last time thing, you know?" I knew, yes, how I knew. I hoped that Eric would reveal more about the details of his day. I'd have to admit I was most interested in comparing our notes. Maybe hearing more of his story would answer some of *my* questions of what was happening to *me* today. "I just kind of wanted to clear my head, to try to figure out how to break all this to six kids." I had forgotten he had two children with each of two wives, and now he was telling me of two more that came later. "Every one of them thinks I'm great, because I've always given them everything they ever wanted. They should all be happy because I'll leave each one of them a *load* of money but I'm still worried about what will happen to them after I'm gone." His sensitivity was visible, and intense.

I wanted to get back on point. "Eric, I'm guessing that this isn't the only place outside Champaign you've been today."

Eric kept looking at the ground. At first, he acted like he had no idea what I was asking. Then, after exhaling a deep breath, he said, "No, it isn't." He looked up at me. "But how do you know that?" He looked torn between a fear of discussing it and getting upset.

"The same way I know I'm not the only person you've seen today that you weren't expecting." Maybe he thought I was beginning to push too hard. I wanted to turn the discussion to *my* medical news, about *my* trip to see *my* daughter, about *my* weird series of interactions today. I wanted someone to hear how *my* day started with the intention of relaxing while playing the last round of golf of my life. We kept walking in the perfect short grass of the fairway and reached my ball first. Eric stopped a few feet before I did; it was noticeable he was moved to say something.

"Maybe you're the first today and maybe you're not," he said, starting to get pretty fired up. "I see you haven't changed much since you were the big boss. Still always think you know everything, huh, Chris?"

"What?"

"Where does that come from, man? Where do you come off always acting like you know everything anyone's ever been through before? You have absolutely no idea. Never have." I slowed my walk, parking the pull cart next to my ball while he hammered away. "And know what? You never will." It was a little hard to consider my approach shot to the green with him starting to rant. "You always gave us that damn *been there, done that* attitude. Trust me; this ain't the time for it now, not anymore, not today." He was steaming. "I don't need it."

"Eric, I don't know who pissed in your coffee, but – "

"*You* did, Chris. *You* pissed in my coffee, just now. You did, just like you did in Nate's. Just like you did with everybody else at the station back in Denver." Just that quick, I went from wanting to help Eric to being attacked by this verbal shelling.

"Nate? Sorry, I'm lost."

"Yeah, you don't remember him, do you? You were just too big a deal then, weren't you?" Eric's best friend Nate was our counter agent for years.

"As a matter of fact I do remember him, Eric." Always bad at names, I remembered this employee. I was raising my voice a bit now in response. "He was a good man." I pulled a 9-iron from my bag for my shot as the breeze in our faces freshened.

"Oh, yeah? Remember why you fired Nate?" I did remember.

"He came to work with the wrong blazer on, Eric." My recollection of the situation was all too vivid. "He had lots of warnings and write ups already. The procedures said I had to fire him – I had no choice."

"You had a choice, Chris, because you were the boss. You had the opportunity to consider that he was a single dad of three kids since his wife died in childbirth. He could have either made it to the dry cleaner or to work on time when his day care opened late that day. He couldn't do both."

I heard him, and I hated the memory. I looked ahead at the large green, sloped from the back toward the front. I hit the ball. It was heading toward the right side of the green. I was afraid it was a little long. The ball bounced on the right of the green, rolling just a little bit, curling a few inches left to a stop maybe 20 feet away from the pin.

"I didn't realize you were such a management expert, Eric. I guess we should have switched jobs."

“There you go again, like you could do my job,” he fired back.

“Is this making you feel better, Eric?” It was *my* turn to raise my voice. “Would you go up there and hit your ball, or do you need me to kick your ass right here so I can feel better, too?” He looked up at me to see I was grinning, but both honest and confident. I motioned him toward his ball. “You know very well neither of us could have done the other’s job. I never said I could do yours but I’m damn sure you couldn’t do mine.” He was quiet until he reached his ball and stopped his cart next to it. He exhaled, deciding he didn’t have the energy to stay mad anymore. I lowered my voice, adding, “Maybe we were lucky to have each other, you ever think about that?” I paused while he pulled the wedge from his bag and finished my thought while he looked over his short yardage remaining to the flag: “I know I was lucky to have all of you.”

“I worked for that airline a long time, Chris, a lot longer than you. But you were there long enough that I feel I have the right to get one thing off my chest before I die.” Maybe I should have been concerned with the connection between what he was saying and the pitching wedge he was gripping, but I was not.

“What’s that?”

He took a couple of practice swings before answering, “You had no right to take credit for the things I did there, not when all you did was hold me down, keep me back.” He couldn’t know how often I praised his work to management above me. At this point, he didn’t need to hear how many times I fought for and won abnormal pay increases and bonuses for Eric and his team. “You changed a lot of lives with all your self-proclaimed *objectivity*. What a bunch of crap that was."

I raised my eyebrows but held my tongue while he took just a second to settle over his ball before swinging. His contact was perfect, taking a long, huge divot of turf that flew straight and high while his ball towered up and up, high above the green. We tracked it and neither of us spoke, both hoping more than believing it would be as good as it looked. Our eyes widened while we followed his ball as it headed down, straight at the flagstick. It bounced on the green, once, twice, and *plunk*! Into the cup. Eric holed the shot. He looked up at me at once. Our eyes met, and I was almost as excited as he. The moment his ball went into the hole he was invigorated. In an instinctive reaction, we slapped our hands together in a solid high five. He still held his wedge, hesitating, not knowing what to do next. He jumped over for a quick hug that I was happy to return.

"Eric, that's an eagle!" I said, with enthusiasm that was genuine.

"I *know*, man! Wow that felt great! You may not believe this, Chris, but I've *never* done that from over 100 yards out! I mean, a couple of times I've made a putt for an eagle, but I never hit the ball in the hole from the fairway for one!" I never saw anyone more thrilled. Given our conversation of moments ago, it was enough that I knew how wonderful he felt, and I considered myself blessed to share his experience. This was without a doubt the last time either of us would be a part of such a shot.

"Dude, that's a hell of a shot!"

He picked up his divot and respectfully replaced it. He smiled and shook his head, still in disbelief. “Thanks, thanks. Man, I’m so glad somebody was here to see it.” He replanted the turf with a tap of his foot. Still smiling, he said, “Doesn’t change what I said, though.” We chuckled while he put his club back in the bag. We walked again but I wanted us to finish the subject.

“When I first took over, we had to make a lot of changes. It was kind of rocky until things got settled. I was there to do a job, not to make friends. I thought once we got rolling, we had a tight group. I think everybody was OK with me. But the reality is, if they weren’t OK with me, the hell with ‘em. We got results, didn’t we?” If I had been listening to myself, I’d know I was just rationalizing my actions.

“Keep in mind one thing,” Eric said, calmer now, as we neared the green and walked onto the cart path. “It doesn’t matter what we thought you should or shouldn’t have done. It doesn’t matter that you excused the things you did as just being objective. There is a bottom line to all this.” He paused and looked deep into my eyes before continuing, “You see, Chris, nothing you did meant a damn thing. You could have been something to us, but you chose to erase yourself from our minds by blowing us off. You meant nothing because you quit us. You didn’t just quit the company, you didn’t just quit *on* us – you quit *US*.”

“I had to. Problem at home. I had no choice.” I didn’t care to elaborate. We parked our carts. I took off my glove and pulled the putter from my bag.

“Baloney.” Eric said, quick and firm. “Happens every day, people deal with their spouse messing around on them without bailing out on a good career, without quitting on the people they work with." I didn't know how he knew more than I thought, but I saw that I wouldn't *need* to elaborate. We walked toward the flag. "A man should have the guts to stand up, be a man, and handle a situation like that and keep going. You tried to be a tough guy at work because you couldn't be one at home." I surprised myself with how far I let him go out of bounds with that. We arrived at the pin, both looking down into the cup to see his ball inside. "And you know what else? We all lasted several more years," he looked up at me and punctuated it, "You didn't." I nodded my response. "I got the watch, I made a fortune on my retirement, and I've got kids that think I'm great." He bent over and picked the ball out of the hole, bringing it to his lips for a quick and well-deserved kiss. "What have you got?" It wasn't a question I wanted to answer.

I looked back at where my ball was on the green. "I've got about 20 feet for bogey." I decided this evaluation of my professional performance and personal decision-making by a line employee was over, despite how profound his observations were. I looked over my line while I walked to my ball. Eric stayed at the flag to tend the pin. The putt would break over a foot from right to left travelling toward the hole. When the ball left the face of my putter, Eric pulled the pin. We watched it roll up and over the grade, then curve down the putting surface. It was a nice putt, but I misjudged the speed just enough that the ball broke sooner than I hoped. It passed the hole on my side, creeping until it quit two feet past the cup.

"That's good," Eric said. He kicked the ball away and back to me, before I could say I'd rather finish it. Given everything that happened on this hole, I decided be glad and take my better-than-deserved 7 and move along.

"Thanks. It's very nice of you to beat me by only 4 strokes on this hole." We laughed together and walked off the green.

We stopped at our bags and Eric extended his hand again. I took it and we both shook, as gentlemen. No words were needed – we both knew that enough had been said already. My desire to "help him" may have been satisfied without mentioning the similarity of our situations. He got a few things off his chest at an old employer. He also had a great experience on a great golf hole, and I was delighted to witness his elation while playing with him. We both were quiet as we headed up the cart path into a tunnel of oaks, both wanting to believe our pairing would continue, but doubtful that it would. Unseen in the distance, but echoing through the woods, we heard the recognizable bark of a familiar dog.

Both of us called the same name together toward the sound: "Ralphie?" Stopping dead in our tracks, our stunned eyes turned toward each other.

I spoke first, my words racing along with my mind. "Ralphie? Ralphie who? What do you know about any Ralphie?"

"How do *you* know a dog named Ralphie?" We were both speechless for a few seconds before he continued. "C'mon, Chris, you've got to tell me, how the hell do you know? Tell me what you know! What makes you think that dog's name is Ralphie?" Eric was trembling, and I was a bit myself.

"Who said Ralphie was a dog?"

"Don't mess with me, Chris. I *told* you I'm having a really weird day." He nodded up the path. "We've got to get moving, you know? Let's walk and talk about this Ralphie, OK?"

"Alright, Eric," I said, turning up the path with him, both of us looking around in earnest for a dog. The driest cottonmouth of my life consumed my tongue. Just ahead, a water fountain along the path was built of flagstone, pyramiding up from a broad base to the push-button faucet and metallic bowl at the top. Eric walked past it but I stopped and bent over for a quick sip. I looked away from him just long enough to take in the cold, crisp water. When I looked up, I was alone in the woods again. There was no Eric, no sound of his cleats on the path, nor the wheels of his cart. After a few seconds of silence, as if it were punctuating the moment, came the echoing single bark of the dog. Ralphie's refrain had a comforting sound to it now. When I heard it, first I wondered, and then I knew: Eric and I would see each other again soon. Very soon.

CHAPTER 17

Standing at the fountain, I looked all around me into the woods, hoping to see Ralphie, or Eric, or maybe even both of them. A bird sang from somewhere above me, providing depth to the emptiness of the thick trees that wrapped around the cart path. I took another swallow of water and carded my score on the last hole, a 7 on my 10th. With a sigh, I continued onward, alone again.

Approaching the tee box from the left side there was a steep drop from the raised teeing ground. The fairway below was once again hard to distinguish from the rough. Yes, I was back in Alabama alright. The land fell away to the right ahead, but then it turned a sharp corner to the left at least 250 yards out. A flickering flag through the woods caught my eye. I looked through thinned tree tops to see the green in the distance. The tee sign marked the par 4 11th hole at 380 yards from the white tee markers.

The forest on the right side was very thick down there at the turn, where the right-leaning fairway preceded the woods with a hard pan surface. A well-hit shot would get ruined if it ran across that hard ground and into the woods beyond. If I were to toss a ball underhanded from the front of the tee box it would roll all the way to the bottom. Something told me to hit an easy 4-iron along the left side and let nature take its course. If I was wrong the mistake would add at least one stroke to my score. I teed the ball low and put an easy swing on the iron. The ball was bouncing and bouncing, rolling and rolling, moving a few inches to the right each ten yards or so. It slowed where the fairway made its hard left, rolling straight until coming to a rest on the other side of the fairway at the corner. I walked off the tee confident I would have an easy wedge remaining to the green.

Pulling my cart down the precarious hill, I thought about Eric again. The similarity of our situations was staggering, so alike it was surreal. I knew it was selfish of me, but still I wished he would have asked me more about myself, about my situation, about my day. It was quite apparent that I wanted to talk about it. If only he could have stayed with me another hole or two, I'd like to know who else he saw today and hear more of his experiences. Maybe Nate was one of them; maybe that's why he was so fired up about my role in damaging Nate's life. I thought of how proud he was of his accomplishments, though, and envied him a little.

As for that "load of money" he spoke of: was it really so important? Eric couldn't be so happy, divorced at least twice with kids spread around to different families. He was alone. There was a brother he wanted to share things with that seemed to want nothing to do with him. He was impressed that his kids thought he was great, but he never mentioned anything about how much they *loved* him. Maybe there was a connection between that and the relationship I had with my own kids. He believed his children liked him because he bought them any and everything they wanted. I thought mine were disgusted with me for buying them so few things they wanted even though I was so committed to get them everything they needed.

Then again, it brought back that long-standing question I asked myself so often since I found out about Cameron's affair. That event always made me wonder if it was possible that "our" kids were not mine. Even though I was confident, I couldn't be sure that the affair I knew about was in fact her only one. Friends and relatives were stricken that our kids neither looked like me, nor did they seem to "get anything" from me. I never looked for a reason why we were so different. Maybe it didn't matter after all, since I was there for them from the time my wife became pregnant through their birth, through everything until now. Right or wrong, real or imagined, I was Dad to Cameron's children. Maybe like Eric, I was looking for my legacies – looking for proof to the world that I ever existed once I depart. It's safe to say this is what many men see in their children. It wouldn't matter so much that Eric's death made his kids rich if they cared very little about him. Neither would it matter one way or another if my kids were indeed not from my loins. My impact on them – positive or negative – has been determined more by what I personally contributed to their upbringing than by my bloodline.

Walking now where the dogleg opened toward the green on my left, I remembered Eric asking me, "What have (I) got?" Perhaps I had a lot after all, perhaps much more than he. It wouldn't be fair to have started a debate with Eric on the subject – it was too late to go looking for ways to be rude. I had to admit, though, it was pretty brazen of Eric to bring up the situation with my wife given his track record in marital relations. Regardless of how my wife and I grew to be so close, I was married to but one wife that I always gave my unconditional love; someone who I believed still loved me today, too.

My ball was safe, sitting where the hardpan leveled out. To the left was an unspectacular view to a large, flat, unprotected green about 120 level yards away. The thinning woods on my left became denser where they rounded behind the green. A full pitching wedge should be an easy shot, so I pulled that club from the bag. I was conscious of the ball being below my feet, but didn't adjust enough for it. The ball headed straight at the right side of the green. In front of the putting surface the ball took its first of several bounces before trickling to a stop a few feet off the right edge. I walked toward the side of the green for my third shot, still preoccupied with my experience with Eric.

Seeing him made me think back to my airline days. It was business before BlackBerrys, cell phones, and chatting with your fingertips. It was a time when office administration and management was computerizing jobs before we really knew what computers could do. Years before the emphasis became interfaces that acted without any manual input, "computerization" pretty much meant typing data into a machine instead of writing it. There were still jobs with names like Data Entry Clerk and File Clerk. Interoffice communication was still done with a cluster of mailboxes. We were using fax machines a lot, some of us wondering why this new miracle could not be combined into that big clumsy photocopier.

It is hard to forget the day we brought in large boxes that were labeled "Personal Computer" and everyone wondered what that meant. The Internet was still a government experiment we never heard of and "wireless" meant put a battery in your transistor radio. Bluetooth meant someone needed a dentist. Productivity management issues like keeping employees off personal phone calls was as easy as watching your land-line telephone logs. No supervisory time investment was necessary to find out if employees were watching live sports or pornography on company time. Social networking was what you did at the coffee pot or in the airport dining room. Every task still had to deal with what would soon come to be called "snail mail", whether we were dealing with customers, vendors, or even for internal communications. It was a big step when we could put beepers on people to locate and communicate with them. The technology that seemed futuristic in those days took just a few short years to first become reality and then become passé.

Despite the now archaic ways we were doing business back then, some management techniques are timeless. I believed I was more than just a very good manager; I was an accomplished executive. One couldn't argue my effectiveness – I got things done for the company that others could not. From the time I hit the ground running out of college, I got the job done. The way I got it done – I *thought* – was being a "by the book" guy. Sometimes, it was *me* writing the book for the company, sometimes I was following the book the company gave to me. I saw myself as implicitly objective. That's why I thought Eric's observations about me as a professional were curious. I'd brag about how I left emotions and personalities out of all decisions, making managerial judgments much like a referee. Where others fell short, where others failed, where mismanagement made a mess, the company knew it could count on me. Call on me, I'll get the job done, the company's profitability would increase, bonuses for everyone above me would get bigger. They knew they had a go-to guy who would get things done by making decisions that most wouldn't be able to do. Others could not, or *would not* do what needed to be done because they could not be objective – they could not look into the eyes of those affected when implementing their decisions.

I possessed a matter-of-fact approach that would not just change employees' job duties, but how they were expected to perform them. Changing employees' schedules was often just a necessity. Saying so meant I could ignore the impact it would have on them. I could and would terminate employees with ease, firing people who "by the book" had earned it. Laying people off was much harder, but if it needed to be done, I did it. I was always "by the book". I created my own vision of myself. I thought these things were what made me so good, what made me so valuable.

How wrong I was. It took me many years to see that. I rationalized my behavior by thinking if my employees thought I was a lousy boss, that meant I must be doing things right. After all, I was so much smarter than them – that's what I told myself, anyway. Perhaps what Eric was telling me today was that my management style wasn't what I'd be remembered for, but it might be why I was so easily forgotten.

I arrived at my ball, just off the putting surface. The grass between my ball and the green was so thin that a putter was the right choice. I could tell from where I parked my bag that it would move just a little right-to-left. With a couple of prefacing practice strokes, I hit the ball, and watched it bounce every few inches until it reached the green, just like I expected. The pin in the hole was never in danger, but it was a decent approach. I hit it far enough, but too hard to take advantage of the break. My ball stopped even with, but about three feet right of the hole.

I was sincere each of the many times I told a group of our employees that they were our biggest asset, that I needed them so much more than they needed me. I meant every word. I didn't see until much later, just as Eric said, the problem was that I carried myself like I thought I knew everything. I had focus groups of employees under the auspices of getting their ideas, of hearing their thoughts. In reality I was looking for a forum where I could con them into thinking something I wanted done was their idea. Without meaning to, I always changed those meetings from open dialogues into my dominating speech to them. Maybe my own successes created my vision of my own invincibility. Like Eric said: they lasted, and I did not. Although Eric rattled my professional cage today, I wondered if meeting him was another faith-related issue. Maybe being put together with him was another way I was being forced to face errors of my past before it was too late.

I pulled the pin and looked at the downhill putt. I was lackadaisical; nonchalant. I stroked it and it turned 90 degrees as it caught nothing but the lip and spun three inches away. At that moment, I was not enjoying the golf, and the golf was my very reason for being here today. The purpose, just like Eric's, was to take my mind off things and enjoy the game one more time. My bewilderment was preventing me from doing either. I sighed and tapped the ball in with one hand. I walked back to my bag, wrote my bogey 5 on the card, and headed back onto the cart path.

It was then that I realized all these wonderful, positive images I had of myself were in times when I was managing people. My precious memories in that world painted a picture of what a young executive dynamo I was. That impressive man I recalled was all about maximizing productivity and getting things done. All my reflections about my career as a good businessman were of times when people worked for me. I was not remembering the failure I became after I blew off my airline career in order to rescue my marriage. Life as an insurance man wasn't worthy of getting much attention. Maybe it was because I was so convinced I found my calling at Mountain West. Maybe it was because, in all truth, I loved it and I never wanted to leave it. Selling insurance looked to me like a way an astute businessman could apply his talents. It seemed like one of those trades that I could make a pretty easy transition into. I thought I could succeed in taking my skills to it. My financial oversight ability was solid, and the direction of sales and marketing efforts were never a problem for me at the airline. I never anticipated the difference doing everything by myself would make. I had to do it on my own. No employees, just a Home Office in Atlanta to keep happy. I thought being a one-man show was how I would solve the hours-worked problem that led to Cameron's affair. I never thought of how hard I would need to work to earn the business of people who knew nothing about me other than my direct-mailed solicitations. I never expected to learn that my aptitude for directing sales and marketing people had nothing to do with my ability to excel at doing it myself. I placed myself in a profession that needed hard work and long hours to get started. I wasn't willing to do it because that's what I was trying to get away from, and because the passion I had for the airline was gone.

I tried to be the best insurance guy I could be, but I missed a lot of things about my airline days. The excitement of an airport was a factor, without question.

The everyday changes in people and conditions, the variety-is-the-spice-of-life stuff. Maybe most of all I missed the respect. In general, people respected me, and I believed I earned it. They showed it with smiles and nods and whispers as I passed, by standing when I entered a meeting, by doing things for me I never asked for nor expected. I thought I earned that respect for the work I did and the way I treated people. Eric made me see that I might be wrong about all of that. Even if the respect I felt was something being shown only for my title, it was better than the solitary professional life I switched to.

I saw insurance as a life raft for our marriage, and a ticket out of Denver. Cameron said she never liked The Mile High City, even though I loved it. If moving would make her happy, though, I believed we could move to New Mexico and start everything fresh: "Land of Enchantment" and all that. We picked a nice place in Albuquerque but I had chosen a business that depended on customers trusting you, knowing you, believing you were part of a community. Just renting space in a strip mall and putting up a sign didn't make up for being a new guy nobody ever heard of who left a huge job with a known company in a respected industry, etcetera, etcetera. In insurance, whether I was right or wrong I felt the disrespect of being a used car salesman. It became another bad personal decision, and it was irreversible.

I needed to suppress all those ego-inflating images I had of myself that Eric was challenging minutes ago. It was time to remember advice my Dad gave me once after he heard me bragging as an adult about my prowess at something in my youth: "It doesn't matter what you *were*, it matters what you *are*." It was meaningless for me to concentrate on having been a successful airline executive with a bright future. In reality, I was nothing more than a dying man with way too many regrets, and too much to do before I died.

Toward the next hole I walked, into the forest again. Going back into the woods, I drew a deep breath, knowing I should gather myself and round up my thoughts. I needed to get back to focusing on relaxing, on enjoying my Alabama golf course. The path between holes was again a tunnel through the thicket, and I knew I could enjoy my day again. I hoped I could. I hoped I would.

CHAPTER 18

Once again, I took in the sounds and the fragrance of the forest. The breeze weaving through the thicket was a calming resonance, disturbing the fallen leaves and the plants in the dim light of the wooded floor that the path flowed across. The aroma was genuine and earthy, refreshed with a hint of magnolia.

After walking a few more steps, those smells went through a rapid change. The air became filled with the salty smell that could be nothing other than an ocean breeze. The farther up the pathway I got, the sounds transformed, too. A different noise was taking over, the din of the woods morphing into a familiar sound like the heavy surf of an ocean. I wondered what could cause that sound here in inland Alabama, thinking of everything from a swarm of bees to a brush fire. Then, I could swear I heard seagulls.

I came out of the woods and back onto the golf course. The grass of the tee ahead was different, a brighter shade of green in the diffused sunshine of a marine layer overcast. The crispness in the air remained, but the breeze was now a stronger wind, quartering into me from my left and ahead of me. I turned to look off to the left. The tee was 100 feet above the water. To be sure, this wasn't Alabama. That body of water out there wasn't the Gulf of Mexico, nor was it Mobile Bay. I was standing on bluffs above the Pacific Ocean. Someone unfamiliar with this spot may have thought it was Monterrey or Newport Beach. I knew it was neither.

Ahead of me was a long fairway sweeping uphill first to the right and then back a little left. It was all bordered on the left by cliffs that towered above the crashing surf of the ocean below. Seeing the distinctive Torrey Pine trees along the right side of the long hole, I knew precisely where this was. Then I saw downtown La Jolla in the distance and felt at home, although I had no idea how I came to be just north of San Diego. If this wasn't Torrey Pines South Course, Number 4, I didn't know my own name. The tee sign confirmed my memory, reminding me with its complex of yardages: Black, 488; Blue, 467; White, 448; Gold, 423; Red, 388.

Something moved in my peripheral vision, and I turned in its direction. Out of a powered cart parked next to the tee climbed a short Italian man. He began speaking before our eyes met in a voice that sounded like someone had just spit in his lasagna.

"Where'd you come from? I'm supposed to be out here alone," he growled. He looked up at me and stopped, frozen in his tracks with his jaw hanging open. He should have been shocked to see me, too. Yes, I knew him; it was Nick Viscotto, a long time ago my closest friend for many years. I hadn't seen him in 15 years, and since then I hoped I would never see him again. We were the same age, but now he looked much younger than I.

I gazed out at the brilliant blues of the ocean and the sky. I drew a deep breath and said, "It's such a beautiful day, such a beautiful place, here on one of my favorite golf holes ever." I looked up the hole toward the green first before turning to focus my cold eyes into his from a masculine stance. "And then you show up and ruin it all."

"Chris? What the hell?" I was familiar with the level of confusion, but was determined to show him no empathy. "Chris, is that really you, man?" He took a couple of steps toward me.

My move away from him was brisk as I walked toward the white tees carrying my driver. I bent down to set my ball on its peg. I was doing everything I could to restrain myself. I wanted to walk over to him and punch his lights out, or maybe even crack his head open with my club. I kept looking away from him on purpose, and said, "While you try to figure things out, I'm playing through." I stepped back behind my ball to look at my target up the fairway. It was such a gorgeous hole I wanted to stop and drink it in for a few minutes, but my desire to get going and get away from Nick took over. I looked over to him with an icy stare and said, "Try to stay out of my way."

Still acting perplexed, he mustered up his trademark soft-toned, smart-ass voice, and while squinting through his Cheshire cat grin, squeaked, "I was here first." I pulled in a deep breath of the ocean air, trying to calm myself down. I was resolved to keep from showing him I was rattled. I wanted to play away with a good ball before he could stop me. "Hey, I told you, I was here before you," he said, coming toward me, incredulous that I was addressing my teed ball through his complaint.

I repeated to myself a tip I heard as a young man, to be used whenever you were stressed over a tee shot: *try to hit your driver as easily as you can.* My concentration was up the right side of the hole at the fairway bunkers on the horizon, hoping to draw the ball back into the center. I tuned everything out, from Nick to the sound of the surf. My full swing felt slow when I hit as solid a ball as I could. I watched it head up the right side before making a gentle comeback into the center of the hole. It was just like my pre-shot routine imagined. It bounced a few times and rolled on the short grass, stopping in as good a position as I might have hoped for. I was sure pleased to have hit this one "on the screws", to stick such a solid one in front of Nick.

I bent down to pick up my tee and moved off the tee box to stow my club in the bag. I turned toward him. "You've told me a lot of things, but now I know better than to listen to you." I grabbed my cart handle and walked away quick. I left the tee and was making good time down the fairway. I knew Nick would have a response of some sort. It would be something on the order of running over me with his cart, or hitting a ball over my head, or falling down crying back on the tee, I just wasn't sure what it would be.

With every step, I wanted to turn around and see what he was doing, but I still faced a combination of emotions that began with wondering why Nick would be included in this day. Part of me wanted to completely ignore him while the other part wanted to go back and beat him to a pulp. Another part of me wanted to give him every piece of my mind I thought of in the past 15 years, while yet another part wanted him to just tell me why he did what he had done. Most of all, I wanted him to feel the disdain I had for him, and show that I could be above lowering myself to his level by getting into an argument or a fight. Then again, for a fleeting moment, I thought *oh to hell with it, I'll just drop a ball and hit it at him, kill him, and dump him over the cliff.* Maybe it was just a fleeting thought, but it *was* there, even if for just a moment. Then I realized that with my luck, he would somehow live through it and sue me for everything I owned.

"O.K., O.K.!" I was far away enough already that he was forced to yell at the top of his voice. "I'm *sorry*!" I wasn't yet ready to turn around and face him. "Is that what you want to hear?" It was, but I wasn't ready to admit it yet. "I don't even know what the hell we're doing here together. I guess I'm having a bad dream or something, I don't know, but I'm *sorry*. O.K.?" It was hard for me to believe Nick could do or say anything without premeditated evil of some sort. That meant I doubted everything I'd seen or heard out of him so far these few minutes, including his demonstration of shock when he first saw me.

Over the years since we last were together, I always wanted to hear Nick tell me how and why he could have taken advantage of me like he did, given that we were closer than brothers for almost 20 years. Although I've always acknowledged that I let it happen, it remained hard to believe that I could have let the savings of my young adult life be stolen by my dearest friend. I long ago accepted the fault for what happened and for what I lost as a result. But I could never forgive him for betraying our friendship. This single event had been the catalyst for an irrevocable change in my life. The way it altered my future was dramatic. I was never the same. I turned and looked back at him on the tee. We stared at each other for a few seconds that seemed like a half hour. I could feel my blood boiling. Then he lifted his arms up away from his sides in silent resignation, a nonverbal reiteration of his apology. Welling up inside me was the desire to launch into him with a screaming tirade. It would start with asking why he thought saying he was sorry would do it for me, and end with telling him he was a ruthless bastard and a con at his very core.

I reminded myself again of my direction to *keep moving*. I yelled, "So, are you playing this hole, or what?" I was far enough up the fairway already that it took the top of my lungs for him to hear me over the wind, but I was still close enough to see his expressions. I saw him smile through a couple of quick practice swings, but I remained hesitant to believe his sincerity. There was little reason for me to take cover; Nick was never a very long hitter, but he was always accurate. I moved over a little closer toward the tree anyway, watching my step walking across its rambling roots in the rough that far preceded the trunk.

His mannerisms on the tee preparing to drive his ball were as familiar to me as my own, despite the passage of years. We played so often together for so long in so many places from coast to coast. I flashed on the many courses we played together, often two or more rounds in a day back then. His short, quick backswing gave me the vision of the two of us in Florida, in South Carolina, New Jersey, California, and Nevada. There were so many other places, too. He made contact with the ball, following it with his characteristic quick, jerky follow-through. The ball flew past me and up the hole, stopping much shorter than mine. It settled just in the fairway next to the rough, short of the down slope that led to the steep drop below.

Watching the ball I thought of how much I missed our friendship, our fellowship – and then snapped back to how it all got thrown away. Our closeness was strong enough to make me trust him, but weak enough that he used it to seize his opportunity. Neither wife was crazy about us as their counterparts, but that seemed normal in a relationship of two guys that were tighter than friends before we met our mates. Cameron expressed her concerns when his business proposition developed, but I calmed her with reassurances that our friendship supported the trust I gave him. I should have listened to her, but I didn't. She had a lot of chances since then to tell me, *'I told you so'*.

"Good shot," I said out of habit, then hoping he didn't hear me. I walked back into the fairway and headed up its hill again. Nick put away his club, got into his cart and drove my way. I could hear the cart's whine moving up the hole toward me from behind. While I walked, I reflected on how my poor decision in the matter had affected so many, so much. Through the years I tried to block out how so many lives would have changed to paths so different, if only I hadn't been so blind. I'd allowed my emotions to cloud my business senses. It wasn't just how much money it cost me. It was more how the quality of life changed, not just for me, but for my wife and my kids. There were so many material things I wanted to give them, but couldn't because of our financial destruction. So much of our futures from that point forward changed because of what I allowed to happen with the decision I made.

"Want a ride?" he asked, pulling up alongside me.

"No," I said in my most forceful voice, "If I walk, maybe I won't be able to hear you, either."

"Aren't you a little old to be walking up a steep hole like this?" His smirk was back.

"Aren't you a little ugly to be out in the daylight?" My straight face shot back at him without missing a step, just like the old days. He laughed first, and I tried not to but chuckled anyway. He drove on ahead and parked next to his ball, surveying his second shot while I kept walking.

When I was back within hearing range, he asked, "What are you doing back in La Jolla?" He knew how often I played Torrey Pines through the years, travelling here often with Scott from Denver. Nick met me here a few times to play, too. Now I wondered if those rounds had been part of his investment scheme, his way of setting me up for the kill. He pulled a 3-wood from the bag on his cart while I kept walking up the right side toward my ball, a good 60 yards ahead of where he stood.

"Maybe you should just worry about yourself. I'm in Alabama right now," I said as I walked past him, "Playing my 12th hole today."

"Jeeeezus," I heard him mutter as he took two practice swings. He addressed his ball while grumbling, "Alabama?" Louder, he yelled, "Alabama? Are you stoned?"

Over my shoulder, I offered a low, "Better keep it to the right up there."

"First you want to bust my chops and now you want to give me playing tips?" He looked up at me while he stood over his ball, ready to hit.

"OK, yank it into the friggin ocean, for all I care." I stopped to wait for his shot, anyway. He moved his feet just a little, realigning himself to retarget his shot the way I suggested. He made solid contact and his ball rolled up the grade to a stop on a plateau above and right of the green. He had about 75 yards remaining to the pin.

"Yep, nothing left but a little up and down for par," he said with way too much confidence. His outstanding short game made up for what he lacked in length anywhere on the course. It was rare for him to be out of a hole because of that talent. Playing with him, you knew you'd better get into the hole before he did. He seldom had long putts to worry about, because from about 125 yards and in, he was deadly.

"Whatever," I grunted, and continued on. I had around 210 yards left to the center of the green, where the pin was cut in the back on the upper of two tiers. I'd missed the green to the left here enough times to know to avoid that at all costs, and being long was suicide as well. Better to follow the advice I gave Nick already and play up the right side. If I used his resting ball as a target, the best shot would hit first there and then angle to the left before rolling up onto the green. I considered the wind in my face before pulling a 5-wood from my bag. I hoped to hit it high with a little draw to get the roll I wanted going once it hit the ground.

"You're going to hit that onto the next tee box – I'll bet you 10 bucks!" Nick would always have something to say just as you were about to hit. I ignored him, and took my swing. The ball flew straighter than I'd intended, so much that I hoped I wouldn't prove him right. It bounced next to his ball, and then turned at that desired left angle, straight at the hole. For a moment I thought it would be too hot and roll too far, up beyond the pin. Just then it ran out of gas and to my dismay began to roll back down to the front tier of the green. The ball was still creeping when Nick's cart drove past me on the way to his third shot. My ball stopped up against the collar, right in front. Thrill, fear, and disappointment had all been involved in that shot. Even though I hoped it would turn out better, it was just fine, thank you.

"Bummer," Nick said and drove on. I wanted to tell him he owed me 10 bucks, but I knew he never carried the money to cover a bet anyway. Out of the cart, he fiddled with the clubs in his bag, deciding how to approach his shot while I walked up the hill. I thought how the last thing I wanted to see here was a repeat of Eric holing his shot earlier. As cool it was to see Eric do it, I felt like if Nick hit his in I might puke. He hit a full sand wedge, very high. While it flew I hoped in silence that it would sail over the green and down the cliff. It did not. The ball stopped on a dime, not four feet left of the cup. Nick looked back at me, and then twirled his club before putting it back in his bag. He stood next to the cart, waiting for me to arrive.

"What, nothing smart to say about that one?" he said, that stupid smirk back on his face.

"Not yet. Let's see how many putts it takes you to get in the hole." I walked past him to the right of the green to park my pull cart. "Nice shot anyway," I paused before adding, "Jackass."

"Oh, how gracious of you," he said, highlighting his sarcasm.

I grabbed a 7-iron and my putter, not knowing yet if I would be chipping or putting my ball. My shot would go up the steep grade between tiers, with a hard break to the left once it got over the ridge. A more accomplished player would pitch it onto the top shelf. I decided to putt it, considering the old golf adage *a bad putt is better than a bad chip.* Kneeling behind my line to review the shot, over the cliffs behind the green I saw a dense, thick fog approaching, coming in fast from over the ocean. So common at Torrey Pines, you could expect this to happen a few times each round. The sun went away, the damp fog swallowed us up in seconds and all of a sudden it was quite cold. I thought of how we used to pack what seemed like an entire wardrobe in our golf bags in order to deal with the variety of elements you could expect when playing here.

I knew what line and what speed I needed for my putt, and settled into my stance. He pulled the flagstick out of the hole without offering to tend it and I wasted no time in making a firm stroke. The ball followed my intended line, up onto the top tier with authority, and then lost speed at the top just like I wanted. It slowed in a curve hard to the left and finished just below the hole, stopping within one foot.

I said, “What, no smart comment of your own?”

Nick replaced his cleaned ball on the green. “That one’s good,” nonchalant in suggesting I pick up the ball. I declined with a glare at him and tapped the ball in with a short stroke of my putter.

“No thanks, but go ahead and try to make yours.” I walked over to pick up the flag, ready to replace it while he looked over his putt. It was short but had a huge break of over a foot from left to right. “Looks dead straight,” I cracked while he looked at it. When he shot me a hateful look before settling over his ball, I hoped that he’d disappear after this one hole, like Eric before him.

The next best thing happened: he missed the putt! Just by a hair on the high side, the putt didn’t quite catch the lip, and settled inches past it. “Bummer,” I said, "But since you lost the hole anyway, I'll give you that one." I replaced the pin in the cup and walked away.

"Up yours," he said, still staring at the hole, confused about how his ball kept from going in. I walked off the green, looking forward with pride to carding my par 4 on this very tough hole. The best part was that I beat him; if I'd had an 8 that'd be alright as long as he took a 9. I replaced my putter and put my glove back on. Nick was already in his cart, driving toward the next hole. At Torrey Pines the next tee box was very close, but the fog was so dense, Nick's cart was only a few feet from me when he disappeared into it. I pulled my bag along, trailing behind him into the fog on the way to the next tee. As much as I spent that hole reminding myself how much I *wanted* to hate him, and fantasizing bad things to happen to him, I wasn't sure how I *should* feel about being around him. I walked with my head down, still hoping I had seen the last of him for today.

Again, I faced my internal struggle between a faith that promoted forgiveness and the emotion of near hatred. Faith says forgiveness should cleanse my feelings, but my pain of his betrayal was so deep. If it was true my faith was what I hoped it was I should be *able* to forgive him. I reminded myself that after all, what happened between us wasn't all *his* fault. I told myself again that it was *my* fault for being stupid enough to let it happen. Just like with Cameron's affair, I was accepting responsibility while I refused to blame either one of them. I suppose by doing that I could avoid the forgiveness I should have given them both.

Just then, I heard Nick's cart tires screech to a stop. Then a yell: "Cool!" I heard him hop out of his ride. I kept moving with curious steps farther into the enveloping fog.

CHAPTER 19

Whether I had pushed my way through and out of the fog or it had just vanished as fast as it came minutes before, I didn't know. Either way, I found myself with Nick again. That misty haze had acted as a time machine to take the two of us to another place where we played together so many times. It was clear that we were in San Francisco. Recognizable in an instant by so many features, this was the tee of the par 3, Number 17 at Lincoln Park Golf Course. The Golden Gate Bridge stood bright and majestic, hovering over the hole, and Marin County was gleaming across the windswept strait that opened to the Pacific Ocean on our left. Next to the tee, steep cliffs dropped away to the water below and took your breath away.

Just like he did 30 years ago, Nick dug into his bag for all those shag balls, the ones you find in a lake or the woods and throw in the bottom of your bag. He couldn't wait to tee them up and hit away perpendicular to the hole, out into the cold, escaping Bay water far below. And, just like back then, I couldn't wait to join him.

The beautiful sight was stunning where we stood along the ledge. The view north, east and west of the

Golden Gate evoked fond memories. Looking to our right toward the hole, the green in the foreground and the tops of the city skyscrapers peeking over the treetops behind it, this was a breathtaking golf hole. My friend Nick and I played here together many times back then. Those were our closest days.

We giggled like children, watching our driven balls shoot out and away over the precipice before falling toward the white-capped, deep blue water. Each of us would tee up and hit another and another almost before our last one reached the sea. Like we had years before, I could have gone on hitting balls there as long as we had them in our bags, but I was afraid of the time we were consuming. *You have to keep moving*, Scott's voice replayed in my head. *Got to keep going,* like Eric reminded me. I urged Nick, "Come on, let's play the hole." My winning par on the previous hole gave me the honor on the tee, so I teed one up and got ready to hit while he sighed walking away from the cliff to join me.

The aesthetic beauty of the hole belies what it is to play it. Playing from the white tees, it measures 230 yards long. A gentle ocean breeze quartered left to right from the water behind me. I wanted to get the ball up and ride the wind, to drop it onto the green in a way not many old men can do with a long iron. I pulled the five-wood from the bag instead and teed my ball low. A grin crept onto my lips. I started an old ritual between us when I went into my shot routine: "This hole for five bucks?"

"Make it a hundred," Nick fired back.

"I'm not going to play for a hundred dollars – five or nothing."

"Why not?" That sneer accompanied his question.

"I don't have that much on me," I said, adding, "And I know you don't either."

"So what, I don't even have five bucks on me."

"Then you can't bet anyway!" I considered daring him to ask me to just trust him, but that line of discussion would just make me madder. "You've never been able to cover a bet you made in your life."

"One needs to be able to cover a bet only if they lose," he said with the tone of a scholar, that smart-ass smirk on his face again.

I was squaring up to hit my ball. Still sighting the target, the flag on the green protected by bunkers in front and behind, I came up with an alternative wager: "OK, then let's do something else. Whoever's tee shot is farthest from the hole can't use their putter." There had to be more, so I added, "And, you have to tee off with an iron on the next hole."

"OK," he agreed. "That *and* a hundred bucks," he added, just when I started to swing. I didn't break my rhythm, making a smooth swing through the ball with a hint of an open stance.

"Shut up, Nick! You don't have a hundred bucks, remember?" We both watched the flight of my ball. It looked so nice I talked to it, hoping aloud, "Don't be too long, baby."

"You may not *need* a putter," he groaned while we watched. The ball was taking a nice fade left to right, heading at the flag stick. It hit just onto the green and rolled toward the pin. Most amateurs know the feeling – sometimes you can't tell just how close the ball is to the hole until you get there. This was one of those. Neither of us knew how close or far away my ball had finished. Then Nick teed his ball up high, barely sticking it into the ground. My eyes widened when I saw he had a driver in his hand.

"Jeez, man, I know you're a weak hitter, but are you crazy?" I shrieked.

"It's a long hole," Nick said as if apologizing, embarrassed at getting caught with so little confidence that he would need his biggest club to go 230 yards with a helping wind.

"Well, if you're trying to reach The Presidio, go ahead." I chided him further, "Hey, maybe you should go up and hit from the ladies' tees?"

"Can I?" he mocked me back and we both laughed. "OK, leave me alone. I'm hitting my driver whether you like it or not."

"I just don't remember this hole being so long," I said, more serious now, "But we were younger then, I guess."

"Well, *you* were," he said, setting up to swing.

Nick was a full foot shorter than me, with a more compact swing. He always needed at least a full club more for the same shot. He studied the tops of the tall trees that imprisoned the hole against the cliffs like he was checking the wind. I laughed at him and said, "What are you, Mister PGA? What are you looking up there for? Worry about if there are any squirrels walking between you and the green. You might kill one of those poor things."

"Piss off," he fired back. While he readied to shoot I stared out at the magnificent vista around us, less concerned with how we got here than being glad that we did.

I heard the sound of Nick's contact with the ball and looked over to pick up the flight of his ball. It was tracking well, still looking good coming down. I was proud of my shot and didn't want him to trump me by besting it. A puff of sand rose from the back bunker when the ball smacked into the sand trap right behind the flag. "Crap!" Nick cried. He had flown right over the pin, carrying the ball long into the hazard. The bunker had sure saved him from going farther, deep into parts unknown.

"Too much club, imagine that!" My sincere-sounding comment made him steam. "Good thing you didn't move up to the red tees after all." His face was redder than that ladies' tee. I continued while he slammed his club into his golf bag, "Well, there is *good* news." He just glared at me. "You kept it short of the toll plaza!" The entrance to the Golden Gate Bridge wasn't really *that* close.

I was gloating when Nick answered me with something to think about: "I *still* might be inside of *you*." He was right, since my proximity to the hole remained unclear from our vantage point. Where he lay in the trap might in fact be closer than mine on the green.

Despite my feelings for his actions years ago, it was still enjoyable to experience again this kind of banter between us. I was reminded again of the camaraderie I missed, much the same as I used to enjoy with Scott. The reminders of our friendship made me wonder about Nick's family, but I was hesitant to ask. He drove the cart slow beside me when we left the tee, and I decided to bring up the subject.

"Tell me about your family," I asked.

"Why? Is it any of your business?"

"Never mind," I fired back. "Sorry to act like I give a damn." I was back to not caring whether he answered me or not. Every time it seemed like I was about to get over our differences, he was quick to remind me less of our past friendship and more of what I detested in him. I took several paces in silence while he slowed to remain a few feet behind me in his cart.

Seeing my irritation, he broke the silence. "The ex-wife is still alive," which was the first news – I did not know about any "ex". Nancy was no "ex" the last I heard. Maybe there were other marriages I didn't know about.

"Nancy's an ex?" I turned to look at him when he pulled up next to me again.

"Yeah." His head was down. "That's about it, though." I took that to mean his Mom and Dad were gone. I thought of them with sadness, not just because they always treated me like one of their own, but they were such doting grandparents to his daughter, Donna. She was eight years old the last I saw them. I thought it would be a positive subject change.

"What about Donna? How's she doing?" When he stared down at the steering wheel before answering, I knew right away I'd asked the wrong thing.

"She would be 28 now." I took several quiet paces. "Not long after the last time you and I talked, we moved from San Francisco to Sacramento." He took a deep breath and continued, "After the business didn't work out, we moved back to my Mom and Dad's house in

Chicago. It took less than a year for my parents and Nancy to have enough of each other, so she left us. One morning I found a note that said she moved back home to her Mother's in Omaha, and when she felt like dealing with Donna she'd send for her." He looked up when we approached the green and crept along beside me to the right of it. "I used that note in the divorce to get custody of my daughter."

We both peeked over the mound while parking, anxious to see our ball positions. There was his ball in the back bunker, and mine on the green. My ball was closer than his, about 15 feet from the cup. Nick interrupted his story long enough to grumble, "Lucky shot."

"You're a real inspiration, you know it?" I wanted to get back to his story, asking, "So, you were saying?"

"Anyway, that made me Mr. Mom, taking care of Donna, getting her here and there, school, soccer practice, band, softball." He grabbed his sand wedge and putter. I peeled off my glove and took my putter to walk across the green to my ball while he stepped into the back bunker. "A week before Christmas, we were late going to band practice one day. She was 15 at the time. It was snowing very hard." A lump was forming in my throat. He took his stance and prepared to hit. "We drove that way three days a week. I still don't know why I didn't see the red light." His full swing took plenty of sand with it, and the ball came out, landing with a nice roll on the green to about four feet away from the pin.

"Nice shot," I said.

"Thanks." He came out of the trap, tapping his shoes with his club to shake out the sand. He dropped the wedge on the side of the green and moved to pull the pin while I lined up my birdie putt. "Anyway, a semi-truck loaded with concrete conduits hit us at full speed – broadside." I couldn't concentrate on looking at my line, afraid to hear what was next. We exchanged silent stares for a few seconds before his eyes turned to the ground.

"She didn't make it," he said, his voice almost a whisper. A chill went through me, thinking of all the times that I saw this wonderful child from her birth onward. Attending her christening, holding her as a baby, and playing with her once she began walking, each moment crossed my memory. It was like having recollections of my own kids. It was hard for me to remember the last time I was with her, given the way my relationship with Nick evaporated so fast. It was difficult for me to speak.

"I am really so sorry to hear that, Nick – that's awful." I stood, with the awkwardness we have when we don't know what to say, when we don't know what to do. "I'm so very sorry."

My ball on the green was in front and right of the pin, so when I knelt again to look at my line to the hole, the view was straight out to the Golden Gate between the pines. The beauty of the moment made me reflect on how truly blessed I was to have never been touched by tragedy like Nick was in losing Donna.

My putt was makeable, flat and a little right to left. I stood over the ball and took an extra deep breath. I exhaled and stroked it. I knew the moment I hit it that I had the birdie. The ball was still rolling when I tried to get us off the accident and asked, "What about your parents?"

"Neither lasted long after that," he replied, and my ball rattled the bottom of the cup. "Good putt," he complimented, interrupting his own story before placing his cleaned ball down for the short putt. I picked my ball out of the hole. He took a quick look at his putt, and then stood over it.

I said, "I'm sure losing a grandchild would be devastating to them, to anybody." I visualized my own sweet grandchild while I picked up the flag, ready to replace it when he finished the hole.

Standing over his putt, Nick said, "It wasn't just that. You see, my parents lost more in that wreck than a grandchild." He paused and stroked the ball. It rolled into the cup when he added, "They also lost their son." I wondered what that meant when he bent over to pick it out of the hole. "You see," he hesitated before finishing, "I didn't make it, either."

I was stupefied, and just stood there with the flag stick in my hand. "What?" I asked, with barely a breath in my lungs. My chest pounded hard.

He dropped his wedge and putter back in his bag and spoke quite slow to reiterate, "Are you deaf, Chris? I said I didn't make it, either. I said that because I didn't. It was a big heavy truck, and it got us both. What did you expect?" I remained still as a statue while he walked off the green. He paused to wait for me a few seconds. He saw my confusion, but offered no more than the shortest explanation: "It was real quick." I still couldn't speak. "If you don't believe my story, call Nancy, if you can find that bitch." We kept staring at each other a few seconds. "You need me to put the damn flag back in the hole for you, or what?"

Still in a stupor I said, "You used your putter."

"Huh?"

"We had a bet. You weren't supposed to use your putter." We just stared at each other. "I was closer to the hole. You weren't supposed to use your putter."

"Oh yeah. Sorry, I forgot. You should have called me on it." He turned away and climbed back into his cart. "See, if you'd have bet money like I suggested, I could write you an I.O.U."

I placed the pin into the cup, still shaking like a leaf. My feet felt like they were glued to the putting surface. "Wait a minute. When we met today, you acted shocked to see me, surprised I could be in La Jolla." It hit me that once again, Nick had conned me. "You *knew*. You knew *everything*. You played me again. You're part of *my* day today, aren't you?" I walked off the green at a quickening pace, my voice quivering as its volume rose. Now I was almost trotting, ready to go after him. He was in the cart with his foot on the gas, ready to escape me.

"Hey, don't waste time with idle chatter. You'll get Scott upset." That meant he *had* to be in on things. "Those were two great holes, Chris. Two holes we always loved playing, weren't they?" He was right. "What's the matter, didn't you have fun?" I got closer to him and he began to pull away again without waiting for me to answer.

"Why? Why didn't you just tell me on the tee back there at Torrey Pines? You could have at least *started* telling me." He was driving onto the path toward the next hole now. "C'mon, man, don't leave now. I'm not finished with you. Don't leave without telling me everything."

I could just hear him say, "You'll find out soon enough."

He was far down the path ahead of me so I shouted, "Is that why you look so much younger than me?"

He rounded the path's turn into the forest. Just as he went out of my sight, he yelled back with over his shoulder, "You're still sharp as a tack, Chris! Nothing gets by you!"

I didn't want him to get too far ahead of me, because I *really* needed an explanation. "Get back here and tell me!" Jogging now while I pulled the cart, my voice echoed through the trees. "What the hell are you telling me? Nick! *Nick!* Come on, man!"

All of a sudden the woods were different now. I knew this San Francisco golf course well enough to realize this was *not* the look of the path to their next hole. I looked straight at one tree and watched as the bark itself changed. My peripheral vision saw the woods make their rapid transformation back to the Alabama forest. The air's distinctive smell, full of the ocean and the eucalyptus trees, was replaced by the familiar smells of Gabriel's Creek. After taking the turn of the cart path, everything I saw confirmed that I was back in Alabama. There was the next hole ahead. Nick was gone.

Several holes before, I stopped trying to understand what *seemed* like travel in and out of Gabriel's Creek. It was still hard to understand why I was interfacing with the people that I was. I wanted the time, the opportunity, to stop and digest it. I wanted to try to answer my own questions about why Nick came into my day the way he did, and why he left it the way he did. I never had time to answer those same questions about

Eric after he came and went. It was not that much earlier that first Scott and later the guys from back home did the same. I wanted to, or even more so, I *needed* to process it. Then there was that ever present warning to keep moving, to keep going, no matter what.

Where the cart path came out of the edge of the woods and opened to the next tee box, a small, concrete bench appeared. Warnings or no warnings, I knew what I needed.

I needed to sit down.

CHAPTER 20

My experience with Nick rattled around in my head while I sat bent over on the bench. If I believed what he told me, Nick was just as dead as Jack was. How could he have zipped with me to La Jolla, and then zapped with me to San Francisco? How was it possible that I could be with either of them, anywhere?

Keep moving, got to get going, echoed in my head yet again. “Just wait a minute,” I barked aloud. With my elbows on my knees I stared at the ground in front of the bench, thinking of so many possibilities for what might be yet to come today, wondering who else might show up. There were some people that I’d *like* to see, but then there were a few others I’d rather not. I gasped just thinking of one of them in particular, somebody I sure didn’t want to see again, to even think of again, at least not until God forced me to. That would be coming soon enough.

Less than an hour before, Nick was on the same list. The previous couple of holes left me relieved enough to take him off it. I felt able to purge the hatred I harbored for Nick all those years. The catalyst for that change of heart should have nothing to do with the tragic stories he just told me, and everything to do with my hope to leave the world without any hate in my soul. "And, no regrets, remember?" I spoke to myself. I shook my head at how futile that thought was, thinking again about my many regrets. I started to think of *that* one – the regret I'd held for so long.

No matter how hard I tried to avoid it, there was no escaping thinking about Spencer Halstead. The fact was I knew so little about him. I learned from news reports after his death that he was a dedicated family man, a veteran, and an artist. They reported his death was self-inflicted, but I knew he was murdered. Despite my years of denials, I would soon be reckoning with my role in his death. I had committed many sins, but this one was the hardest for me to face.

Spencer was a life-long Denver resident. Ten years older than I, he was a semi-retired real estate developer and part-time sculptor. Business took him to many western cities, all of which our airline served. His role as CEO of Halstead Enterprises required far less of his time when we met than years before when he built the company. He surfaced only in the rare occasions when his day-to-day management team needed his visibility. He used our airline for many years while pursuing both his business and artistic interests. He racked up frequent flyer miles flying to Boise and Billings, Portland and Spokane, Albuquerque and Tucson. On paper the match of passenger and carrier was ideal. On paper was where the love in our relationship ended.

Keep moving, got to get going. I shook my head and looked up. From the bench, I saw the next hole had a sharp rise in front of the tee, going up to a narrow opening in the woods where the hill crested. It was a good 250 yards to that horizon, where the fairway was punctuated by the golfer's target, a large pole in its center. The tee marker said the 14th hole was 510 yards long from the whites. It was fruitless to wonder what was beyond the top of the hill; I'd just have to find out when I got there. A few bright white cumulus clouds above gave contrast to the deep blue of the sky and the lush green colors of the woods. It wasn't far to pull my cart alongside the teeing area. I took out my driver, hoping I could hit my shot close to that pole. I teed the ball high and stepped back behind the ball to sight that target for my drive. The relaxed swing I put on the ball sent it high into the blue sky, straight as a string. It bounced near the crest of the hill right in the middle, making me think for a second I might hit the pole. My ball struck nothing but short grass, moving just right of that stick by a yard or so before it disappeared out of sight. It was a solid tee shot, and I walked off and up the middle of the fairway pleased. The memories of Spencer continued.

Years ago he had an awful trip with us that involved everything from departure delays to equipment changes to being denied a First Class upgrade just before he discovered that cabin almost empty. Spencer marched into our Administrative Offices at midday demanding to talk to Adrian Fourcade, my predecessor in the Station Manager position. Fourcade's retirement created the opening that my promotion to Denver filled. Marianne Sailsbury, my secretary, reported that Halstead was waiting to see me without an appointment and why. She let me know there was a history with him and anticipated my next question by handing me his very thick file. Airline management knew him as a chronic complainer. He would file his grievance, get some kind of compensation, fly with us again, complain again, and the cycle would continue. Marianne reported that everyone at the airline knew him, from the curb to the counter to the gate to his seat. He even tore into Eric once about the cleanliness of a cabin, and Eric had to be restrained. Most of all, his loud, caustic and belligerent attitude meant that everyone dreaded dealing with him.

I was in the job less than three months that day when Spencer became *my* pain in the butt. There were a lot of ways I could have handled this customer that first day we met, but I was determined to establish my turf and set the tone that change had come. I saw a chance to make some positive points with the entire Denver staff. I thought it important to show my employees that I wouldn't always take the customer's side, that I was willing to back my staff up, too. They needed a morale boost in advance of the changes to come. My mind was made up that I was going to be the one that stopped this goofball.

"Tell Mr. Halstead I'll be with him when I have an opening in my schedule," I told Marianne. "Tell him if he would rather make an appointment another day, he is welcome to. Otherwise he will just have to wait." Marianne sighed knowing she would suffer the most from my decision. He would have to wait a very long time to see me that day.

"I guess you know, he's not going to like that," she said.

"That's not all he's not going to like before I get through with him." My chest was sticking out. I was proud of myself in advance. I was fixing this problem once and for all, for everybody.

I finished my rounds after 5 o'clock and came back to my office through the private door. Marianne's note in the center of my desk said that Halstead was still waiting, and he refused to leave without being satisfied.

I buzzed her on the intercom to confirm he was still there. I told her to show him in, but also to bring our Dictaphone recorder and sit in on our meeting as a witness.

Halstead came in fuming. He was neither interested nor impressed with our introduction. I interrupted him before he had a chance to vent his specific complaint. I told him in no uncertain terms that he would no longer control our airline, than his free travel for being a loud-mouth was over, and on and on. I dominated the conversation and talked over him, leaving him no opening to respond while I told him the way of the world. Through it all, Halstead was ready to explode and Marianne just wanted to hide. When I finished I asked him if he understood me in my firmest tone.

He was calm when he turned to Marianne and said, "Make sure you've got plenty of tape in there and that it's recording. Take good notes. Get my statements exactly – verbatim – so that I'll be on record when I keep the promises I make here today." Then he turned to me. "I understand that you have no idea who you are talking to," he said, quiet at first. "I understand that you want to make a name for yourself, and you just have." His volume escalated with each word and he began pounding my desk with his right fist to punctuate his points, a little harder each time. He continued, "Welcome to Denver. Between now and the time that I have your job, you will have to deal with people who have been my friends since before you were crying about your loaded diaper." It went downhill from there. When he wasn't pounding, he was pointing his finger inches from my face. He emphasized his threats would be carried out not just in Denver, but in our other cities as well. He was at his loudest when he stood and reminded me, "Every time I travel, every single passenger I bump into will hear about what an imbecile you are. Anywhere your airline's logo is, I'll be there finding something your boss will not be happy with." His tirade complete, he headed for the door. He paused to turn back toward my silence and asked, "Now, do *you* understand *me*?"

In a reconciliatory voice I said, "Mr. Halstead, if you hate us so much, why don't you just take another airline?"

"Because it will be too much fun ruining your career," he sneered back, and slammed my office door behind him. Marianne and I just sat and looked at each other. Much like a common unhappy customer, I expected he was just blowing off steam. I was comfortable, confident that I achieved my goal of drawing a line in the sand with this sword-rattler, and I didn't expect to ever hear from him again.

How wrong I was. The phone calls started coming every few hours, from Denver City Hall and the FAA just as warm ups. I began to fear I'd underestimated Halstead. When it moved further to authorities in all the cities he continued flying to on a regular basis, I saw that maybe I'd fanned a fire I shouldn't have. When three months later I was spending half of every working day dealing with inspectors, auditors, and fire chiefs, I knew I'd made a mistake. Every day there were demands for written responses to a flood of complaints required by our corporate customer service department. The impatience of my superiors grew. Every work day grew longer and longer.

One day was the worst yet. The problems Spencer caused started with my signing 15 apology letters to customers from a single flight they shared with him. It continued with an inspector from the Health

Department having to wait for me while I dealt with a surprise FAA engine maintenance audit. The topper was the call from the city that out of the blue put a stop work order on construction that started that day on improvements to our central hangar doors. It was the wrong time for me to get a call from Jaromir Madzinski.

Cresting the hill of the 14th hole, I thought of Jaromir for the first time in years. The terrain of the hole sloped down from the target post, flattening out to a plain as the tree line holding the fairway widened to allow the placement of a small pond. The water was on the front right side of a long and narrow undulating green 250 yards from where I walked. Several yards ahead sat my ball in the middle of the fairway. I reached the white pellet and stopped to think about my next shot. With my hand on the 3-wood I stared at the pond before discarding the thought of hitting a shot too risky at my age. I let go and pulled out a 5-iron instead, embarrassed that I was choosing to lay up.

Madzinski called me that fateful day as a courtesy to tell me that he and his partner, Buck, were going out of business, at least in the United States. A combination of factors led them to find "opportunities to make a very good living" in Eastern Europe. He would tell me what those "factors" were if I asked, but I honestly didn't want to know. I already knew more than I wanted to about their experiences as mercenaries around the world. He added that he was looking forward to showing Buck around his ancestral homeland.

I aimed the 5-iron up the left side of the fairway and struck it well from my elevated position. It flew nice but longer than I wanted and hopped just into the thicker grass of the rough. I was in pretty good shape with about 70 yards remaining to the green. At least my ball was dry.

Jaromir was a business contact that grew into a business friend but there was no personal connection between us beyond small talk. I was introduced to them by an independent auditor we used my first month in Denver. There were some internal theft issues I wanted to clean up. I was looking for someone experienced in "shopping" counter agents and in-flight sales. I was told these two could remain inconspicuous while spotting a thief a mile away. Their work went on for several weeks. "Mad Dog Investigations" was the business name our checks were made out to for the work Madz and Buck performed.

Madz was a huge Polish man from Philadelphia, standing just less than seven feet tall. He was all muscle but weighed at least 350 pounds. He was as comfortable in a suit as he was in fatigues or a T-shirt and jeans. I never knew Buck's last name, doubted his real name was "Buck" anyway, and felt the less I knew about him the better. Buck was an aged Hippy, about 6'5" tall, weighed about 160 pounds at the most with long dirty hair and very few teeth. He lost half his right arm in Bosnia, replacing it with a prosthetic device that allowed him to change the end of it to suit his needs. I heard too many stories about things Buck did with different attachments on the end of the arm. The most gruesome tales were when he would use "the hook". Suffice it to say you'd want neither of these two as an adversary.

Jaromir was quick to detect my anxiety in our phone conversation that day. He asked what was wrong, and I was foolish enough to talk about the antagonist that was making my business life Hell. I thought it was just one of our ordinary chats, so I described in limited detail my experiences with Spencer from our first meeting to what my every-day life was like since. In a brotherly tone Madz said, “Chris, I hate to hear you like this.” I became concerned when he asked, “Is there anything I can do?” I remembered the many stories I heard of how he “took care of” various situations for people.

I tried to change the subject, but my Polish friend pressed me. “Look, Chris, I don't know when I'll ever see you again,” he pleaded, “So just tell me about this guy, and maybe I can suggest a way to calm him down.” He sounded sincere. I hoped he was going to just refer me to a lawyer or someone to handle him in a normal way.

“And no Jimmy Hoffa stuff, right?” I asked.

“Aw, Chris, don't hurt my feelings.” I swear I could hear him smiling. “I'm just a little immigrant business man.” I don't think he heard me gulp. My restraint fractured and my frustrations poured into the phone. I told him Spencer Halstead's name without realizing that he was taking notes. The moment it came out of my mouth he said, “Oh, yeah, I've heard of that guy. I've seen his name in the paper.” He began laughing in a way I knew wasn't good, and then he became more serious and more inquisitive. Each time I tried to change the subject, his investigative questions went deeper. No, I told him I knew nothing about Halstead's personal life. Soon I thought of a reason to excuse myself and told him I was late for a meeting. I apologized for venting about Spencer and asked him to forget I mentioned it. It sounded like he agreed to. We exchanged best wishes and the call came to a warm end.

Two weeks later, I received surprising calls from several city offices. Permit problems with the Denver hangar, a proposed parts warehouse in Salt Lake City, and call centers in Portland and Tucson were all solved. Building, food, and maintenance inspections were complete and satisfactory, or cancelled. Just like that, all was well with the world, all in that one day. For a moment, a connection to Madzinski crossed my mind. I thought of calling to thank him for whatever he did, but our goodbyes had already been said. I even considered calling Spencer to apologize, to bury the hatchet. I decided that would be too wimpy, choosing instead to be impressed with myself that I won our battle.

A few days later, I opened my morning newspaper to be stunned by the headline "Developer's Suicide Puzzles Police". The front page of the Rocky Mountain News had a large portrait of Spencer above the fold. The cut line showed his name followed by, "Developer, Artist, and Long-time Resident". My eyes raced to the article where I read with horror the details of Spencer's death. I stopped and picked up the phone to call Jaromir, to ask him what the hell he had done. His number was already disconnected. My pulse sped. I couldn't draw a breath.

The opening paragraphs of the article spoke more to how the man lived than how he died. Spencer lived in an old established Denver neighborhood, where big yards surrounded small comfortable homes with high-pitched roofs and detached garages along wide, oak-lined streets. He and his wife were empty-nesters, the youngest of their three adult children in her last year at the University of Colorado in Boulder. Their other two kids were both married professionals and lived in the suburbs on opposite sides of town. There were two grandchildren from a daughter who was the eldest child. Their middle child, a son, had his first baby on the way. The paper said Mrs. Halstead was a Registered Nurse at a nearby hospital despite years of suffering from rheumatoid arthritis.

Approaching my ball in the left rough, I vividly remembered how I almost ripped the paper apart turning to the page where the story continued. I glanced at the long green with the pin cut in the center of the back quarter of the putting surface. I paid no attention to the nearby pond or the woods beyond the green. The word "*suicide*" in the newspaper that day was superimposed in bold print across my field of vision when I looked again at my target, wedge in my hands. My mind was stuck on Spencer's death, and the attempt at an easy approach shot was pathetic. The ball fired away low to the right, never bouncing before drilling straight into the middle of the pond with a loud *ker-plunk*. I took out a second ball. I kept the same club in my hand and walked the 25 yards to the shore of the pond, dropping the ball two club lengths behind the point it crossed into the hazard. This time the shot was relaxed, the ball flew nice and high and dropped into the center of the green, rolling just a few inches to a stop about 15 feet short of the cup. I bagged the wedge and pulled off my glove. I parked the cart next to the green and grabbed my putter. My ball laid five, with a tricky putt to come.

The story in the paper years ago continued into the details of Spencer's death on page 5A. It covered most of the page along with more pictures from Halstead's life: in front of a new office building, presenting the governor of Montana with a commissioned sculpture, a family photo from a weekend in Vail. A picture from his military days showed him in a training exercise, his pistol drawn and pointed in a "don't move" stance. The story described how a middle-of-the-night gunshot startled surrounding households awake, but Spencer's wife slept through it. One neighbor called police to investigate. At 3 a.m. they rang the doorbell at Halstead's home to inquire. Mrs. Halstead was surprised that her husband was out of bed this late. Their detached two-car garage was both Spencer's workshop and sanctuary. It was common for him to spend late hours out there, but just as typical for him to crawl into bed without her noticing a little after midnight. Tinkering with cars helped him think and relax, and he used the garage as his artist's studio, too.

Police followed her into the garage to find his lifeless body slumped over the fender below the open hood of his car. Blood from a single gunshot to his temple ran across the engine on its way to a pool on the floor. A revolver he owned since his young days as an Army MP was in his left hand. A small, crumpled slip of paper was clutched in his right hand, onto which nothing but the words "I'm Sorry" were scrawled. There were some unexplained fresh marks made by something metallic on the hood and fender, but police thought nothing of it. There was no sign of a forced entry, nothing else out of sorts as detectives began their investigation. Neighbors rolled out of adjacent houses, trying to console and comfort the delirious Mrs. Halstead. The entire street was wide awake as local news trucks arrived ahead of the Medical Examiner.

When the light of dawn began to glow above the eastern horizon, a respectful investigator approached the group huddled around the new widow, and asked Mrs. Halstead which hand her husband wrote with. "He wrote left-handed," she sobbed. The detective thanked her, excusing himself again to return to the crime scene. He was satisfied now, because of where they found Spencer's gun. The very instant I read this fact that morning I felt like I was being choked. Why would Spencer have pounded my desk with his right fist? I visualized him shaking his right finger at me. Part of me wanted to run to the phone and call the authorities, the other part wanted to find Madzinski first. I couldn't be the only one confused after seeing the old photo of him preparing to shoot right-handed. I didn't know what to do. I kept on reading.

The next shocking news was still fresh to me as I thought of it now, kneeling behind my ball on the green, trying to see the line of the putt through my misery of recollection. The putt was a bit uphill, and might break twice over its 15-foot length. My mind stayed on the story and how I learned more about Spencer's death. I gave the putt a firm stroke. It broke once a bit to the right and then again a bit to the left and stopped about a foot short and right of the hole. I stepped up to the resting ball and gave it no further consideration before I stroked it straight and smooth into the cup. Considering the blind tee shot and my awful third shot into the pond, a double-bogey 7 was just fine. Too bad it was my second double on a back nine par 5 already.

Police decided there was no evidence of anyone else being involved in the shooting. A pencil on the floor of the garage had been matched to the note. Analysts concluded the brief note was written right-handed, but that was dismissed as having been authored under duress. Their theory was that Halstead was depressed during his final days, with the kids grown now and away from home. His wife was struggling to get through each day of work with her affliction, and he wasn't needed by his business so much anymore. They believed he wanted to find a way to provide for his wife so she could stop working, even though she worked for purely social reasons. His insurance policies were violated by his suicide, but his wife and kids would see a generous profit from the liquidation of his assets.

Far into the newspaper story the writer theorized what may have been the most depressing thing Spencer faced that no one could have known: he believed the life of a grandchild was threatened just a few days before he took his own life. When I read that one single point I felt like I was the one who pulled the trigger of Spencer's gun. The theory was based on facts his daughter shared with police when she arrived at the scene. She told them her father rushed to her house a week before and was very emotional when he swept her newest born child into his arms. He cried, hugging the young girl while admonishing his daughter that she could never say anything to anyone about his outburst, repeating over and over that he already "took care of everything". He shared little with his daughter beyond the fact that everyone would be safe now, because he made sure of it. He would never let anything happen to his family, ever. He swore his daughter to secrecy, but she shared it now with police and the newspaper. Everyone just wrote it off to the suicidal depression he was in, and they investigated no further.

No one knew about my phone call with Jaromir but me. I couldn't help but believe he and Buck were repaying what they thought were debts to me in the best way they knew how. Sure, I gave them lots of free flight vouchers and arranged discounted or complimentary hotel rooms for them in a variety of cities many times, but I never thought they "owed me" for anything. They must have threatened the grandchild's life to get Halstead to stop his attacks on me. After he did, they must have killed him on their way out of the country, maybe just for the fun of it. Spencer's blood was on my hands. If I possessed any of the integrity, the courage, the ethics that I put myself forth as having, I would have gone straight to the police and told them everything. I did not.

I walked off the green and wrote down my score. I went back to the cart path with my head hung low and moved on to my next hole. Looking at my role in Spencer's death, I knew a stronger person would have resisted Jaromir's persistence on the phone that day, and wished him a nice trip to wherever he was going. A person with a stronger faith may have dealt with Spencer by praying that he could turn into a nice guy, would have wished him no harm, hoped that the worst thing that could happen to Spencer is he would wake up one day filled with love. Some may even have dealt with him directly, perhaps even finding a way they might peacefully coexist. Or perhaps just kicking his ass would work.

I could do nothing about it now. After all, maybe Spencer *did* kill himself. In my heart, I had a responsibility to face. It would be worthless to point out the possible involvement of Madzinski and his partner to anyone. Even if authorities could find them, having them punished was not the point anyway. Focusing on the two of them would be little more than an attempt to shift the blame off me again. To me, *their* involvement wasn't the point – *mine* was.

Following the path into the trees again, the answer became clear. I decided I wanted to "come clean", whatever the consequences. I made up my mind that when I got off the course later, I would call the police in Denver. I needed to convince them to have a detective interview me by phone as soon as possible because I wasn't sure when – or even if – I'd make it back to Albuquerque, much less Denver. I'd have to tell

Cameron, of course. I had to count on her understanding why I needed to clear this up, to at least make an attempt to gain peace with myself over what I felt was among the worst things I ever did. Maybe it was nothing to a lot of people, but it was a big deal to me.

Cameron wasn't going to like learning I kept all of the events leading to Spencer's death a secret from her. At the time, she endured listening to my ongoing complaints about how his efforts were making my professional life miserable, but I never told her about Jaromir's call, or how I felt responsible for his death. I had to tell her now that I was going to the police, without having any idea how they might react.

Ahead in the woods was the opening to the next tee. There sat a little building, a small maintained version of that tattered one back near where I met Eric. My wish came true when I got closer and saw the "Restroom" sign on its door. It wasn't long until my round was over, but it was too long to wait. I parked my bag and pushed the door open to go inside.

CHAPTER 21

In contrast to the Halfway House I found back after Number 9, the amenity in the clearing ahead was in every-day use. I found the inside of the restroom to be spotless, just what I had come to expect from Skip. The tile floor was a challenge to negotiate with golf cleats. The urinal was a simple tin trough that a tiny trail of water would rinse with a turn of its valve. A single toilet sat behind a simple modesty panel. A sink with a half-used bar of soap sitting on it had a small mirror above it and separated the relief stations. One small window on each side of the room was opaque and closed, each secured by a plain swing latch. The tin roof above had a gentle pitch to it.

Standing at the urinal I was sad that I just had a few holes remaining. I thought of how quick I was running out of days, out of minutes, out of seconds. My musings were interrupted when a fierce wind came up outside. I could hear the trees as they whooshed and swirled around. What sounded like pine cones and needles pattered as they pelted the roof. The small building resisted, pushing back against the gale, heaving enough to inspire me to zip up and get going. It was a beautiful, clear day with puffs of cumulus clouds when I came in just moments before. The windows were darkening more by the second, and I could see spats of water spraying with some force against them. I hurried to rinse my hands at the sink, annoyed that the elements had changed so fast, and that I was so unprepared for it. Then, in the reflection of the mirror I saw clothing hanging on a hook behind me on the back of the door. I didn't see it earlier. How could I have missed it? The tempest continued outside, the fury growing even louder while I stood gawking at the hanger. I moved over and reached to touch a warm, wool-lined water-repellent rain suit on the hook. Just as I did, a loud voice shouted from outside, screaming against the storm with as thick a Scottish accent as any I ever heard.

"C'mon Mr. Collins, we've got to get moving! If you'd be so kind to get your suit on, I'll need ya to hit away, please sir." I had no idea who the voice could be, and I still was not sure how the rain suit got there, but the pounding sounds of the weather were enough to make me put it on anyway. Then, the same voice grumbled in a muted volume that meant the speaker hoped I couldn't hear him. "Damn Yank tourists come over here wantin' to play in a bubble. Think they'll be playin' one of their pitiful little American kiddies' parks they call golf courses with such utter blasphemy." He sounded less like he was talking to someone else than he was just blowing off steam, irritated at waiting. "If I'd known when I started doing this 40 years ago that it would get so easy for all these bloody babies to get here from the USA, I'd have taken over the cobbler business me uncle had. Used to take days on a ship to get here, now the spoiled whiners are here in a few hours."

While the voice rambled, I pulled the pants on one leg at a time, over my shoes. Zippers on the sides of the pants helped me avoid the cleats. The jacket was a perfect fit, too, and warm when I zipped it up to my neck. I came out of the shack to enter a different world. It was another waterfront hole, but this time I was nowhere I had ever been before. An angry ocean curved the length of the right side of a short par 3, at the end of which a small peninsula held a small, well-contoured green. There, the shoreline turned back and around behind the green, perpendicular to the length of the hole until it disappeared. Tall, ancient trees bordered the entire left side all the way to the water, swirling at their tops in the strong winds. If I didn't know better, I would think this was Scotland. With everything that had happened today, maybe it was true that I *didn't* know any better.

I looked at the sights around me when something tapped my body's midsection. I looked down to see the head of a 5-iron. I lifted my head to see a thin, tall and leathery man handing it to me. He was much older but much more fit than I. Dressed like a playing partner, he was ready for the types of elements engulfing us now. A cap was pulled down tight against his skull, the brim just above his eyebrows. His wind-shirt was embroidered on the sleeve with a logo that read "Kingsbarns Golf Links". Below the course name, the shirt was inscribed with two more personalizing lines, reading "Finnean Macalister" and "Senior Caddy". Like my new suit, his clothing beaded the rain that was pelting us. The same bag I pulled on the cart all day was now slung by its strap across his shoulder, a rain hood covering the top end. I was certain that the club he poked me with was from Skip's set that I'd been playing with the past few hours. The man held the grip with a towel to keep it dry and wiggled the club in a motion for me to take it. He stood strong in the storm, more irritated than befuddled by my confusion.

“Hood it a little and knock it down into the wind,” he directed, nodding toward the tee. I took the club from his hand, and he kept the towel. He acted like we had known each other a long time, or at least like we’d already been together for much of the day. He sure didn’t react to me like I just popped into his day the way I believed I did. “Aim it at that back left bunker and you’ll have a chance to keep us out of the North Sea there.” He pointed toward the churning surf beyond the far shoreline.

Still just a few steps outside the restroom I gripped the club. The caddy prodded me again, “If you’d scurry onto the tee, Mr. Collins, *please*. We’re behind pace as it is with your potty stop and all, sir. We’ve only reached the 15th hole, after all.” We stared at each other a moment before he glanced down to the club in my hands, continuing, “Dally around any further, this rain will get those grips slick as a whistle on you, too.”

A plain but attractive tee sign in front of us with a Kingsbarns logo matching the one on the caddy’s sleeve marked the 15th hole as a par 3, 151 yards from the “Regular”, or white tees. I walked between the white markers, looking around for playing partners that maybe I just didn’t see yet. Finding none, I looked at Finnean with stupefied glance of wonder.

“It’s *still* only the two of us, Mr. Collins.” His eyebrows rose. “Now, sir, please, if you’d step to it?”

I teed up my ball, but decided to ask, “Don’t you think a five-iron’s a bit much for 151?” Bad idea.

The veins in his neck bulged and his look was incredulous when he fired back, “If I thought you needed a different club, I’d have bloody well handed you the bloody thing! The Mashie, that’s the club here.”

The wind pushing the ocean's spray slapped my face along with his words. "Sorry, I'm not used to having a caddy," I sighed, to which he growled with disgust. The wind peppered my exposed skin with speckles of sea water, a salty feeling that was somewhere between stinging and refreshing.

His frustrated tone became reconciliatory. "You want anything from a Brassie to a Niblick, you say the word and I'll hand it to you, Mr. Collins." The old Scottish golf club names were not as recognizable to me as I wished they were.

"Thanks." Thinking back through the day made me want to trust this newfound acquaintance and try to follow his direction. I reminded myself that I was the one here who had no clue what was going on. This had to be Scotland, though. I recalled the name "Kingsbarns" from those times I planned the vacations that never happened. In fact, I was pretty sure my uncle recommended it to me. He toured the British Isles several times on golfing holidays, and was therefore a great source for the wish lists of my proposed pilgrimages. This classic links course was very near St. Andrews, the birthplace of golf, the Mecca for golfers. I remembered the course dated from the 1700's, and that it ran along the North Sea.

"Mr. Collins, if you bloody well *please*, sir?" Finnean was begging me now, having caught me daydreaming of those distant memories. I rushed a couple of practice swings next to my teed ball, trying to follow Finnean's instructions. The damp squalls coming straight at me off the sea made my eyes tingle when I looked at my target. I thought back to those knock down shots into desert winds many years ago, and concentrated on keeping my leading elbow out in front of the club head as I swung.

The result was disastrous. I kept it low all right. It shot forward, a bullet that flew several feet off the ground with nothing but topspin. At least I hit it straight in the direction I was aiming. It began bouncing half way down the length of the hole just inside the shoreline on the right, splashing along until stopping in the wet grass about 30 yards from the hole.

Finnean was quiet but disgruntled when I turned around to hand him my club. “Well, we’ll have a bloody fun time with your next shot,” he said. I had no idea just how scary a shot it would be when we walked off the tee together, both silent.

Ahead the green rippled with twists and turns. It stood on a cape into the North Sea, jutting to the right away from a bunker that was my target. My chip to the green would be across the strong wind onto a putting surface that wanted to pull the ball from one slope to the other and off into the drink. Our walk up the short hole required us to lean into the wind to fight against it. I was sure glad I had the rain suit, wherever it came from. I looked out across the churning sea bordering the course. I had to reach up and grab the brim of my hat, to snug the bill of my cap down onto my head.

“We won’t be trying one of those cute American flop shots here, will we, Mr. Collins?” No, those gentle, high-flying lob shots I enjoyed trying so much would not work in this hurricane. I looked over my shot, deciding what to do when Finnean took out a six-iron, the Spade Mashie. I was pretty sure I knew what he wanted me to do with it, but gave him a pensive stare nevertheless.

"This is real golf here in Scotland, laddie. Keep it low. Chip it up there about halfway and get it to stop rolling once it gets on the green or you'll be among the fish. Remember the wind will offset how wet the rain has made the grass." After a moment of hesitation, he laid the golf bag on the ground behind us out of the way, and reached into his pocket. He dropped a ball on the ground next to mine and his tone changed to a fatherly sound, like wanting to be helpful. Instead of handing the six-iron to me, he gripped it himself. "Let me show you, Mr. Collins," he said with a grin.

Without hesitation he took a balanced stance next to his ball and braced himself against the storm by shifting his weight to his left, toward the flag. A glance at the pin and back down at the ground, he pressed his hands ahead of the ball. He made a relaxed, short backswing before hitting down on the ball, looking like he didn't want to hurt it. His follow-through pointed the club straight at the fluttering flag. The ball sailed low to his landing area. It bounced a few times as it splashed closer to the green. It reached the putting surface and hopped as if hitting a wall, creeping to within six feet of the cup. I was impressed that he could hit such a great shot in these conditions, seeming to do so with such effortless ease. I appreciated the relaxed perfection of Finnean's shot while I prepared to try and emulate it.

"Just like that," spoke a new voice, one familiar enough to startle me. The voice was loud and clear, and felt like it was right next to me. I wheeled my head around quick to look at the caddy. The club was being handed back to me by a grinning Finnean, but the voice was not his.

"Nicely done, Mr. Macalister," I complimented the caddy on his shot. "Did you say something else?" He was stoic, anxious for me to take the club back from him after his demonstration. He believed I was standing there frozen because I still feared trying the shot. After a few seconds, he answered me.

"No, Mr. Collins, I said nothing else. Now give it a go, would you?" I gripped the club. I was looking straight at Finnean when the voice came again.

"I never had a chance to show you a shot like that back in Weatherford." Finnean's mouth did not move. The caddy stood staring at me like I was another crazy American. He was neither speaking the voice nor hearing it. Surrounding me was the chuckle of the wonderful, strong baritone that fell silent with his death 30 years before. Without any doubt, the voice was my Uncle Clyde. That's when I saw him standing on the large rocks at the back of the green some 60 yards away. I wanted to run to him and shake his hand, maybe even to hug him. "Don't think about coming over here, because we can't get together right now. Come on, Chris; let's show him you can do this. Make this shot!" Finnean's glare showed an increased level of concern for my mental health, and I feared it might be well-founded. "Nobody else can hear me, Chris. You wanted so much to play in Scotland, and now, here you are!" My uncle's voice still sounded like it was at my shoulder. It wrapped me in warmth. "C'mon buddy, you can do it!"

Uncle Clyde was a big man. He stood 6'5", a fit and muscular 230 pounds even in middle age, even as he fought the illness that ultimately took his life years ago. My grandparents named him befitting their Scottish lineage, but family members were the only ones who called him by his given name. The reason that everyone outside of family knew him as Dick was a tale I never grew tired of hearing.

When he was a young man, my uncle was serving in the U.S. Navy in the fall of 1941. That December, his ship was at sea out of Pearl Harbor when Japan's attack took place. The graphic tales he told of returning to port aboard the USS Lexington a few days after the ambush made an impact on me as a youngster. He remained on that ship through being wounded in action at the Coral Sea. That put him not just out of the war but out of the military for good. The silver lining to his horrible experience in that final fray was that it introduced him to the woman who would become his wife, and also had the consequence of attaching to him a nickname that would stick forever.

Uncle Clyde manned a gun the day Zeros attacked his ship. One Japanese pilot flew straight at him. "We stared each other in the eye while we shot at one another," he would tell, "Right up until I won." Debris from the exploding aircraft peppered the deck of the ship. Many sailors were unable to avoid the wreckage, larger pieces killing some of his crewmates. A mist of white-hot shrapnel sprayed across my uncle when he dove for cover, just in time to get behind a wall to protect his torso. Bad luck steered many of those tiny fragments to penetrate several spots between his waist and his knees. He hung on while the ship then sank, abandoning the deck to be plucked from the warm sea along with hundreds of his fellow sailors.

Recovering in a Pearl Harbor hospital, a nurse helped him through the slow healing of his wounds, first his legs and then his more embarrassing injuries. Suffice to say a couple of poorly placed shards of metal had rendered him impotent forever. He struggled to accept the permanence of his reproductive injuries. In time, the two built a relationship where each appreciated the other's sense of humor. She got ahead of the jokes of others in their wing of the hospital, beating them to the punch when she hung a sign on his bed that read "Dead Eye Dick". The double entendre both complimented his shooting ability as a gunner and made light of the body part made useless. Before he knew it, the name stuck, and everyone called him Dick instead of his given name. The bond between the two was even stronger after that. They thought of nothing but each other when he returned stateside after his decorated discharge. Letters went back and forth with greater frequency, and the growing intimacy in them became more meaningful to both. V-J Day came, and fate took over. As if serendipitous, Nurse Jane was transferred to San Antonio, Texas. Within weeks they were married. The large framed wedding photo in their living room showed the newlyweds smiling over a cake that read, "Good Luck, Dick and Jane".

"Now you give it a try," my Uncle told me, just like hundreds of times in my youth when he taught me so much about golf. He was the most positive man I ever knew, always encouraging in a voice with a distinctive native Texan drawl.

I hesitated, and then said, "Gotta keep moving, you know."

Finnean responded, "Yes, sir," just as my uncle's voice said, "Yes, Chris". I gripped the club with a broad smile just as a strong gust caused both the caddy and I to catch ourselves before falling.

"You can do this," my uncle encouraged. The wind howled again. "There, feel that gust? Try to time it – hit the ball just after the wind calms down. Relax your hands. Get balanced. Give it a try. Don't look at the water; look at your target, about halfway to the green. Finnean's rooting for you just like I am. The quicker you get in the hole, the sooner he'll be sitting by the fire." I replayed in my mind the caddy's shot that knocked it so near the pin. I lightened my grip and balanced myself once more. I shifted my weight onto the inside of my left foot, pressed my hands forward and swung the low-lofted club. The ball clicked when I hit it and began a flight so perfect I thought it may bump the one resting on the green. It rolled just past the caddy's demonstration ball to a stop a mere three feet from the cup. My uncle applauded with a golf clap while Finnean just smiled, nodding in acknowledgement of my accomplishment. He extended one hand to retrieve the club. With the other, he reached his fingertips to the brim of his cap and graciously tipped it.

"Bloody well done, sir." Finnean went to the collar of the green, pulled my putter out, and laid the bag on the wet ground. He walked onto the green and picked up his ball, then marked mine with a coin before cleaning it.

"See there, I knew you could do it!" Even if I had made a horrible shot and muffed it, my uncle would have something good to say. I walked toward the green beaming with pride, wanting to walk over toward the surf to try and talk him into playing a hole with me.

Behind the green my uncle was shaking his head, declining my unspoken suggestion, somehow knowing the thought was in my mind. "No Chris, I can't do it, but get up there and hit that putt like we've got a Big Red bet on it." I walked onto the green where Finnean handed me the putter and I looked at the line. A short three feet away, it should be simple enough, but the full force of the storm was upon me.

"Knock it in, Mr. Collins," Finnean held the pin in his hand, showing his expectation I would make it.

"Like he said, Chris," my uncle's voice echoed. "Spread your feet wider than normal to anchor yourself against the wind. Then, just give it a solid stroke right at the middle of the cup. Hit through the ball and nail it to the back of the cup." These instructions were the same as he gave me long ago when we played in the winds of West Texas. I heeded the advice, and the ball rattled in the bottom of the cup for a par.

"Well done, sir," Finnean complimented me. I beat him to the hole to pick out the ball. He replaced the pin into the empty cup.

"Atta boy," said my uncle.

"Thanks," I said to both. "Couldn't have done it without you." Finnean nodded, not knowing that I was talking to both of them. I hesitated, exchanging smiles with my uncle while we stared at each other in silence. Finnean believed I was looking out at the sea and was courteous to wait, allowing me to enjoy the spot before walking off the green.

"I'm so glad you had a chance to experience that, Chris," my uncle said. "And to make such a great par here. What a thrill!" He was right about that. "My brother is anxious to be with his son again. We'll all be together soon. So soon." I so wanted to answer him but I kept quiet. The last words I heard from him were those resounding two words again, "So soon."

After trading final glances of non-verbal communication with my uncle, I turned to see the caddy motioning me ahead. He waited while I stepped past him and we walked along the shoreline toward the trees. I wanted to look back once more for Uncle Clyde, but I knew he was gone. We stepped onto the path entering the forest ahead, the caddy following me a stride or two behind and to my right. I was anxious for the protection of the woods, to get out of the elements for a couple of minutes before whatever came next. It was a simple dirt path that we stepped onto at the tree line, well-worn from many years of use. After a few paces, small natural stones made the walkway negotiable in the rain. The grade increased to go a bit uphill. I thought of how precarious walking on it with cleats would be before I realized that thousands upon thousands of golfers had walked this very path through the hundreds of years the course was here. It was at the very moment I stopped worrying about my footing that I fell.

There are those moments when we are neither asleep nor awake, when what feels like seconds turns out to be minutes, or hours, or days, or years. Sometimes you're not sure if you're still sleeping or not, when you peek open one eye to find your alarm is set to go off in three more minutes. These were my sensations just before opening my eyes, when the warm wet tongue of a dog licking my face startled me back to consciousness.

CHAPTER 22

It was that kind of accident where you don't realize you blacked out until you regain consciousness and wonder what happened. I opened my eyes. The weather was calm, not the North Sea day of a moment ago. There was no rain, no sound of the surf. There was no Finnean, and no Uncle Clyde. Lying on the ground, I felt the warmth of bright sunlight. I heard the chirping of birds and a breeze in the trees.

And, there was a black and white dog licking my face. Ralphie was bringing me back to reality with a gentle lapping. The dog's eyes met mine with a look that said, *'Hey, are you alright?'* I wondered where we were now.

"Hey, boy." Ralphie stopped and cocked his head when I sat up. I checked my arms and legs for the bloody scrape or two I thought I'd find from my fall. There were none. I ran my hand across my head expecting to find blood on my scalp and again was surprised there was no damage. "I'm pretty lucky for an old klutz, huh, Ralphie?" I was embarrassed about my clumsiness, especially since Finnean and Uncle Clyde might have seen me.

I scratched the dog between the ears in thanks and then took my time standing up. My bag was there on the cart again, with beads of rain and pieces of cut grass on it. The Border Collie stepped away to sit next to my cart but kept an eye on me. I wore a wet wind suit that bore a Kingsbarns Golf Links logo. I hoped for a dry towel when I reached into the zipped compartment of the bag and found one. I wiped my face and skin first, before the damp golf bag. Then I dried the rain suit before peeling it off and putting its pieces into the bag.

My surroundings were still unclear but I felt this *could* be Gabriel's Creek. It sure wasn't the stormy Scottish landscape I was enjoying before I tripped. I regained my senses, certain of the fact that we were back together again: Ralphie, the bag on a two-wheeled golf cart, and me. "O.K. boy, break's over," I sighed to the dog. "We'd better get moving." I was concerned about how much time might have passed while I was lying on the ground.

We followed the path deeper into the woods. A gentle chirping echoed, not to break but to accent the calm while we walked. The underbrush was silent, serene. Above the treetops, the daylight struggled to reach down to us, lending little light to our steps in thin rays between the tree limbs. Within a few yards, the dry warm sunshine transformed to a dense fog that swallowed Ralphie and I with a cool dampness. Quick changes like this didn't surprise me anymore. The dog panted, smiling up at me while we walked. The path curved ahead around a wide tree trunk. Past it, there was an inviting water fountain built of flagstone next to a small stone bench. I parked the cart for a moment to take a drink in the wooded cool of the foggy forest. Ralphie jumped up onto one end of the bench and sat, looking at me.

I bent over to use the fountain, saying, "I sure would love to have someone to play with on just one more hole. There aren't many left before I'm done." I sipped the water and paused before I said, "Of course, who knows what's around that next corner?" I drank again.

"I do," a mature male voice said. I looked up from the fountain, the water still flowing while I held the button down. The voice wasn't familiar this time – it sounded like the voice-over narrator of a documentary film. I let go of the fountain and turned all the way around, squinting into the fog as far as my sight allowed.

"Hello?" I said once, and then louder, "Hello? Who's there?"

"You don't need to raise your voice, Chris, I'm right here." Much like my uncle's distinct voice on the previous hole, this new speaker was close. Very close. This time, though, I could *hear* it, and *feel* it, but I couldn't tell if someone was talking or if it was in my head. "Chris, look at me." Now I caught the direction from which it came. The voice was coming from below my height. It was coming from the bench. Great: it was coming from the dog.

"Oh, come on," I said, incredulous. I looked at Ralphie, who was just sitting there panting and smiling as always. "Don't even start that with me." I gazed at him with a nervous smile, trying to prompt another response.

Ralphie's eyes stared hard into mine. There was no motion picture special effect-type moving of his lips or his tongue, nothing physical to indicate that a dog was talking to me. But then Ralphie – or somebody – said, "Look, I know this is kind of weird, but just go with it."

I flopped down onto the bench next to the dog, and our eyes were fixed into each other's. "Kind of weird? Is that what you said? I've seen you off and on for hours, and now you, a dog, are talking to me?" I was almost at a loss for words, repeating, "Kind of weird? With the day I'm having, kind of weird? You know, you could have just asked me to pass the pepper back in the grill and I'd feel a lot better now."

"Hey, don't blame the dog, Ralphie is like –" and there was a thoughtful pause, "Like an instrument. He's allowing me to use him to speak to you, because he's with you." Silence, while I tried to figure out what that meant. "Ralphie doesn't hang around anybody he doesn't like."

"So, you're not Ralphie?" I asked.

"Well, let's just assume I am," the voice said, "But perhaps I'm not."

"Thanks so much for that clarification," I said, standing now and getting a little irritated, still staring into the dog's eyes. I have always talked to dogs, so that never bothered me, but carrying on a two-way conversation *with* an animal was too much.

The dog hopped down off the bench and back onto the path, taking a few steps before turning around to look at me again. The voice continued, "Look, let's not waste time that you don't have with details." Ralphie motioned to suggest I needed to come with him. "Besides, you need to remember to keep moving."

"Or what, if I stop I'll imagine that dogs are talking to me?" I took a stubborn stance that implied I wasn't going anywhere. "Come on, for crying out loud, you're making me feel like I'm in a cartoon! So what now, are we going on a picnic together or something?"

"Christopher, c'mon, walk with me," and the dog took a few steps and stopped to turn, took a few steps and repeated. "*WOOF!*" a loud bark came from Ralphie's mouth. The voice said, "See, now you're starting to irritate the dog. Come on. You'll be glad you did, I promise."

"Whatever," I said like a teenager, pretty much because I was annoyed and didn't know what else to say. I grabbed the cart handle and shuffled off to follow Ralphie.

He stopped ahead on the path, waiting for me to catch up and stop with him. I looked down, and there was genuine warmth in Ralphie's eyes. "Your wish for another encounter has come true." The voice returned to a gentler sound now, and continued through the dog's panting. "You must understand, however, that you *must* keep going, you *must* not stop, nor try to prolong the next hole. You will want to but you cannot. You haven't yet been told the ramifications of delaying today, so I'll tell you now: you will risk losing the chance to be with anyone when you reach the other side. If you do as you are told, the experience you are bound for in heaven will include all the souls you've hoped it would." He began walking again, and I joined him while I listened. "If you ignore this direction, you'll still go to heaven, but the *kind* of heaven you've earned will be lost." We were approaching the point that the cart path was returning to the course. I hoped that the fog would lift and we would be back in Alabama.

With that, like breaking through a banner at the start of a football game, we were out of the fog and out of the woods. The cart path exited the trees and curved around to the right toward the next tee box ahead. We approached the 16th hole from the side before the path turned right to parallel the tee. Ralphie dropped a couple of paces behind me when we rounded the corner and came to the tee. My mouth fell open. When I saw the hole I knew that once again I was not at Gabriel's Creek. I knew right where I was – this was Denver; this was Antelope Run.

The familiar homes that surrounded this hole when we lived on Antelope Run weren't there, but their *shape* was. The neighbors were nowhere to be seen. The dwellings were muted into a translucent form, constructed from the fog we busted out of moments before. If you didn't look right at the cloud you almost felt the houses bordering the hole *were* there. It was like stepping into a hockey rink, the fog representing the houses much like the half-wall dasher boards and glass keeps the players on the ice. In place of a crowd above the boards of a hockey arena were the majestic Rocky Mountains in the distance. The deep blue sky straight above us had that Colorado crispness in it that was so familiar to me.

This was the par 4 16th hole of the course in the Denver suburbs, the very one that The Boys and I would often go out on late in the afternoons. The 395 yard hole was straight, and for the first 200 yards it was flat. After that a gentle slope carried it down to where a creek cut across the fairway just a few paces in front of the green. The character of the hole was a huge tree that stood tall and wide just left of the center of the fairway, about 175 yards off the tee. It was a 60-foot sentinel, determined to block direct access to the green. Getting into that tree and falling under it was easy, but getting out and back into play was not. If you tried to go around it too wide, ankle-deep rough would swallow your ball. The *right* shot shaped around it would render that same tree a simple conversation piece and lead to an easy par.

I was excited to be here, and was ready to tee one up. I took a 5-wood out of the bag, knowing I could start my ball high and right, drawing it just past the tree into the center of the fairway. Over the many times I played this hole, I learned that this club would catch that downhill slope with a nice roll and take it to a stop short of the creek. I strode onto the tee, reaching for the ball in my pocket while Ralphie smiled and sat a respectful distance away, parallel to where my stance would be.

“Wait a minute,” I stopped and looked over at the dog inquisitively, “I thought you said I had another encounter coming here. Didn’t you say that?”

Now Ralphie gave a “*BARK!*” once, then twice. He was louder than I heard him bark all day, like he was calling to someone at a distance. After each report, he motioned his head back toward the woods where we just came from. I looked in that direction. I was stunned. Through that wall of fog ran, sprinting as fast as they could manage, a Basset Hound and a Retriever – it was Houston and Tyler!

The club dropped from my hands and I fell to my knees, tears welling up quick as my dogs ran toward me. Tyler was so much faster a runner than Houston, but they both came as fast as they had ever run in their lives, and their barks were happy and strong. Ralphie barked along with them, looking pleased to witness our reunion. Tyler reached me first, leaping the final several feet into my waiting arms. I fell onto my back with him on top of me. He licked my face wildly while I hugged him, rubbing his coat and keeping an anxious eye on

Houston. When the hound arrived, he climbed up onto me along with his brother. I cried so much with sorrow when I lost them, but now I cried with joy.

The three of us swirled on the ground in a genuine love-fest, Ralphie still barking away his approval. As much as anything that had happened this day, seeing my boys had to mean this was a dream, but it was so *real.* I could *feel* them, the warmth of their coats, the wetness of their tongues. I could *smell* them, that unique my-dog smell that Cameron hated as much as I loved. It seemed I could *taste* them. It was one of the most wonderful moments I ever experienced. They were so *healthy.* Just as I knew how long they had been dead, I knew this *had* to be real.

Tyler and Houston each hopped off me and went over to Ralphie, showing their appreciation by exchanging loving, thankful touches with the black-and-white dog. We were all thrilled to be a part of it. My face was wet in a combination of my tears and all our saliva. Then Ralphie and I connected with our eyes and I knew it was time to move along.

I picked up my club and stood while the dogs still jumped around, smiling and panting hard. With a wink at Ralphie, I reached in my pocket for a ball and a tee. "Hey guys, whattaya say, wanna play this hole the way we used to?" Both barked their agreement and took their seats on either side of Ralphie next to the tee marker, waiting for Papa to hit. I could only hope heaven was like this. I wanted to play the hole well, both for the boys and for me. My emotions made it difficult to relax over the ball. There was no better example of why you follow a pre-shot routine. I needed to calm down and focus on this hole with the enormous Christmas-tree looking obstacle trying to block the fairway. Standing over my ball I kept repeating over and over to myself, "You'll see them again, you'll see them again. Just don't screw this up – keep moving so you can see them again."

I drew a deep breath and let it out slowly. I could feel three dogs ready to bark in an order to hurry up and get on with it. I focused on not taking the club back too far before finishing my swing nice and high. Three heads swiveled to follow the flight of the ball with me. It started its flight down the right side. Just as it reached its apogee, my ball began to draw left more and more. It bounced beyond the big tree but took a big kick to the left and went out of sight. I was sure I would find it in the short grass of the fairway.

Houston lumbered away at a brisk pace – brisk for him anyway – leaving the tee down the left side, ready to begin one of his scavenger hunts. He looked a little confused since there were no neighbors to beg from. Tyler took off like a shot, sprinting the first 20 yards or so as if chasing my ball. That's about as far as he could ever focus, taking about that long to find something, anything more interesting along the way. We called Tyler "our A.D.D. dog". Moment to moment, he might decide he would rather pursue a butterfly, a flower, a pine cone, anything, and then return to wanting to be the first to reach my golf ball. Assuming the role of overseer, Ralphie loped off the tee straight up the middle of the fairway with his head held high, turning it left and right to keep tabs on both of my boys. Like a hall monitor, now and then he would bark encouragement at one or the other of them to *keep moving*. It was believable that Ralphie had an arrangement with the boys similar to the one he had with me.

I began following the three dogs up the fairway. I couldn't help but to think that things were, at that moment, *just like they used to be*, only better. We were together like we were long ago, except now with Ralphie we were four. Ahead, Tyler stopped whatever he was doing, looked up the fairway, and took off, sprinting to a screeching halt. It was obvious he had found my ball.

I was conscious of walking slower than usual, and I was having a hard time taking my eyes off the boys. Tyler wagged his tail with pride and sat statuesque next to my ball, which was in pretty good shape. Houston was more interested in what he might find in the shady grass of the big pine tree. He hunted like he wanted to find a turtle or a squirrel to play with. Up ahead, Ralphie sat in the center of the fairway parallel to my ball. Our eyes made contact again. The voice spoke, "I see what you're doing, Chris. C'mon, step it up, let's get going." I nodded in acknowledgement and resumed my normal gait. I looked ahead to Tyler, dutiful while waiting for me at my ball, smiling and panting with his haunting handsome face that has stayed with me since the day he died.

When our kids were toddlers, I had visions of future years of our family out on the golf course together. I dreamed of my eager children, looking up at their father like he was a saint sent to them straight from the Golfing Gods. Patiently, they would wait their turn for Daddy to come and help them. They would stand all together in awe to watch him hit a golf ball in a way they would describe to others for the rest of their lives. It had forever remained just that, just a vision, just a dream. My kids never looked at me like that, but my dogs always did.

It is possible the kinship with my dogs was a substitute for how my relationship with our kids should have been. Looking back now, I missed the closeness with my kids that every parent wants. In those years that I over-prioritized work, when 80-plus hour weeks were common, everyone at home must have felt slighted. The baseball and soccer games missed, dances where all the other parents were chaperones, meetings with teachers, Scouting events – all the things that give a parent a chance to build their bond with their child in their formative years, I wasn't there very often. I miss-prioritized. I prevented myself from being there when I should have. Through all that, when I would get home the sad faces of my wife and children were replaced by the smiling, unconditional love of The Boys. Most would say it wasn't a very good trade. With a misplaced work ethic, I drove my wife into an affair, lost the adoration of my children, and ruined my career with the wrong kind of fix. Through all that, though, there were two dogs that somehow loved me no matter what.

When I arrived at my ball, Tyler moved over to lie in the rough, about 20 feet away. The 150-yard post was less than 10 yards ahead. Down the slope, the small creek just short of the large flat green was not very threatening. On this hole, once you got around the big tree and kept from running your tee shot down into the creek, you were pretty safe. Ralphie sat facing me from his spot in the middle of the fairway. Houston was behind us but we all knew he would be here by the time we got moving again. He would stop here and there to stare into that fog bank, wondering how he was supposed to get a snack out of it if nobody was there to give it to him. I parked the cart and pulled an 8-iron out, swinging it to just clip the fairway grass a little with a couple of practice swings.

"I know you understand how special this is to me," I said to the listening Course Dog or Ralphie or whoever the voice was. I hit the ball with the same snip of the turf that I practiced, sending the ball high toward the green. It landed pin high, about 15 feet right of the flagstick. My two dogs looked happy, but Ralphie waited for me to continue my point. "As much as I don't understand why I deserved anything that has happened all day," I said, sliding my club back into the bag, "I have no idea what I ever did to deserve *this*." I motioned toward my dogs. Tyler was already off again, on his way to the green, and Houston just waddled between Ralphie and I on his way to join his brother. "I mean, unless they're here to take me with them, I don't know how I can let them go again. In a very wonderful way it hurts to see them, to be with them." Ralphie was listening like the close friend he had become. I added, "And as far as that goes, after how you and I have spent the day together, I'm not going to be real crazy about saying goodbye to you, either."

"Aw, you're makin' me tear up. Got a tissue?"

"Smart ass," I smiled. I grabbed the cart handle and started to walk toward the short footbridge that crossed the creek ahead on the left side of the green. Tyler was already across and Houston was nearing it. Ralphie joined me and the voice returned to a more serious tone in reply.

"You should have paid more attention to your family, your wife, and your kids, but you know that." Whoever this voice is was pretty astute, I thought. "But there is value in the fact that you tried. You did what you thought was the right thing. You thought you needed to work hard and be a provider." I motioned Ralphie to cross the bridge ahead of me before I followed. We were across it in five of my paces. "The dogs were not a *substitute* for your family. They were an important *part* of your family, a meaningful part of your kids' young lives. They are proof that you're a good man, Chris. You did not *have* to add dogs to your family, but you did. You could have purchased pure bred dogs while two other mutts perished. You could have picked anybody else when you went to the pound that day. What happens to Houston if you don't take your family there that day to adopt a dog?" It was a good point. "And then there's Tyler." The Retriever was laying with paws in front of him, haunches next to my ball on the green. I pulled my putter out and took off my glove while Ralphie and I walked onto the putting surface. Houston was sniffing around behind us at the bottom of the surrounding fog bank. "What happens to Tyler if you don't buy him from the kids on your porch?" I thought of what may have happened to both.

"Think of all the things that you did for them through their lives, long lives, I might add." I thought of the illnesses and injuries and pills and tooth cleanings and gland expressing and pedicures and wounds. I remembered emergency room trips and regular doctor visits. I visualized the blankets straightened and toys and treats and water bowls and poop scooped and baths and car rides and walks in the parks.

I looked at my 15-footer for birdie and stepped up to the ball. "You know they say the hardest putt to make is a straight, flat one." I felt Houston mosey up and stand quiet, waiting at the edge of the green.

"Knock it in," encouraged the voice. Tyler stared at the ball with his tongue hanging out like if I didn't make the putt, he was ready to eat it. I started the ball rolling at just the right speed, but just ever so little off line. I pulled it just enough that it rolled an inch outside and about three inches past the cup and stopped. I walked over to tap the ball into the hole.

"Here's the thing," I said to Ralphie. "They deserved it. They loved me like I could never expect anyone to. They loved the kids, they loved my wife, they loved everybody. There were a lot of lives that were a lot better because of these two creatures. Mine included, yes, but there are so many lives they touched."

"Then you *do* understand after all. It's one big circle, isn't it?" When the voice finished, Ralphie looked at my two boys and gave a *BARK*, once, then again. Houston and Tyler looked first at each other, then at Ralphie, then at me. They began wandering around like they were avoiding the open door of the Vet's office. Ralphie gave another *BARK*, but this time it had a gentler sound to it. He was telling them it was time to go.

My two dogs came to me together. Each barked once and looked up at me smiling. I took their looks to say, "Goodbye for now, Papa, but we'll see you soon!" Before I could reach down to them for a departing caress, they turned and ran ahead together, Houston trying to keep up with Tyler, as always. They galloped down the cart path and into the fog bank. Just like that, they were gone.

"I'm not crying again, you know." I looked at Ralphie with conviction. "Nope, not going to do it. I'll see them soon. I will. You tell me one more time that I will." I fell to one knee on the green, fighting back the tears that wanted to come. Ralphie came and circled me, swirling his coat over and around my legs. I stood up again and he jumped a couple of times at me. He was smiling. He helped me decide I should be happy, too.

"Be happy, Chris. You earned it. You *will* be with them soon." With that, Ralphie took off ahead of me again, down the cart path into the fog, right were the other two had run before him. I walked off the green, bagged my putter, and slowly pulled my cart down the path with my head held high.

CHAPTER 23

The romp with my dogs on the last hole left my emotions drained, but I was far from sad and depressed. I was happy to be walking through the now familiar fog on my way to Number 17. I had no illusions of catching up with Houston and Tyler, although I hoped to see Ralphie again before leaving the course. I burst through the fog and back onto Gabriel's Creek to finish my round.

The recognizable tee sign confirmed I was back at Skip's place. The gorgeous hole was a par 4, said the sign, 446 yards from the tips, 414 yards for me from the white tees. There were two sizeable lakes. The fairway weaved through them, first to the right, then left, then right again to the green. The nearest lake began in front of and left of the tee, running to about 225 yards up the left side. That was the landing area, where a second lake began on the right. Its bank curved away in the opposite direction, all the way up to the side of an undulating green in the distance. Around the green, moguls made a bowl's bottom out of the putting surface. A culvert below ground must have carried the water flow from one lake into the other since no creek was crossing the fairway. The customary forest of tall pine trees encapsulated it all. The challenge to escape the two lakes made me think one thing.

"Double Trouble," I said aloud.

"Good name for this hole." I was startled by a voice just behind my right shoulder.

"Holy crap, Scott," I sighed, calming down. "You could give me a little warning, you know. You scared the hell out of me."

"Sorry," he chuckled.

I pulled a 3-wood and walked onto the tee. I looked over to see Scott's bag on the same pull cart he had when we were together earlier. "I didn't expect to see you again, but I'm sure glad you're here." I teed my ball and surveyed my shot. "I gotta keep moving, you know."

"Yeah, I know," Scott said, standing a respectful distance behind and within my vision.

"Playing or just visiting?"

"Sure, I'll play this one with you."

I took a deep breath and aimed right of the nearest lake, setting up to draw it just a little following the fairway between the banks into the desired landing area. Scott pulled a club up out of his bag after I swung away. The departing flight path of my ball looked like it would finish just right.

"Nice shot."

"Thanks." I walked over to put the club in my bag. Without fanfare Scott teed his ball and hit away, landing his shot just behind mine. It rolled up between the lakes and a few yards past my ball to a near-perfect position. He grabbed his cart and we walked off the tee together.

"Chris, you know this is the 17th hole. Time is short."

"Yes, it is, in more ways than one." We both smiled. "It's a little like nearing the end of the gangplank."

"Have you learned anything of substance today?" Scott was cutting to the chase.

I looked at the ground in thought as we walked. Since Scott seemed serious, I felt I should be, too. "I've been reminded today of something my Dad often told me: no matter how bad you think things are for you, it's always worse for somebody else. I've realized how truly lucky I am. I think about those who've dealt with long illnesses, with various forms of cancer in particular; my parents, family, friends, and other people I've known. What they faced: long painful treatments, feeling worse and worse and then better once and a while, never knowing whether they were going to live or die in days or weeks or months or years. I've been so blessed that I'll not have to go through what they did. I feel like I should trade places with someone."

"That's normal, but you don't have a choice. What else – any other epiphanies?"

"Why, did you come back here to test me?"

"Maybe," Scott grinned.

"I feel like I've learned things today I should have learned a very long time ago; I've learned so many lessons of life too late. I want to pass them to someone else, so they don't face the same realities years from now. I have no more time, though. My life is over. It sucks."

"There's no way for you to know that these lessons will *not* be passed on." Scott's head was down, too. We walked a few silent paces.

"I've proven true the old saying that God will make us live long enough to see how many stupid things we did. Maybe the more dumb things you did requires you to live longer so that you have to reflect on them. I've lived pretty long, so that makes sense, I guess."

"You think that might be put a different way?"

"I suppose it could. Maybe I wonder if the time we are given here is to reflect on our life: to come to grips with the consequences of our actions, to learn, to understand, to reconcile our actions, to see our wastes, to mount our regrets, to see the wrong road taken in the yellow wood. I wonder if all those things are divined as preparation for our Judgment Day. Since we're sure to be questioned, maybe God is giving us time to practice our answers?"

"You sound like you've come from some mountaintop in Nepal. You're speaking as if communal but you mean it as an individual. Don't say that like you've found some sort of esoteric mystery. You're wondering if you're getting all this stuff thrown in your face today for a reason. You can just say that, you know." The gentle breeze pushed up little waves in the lakes that lapped at their banks while we walked between them. A family of ducks was nonchalant as they paddled in a line through the lake to our right. The scene around us was tranquil while we headed for my ball ahead in the fairway, twenty yards short of his. I could tell Scott was beginning a soliloquy that I'd better not argue with, but listen to.

"So what do you think the whole point of today has been? Do you think the whole purpose has been to drag you back through your mistakes and the stupid things you've done your entire life? Are you waiting for this to turn into *It's a Wonderful Life*? I'm not Frank Capra, Chris." He wasn't scolding me as much as leading me. "Do you think all these people today have been the ghosts of Christmas Past or something? That's not it at all." He saw my confusion. "Besides, who says this is all about you anyway? Maybe it's about everybody else you've seen today. Maybe *you've* been put into *their* day. Maybe you're part of Nick's day, of Eric's, of Jack's. Maybe you're even part of *my* day." I thought I was starting to get it when he said, "But then again, maybe it *is* all about you."

"You're killing me, Scott." We chuckled together. "You're just killing me." We both found humor in the irony of my comment.

"Maybe today has been about exactly what you just told me – you've learned lessons of life. So what if they're too late? When we're young we do stupid things. When we're old, we reflect on both what we did wrong, but also what we did right."

"I think I've seen a little of both today, you're right."

"And by the way, I know you're concerned about your involvement in what happened to Spencer. Your faith should remind you that you're not in charge of judgments. You've been judging yourself all day, thinking too often about your regrets. You've second-guessed why you did this or that. Sometimes you've sounded like you envy the lives that others have lived.

Why? It's unnecessary for you to evaluate your own life, to think that your accomplishments are diminished compared to theirs. You can't know whether or not the value of your contributions are just as important, just as meaningful, as those of others. Your faith is strong enough that you shouldn't question what your God's plan has been for you. For all we know, everything that you *should* have done *has* been accomplished." He paused to catch his breath.

"I hope you're right."

"Stop and think about it. This entire day has *not* been about making you review the crossroads of your life; it's more about giving you the peace of not needing to worry about how you handled them. What did or did not happen, the decisions made right or wrong, the choices you made or did not make – very few of those are important now. You see, it's not even a matter of believing or not believing. One person has deep religious convictions, while another believes a bird crapped on a rock and the sun hatched us. God oversees them all. The events that lead each through their lives are there for a predestined reason. To scoff now at the notion God had no plan for you, no reason for how you got here, it's foolish. You lived this long for a reason. You'll live no longer for a reason. You're going where you're going for a reason. It is not a good application of your energy to try to figure out why. I know you appreciate what you've been through today." I nodded in agreement. "You've had a good day golfing, yes, but so much more. You've had interactions with friends, even family, both living and dead. You've experienced again places you know and love, and been places you wanted to go but never did."

Scott stopped and stood in the fairway, making me realize we were at my ball. "You've got 170 yards left. Hit the 5-iron." His distance estimate looked right on. I couldn't be sitting in a better position for my approach to the green. I would only have to deal with the second lake if I pushed a bad shot to the right. Unless I missed by a mile, the mounding around the green would help more than hurt. The flag fluttered in the breeze, swishing one way then the other. I still wanted to hit a 6-iron.

"I'm hitting a six."

"Hit the five."

"What are you, a caddy now?"

"The Scotland thing with Finnean was pretty cool, wasn't it?" He seemed quite proud, like he put that one together.

"I think the five is too much, I want to hit the six."

"Hit the five," he growled.

"You sound just like Finnean," I mumbled. I relented and pulled Scott's choice from my bag. I stroked the 5-iron with crisp contact. Right away I knew it was too much.

"I *told* you, Scott," I whined with feigned frustration. We watched the ball look like it was going to sail way over the green. Scott laughed harder the farther it flew.

"Gotta let me have a little fun once in a while, Chris." About then, the ball came down, well beyond the putting surface. It hit into the top of the highest mound behind the green and hopped high into the air before coming down. It bounced back toward us several times, nearer the green each time. It settled where we could still see it, just on the back collar of the green.

"See!" Scott acted like he was thrilled. "Isn't that a lot more fun than dancing a perfect 6-iron up there?" We laughed loud together. I replaced my club in the bag and stomped down my divot. Scott walked the 20 yards ahead of mine to where his ball lay, pulling a lofted club out of his bag. I began walking to join him when he stopped and took his stance, talking as he got prepared to hit. "OK, so you're wondering what you did to earn what has happened today. It's not a matter of you *earning* anything. It's more that you are *part* of it – each and every one of us is. The interface between souls is not restricted to our life on Earth." Scott swung and the ball flew straight away, right at the flag. "Every soul's human existence, whether we live hours or a hundred years, each and every experience of billions of lives have been intertwined."

I watched his ball fly, still trying to grasp what he was telling me, still trying to get my arms around it. "But I've seen so many people today that I *know* are dead." His ball danced to a stop just five feet from the pin. "What did you hit there?"

"8-iron."

"That's some 8-iron. Do you ever hit a lousy shot anymore?"

"Not often." He chuckled while I just shook my head.

"Anyway, then there have been others that I see how they have or haven't aged, and that makes me *think* they are dead, but I'm not sure. Others, there is no way I know that they could physically be there." The calm understanding in his eyes told me that he saw the sincerity of my lament.

He held up his hand to stop me, to inject. "Listen to what you said – *there's no way you know.*" He was slow and methodical as he repeated again, stopping on each word for emphasis, "No – way – you – know." He saw my enlightenment. "OK, now realize that you see me – *ME* – here and now, because you are supposed to see me here and now. Get beyond the visual restrictions of your earthly existence."

"But I saw so many others besides you."

"With enough souls I can show you a marching band if you want," he smiled. "Perspectives, Chris, perspectives." There was a pat on my shoulder and we were on our way again. We kept talking.

"So, you just round up some souls that aren't doing anything and have them come act like people I've known though my life?" I asked.

"That's not what I said. Why would you think that those souls were not the people you always knew?" He didn't wait long enough for me to answer. "Each soul is in spirit before their time on Earth, and each soul will be in spirit after their life as they know it here ends. Understand that we're talking about dimensions of time and existence that there is no way to explain, no way for you to experience, until..." Now he paused, "Until soon." His expressions became very calming as he punctuated, "Very soon."

"I see people that have aged just like I have, and some – even my dogs – that didn't show aging past a point," I said.

"When we pass, and this includes animals, the body decomposes, deteriorates, and returns to the earth; dust-to-dust. The life of the body stops developing, it stops aging. The soul doesn't need the body as a vehicle anymore. The last way we look in our life on earth becomes the last frame of reference that can be attached to that soul." Scott continued, "For example, I can't show you Payne Stewart at age 70, because he died at 43. The soul has no *age* per se, so you could encounter his soul at any point. But if you were to see him embodied, be around his physical representation, he would look no older than 43. Keep in mind, too, that when you cross over, *years* mean nothing anymore."

I was just as confused about something else. "What about places, like the courses I feel like I've been to today?"

"You must have some point of reference to be put into someplace. You've either been there before, or there must be some way to send your mind there. Vacation brochures, your uncle's photographs, or someone's detailed description to you in your past of a particular place."

"Like Scotland?"

"You got it."

"But to transport me, and any of the others, to put us together," he was starting that grin again as I inquired, "To pull us from different places." Scott slapped me on the arm.

"Who said *anyone* was 'transported'? You are still thinking with earth-borne logic – that doesn't apply." He was right, and I knew it. "Keep in mind that it was no accident, no coincidence that you *decided* to drive past the turn off to Hampton Cove and come instead here to Gabriel's Creek. It didn't *just happen* any more than your whole life didn't just happen to turn in a different direction." I began thinking of crossroads in my life that might have taken me on a different path. Until that moment, I always thought of those times in a different way, seeing my life's path as a product of my own decision-making. We talked about a few specific examples. He was making me look at it from a different point of view. We walked away from the lake to the left side of the fairway.

"Is it predetermined that I would think so much about what I'm leaving behind?"

"How do you mean, Chris?" Again Scott asked like he knew the answer already.

"I've reflected a lot on whether or not I'm leaving anything that says I was here. I'm not sure there is any proof that I *was* here. I'm not sure the world or the lives of anybody in it is any different because I was here."

"Are you worried about what will be said of you, Chris? Tell me, what is it that you think people will say about you, about your life, about your impact?"

"Not much, I guess. Not much."

"Is it relevant what people will say about you when you die? Do you think it matters?"

"Yes, I think it matters. But now I also see that the time to worry about what you will leave behind and what people will remember about you is when you are young and have your life ahead of you. When you are too old it's too late to do anything about it. Maybe that reality is what impresses me now."

"That's very intuitive. I have a proverb for you to think of. Listen to this, and let it sink in: *your reputation is what people think about you; your character is what God knows about you.*" He paused for effect. "So yes, it would be great if your passing was a news item, a cause for public mourning, a day off for a parade, but none of those will happen, will they?"

"No."

"What you've done, what you've left behind, they are at the pleasure of a higher power, Chris. You will find that you satisfied your purpose, and that's what's important."

Reaching the front of the green we picked up the cart path again and headed around the left side between its protecting moguls and the woods behind. We parked our carts and stood next to our bags. There was another subject I wanted to talk about.

"To be honest, Scott, I can't seem to get over being scared. Maybe 'scared' is the wrong word anyway because it's more like apprehension. I've always been concerned not so much about dying as the changing of life from this world to the next. It's the process itself. Does that make sense?"

"Sure it does. Remember one thing, Chris: this is something that bonds everyone who ever spends time on Earth. Every single person who has ever lived has or will experience death." That was sure true. "Think about it – why do you, or why do any of us fear death? The fear has its roots in many things. Maybe it's the fear of the unknown. Neither the most pious theologian nor any other living person knows what's about to happen. Granted, it may be a matter of degrees, but anybody who tells you they experience no fear of dying at all is not being truthful. There's fear in everyone when it comes time. Even the guy jumping off the bridge to his certain suicide; you think just before the moment his feet leave the bridge he doesn't feel at least some amount of fear? We all have it." He turned his head to me and our eyes met. He said, "I sure did." It was too late now to be shocked by his statement, and I decided not to try to learn any more about it.

I pulled a 7-iron for my chip and a putter, and noticed Scott was walking onto the green without one. At just the moment I was about to ask if he wanted me to grab his putter for him, he extended his arm and opened his palm. He showed me a ball in his hand.

"Thanks for giving me that short putt, Chris." We laughed. "Remember we're talking perspectives and dimensions, Chris," he said. I just sighed. I walked to the back of the green to look at my forthcoming third shot. Scott headed for pin-tending duty and continued, "We are trained our entire lives that death hurts. We see indescribable pain come to everyone connected to someone's death. Acute grief is an expectation. The ones who remain are the ones who feel death. The pain of our sorrow is deep when we focus on losing those we love. Part of our fear of death is that we know our passing will cause loved ones to feel pain: the handling of the funeral, someone having to deal with our personal effects, the sadness felt by those we love. As much as anyone wants to have their things together in advance, almost no one will approach achieving it." Those comments seemed somewhat personal, I thought.

"Too bad I didn't get to see you putt to get some help on this read," I needled Scott when I looked over the undulating green. My chip would have to roll to the hole like a putt once I got it over the collar.

“Breaks both ways, but it will end up going to your right more than you’d think,” Scott said.

“No it doesn’t, the water is to my left. It’ll break that way.”

“If you’re so smart, why did you ask me for help?” He had a point. I would chip it just to get it onto the putting surface and trust my read that it would go more left than right. Every foot it rolled I could see I was wrong. My ball crept to a stop almost as far away from the hole as I was before my chip. Now the long putt for my fourth shot would be downhill toward the water. I looked at Scott as he just shrugged. “Not everything is what it appears to be.” I walked to my putt.

“You couldn’t just blink mine into the hole like you did yours?”

“That wouldn’t be fair, Chris. Besides, how do you know I didn’t putt it?” He was fighting to hold back his snicker. I dropped the 7-iron, knelt for a quick look at the winding 20-footer, stood and stroked it. The ball trickled right, then left, then straight as it rolled, tracking like it had a chance to go in. The speed was good, but it was just a tad offline. It slowed and stopped just a foot past the cup.

“I’ll give you that one,” Scott said and moved like he was going to kick it away.

“No, I can do it all by myself, thank you.” Scott pulled the pin and held it with a smile as I walked up to tap in the short putt. Into the cup went the 12-incher for my five on the hole.

"Hey, it could've been worse, you know." He was trying to sound both consoling and encouraging. "Maybe your 18th hole will be better."

"Thanks. I hope so." We walked off the green, back to our bags. I put my clubs away and marked my scorecard.

"You know this fear of yours, your apprehension, whatever it is; it's not an indication that your faith is weak. I know that's bothering you. You're just trying to explain your anxiety. If we were able to see what happens next, survivors would cheer in celebration. Hospitals and other places that death visits so often might become happy places. Maybe we are trained for death the way we are so that we avoid taking it as an easy way out. It is desired that we stay here until our God wants us to stop being on earth, until it is time for us to go elsewhere."

"What are you, a missionary, or something?"

"Kind of." We took our carts, pulled them onto the path and began walking again, toward the woods. "What we fear most about death is the coming accountability. We fear having to answer for so many things we've done, for all our little secrets. Even the most devout will fear their Judgment."

We entered the cool and damp forest. I knew I was enjoying the last of these winding, relaxing transitions between holes. We headed for my final one, Number 18. "Thanks for everything today, Scott. It's good of you to be here with me now, too." We both looked down while we smiled, walking in quiet toward the opening back onto the course that was ahead.

CHAPTER 24

Scott and I came out of the trees into bright sunshine bathing the finish of Gabriel's Creek. There was beauty in the utter simplicity of the 18th hole, no more than a mowed pasture. It was the reverse image of what I saw earlier from inside the grill, as peaceful now as it was hours before. The path stopped at a wide, mowed flat spot that was the tee box. The flag fluttered atop its pole 415 yards uphill from the back tees, so the sign read. The signature creek was trickling from one side to the other little more than 50 yards away, in front of the ladies' tee. I pulled the driver from the rental set and fished for a ball and tee in my pocket, waiting for Scott to take his place with the honor he earned with the better score on the previous hole.

"Sign says it's a par 4, but it looks like about a mile from here," I remarked, squinting into the distance.

"It's not so bad, it's an easy hike," Scott said. "It's just 380 for you from the whites."

"You mean for *us*, don't you?" That's when I noticed Scott's bag and pull cart were missing. I wasn't surprised, but I was disappointed.

"No, Chris, this is where I get off. Think of it like a big tournament, where they let the champion walk ahead of everybody else, to enjoy the moment, to savor the finish."

In an attempt at a joke, I asked, "Do you mean of the round today, or of my life?"

"Both." His quick and serious response killed my levity.

"I'm sure no champion, but thanks anyway."

"Don't sell yourself short, Chris. The last thing I want to tell you is this: relax about what's coming. Don't fear it, embrace it. You got me?"

"Yeah, Scott, sure. Got it."

"Now go ahead and tee it up. Grip it and rip it, buddy." Scott tipped his visor. "Hit 'em good, Chris. Hit 'em good." With reluctance, I stepped onto the teeing area, walking to the spot between the markers. I remembered back to Number Four, where Scott got away before I told him what I wanted to say. I still needed to tell him that I was sorry for bailing out on our friendship years ago. I wanted to apologize for not being there for him, and for his family. When I turned around to say it now, he was gone.

Alone again, I resolved to take Scott's advice and enjoy this hole like it was the finish to winning the Masters. My game was better than it should have been all day. It was a long time since I'd played this well through an entire round. I wanted to keep it going for just one more hole. I teed the ball high and settled into my stance. I thought little more than to just hit it sweet enough to clear the creek one more time. Scott's suggestion to *rip it* was one I should have ignored. Instead, I tried to hit the ball too hard and the contact was less than pure. Off the bottom right of the driver's face the ball shot low and up the right side. Because there was so little danger here I was safe, but still much too short for a long-playing hole.

"Hey, at least I cleared the creek," I said to myself, and put the driver into the bag. I headed for the crossing over the calming brook to walk up the hill to my ball.

Today, the metaphors were so thick you could cut them with a knife, but this 18th hole was the perfect analogy for my life; the last destination in sight, the end of an uphill climb. I could go on and on.

Through my entire golfing life I never had a bad walk up an 18th fairway. For me, there never was an adoring, cheering throng to receive me when I finished a round, never a gallery of faces smiling in appreciation. Just as satisfying, though, every now and then my wife or the dogs would be waiting at the final green. Not often was I glad to be finished with the course for the day. Like a fisherman bringing his dinghy into port or walking home carrying a pole with a string of fish, your day was pretty much over but you weren't done quite yet. There were still things to do, but you wished you were still out there. That's how I was on most of the 18th holes of my life; I wanted to keep going.

Once in a while through the years, the coming of the 18th was good because it meant a lousy round was ending. On those days, we just remind ourselves that the worst day golfing beats the best day working. Often enough, though, it had been the opposite, the end of a good round. When we're playing well, no golfer wants the day to end. Today, I didn't play *that* great, but all things considered, I'd scored pretty well. A quick look at my scorecard reminded me again of Uncle Clyde. When I was in grade school, he taught me a simple method of keeping track of your score through a round. He'd say, "If you get a 5 on every hole, that's a 90, and that's good!" Plusses or minuses to a five on each hole would be added or subtracted from 90 to tell you where you were. I could see a bogey on this final hole would give me an 83 I could be very proud of. It didn't matter to me at all that it might have been a 99 on a tougher course; I was happy with both how and where I'd played this day.

My faith was much stronger since I came to this place, I thought. Before this day, there were times since the doctor gave me the news that I stopped and asked myself something: what if non-believers and those of so many religions are right, that when we die, there actually *is nothing?* What if we live, we die, and that's it? Today I was successful in shaking away those thoughts and was more convinced than ever there was a hereafter coming next. The little clubhouse up there made me realize that just beyond, there were so many that I was anxious to see again. Friends, family, beings, souls, so many things to call them, my eager anticipation was building just thinking about them. I felt warmth in Scott's direction that I should embrace what was coming.

The end of my round made it natural to concentrate on the coming end of my life. I thought of my plans for what little time I had left. I could check off playing one last round of golf. My mind began running through an updated mental list, visualizing what I would do after leaving the approaching final green. First there would be some time in the clubhouse with Arnie and our ice-cold bottles of Nehi. I'd convince him to let me pay for *something* today. Then there would be the drive back to Shannon and Dan's house. During that drive I'd need to give some thought to when and how I should describe my day to Cameron. That conversation would include my plan to talk to the Denver Police; a phone call I hoped could wait until after we got home to Albuquerque. There would be difficult goodbyes to say to A'Dell and to my daughter. I wished there was time to stop awhile in Weatherford on the way home, but there wasn't. There were things to do back home. It was so long ago since I'd done anything about my death preparations; I wanted to work on getting my papers together, and to visit both my minister and the funeral home to finalize my arrangements. There was also just being back in my adopted New Mexico home of Albuquerque; at least one more date with the green chilies I'd find a way to work into every single remaining meal I'd enjoy.

My ball rested about 200 yards from the green over on the right side. There was no breeze to speak of. I didn't feel like hitting another fairway wood, despite how long this shot would play. I took a 3-iron and stroked it smooth but started it right of my target. The ball came to a rest on the right, again much shorter than I wanted to be. Maybe my subconscious was lengthening my day's finish, avoiding the inevitable, like when Ralphie busted me walking too slow with my dogs a couple of holes before. I put the club back in the bag and kept moving up the hill.

My mind reviewed the many 18th holes of my life. This one was so much the same, and so much different. Hovering just up another rise to the left of the green was a simple scene, fitting for the end of a simple golf course. There was Skip's little grill and golf shop, a nondescript little shack next to a plain and flat 18th green. Maybe because its plainness reminded me so much of Higdon Park, I had to smile. Today it was more. It was my majestic structure awaiting its course's conquering hero. It was the monument that punctuated a great golf experience. Walking up this 18th hole toward my ball, Skip's building up there was now my Olympic Club, my Shinnecock Hills, my Colonial, my St. Andrews. The dramatic contrasts between Gabriel's Creek and those spectacular golf finishes brought into focus some of the juxtaposition within my life. I'd been at both the top and bottom of my profession, experienced both the good and the bad in personal finances, enjoyed the finest and not-so-finest of living, and played both good and bad golf.

Then there were points of my life terrific enough to defy any contrast or comparison: I was raised by two loving parents who lived into my adulthood. I loved my one and only wife and we'd stuck together through everything. I raised two fine children that I hope will feel a positive twinkle in coming years when they think of me. I lived long enough to delight in seeing the birth of a wonderful grandbaby. And perhaps as important as all the rest, I enjoyed the unconditional love of two dogs that enriched my life and kept me on track when I might have strayed.

Seeing all of this combined to make me wonder why I deserved to be so blessed. It seemed like an awful lot of good things to happen to one man, one sinner. But, amidst all the positive experiences of this day that led me to recall the good of my life, there still remained one dominating question: what did I accomplish? The answer was perhaps still too clear: 'very little'.

Trudging up the slope was the first time all day I began feeling tired from the hike. It took a lot more effort to get up the hill, more like what I expected at the start of the day. Scott told me on the tee of this hole that it was "not so bad" – funny guy. I was surprised at how far my ball still was from the green. My third shot had at least another 60 yards to go. I pulled my pitching wedge, and told myself to not push the ball to the right yet again. I put an easy stroke on it, and watched it sail the perfect correct distance. It was pin high – and left. The ball bounced a couple of times before settling just off the left of the putting surface, on what was a stretch to define as a *collar*. I bagged the wedge and headed on.

Maybe the purpose of my life was to see its reflection on this day, to review it this way at Gabriel's Creek. Preordained or not, it was that extra little drive following those signs farther down the road that gave me the opportunity to see them: Arnie the Pro, Doug the Kid, and of course Ralphie; then there was Scott; Jack, Terry, and Ned; Eric; Nick; Uncle Clyde; and maybe most of all, my Boys.

I met so many at Gabriel's Creek – maybe I even met myself.

I spent a lot of this day rehashing things I did right, and so many things I did wrong. Now I began seeing those events of my life in a different way, more like my life took its path because it was my destiny, my purpose, God's will. I saw with more clarity now that my life was blessed with so much more than so many people had. Through the mystery and confusion of the past few hours, every revelation, every re-acquaintance, each one of those flashbacks were all worthwhile. They helped me see my life as being complete. I wasn't giving up, not giving in or quitting, but accepting my fate with a different perspective. If the end was to be now, I was lucky for everything that preceded it. Every day of my life had, in fact, been a gift. How blessed I was to have Ralphie and Scott as my guides, to help me see all of that.

I parked the cart and bag next to the green below the bordering berm that made a natural amphitheater of the green. It was just a short stroll down from the clubhouse. I was ready to pull out the 7-iron for a chip since I was a few feet off the putting surface, with about another 40 feet to the flagstick. The grass around the green was short enough I decided a putter would do the job. I pulled off my glove, stuck it in my back pocket, and studied the line from one knee. It was a simple green, yes, but I wanted to finish with no worse than bogey – that meant I had to keep it very close if I didn't sink it for par. It was a long putt with a slight left-to-right turn in it. I steadied myself and stroked the ball, making sure I didn't leave it short. I hit it a little too hard for the ball to break like I read it, though. The ball sped past the cup on the left side, stopping about four feet past it.

I turned and looked back down into the valley, thinking of how many times across a continent I stood on a final green and looked back at the hole, reflecting on the round. Just like this moment, those were times when I wanted to lock the whole day into my memory, to freeze the entire experience. There were different reasons for those moments, like the camaraderie with fellow players or the competition of that day. Maybe it was the good done that day by playing in a charity scramble. Sometimes it was the mental picture of the place you wanted to capture and keep forever, a moment I experienced at so many wonderful courses. Then, like so many golfers, there were lots of other places around the world I never made it to see in person. Like the 18th at St. Andrews, I'd never enjoyed those sights.

At that moment, looking out across Gabriel's Creek, I doubted that I would relish any of those other places more.

This day, maybe the reason for the pause was to appreciate how this magical place had forced my introspection, had extracted my thoughts using interfaces with all these people. It was worth stopping to cherish that.

Suddenly there was a swirl of scenery and everything began a rapid change. The sky, the air, the forest, the ground under my shoes; everything swirled around me. It came upon me as quick as a dust devil, and I was at the center of its rotation. I sensed no one else could see it, hear it, feel it – it was a special performance just for me. Inside the walls of this mini-cyclone I saw scenes from my life. With each couple of seconds I was on yet another 18th green. Looking back down the valley toward the tee at municipal courses of my youth; to desert courses of the arid southwest, to ocean courses lush with vegetation; to an eddy of old friends and faces long lost from memory flashing before me, a time warp of "good game", "nice playing with you", "thanks for the round", "great day", "how about a drink", "you owe me ten bucks", all those final parting words uttered on the final greens across a lifetime. The orchestration rushed through my life's memories second by second, from one coast across to the other, from the young part of my life until now. They were all buried treasures in the depths of my experience before this event brought them back.

Like being stuck within the impressive special effects of a movie, everything whirled faster and faster.

Snapshots inside the fury froze around me, each for milliseconds at a time. Here came those visions of an entire lifetime: so many places, so many people, from my earliest childhood days up to recent times. Grade school class photos, family vacations with fish on a string. A Junior High School talent show program and Instamatic pictures of pee-wee football games. I saw myself in the gallery at Colonial with Uncle Clyde, leaning over to see Gardner Dickinson and Jack Nicklaus in a stressful Sunday battle to the finish. I saw flashes of me walking in practice rounds alongside Lee Trevino, Billy Casper, and Ben Crenshaw, soaking up the experience. There were High School baseball games, senior prom pictures, and so many more images from our yearbook. Several TCU students dressed up as Horned Frogs for Homecoming, with me in the center. There was Cameron, so beautiful for our wedding, smiling family members from both sides all around us. I saw the births of our children and their lives in a sequence all the way through A'Dell's arrival. I blinked through televised images from that old Wonderful World of Golf through last year's British Open, knowing that each time I wished I wasn't just watching but playing.

Like the overused old cliché we always hear, my life was flashing before me.

The rushing, spinning myriad of remembrances that rushed in seconds like a tornado both around and through my soul stopped in an instant to create an eerie silence. I again smelled the pines, again heard the same birds chirping that I'd listened to throughout the day, again felt the southern heat and humidity replace all those climates I'd been back through today. I knew the time warp was over, but something else was beginning.

Movement at the clubhouse caught my attention. A player held the door to the golf shop open and pointed in my direction while Doug ran out of it. He sprinted at full speed down the hill toward me at the green. He was screaming as he ran, “Mr. Skip! Mr. Skip! The green, the 18th green, you’ve got to come NOW!” I saw the Pro sling the grill door open and he ran the best he could with his limp, following Doug with all his might, heading out to *me*.

“Claire!” Arnie screamed back toward the grill, “Claire! Call 9-1-1!” I wondered what was wrong, what were they all so excited about? My perspective looking toward the scene began changing – it felt like I was rising to look at them from a higher point than standing next to the green, like I was being lifted by a cherry picker. First I thought maybe I had moved to stand atop the berm, but then I rose higher and higher. I was looking down at Doug as he ran closer and closer. I was seeing him from above. The Pro was still running to catch up with him, but they were underneath me, below my feet.

Doug slid to a stop on his knees there. I looked down, and to my shock saw...myself. Could that be me? It looks like me, he’s dressed like me, a body lying face-down on the ground next to my golf bag and not moving. Wait a minute, I’m right here, that can’t be me, I’m right...

I went to pat myself, to bring my hands to my body. I tried to touch myself to prove that wasn’t me on the ground. That’s not me, it can’t be me, I’m right here, I *know* I’m right here. See, I can feel my body...but I couldn’t after all. There were no hands, there was no body. Like I was now a cloud, I still had the sensation of being myself, having eyes to see, senses to smell, to hear, to feel, but I had no body to contain those senses. When Doug and Arnie rolled over the body below me, I stared at it from above, from farther and farther away. I knew now just what they were all excited about. Still clutching and a putter in one hand, there was now no doubt at all: the body was me. Eyes frozen open. Motionless. Lifeless.

My perspective above the scene rose even higher. There were others who were curious, coming out of the clubhouse, peeking from the parking lot, looking around the corner of the building from the practice green. A few ran after Doug and Arnie to the side of the body below, looking for a way to help. Light around me grew brighter and more intense, beginning to wash out what I could see of the action below. The light grew stronger and stronger. I felt motion now as if being pulled away from the scene like a subway train pulling away from a station. I thought of my wife and our kids. Oh, how I wanted to be with Cameron, with Shannon and Austin now. I knew, in the words of Doctor Crosland, I was "done". I was finished; this meant I had seen them for the last time.

The earth below disappeared into the brilliant light. I was no longer a body now but a mass on a train accelerating through a tube, being sucked through a straw. I felt like I was riding a bullet train underground, speeding through the twisting walls of an imagined tube. A pinpoint far ahead implied an end of the tube was coming. Gradually, that dot grew just a bit bigger as I flew even faster through the conduit. Now, every color imaginable was mixing with the pure white of its walls: brilliant blues, oranges, greens, yellows, and streaks of red all accented the tube with a gentle churning as the speed I felt kept increasing. As that ending speck grew larger and larger, I began feeling extreme happiness, a thrill and peace beyond any I ever dreamed.

Appearing in front of me like a screen on the bridge of a motion picture's spaceship, I saw an ambulance pulling away from the 18th green of Gabriel's Creek as a small crowd dispersed. A Sherriff Andy Taylor look-alike finished writing his report on a clipboard leaning against his patrol car. Cleaning up the scene meant Doug needed to collect the clubs and cart. He spotted my ball on the green, four feet away from the pin, and looked to Arnie for what to do. The Pro sighed, and then walked over to the pull cart where my scorecard was attached to the handle. He grabbed a pencil and the card and told Doug, "Go pick it up with respect, son. We're giving him that one whether he likes it or not." Skip wrote down my bogey five and the image blended back into the blur.

Surrounded by the swirl of beautiful colors, I sped even faster, feeling not taken by, but a part of the motion. Pure pleasure overcame me. It came with the knowledge that when loved ones follow this way in the future, they will experience the unprecedented joy I was feeling. I thought how I hoped to meet my wife in the future, to receive her as she comes in, to see and share her unbridled euphoria upon taking this same journey.

Faster and faster toward meeting my God, a rush I'd never known consumed me, knowing that I was about to see so many loved ones that passed before me – my Mother, my Father. How would "seeing" them now be manifested? What shape, or form, or being would "being" now be? Regardless of what it was, I knew – I *knew* – I was about to be with them. I realized I could now be with all of them, in whatever form they would take. Uncles, aunts, and, grandparents. In-laws and friends. Professors, teachers, fellow students, co-workers. Scottish shepherds that once hit a wad with a stick while herding their sheep. Golf buddies, golf legends. Payne Stewart – I want to spend some time, whatever that is, with Payne Stewart. What would "time" be now anyway? Will there be any measure, any sense of what I was thinking of as "time"?

The pinpoint of before became a large disc. I grew ever closer to it before it swept into a huge globe enveloping me, suspending my formless being within it. A rapid expansion of the shell now surged outward, the light becoming sheer magnificence all around me. I felt the presence of a rainbow.

I heard a dog bark – once, and then again. First the sound was distant, then a bit closer, and then closer still. Then a second dog joined in, not just barking but as if singing in tune with the first. My ecstasy accelerated. How familiar was the sound of these two, for they were my two canine loves. I knew they were *my Boys*. Then I *knew* I was about to meet my God, and He would be receiving me with favor. I knew, because he had my dogs waiting for me.

There was no doubt at all: I was indeed entering Heaven.

EPILOGUE

The room set up for the memorial service at the funeral home was pronounced perfect by its director. Across the front were many framed photographs and posters, trinkets and keepsakes remembering Chris Collins. There were just a few sprays on stands and a couple of potted flowers, but each was beautiful. At the center of everything, a beautiful Navajo urn containing the cremated remains of the departed stood on a simple stand next to a speaker's lectern. The items up front outnumbered the chairs that were lined into two short rows, ready for attendees. Mrs. Collins simply didn't expect many to attend. Her husband had few friends in the Albuquerque area.

The framed pieces included Chris' wedding photo and a huge family collage that seemed to include as many photos of dogs as it did children. Every picture in the collage showed a happy Collins, as a businessman, as a parent, or with a dog or two. His college diploma hung prominently, draped with a purple felt TCU Horned Frogs pennant his parents gave him when he was a freshman. One frame showed Chris' favorite golfer in a series of pictures reliving Payne Stewart's putt on the 18th green of his 1999 U.S. Open win at Pinehurst.

Trinkets included divot repair tools and ball markers and pencils collected from places he'd played like Canterbury Golf Club in Cleveland and Torrey Pines outside San Diego. There were scorecards from all over the country, some as far back as when he was in grade school. His Pat Neff High School yearbook was there, open to the page where he and his Golf Team buddies displayed broad smiles. It lay next to the college yearbook from his graduating year. Standing on an easel was a cork board with a few more photographs tacked up with push pins. They went back to his childhood, remembering family, friends, and places he loved.

Outside in the foyer, Cameron Collins sat to talk with her brother-in-law Chad, who had just arrived in advance of the service. They finished a brief walk through the prepared room, where Cameron gave the director her final approval. She was waiting for the minister from their church to arrive. Chris's wife knew her husband would want his pastor to conduct the memorial. There was little activity in the funeral home this day, so the two of them sat together for a soft conversation on the couch in the lobby. Recorded mortuary music played from ceiling speakers above them.

Everything was so hectic a few days ago when Chad got the call from Chris' daughter Shannon about his brother's death. Shannon took charge of notifying everyone she could, which was difficult given how distraught she was. That phone call had been all about the ambiguous details of the service. Pretty much all she knew at the time was that it would be in Albuquerque. She recalled how a few days before, she had asked her Mom to come to her house in Huntsville after Dad was done at the hospital. They would never make it past Houston. She was trying to figure out whether she could afford to bring Dan and A'Dell to the funeral with her. She wanted to be, she *needed* to be with her mother.

Albuquerque had become home, so home is where Chris pre-planned arrangements with the mortician months ago. This seemed the right place to have a service; not Denver, not Weatherford. After the police approved it following their routine investigation, Chris was cremated right there where he'd died in Houston, because Cameron said it cost too much to ship his body back home. She brought his ashes back to New Mexico for the service, after which someone else would take the remains to Weatherford in accordance with his wishes sometime in the future. The details of that trip had yet to be worked out.

Chad broke the ice first. "It's good to see he was still into golf."

"He hasn't played twice since we moved here, and that's been many years," Cameron said. "It was still about the only outside thing he cared about, though."

"I hate to bring this up, but could you tell me what happened?" This was Chad's first chance to learn from his sister-in-law the details of how his brother was found dead in their hotel room.

"He was so exhausted from the trip to Houston, and then that damn air conditioner in the room thumped so loud all night neither one of us could sleep much. I think he was a little nervous about meeting this Doctor Crosland, too." Chris' home cardiologist had referred him to the doctor in Houston to oversee a series of tests that would confirm suspicions about an advanced heart disease. The trip to go take the tests was scheduled the same day. The Albuquerque doctor told Chris he was certain that his condition would kill him soon if it was left unaddressed. "I woke up the morning of his first appointment hoping to go over his test schedule together with a cup of coffee. Chris was sitting up on the couch with all this stuff spread around him. I thought he was sleeping, because he slept just like that on the couch so often." She told how it was common for Chris to get up during the night and do something for a while when he couldn't sleep. "I was trying to be so gentle in waking him; I just thought he was sleeping." That he was. He was dead.

Preliminary reports confirmed that his heart just quit while he sat there. The things scattered around Chris when he died told Cameron that he was reminiscing of people and places while he fought sleeplessness during the night. Around him were lots of photos he must have brought in his luggage. "I didn't realize he had all those things with him," Cameron told the brother. "Why would he have these? Why would he bring them on a trip for medical tests?" She recognized few of his old friends' faces because she'd never met many of them. There were a few golf magazines around him that he bought in the airport, too. One was open to an article about an ancient seaside course in Scotland.

"I called the doctor's office the next day to tell them what happened. They talked to the coroner, but I don't know whether they learned if anything was actually wrong with him anything or not. I wonder what the tests would have shown if Chris had ever gotten the chance to take them. I guess it really doesn't matter anyway. Either way, he's still dead." Her frustration was visible. "We went down there to try to find out what was wrong with him, and he never even made it to meet the doctor. I guess it was all nothing but a big waste of time," she said. She told Chad what other notifications had been made. "A neighbor wrote an obituary. We sent it to newspapers in Weatherford and Denver. The funeral home posted it on their website. I got a sympathy card today from some man in Texas named Terry Travis, but that's about it. I called the Home Office to file the claim on his life insurance policy, but they seemed more concerned about how Chris' death affected their business. They said they sent an email to let his customers know an agent in Las Cruces will take care of them until a new local rep is found."

While he listened, Chad grew sad that he'd be the only one of Chris' siblings attending the service. He didn't know how to contact one sister, and he knew the others would spend neither the money nor the effort to get there. He wanted to change the subject. "This is nice, having a memorial in the funeral home." A compliment should precede his comment, he thought. "I'm surprised he wanted to do this, though. I'd expect he'd rather have it in a church."

"I thought so, too. But when we talked about such things last year he said that since we only attend Sunday services once or twice a month we shouldn't put them through the trouble of hosting a funeral."

Chad chuckled, "That sounds just like him."

"I told him I felt like for all the money we put in that church's plate, we deserved to have it in their chapel. But Chris said that wasn't what makes you part of a church. He just kept saying he didn't feel he'd earned having a service there." She sounded bitter, Chad thought. "He sure was emphatic about having our pastor speak over him, though," she said, looking at her watch.

"By the way, is that your dog outside?" Chad asked.

"No, what dog?"

"Little black and white dog, just outside the front door. Border collie, I think."

"Chris' dogs died several years ago – it must be a stray."

"I don't know, but he kind of acted like he was there to hold the door open for me, to greet people or something." Cameron looked at Chad like he was nuts. "Anyway, the dog looked like he was ready to sneak in with the next person that showed up. I didn't let him in, though."

"That's strange."

"He's nice and clean, too. Friendly looking, you know?" Chad wished he hadn't mentioned the animal at all. He wanted to get back to finding some way he could help her.

"Tell me what can I do?"

"I don't know. I'm still concerned about what he wanted done with his ashes."

"What do you mean?"

"He wanted his ashes combined with the dogs'." Cameron looked like she just swallowed castor oil. "That's so gross. I just don't know if I want to do that."

Chad smiled. "I remember him telling me you would say that. May I ask you; are the dogs' ashes still important for you to have around?"

"No, not at all."

"What about Chris' ashes? Are you still OK with them going to Texas, or would you prefer to keep them with you?"

"In the house with me? Are you kidding?" She snapped to the realization she was talking to the dead man's brother. "I'm sorry, I mean no, I don't."

Chad smiled, like her response was another thing Chris told him to expect when the day came to talk about it. He took her hand in a consoling gesture. "Seems like since that's what he wanted, maybe it's a way to put them all to good use. I'll take care of it for you if you'd like."

"Thank you."

"Cameron, I didn't talk to my brother often enough anymore, maybe once every couple of months on the phone, if that. You know how it is. We get busy; we forget how precious time truly is. Our parents tried to teach us to always treasure family, but we never practiced it very well. I know one thing though: there were a lot of things Chris was not, but he *was* a loving man. How can that be bad?" Cameron nodded. She knew Chad was sincere when he looked into her eyes with pure compassion.

"I can tell you what he told me every single time we spoke: he loved you more than anything in the world." He offered her a handkerchief – she had finally begun to cry.

GABRIEL'S CREEK

ACKNOWLEDGMENTS

Gabriel's Creek Golf Course and its holes are a total fabrication of my own, creations helped by memories of holes I've played around the United States.

The holes from other golf courses that characters in the book appear on while playing Gabriel's Creek are real. I've played them all with the exception of Kingsbarns in Scotland, the vision of which came from their website. I hope the owners, operators, members, and/or regular players of all these courses feel I have treated them with their deserved level of respect.

The Alabama Golf Trail, including Hampton Cove outside Huntsville, Alabama, is indeed real, and is a wonderful project worthy of consideration for any golfer's vacation.

Higdon Park Golf Course is a fictional name for a real place, at least one that existed in my childhood as a municipal course on the west side of Fort Worth. It was there that I grew up playing with the people upon whom the characters of those two chapters are based. The actual course is reported to have been recently closed by the city in favor of urban development At least it will no longer have to survive by catering to young broke hacks like me and my buddies were back then.

Weatherford and other noted cities and towns are real. Much of what I placed in them is purely fictional, including Misty Lake and Pat Neff High School.

The Denver subdivision of Antelope Run is completely fictional. I admit that I based both the development and the hole the main character plays there with his dogs upon a real community in Ocean Springs, Mississippi where we lived a few years.

Mountain View Air is my own fictional creation. I have never worked as an airline executive, nor have I ever worked in insurance.

All of the characters in the book are fictional creations of mine. Many are based on real people, some still living, some not, and some with status unknown. If you're one of them, perhaps I'll admit it to you.

This book was written through its first completed draft before I was diagnosed with cancer. That means the concept of the book and perspectives of the main character were initially written without my real personal insight of what it's like to hear such "news". Once I had, further editing preserved the thought process of this story's main character, which my experiences proved to me are quite accurate.

I was fortunate that the negative opinions of Las Vegas oncologists were rendered inaccurate when I was introduced to the Mayo Clinic in Arizona. A word of special thanks is appropriate to Dr. Nabil Wasif and to Dr. John Camoriano and their staffs at the Mayo Clinic Hospital in Phoenix and the Mayo Clinic in Scottsdale respectively. When we first discussed the poor survival odds I'd been given in Las Vegas, it was Dr. Wasif who said, "I think we can do better than that". He turned out to be right. Dr. Camoriano's oversight of my condition through and after Dr. Wasif's surgery has been worth every trip to the Mayo. I know you people don't want the credit, but in my mind, you're responsible for me living into "bonus time". Thanks.

The Boys, the dogs of the book known as Houston and Tyler, are certainly based upon my two real female dogs. My Girls are gone now but both lived until each was almost 15 years old. Their names were Misty and Lilly, a beagle and a "white dog" of questionable breed. I've had no better friends in my life – in fact, they were more like daughters. The feelings of the book's main character regarding the loss of his dogs are an accurate reflection of my personal experience.

No one knows that as well as Misty and Lilly's Las Vegas veterinarian, Dr. Cynthia Lopez. Dr. Lopez earned her place as a friend to and lover of animals long before we came to her as refugees from Hurricane Katrina. Her care for my dogs through our Las Vegas years remains a very big deal to me. We share both a love for my departed dogs and a passion for college football. I hope that means we'll remain friends for a long time.

Texas Christian University (TCU) is, of course, real. As full disclosure, though, I am an alumnus of The University of Texas at Austin. Hook 'em. TCU was near the home where I grew up in Fort Worth and where I hung out a lot as a kid, for a lot of reasons. It fit the fictional development needs for the young years of the book's main character. It is also the alma matter of two people who provided me with critical spiritual support in Las Vegas before their retirement, oddly enough, back to Fort Worth. I wrote the TCU-related parts of this book before getting to know the Reverend Doctors David and Ginger Jarman, but admit that part of why it remains written this way is in homage to them. I am proud to call them my friends. So there.

Ginger also read of one of the earliest completed drafts of the book, and provided ample encouragement toward its eventual completion and publication. Whether she should get credit or blame for that remains unclear at this writing but her intentions were most assuredly well-placed. David's contributions include leading me to participate in his "Through the Fire" support group, which I credit greatly with my recovery. They have my eternal thanks.

The cover was created by Michael Leadingham of Las Vegas, Nevada (michaelleadingham.com). I greatly appreciate his artwork on my behalf. He also provided helpful input on late drafts of the book which were most valuable.

My affair with the game of golf began before I was ten years old and continues to this day. A father with polio was envious of anyone's ability to play the game and always encouraged me to stay close to it. His brother, my uncle, provided a worthy surrogate to peak my adolescent interest. He was a recreational golfer who taught me the point was to have fun, and gave me a family golf idol to look up to. Those two men are long gone, but I thank them just the same.

How I managed to grow up in the footsteps of Ben Hogan and Byron Nelson, closely follow Ben Crenshaw and Tom Kite at UT, but still play like I always have makes me no different from millions of others. We prove you don't have to be a quality player to still love the game, its history and its characters.

Finally but most importantly, this book would be impossible in so many ways without my wife, Mary. Of the many things with which I've been blessed, her love is at the top.

www.ingramcontent.com/pod-product-compliance
Lightning Source LLC
Chambersburg PA
CBHW030820310726
48980CB00006B/560/J

* 9 7 8 0 9 9 1 5 6 0 5 2 3 *

PRAISE FOR PYROTECHNICON

'A rich dessert of a novel, filled with finely crafted wit and adventure — Adam Browne has resurrected Cyrano in fine form. Delightful!'
Greg Bear — Hugo and Nebula award-winning science fiction author

'Cyrano de Bergerac returns to science fiction after far too long an absence. *PYROTECHNICON* is a shadow play of clockwork whimsy, strange invention, and baroque puns. Browne zestfully steers his lighter-than-air word-balloons through a vast and improbable universe of plot. Sit back and enjoy the ride.'
Michael Swanwick — bestselling author of *The Dragons of Babel*

'It is three centuries before Apollo 11, and there are half-angel-power spaceships, angst engines, and even perfumed cannons. *PYROTECHNICON* is a fantastically surreal and entertaining tale of improbable sciences, unheard-of technologies, and very original adventures.'
Sean McMullen — Aurealis and Ditmar Award-winning author of the Greatwinter and The Moonworlds Saga series

'The title does not mislead. *PYROTECHNICON* is a literary cabinet of curiosities filled with lush imagery and exotic notions. A delicious concoction of swashbucklery and delight. Highly recommended.'
Jeff Vandermeer — World Fantasy Award-winning author of *Finch*

'Simply dazzling. *PYROTECHNICON* is an audacious triumph of the imagination.'
James Maxey — author of the Bitterwood Series

PYROTECHNICON

PYROTECHNICON

BEING A TRUE ACCOUNT OF CYRANO DE BERGERAC'S FURTHER ADVENTURES AMONG THE STATES AND EMPIRES OF THE STARS

by

Himself (dec'd)

(Englished from the French by Adam Browne)

First published in Australia in 2012
by coeur de lion publishing
www.coeurdelion.com.au
Please direct all enquiries to the publisher at:
keith@coeurdelion.com.au

ISBN 9780987158727

This project has been assisted by the Australian Government through the Australia Council, its arts funding and advisory body.

Illustrations by Adam Browne
Cover and internal design by Keith Stevenson
Printed in Australia by Lightning Source

National Library of Australia Cataloguing-in-Publication entry:

Author: Browne, Adam, 1963-

Title: Pyrotechnicon : being a true account of Cyrano de Bergerac's further adventures among the states and
empires of the stars / Adam Browne.

ISBN: 9780987158727 (hbk.)

Subjects: Science fiction.

Dewey Number: A823.4

For Julie

TABLE OF CONTENTS

A NOTE ON THE TEXT

Although Cyrano de Bergerac's sprightly space adventures, posthumously published in two volumes in 1656 and 1661, belong to the tradition of all fantastic tales, ultimately they came to be classed as science fiction. We can imagine Cyrano himself finding this categorisation restrictive, a quality the genre characteristically abhors, as did he, a notorious freethinker.

Perhaps it was because science fiction publishing seems so enamoured of trilogies that speculation arose about the existence of a third volume in Cyrano's series. When efforts to find it came to nothing, however, the consensus was that the manuscript was lost or destroyed, if it had ever been written at all.

Then came the United States *MER-V* Mission to Mars, its rover robot famously rolling aside a small boulder on the Meridiani Planum to uncover the text you are about to read. Predictably, doubts have been raised about the discovery and the authenticity of the text. As one observer has commented, aside from its innumerable scientific, cultural, linguistic, social and political anachronisms, it appears to be legitimate in every way.

This is a debate best left to others. We present the story found there without speculation or comment, except to quote the Demon of Socrates in Cyrano's first adventure: "If there is something you men cannot understand, you either imagine that it is spiritual or that it does not exist. Both conclusions are quite false. The proof of this is that there are perhaps a million things in the universe which you would need a million quite different organs to know . . ."

Adam Browne

CHAPTER THE ZEROTH:

DAWN

Le 28 juillet de l'an 1655

Dear Reader:

My nose surfaced first, rising from slow waves of sleep, from darkness into darkness.

The hour was early. My feet were cold.

I heard a baker's horse clopping through the Toulouse streets, and a costermonger's soft singing as he prepared his stall. Then a ragged clatter of footsteps, and the laughter and drunken shouts of revellers leaving a tavern after a long night. I heard one of them spewing into the gutter, and by the grunts forced out of him as he heaved — the shapes of them, as it were, the grunted consonants, the bowely vowels — I knew the fellow for a Gascon.

I smiled in the dark, remembering my confrères, d'Artagnan and le Bret and all the others at Arras.

The revellers departed. There was silence.

My eyes wandered, focusing for a moment on my nose, proud, flexuous, faintly luminous in the gloom — and ah, reader, what a nose!

Had you been there, you might have missed me in the darkness, but never my nose, the most eminent member, great in size and noble of form, and conspicuous to the highest degree.

Did not a wise man once declare that a large nose is the mark of a witty, affable, generous and liberal soul?

Is it not said that the Emperor Heliogabalus made choice of big-nosed soldiers, who are known to possess stout hearts sure as redheads are fair of skin?

Mine is the bravest of appendages, always going before me into peril. Had I a selection of noses, I would pick this one every time.

It is my mark, my emblem; it is my *grande panache.*

By my nose you may know me. Cyrano de Savinien Hercule de Bergerac, lover, poet, inventor, swordsman — the great Captain Satan — a man of ferocious blade and pretty talent!

Là! I threw aside the covers, threw on this item of clothing, and this. Thus, I strode to the balcony, facing east, with a view of the fields past the town.

Where I sensed a softening of the night on the horizon, the first pink hints touching the sky. A fine glimmer against the most distant hills, approaching, touching a ravine, now a knot of cascades, brawling waters flinging rainbows skyward.

I returned the dawn's grin.

For the approaching day, I knew it, would be a splendid one, as would all my days forevermore, since I had proposed marriage to the choicest of earthly beings. Mademoiselle Magdelaine Robineau de Neuvillette, known as Roxane.

My kissing cousin, a lady so fair that even her mirror was jealous of her beauty.

My dawn, my Juliet . . . That she returned my love in good favour was still a source of wonder to me.

But with the *fact* of the wedding settled, there remained the question of *when.* I confess, reader, to an odd reluctance.

I was the hound who corners the lion, then wonders if it is up to the next step . . .

But enough. More of that in its place . . . For here it was. Here, now. The sunlight, its molten colours spilling over the fields to the outskirts of the town. I readied myself for a ritual in which I sometimes indulged, and which I share with you now.

You should know, reader, that as other men were samplers of wines, I was a connoisseur of dawns. A fine nose is of benefit to both pursuits.

'Twas a matter of length. Of distance . . . Isaac Beekman purposed to reckon the speed of light with twin cannon, mirrors and a measure a mile in length — any less, and the readings would have been impossible to take . . . (Beekman's conclusion was that light "be extraordinarily rapid", a result agreed upon by subsequent experimenters).

So it was for me, with the reach of my nose such that I could stand in yesterday while the tip extended into the morrow, the sensitive member dipping into the day to come, wherewith to judge its qualities . . .

As for those who insist, against reason, that this practice is but one of my jests, or worse, a delusion, I have but this to say . . . but ah, no time! For here it was! The dawn!

The day! Coming! Dashing and gushing! Splashing over the grounds of the château!

Which would it be? A red, a white? Crisp as a Chardonnay? Earthy and oaken as an old sherry? Would it possess, like to the day I proposed to Roxane, a scent of dusky roses and cherries with glints of liquorice . . .?

It was upon me, it was *here*, it was now . . . The moment. The shimmering instant with sunlight warming the end of my nose, but not yet touching the plane of my face.

I smelt futurity. I drew it in, warmed it in my sinuses. I asked of it the question: Would the morrow be a happy one?

And even as the negative, the bitter, the stinging answer came, I saw, over the château wall, the façade of the neighbouring hôtel — Roxane's hôtel — and a darkness, a creatured darkness descending upon it . . .

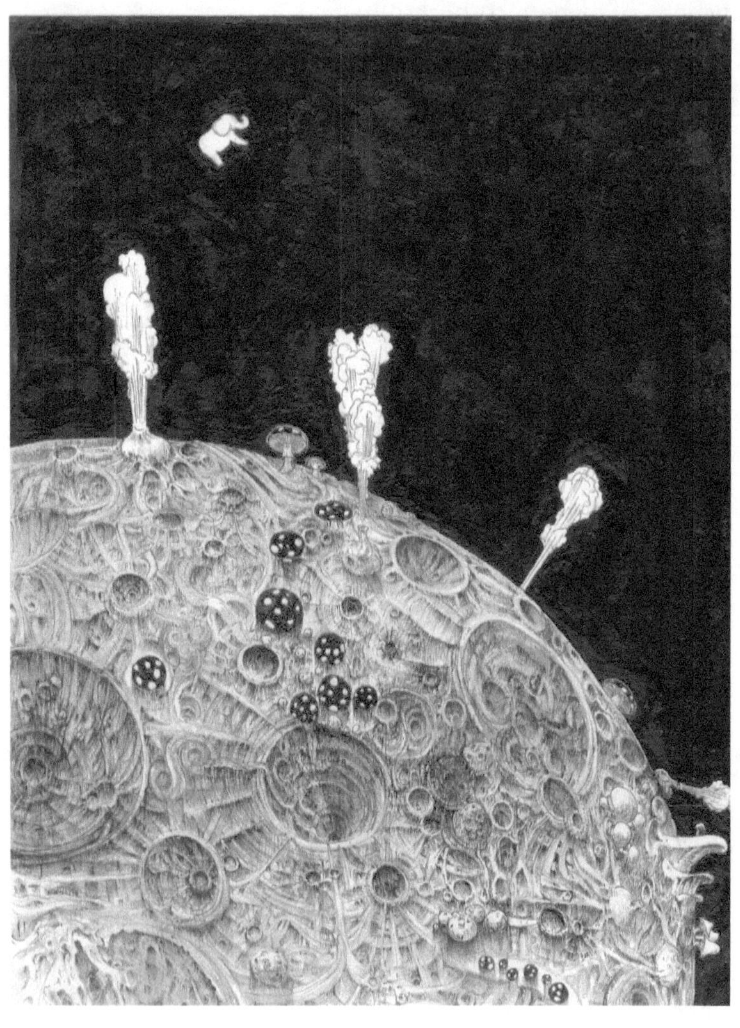

And still upward in my elephant I rose, away from that oozy zoo; up, up, delivered from the fog, nimbly, trunkfirst into a lightly nightingaled sky.

1ST DAY

CHAPTER THE FIRST:

THE CONFRATERNITY OF THE PASSION

Make haste, reader! What, you are still in the room? Là! Long empty! Look you, through the window! See, I am already racing through the château's courtyard, barrelling through the property owned by my friend and patron the Baron de Colignac, once the home of M. Adhémar Montiel de Sainte-Blandine, the Mad Count of Toulouse . . .

Past the observatory, the tumbledown library, the château and grounds a mazy map of madness writ in stone and wood. Now past the famous pond, its water imported from the pool outside the Taj Mahal, skimmed from the pool's surface with infinite care; but whether the Count had achieved his goal of acquiring the reflection of the Taj (a glimpse of minarets in the stagnant water, perhaps, a hint of the hot white skies of Ind in the strew of lilies?), I could not say.

For already I was gone, out the gates, rushing through the streets of Toulouse. Now an avenue, now a boulevard, now the rue Gambetta. Now the hôtel where my love was residing, where I had seen that darkness, descending . . .

I banged at the front door. I pushed past the sleepy domestic who answered, through the entry hall, past more startled factotums and dogsbodies of various breed and pedigree — up the staircase, into her bedchamber.

Quiet. The cats asleep, the curtains drawn, the candles snuffed . . . but there was a light in here nevertheless.

"Roxane."

She stirred, glowing, pinkling roundnesses and roundling pinknesses, my precieuse in delicious déshabillé.

"Cyrano?" She rubbed her eyes.

I stepped closer, rapt as any astronomer, gazing on the firmament of her face, the orbits of her eyes. The world upon which my destiny turned, drawing me down.

"Forgive me, my dear, for entering unannounced."

Her hand was milk-cool in mine — "Cyrano, your entry will always be welcome." — but in her eyes was a hot look, and she leaned forward, her nightgown parting to offer the merest hints of the terrain beneath: the soft hills, the furzy dales.

She smiled.

She touched a finger, just once, to the length of my nose, a sensation of such unique and delicate pleasure that the Church would have declared it a sin on the instant had it known.

My earlier urgency was forgotten, replaced by another. That we must wait was intolerable, a nonsense. It would be sin *not* to sin.

I moved to meet her lips . . .

"Sir!" She sat back, scandalised. "Not until we are wed!" She clutched one of her cats to her breast as a shield.

"But, my dear, I —"

"And when will that be, may I ask? Oh dear, I forgot, Patapouff!" — this to the cat. "He has not set the date! What's that?" she said. "You say he does not love me? You think he is not resolved to marry me at all? Oh, Patapouff!"

"I assure you, Patapouff, my resolve is of the stiffest sort."

Roxane glared. She said nothing. She did not need to. She had said it too many times: "When first you asked for my hand, I refused, do you recall?" — this was what she did not say. "Not because I did not love, but because I loved too much," she did not add. "I feared I would be your widow almost as soon as I was your bride. But you vowed you would forgo your sword, Cyrano," she did not go on to say. "And now I see you stumbling about, sword in hand —"

But hold —

I looked about.

"What is it?" Roxane said.

Something. I stood away from the bed.

She stared. "What folly is this?"

"There is some danger . . ."

"Fie! You are drunk! You have been on a carouse with your friends again!"

"I am in earnest, Mademoiselle. There is something terrible . . ."

"Truly?" She laughed suddenly. "Is this the beginning of one of your adventures?"

"I hope not."

"Oh, you love adventure!"

"Not a bit of it."

"Will *I* be in this one?"

As children, I had sometimes allowed her along on a quest — the two of us in a forest or meadow, playing as musketeers or crusader knights or soldiers, armed with reeds and helmeted with cooking pots.

I had regretted it every time. I forever had to remind her not to titter while we were locked in combat with some imagined foe; nor could I insist that she not treat it as a game, for she would return that it *was* a game, was it not . . .?

"What is that smell?" she said.

Yes . . . How could I have missed it? That yellow smell: opium, no question. A strong blend, by the scent; no dross, thick, potent. My eyes burned . . .

And now, swelling from the shadows, a gallery of grotesques . . .

"How now!" I cried. "How durst you to enter this

room?"

The figures moved not, nor answered: a *tableau vivant* of strange, staring fellows dressed as for a masque; actors, by their habits, of the type called Frantics, some in close cuirasses to signify Madness; others costumed as for female rôles, disquietingly pretty, their bodices contrived into well-favoured forms.

"Come . . ." I coughed. The air was thick, the tarry, Eastern sweetness reaching into my blood. "Come," I began again. "Open your throats and answer, lest I open them for you. How come you to enter this maiden's chamber?"

"One might ask you the same question, Monsieur de Bergerac."

Through a wrack of corrupt clouds there stepped a man.

My sabre flashed an inch from his throat. My mustachios bristled. My nose (I knew) was terrible to see.

The man smiled, a yellow crescent. Fat he was, as an Amiens pâté, and cue-ball bald. His costume was less splendid but more curious than those of his confrères, with culottes and jerkin of gooseturd-green baize scuffed and dusted with pale blue chalk, the whole cut from the playing surface of an old billiard table.

Nor was he unlike a billiard table in heft and general geography: massy, oblong, set upon heavy pedestal legs.

"Calm yourself, Monsieur," he said. "We are but harmless entertainers, members of *La Confrérie de la Passion*, engaged to stage Mystery Plays in this establishment."

"I care not a cucumber for your plays." The point of my sword pricked his bosom at the spot where the white ball is placed at the start of play. "You will tell me, Sir, why you are in this lady's room."

"Fie." He chuckled around his long and elaborate pipe. "Why do you protest? See, your Dulcinea is unharmed."

I made out Roxane in her bed. I saw fear in her eyes,

but also a measure of excitement . . .

I noticed the fat man looking at her also. I lowered my blade to his breeches. "Have a care where your eyes wander, Sir, for what is a billiard table without its balls?"

"Pray, allow me to explain," the billliardman said, "I am a student of sleep, and of dreams. This substance I am smoking, for instance, it is not opium, but a gum derived from dreams. 'Tis the brownish resin one finds accreted upon old pillowslips and unwashed nightcaps, collected and rendered into an intoxicating paste." He puffed away, the pipe's fumes wreathing bluely. "Pipe dreams, Monsieur de Bergerac. They make for a sovereign smoke . . ."

The fumes thickening, entering my senses; a fizzy, fatty, eelish feeling, a slow swell of liquid electricity salamandering up the staircase of my spine. "You know my name," I managed, "but who are you?"

"I am the guild's Master of Secrets," he said with a bow. "With my mechanisms, my smoke and my mirrors, I bring life to the theatrical dreams our public so enjoys. But they are fools who think the proscenium keeps those dreams from oozing out into the world. You, Cyrano, are you sure you did not wake this morning to find yourself still asleep? To me it seems a most dreamish situation."

"This is no dream," I said. "This is the wake-a-day world."

"As to that, we shall see."

He glanced at his watch, a heavy, misshapen mechanism which I will not trouble to describe except to say it was exactly the timepiece one would expect a billiardtable to carry. " 'Tis time," he declared. "A five-act play, I think — five days in one, a million years in a moment — the hero suffering many and various reversals . . ."

Roxane gathered her bedclothes about her. "What is he prating about, Cyrano?"

"He is speaking his last words, my dear," I said. "As

a rule, Sir, I am loath to kill an unarmed opponent, but I shall allow the exception to prove the rule."

I leapt and swung . . . or made to do so . . .

Was it my blade or my hand that was so hesitant, wavering as if viewed through water?

Again I tried to strike. Again I could not.

I glared at my blade. Still it lolled weakly, as if drunk. My sabre was not sober.

The Master of Secrets laughed. "Well, then! This has been most satisfactory as a prologue, but as with all dreams and scenes, our meeting must come to an end. We should strike the set *strikingly*, I think. I believe *periaktoi* are the best mechanism here."

"Cyrano!" Roxane's voice. "They are coming closer!"

I could not see her . . . the mists, the darkness.

Again I lunged. I stumbled; I who had put a hundred men to the rout at the Porte de Nesle. I staggered like an infant. My sword was one half of Fate's Shears. It flailed. I tripped over a cat.

"If you are unfamiliar with the term, Cyrano," the Master of Secrets said, "*periaktoi* are those collapsible equilateral flats one sees at the rear of the stage, closed like a set of shutters — *thus!*" And he reached up and plucked at the corners of the darkness and folded it and, with a creak of canvas and hemp, packed it neatly away, folding it all, the Frantics, the smoke, even himself, into a rectangle that closed in and in on itself until it was no more.

The Master of Secrets had vanished, and Roxane, her voice trailing behind her: "Cyrano . . . Help me . . . he is taking me . . ."

She was gone. The bedchamber was empty. I was alone.

CHAPTER THE SECOND:

OMNIUM SOMNIUM

I remember bursting from the room; downstairs; the lobby, hoping there to see sign of her or her abductors, in vain.

I remember thundering curses, raining threats.

I remember staff rushing out, some with umbrellas, thinking a storm must have entered the hôtel.

How I roared! How my sword flashed, how it flickered!

Some of the staff fell back, others laughed, making game of me. Some made bold to declare me mad.

I snatched up the nearest, a serving boy, his hair blowing in the gale of my rage; I demanded on pain of death he tell me all he knew of *La Confrérie de la Passion*. In sobs (how it shames me to recall his terrified face!) he swore he had never heard the name.

Disgusted, I cast him away and caught another. He too claimed to know nothing. I called him a liar; I described the Frantics and the billiardtablish Master of Secrets — and now the servants no longer thought me mad, but were sure of it.

Dismayed, the storm departed.

I fell through the streets as if the town had been upended. I tumbled into the château, crying out for my friend, the Baron de Colignac.

He emerged from a doorway, shocked, and guided me into the atelier where he kept certain of his curiosities. Here my woes poured from me and, as I spoke, the cramped chamber began to seem an embodiment of my state of mind — trapped, lost among gimcracks and dusty shadows, ormolu whim-whams, nightmare gewgaws, nonsense and horrors . . .

Through it all, my friend the Baron stood by the hearth, calm and strong, listening carefully.

The Baron de Peyrescous de Colignac was, all agreed, the finest of fellows: a scholar, stout swordsman and worthy ally. We fought together at Arras: more than once he had saved my life, and I his. It was a signal honour to be friends with a man of such kidney, and he proved his worth again that day.

No sooner had I spoken than he took action. Gathering certain of his servants — dark-faced men with a set to their jaws and roughness to their ruffs that suggested they were men who knew which end of a cudgel was which — he tasked them with a search through the town's demimonde. They were to sweep the taverns, bawdy houses and other low places where such villains might congregate.

And for this I was grateful, but I knew the men would be gone for hours or longer. What might happen to her in the meantime?

I fretted. I put energy into it. I sat, then stood, then sat again. I got up and picked up a mummified toad from a display table. I read a tag on its leg, which claimed it had been born of a Gypsy woman. I put it down. I sat.

"Listen," said de Colignac at last, "here is an idea. When one desires information, where does one go but a library?"

"You are suggesting I wile the time by reading books?"

"I am. Specifically, why do you not try the library on my estate? — no, do not answer that — there are many reasons why you might not. It is in sorry shape, I know. As for the librarian, he is, I cannot deny it, a lunatic. In his defence, however, he also stinks."

He paused for some snuff, returned the box to his breast pocket, sneezed.

"Now then . . ." he said, and paused again, clearly

forgetting the thrust of his discourse.

"The library," I said, with restraint.

"Ah, yes. My friend, I know it sounds odd, but there is something *to* this library, something strange . . . Suffice it that I am not suggesting this merely to distract you from your worrying." He smiled. "Or not entirely for that reason, anyway."

De Colignac's manner was so earnest that it compelled, if not belief, then a little hope, and if I consented, then at least the poor fellow would be spared a few minutes of my fretful company.

"In truth," I said, standing, "I have found that when things are at their darkest, books have often served to light my way. Perhaps they will do so again."

He grinned and thumped me on the shoulder. "Just so!"

The library was in the poorest repair, having received no maintenance since the Mad Count's disappearance. It was an architecture in which one felt as much outside as in — an eccentric, domed edifice with much of its structure collapsed or eroded away, the remains of its ceiling supported by the idolatrous masts of Byzantine ships defeated in war. The weather, offered little disincentive to enter, had composted many of the books to a rich, wordy loam, the lot of them piled in a shambolic mountain that leaned hugger-mugger against the northern wall with, incredible to say, a tree growing near the summit, its roots tangled among volumes touching, one fancied, on agricultural matters.

Grootschalk, the librarian, greeted me as I entered. An eccentric, domed edifice of a fellow, but his grin was bright, infested as it was with a species of phosphorescent tooth-moss. "*Guten tag, mein Herr.* How may I be of service?"

I told him I required information regarding the actors'

troupe known as *La Confrérie de la Passion*, and quick about it.

"*Oh, nein, nein!* The library, ha ha, she mislikes such a . . . blunt approach." Mosquito larvæ wriggled in the spittle of his tongue.

"I warn you, Monsieur," I said, "I am of an ill-humour."

"But you must understand, this is a most *sensitive* library. To enter into her — well, a man of the world knows such things he must not rush, *ja?*"

Enough. I grabbed the fellow by his academic gown. "You seem determined to see me draw my sword, Sir."

"Ha ha! I see you are in character, *Herr Cyrano! Ja*, look not so surprised. Your books are in here also. Your adventures, your poems, *ja*. How amusing it is to see you make of yourself *eine Karikatur* — flinging people about, *ja*, collecting foes as others collect flowers, ha ha."

He freed himself at the expense of his already ragged robe, leaving tatters in my hands. "*Es ist* all just information, *ja? Die Informationen*, flowing all about *und* through — seeping like a moist heat through *die Bücher*."

He backed away, his laughter roman-candling the gloom with psychotic crocodile-green spittle. "*Informationen*," he said, "it is physical, *nicht wahr?* It is the vital humour — like the phlegm, like the yellow bile — like the man-seed, ha ha . . ." He leapt upon the base of the book-mountain.

He ascended, the lower slopes dotted with missals like Alpine flowers. "It is a ghostly liquor, *mein Herr — perspiratio insensibilis*. It is the generative principle, ha ha; *und* the knowledge in this library —" his grin brightened — "it is *carnal*."

Navigating by toothlight, he achieved the middle heights. "All *Kreation* made of it, ha ha, the male *und* female principles heaving *und* pulsing. The *Informationen*, the quickening seed," he said. "The germy moisture, *nicht wahr?*

— coursing through the library, downward and down, ha ha, through her crevices *und* intimacies."

He stopped suddenly and began digging through the books at his feet, calling out their titles: the great *Monstrorum Historia* of Ulisse Aldrovandi; a document by Galileo on the dimensions and location of Hell; another, telling of fowl born from barnacles, the Ezox Fish, which tastes of pork, and the vegetable Lamb of Tartary (fabulations, I believe, invented by clergymen and other humbugs who wished to eat meat on a slow-moving fast-day).

He froze. He dipped a finger into the interstices between the books. "Under the influence of the *Lebenwärme* . . . Worms and innumerable other creatures, they arise. Just so, *mein Herr, mit die* informational humours. Hot *und* wet, eddying through the library — causing her to beget . . ." — he plunged his hand into a damp cleft, as if trying to haul a root or corm from maternal clay — ". . . this!"

Triumphantly, he delivered forth a small text from the side of the mountain.

I peered. He came down, presented it to me. I misliked to touch it. It was a scurvy, sorry tome, and by the title, *Omnium Somnium*, it seemed to have precisely nothing to do with *La Confrérie de la Passion*. "You say this is the book I am looking for?"

"*Nein, mein Herr!*" he cried, loosing a mad green coil of laughter into the air. "*Hier ist das Buch* that for *you* was looking!"

In open affront to my feelings, the day was blithe, the château grounds filled with a poetic light. 'Twas like to the grin of an idiot at a funeral.

I sat in a bower to study my prize.

The cover was damp and embossed with letters of what looked like eczema. I opened it, expecting little, which expectation was roundly met.

I shall spare you, reader, a minute account of my efforts to make sense of that wet jumble: a transcription of the witterings of a Fourteenth Century convulsionnaire, a nun, Sister Marie Jakob-Lôrber. A victim of the "sacred disease", her ecstasies had wrenched her mind from her person, her soul purportedly rising from its cage of flesh to wander the spheres of the Heavens . . . Clearly, she was what our more enlightened age would recognise as a sufferer of the hysteric ailment, come of her womb, which Galen tells us delights in fragrances and is averse to foetors, moving of itself about the flanks, or obliquely to the liver or spleen.

I cursed that already-cursed woman. I'd been without hope, and now even that was dashed.

I spat and flung the book to the grass, where it fell to pieces, its pages borne away on the breeze — all but one, clinging to my ankle.

With a shout of disgust, I reached down to peel it away. As I did so, my eye fell on a certain passage. My anger dissolved.

I read more closely. The passage came in the Sister's observations of the inhabitants of the planet Venus.

I have it still, and reproduce it here in full:

"It was granted me of the LORD," she wrote, "to beholde these Creetures right clear, and to Know they had Tyred of their Rightfulle Spouses in their Beddes, and so had Polluted the Bedde Steads in their stead; and not just the Beddes; they had their Wicked Way with other divers Objectes be sides; *Ward-Robes* did they Abuse, and *Psalteries*, and *Chamberpottes*, and *Sun-Beames*, and *Fog-Whisps*; and all Manner of Thing and Stuff; and in *Due Season*, these Actes resulted in Offspring, and the sin of the FATHERS was visited upon the CHILDREN; who bear yet the Marke of their parents' Iniquity; Possesseth they a Family Resemblance to the Objectes so used; Ill-favoured

Creetures, neither this nor that: Housemaids, there are, like unto Hatstands; Swains like unto Hay-wains; and *Theatrical Impresarios resembling in every particular the Tables upon which Noblemen play at Ball-games with Billiards . . .*"

I looked up, head swimming.

This last, if it was not in italics, appeared so to me, tilted with the world . . .

The likeness to the Master of Secrets could not be a coincidence . . . or if it was, it was the kind that was too compelling to be denied.

I felt the binding of the ties of fate. Very well then. I stood, feet planted wide apart, hands on my hips. I grinned at the sky.

So. Venus. All that remained was the matter of getting there.

CHAPTER THE THIRD:

L'ELÉPHANT AÉROSPATIAL

Many years before, the Mad Count of Toulouse had caused to be built in the grounds of his estate a zoölogical garden, with the aim of stocking it with every manner of beast. But like many of his type, the Count was a fellow of enthusiasms as suddenly adopted as they were abandoned.

The place had fallen into disrepair not long after the making of it, and by the time de Colignac had purchased the property, such animals as there were had been sold off or died of neglect; some, it was suggested by the bailiffs, may even have been consumed by vagabonds.

Now, as it was for the Count's library, so it was for his zoo, where the only beasts that remained were the vermin that may be seen in any ruinous place.

The outer wall was broken, the grounds were exposed to frosts and fogs, and Decay had been allowed to stride about adding her fantastic touches to the already grotesque fancies of the cages and ménageries — among which may be counted the Animalcule House.

In design, I should say it was not the most curious building to be seen there, but the intention behind it was such that it alone would have sufficed to label its author mad.

Built in the likeness of a microscope — the 'eyepiece', an angled, cylindrical tower of brass and teak, rising above a boxy 'stage' where the specimen was stationed — it was made to house the results of the Count's foray into the then new discipline, now called *Microbiology*.

Or perhaps the term is not apposite here.

For, shunning the magnifying lenses normally

considered indispensable to that science, the Count had opted instead to breed, "these lyttle Creatures to a Bigness more agreeable to Studie and Admiration", as may be read in his notes preserved in de Colignac's library.

This procedure, the Count reasoned, should take but a week to achieve, as the animalcules' generations were a mere five-and-twenty minutes long.

As for the outcome of this enterprise, there was nothing in his notes signifying success or failure, but there was dark talk among the staff, tales of shapeless *things* sighted in the night — reports of noises, lights — of cats and dogs straying in, never to be seen again, or their raddled skeletons found days later . . .

Faugh! Peasants' prattle!

But at the fall of night, when the mists rolled in, I confess that the sight of that great eyepiece, the very upthrust finger of Reason, touched my heart with a dread that reason could do nothing to dispel.

I looked forward to lifting off and away from the place as soon as possible.

After my revelation in the gardens, I had hastened back to de Colignac, and breathlessly told him of my plans to travel to Venus. Whereat he had proved himself yet again to be the very definition of a friend.

Neither did he scoff, nor stare, nor even hesitate, but pledged to put all his considerable resources at my disposal, for which I remain forever indebted to him . . . But let it be said, also, that as we set to devising the manner of my voyage, I looked up more than once to see him regarding me with a certain crooked smile, the same, indeed, he wore when considering some choice bit of lunacy from the Mad Count . . .

My friend's ruling passion was for the bizarre, and sometimes I suspected he saw me merely as another oddity for his *Wunderkammer* . . .

No! It was an unworthy thought, and I cast it out as soon as it occurred . . .

To the matter of my vessel:

For the hull, I had decided on an old orangery in the eastern corner of the zoo. It was of lead-framed glass, in moderate poor repair, shaped into the likeness of an elephant, its trunk arching to spout a fountain of grass and flowering weeds. De Colignac had set his domestics to scrubbing and cleaning, and an engineer to separating its legs from their foundations. We ourselves fitted out the interior with optical and astronomical instruments; comestibles stacked in crates; some warm garments; a few books to pass the time between the worlds; a comfortable armchair, securely fixed to the floor — and, lastly, a box of rocks, mounted on sturdy oaken girders at the cabin's mathematical centre.

Our main preparations finished, we paused for a meal late in the evening, using an invention of my own devising, being a fine copper webwork of heat-conducting wires pierced through a haunch of lamb, so that a single candle flame sufficed to cook the meat in a minute or so.

While we ate, I noticed de Colignac studying the box with interest.

"Meteorites, are they not?" he said, studying the rocks within.

"They are," I said. "Gathered by myself some years ago from a strewnfield on the Dar al Gani Plateau. Note the venereal gleam of their crystalline facets, glittering the very colour of the Evening Star."

"You mean . . .?"

"Yes, my friend. From studies of their micro-pockets of fossil-gases, I have determined that these stones derive from the planet Venus, likely blasted here when that world was full-struck by a planetesimal or comet."

"I see," he said.

"Ah! But do you see how they will help me in my journey? Know you the gravitational theory formulated in Plato's *Timæus*? *Like attracts like*, that is the rule. It is the tendency of bodies towards their kin that gives them the property of weight: just as the kinship of terrestrial stones with our Earth causes them to fall to the ground, so too will a rock from Venus be attracted to its mother world."

"But how is it these stones did not rise to Venus before this?" He took a bite of the meat, grimaced, and began picking fine copper wire from his teeth.

"Come, friend," I said, "has fatigue so blinded you? Can you not perceive that they are clotted with terrestrial soil? As soon as I clean them of earthly matter, they will begin their ascent towards their mother world."

"Of course! Most ingenious!" That crooked smile again. "And you happened to have these stones with you?"

"I carry many things against the possibility they will prove useful. What of it?"

He but laughed, and shook his head, and I was about to say something a little sharp in reply, when from without there came a *clang!* — then another; and now a *crash!* as one of the elephant's glass panes was smashed asunder!

I snatched up a lantern. We hastened outside.

The fog! It was so thick! I'd never seen its like . . .

Then again: the whistle of a missile — a projectile passing fearfully close before it crashed against the orangery . . .

It fell to the ground, and I retrieved it. A crossbow bolt, a heavy, unsubtle thing, its shaft improvised from what seemed an old billiard cue. Doubtless the work of my enemy.

Another bolt sizzled past. We fell to a crouch. Yet another zinged off the stones an inch from my fingers.

Glancing up, I noticed the arrows' paths remained clearly discernible in the fog minutes after the arrows themselves had passed.

I looked a question over at de Colignac, who nodded. He had noticed it too. Stout fellow!

Plucking up our rapiers with our courage, we rose, and in a crouching jog, followed the arrows' converging wakes.

This was a long, terrible run, every twist of the mists a seeming face — cages drifting, louring, ghostly . . . The *Musée des Hommes*; a great broken crab; the Monkey House, a dead baboon grinning within like to madness manifest in the mind of a soft, sick fog god . . .

"*Here*," de Colignac whispered. He had found the end of the arrows' paths; or rather, their beginning. There was nothing.

A shaped nothing, a hollow of clear air with a not-unbilliardtablish form.

The fat man had stood here, firing at us.

My sword found but thin satisfaction in the mists. "Come out!" I cried. "Show yourself, poltroon, and I will have the head off you!"

By way of answer — *whissst!* — a bolt from another direction . . .

We traced the arrow's trajectory, coming again to a Master of Secrets-shaped hollow, arm raised in a vulgar gesture. A smaller hollow billowed in the fog before his mouth. The shape, I fancied, of mocking laughter.

"This seems a slippery enemy," said de Colignac.

"Slippery and terrible." I looked at him. "This is my fight, my friend. You should leave me to deal with him."

"Oho! Whence comes this selfishness?" de Colignac said. "You have had all the finest battles to yourself — more than a thousand, by my account — surely you do not mean to claim this little one too?"

"You do not fear this fellow's crossbow?"

"Heaven forfend! In any case, his bow is less to be feared than his arrows."

We laughed, then ducked as yet another bolt lisped past.

De Colignac stood. "He is the trespasser, not I. 'Twill not be I who leaves, but he!"

I clapped him on the shoulder. "Excellent friend!"

We set off, following the arrow's paths. Shadows and vagaries; masses rising and falling; a tall form rising before us, a columnar shape in the fog.

With a feeling of inevitability I recognised it as the Animalcule House.

"Ah." De Colignac paused. "Suddenly this game has lost a measure of its fun."

"The bolts were fired from within," I said. "As I see it, we have little choice."

De Colignac looked as if he were about to speak, then nodded silently.

The door to the building hung open. The clouds parted as we stepped within, the Moon staring down the barrel of the eyepiece, fixing us in its blanching gaze.

Never have I felt so exposed, so tiny, so helpless . . .

We moved on, into the microscope "stage", being a rectangular building of dark wooden panels, flat-roofed and almost entirely given over to decay. The footing seemed greasy, which I attributed to moss until I spied the light of my lantern reflecting from the floor. " 'Tis of glass," de Colignac whispered, "the microscope's specimen-slide —"

Hush! A noise! A creaking as of old leather.

I shone my light forward, seeing only shadows. The creaking ceased.

"Rats?" I whispered.

"Have you not noticed?" de Colignac replied. "There are none in here."

True. Odd. The rest of the zoo swarmed with them.

We resumed our progress, through shadows and rot and dripping water.

Whisst! — an arrow! It struck the lantern, which smashed on the ground, extinguished.

We squatted beside it, facing either way, swords raised. Moonlight diffused through the mist, the holed ceiling.

Again: that leathery noise. Vile, appalling. A rhythm to it now. The sound of a dead goat's laughter; of an octopus eating a watermelon.

Although I style myself a man whose heart is enticed above all by the acquisition of knowledge, I felt I could live out my days in happiness if the source of those sounds remained a mystery forever . . .

Whisst, whisst, whisst! — bolts from the right, one passing so close I felt the breeze of it on my cheek.

De Colignac was not so fortunate. He grunted and fell to one knee.

I knelt beside him. He was breathing shallowly. A bolt protruded from the right side of his chest. "It is not deep, I think," he said. I felt it with my hand. Only a little blood where the shaft met his body. I took hold. De Colignac tensed. I *pulled.*

It would not budge. It was buried more deeply than I had supposed.

Taking a firmer grip, I pulled again. His breath hissed between his teeth, a sound more expressive of pain than any scream. I marvelled at his courage; feeling the bolt move now, grudgingly, grating against a rib; his agony shivering through the wooden shaft as it shifted an inch, another . . . then at last, all at once, it was free.

There was a long silence.

"Are you all right?" I said at last.

"Quite, thank you," de Colignac replied. "But I fear my snuffbox escaped not so well as I." He drew it from his breast pocket, shattered.

"On my word," I said, "I shall get you another."

"I declare I shall be happy if . . ."

He cut off. The leathery sound came afresh — no, not afresh — nothing *fresh* here . . . A sickly light swelling, a light like a stink, affording gangrene-coloured glimpses, forms within forms . . .

And now an actual stench: fungus, mustard, dung and sick sweat . . .

De Colignac was not ready to stand. He would have to anyway. I eased him to his feet, which caused him more pain than any that had come before.

We hobbled away from the glowing things. And the crossbow, where was that?

I spied the doorway, a distant grey rectangle, a sign of hope, slowly approaching . . .

Then hope was taken away.

A figure moved into the light, and even had I not recognised the silhouette, I would have known the Master of Secrets for his ivory laugh.

Despite everything, de Colignac was rapt. "There he is! The Billiardtable Man, just as you described! What a marvel! A true nonesuch!"

The fat man raised his crossbow . . . then paused at a voice outside.

One of the Frantics, shouting to his master. The fat man turned to answer, then looked back to us. "It seems the tide is up," he called. "Sadly, I must away. Well, I am glad enough to allow the animalculæ their sport. I shall give my regards to your fiancée, Cyrano!"

I cursed. He slammed the door as he left, though there was no need . . . Things half-seen were massing over the path, others closing in all around . . .

"It seems your friend has us snookered," said de Colignac.

"Never."

I thought hard. I cast my mind back to texts on the subject of microscopic fauna.

I remembered the classic texts by Marcus Varro, by Augustine; the volume called *De Contagione*, by Fracastro, who proposed divers means of averting diseases. Mercury served, apparently, as did vinegar. Neither of which I had to hand, regrettably.

The leathery sound grew, the bluegreen light pulsing to all sides. "If you have a plan," de Colignac said, "should we not put it into effect sooner rather than later?"

I nodded abstractedly. What else had Fracastro suggested? Boiling water. Certain herbs, some fungi . . . Then I remembered.

"Make haste," I said. "Back the way we came."

I drew him on, sword at the ready — only to halt at de Colignac's cry. He was pointing upwards . . . Overhead, like snot, like the underside of a schoolboy's desk — sagging, blistercoloured, it flapped down at us, a dim wet muddle, lollingly obscene.

We fell back.

I saw inner organs sluggishly chuggling, something stiffening to the rear of it — the flagellum twining serpentwise — it whipcracked out.

I dodged. The member paused, arched; a brief refractory period, chymical clockworks rewinding — I danced, stabbed. The flagellum flailed spastically. I stabbed again. A slap of stuffs on the floor, a flap of blype, a slubbery gush. I pressed deeper with my blade — another soupy splash, the sword finding an inmost sac packed with greasy helices. Nausea transmitted itself in a wave through my blade to my hand.

The flagellum slackened. The organs wound down, were still.

I heard de Colignac calling for help. I whirled. One of them had him, was wrapping itself about him. Horrid!

Rapelike! Blebs and phlegm, cottony mucus, cilia snugging suctorial tips into his breast. De Colignac yodelled with horror, slashing unhandily with his blade . . . I could do nothing, for I was checked by yet another of them, larger, squarish, an old wound on its outmost membrane, infected — an irony — overrun with animalculæ of the normal size.

Its flagellum cricked, wracked, I dodged, essayed an awkward blow that glanced from its hide, it struck again, its movements difficult to predict, a blow to my leg, I staggered, more from revulsion than the impact, I saw a barbed sting in the fabric of my breeches, some globular nonsense at the end pumping black from the tip.

I shook it loose. I cried out. I gave the thing due return, hacking until it was aspic and ribbons. And de Colignac, where was he? Ah, there — being dragged towards — towards — even now I do not like to think on it. Huge, deep and wide, burrowed partly into the earth. Snailtrails, webs and films between floor and ceiling. A socketed hive, a mucous nest, trafficked by things that dwelt in dark and therefore had no use for beauty . . .

De Colignac's monster was humping towards it, bearing its prize homeward. I ran, lunged, ran it through. It convulsed. I lanced that boil again. It heaved, delivered my friend to the ground, sobbing, wrapped in slobber.

The hive was astir. Others were coming.

I hauled de Colignac to his feet, bore him along, scanning the floor.

I found our lantern. I snatched it up, shook it, grinned. The fuel reservoir was full.

They were upon us, terrible jellies, slubberdegullion throngs . . .

I opened the lantern, flung the fuel left and right; I struck my pocket flint, cast it forward. The flame caught. It spread. The animalculæ retreated, too slow. There was a wet report as one, its fluids heated to boiling, burst asunder — then a second.

Organs thudded down around us, some still chugging out porridgey glop . . .

The fire spread further. A beam crashed to the floor.

"This way!" I shouted. We moved in what I hoped was the direction of the door. I was mistaken. There was no door, only wall.

I felt heat at my back. I looked behind. The flames were so close! A piece of ceiling came down.

Desperately, I punched at the rotten boards of the wall. They gave a little. I hammered with the pommel of my sword. Chunks came away, a hole forming. De Colignac tore at the edges, and I kicked, enlarging the gap until it would let us through.

We scrambled out a moment before the roof collapsed — followed by the great eyepiece, the flaming barrel smashing to the earth.

We staggered away, gasping for air — but our gasps did not cease there, for the wonders and horrors were not at an end . . .

"My god!" De Colignac was staring into the sky. "My god!" I looked up, seeing nothing — but heard . . .

Shouts, the shouts of sailors, the clatter and creak of rigging . . .

And then there it was, heaving into view, crossing a gap in the mist . . .

A ship. Its sail aglow, its keel stirring the fog, buoyed by the night . . .

For a moment I could but stare . . .

Then I spied the Master of Secrets at the stern. The object of my hot hate, laughing as he made good his escape.

I raged. I called Roxane's name, sick to think she must be somewhere aboard . . .

"Come, man, fly!" De Colignac was shaking me by the shoulder. "Give chase! The hunt is on!"

"Your wounds . . ."

"Fie! They count for nothing, less than nothing!" He grinned. "Bid me adieu, and off with you!"

He took my hand and we shook, and though our smiles were brave, our hearts were heavy that we should part so abruptly.

And I turned and hurried away — through night and fog — to the elephant; inside; thence to the box of meteorites, my scrabbling fingers cleansing them of terrestrial matter . . .

The rocks stirring and tumbling in their box, throbbing like to little mineral headaches . . . Venus drawing her kindred homeward, upward . . .

The stones rattling, rollicking, and then all at once, they flew to the upper lid of the box.

A strained moment.

The ship bumped, slid a few feet to the side — and then rose. Or else it fell.

A feeling as of plummeting; which I was indeed. Plunging for Venus . . .

The zoölogical gardens receded. I made out de Colignac, laughing, waving farewell and, not far distant, his servants, alerted by the fire, running to help him.

And still upward in my elephant I rose, away from that oozy zoo; up, up, delivered from the fog, nimbly, trunkfirst into a lightly nightingaled sky.

CHAPTER THE THIRD-AND-A-HALFTH:

A RIDE ON A MENSTRUAL CYCLE

Thus did I cast myself upon the stars.

Through fog, clouds, flinging myself elephantly fateward to slap my tale across the face of the heavens . . .

The world a map, a globe, all Earth below me. She fell away, her seas ornamented with serpents and schooners, the Four Winds standing puff-cheeked at the points of the compass . . . There — Europe, and there — dark Africa, and now the old Orient heaving into view, warrior gold and benevolent dragon red. And there, off in the distance, the coastlines of continents yet undiscovered, hazy and vague . . .

All diminishing, the world closing in on itself. Less than a world now, a minor planet, a pallid irrelevancy, giving the lie to those egocentric geocentrists who so fear their own insignificance they must place themselves at the centre of all things.

The ship still rising, and my spirits with it, I stood, stretched, grinned and poured a brandy. *Et voilà.* What else would this night bring?

I walked through a seeming rain of starlight to the elephant's head, the right eye, where I'd set my telescope, and through it, my destination was quite visible: Venus dead ahead, a pink, blowsy world, her axial repose at 177 degrees, reclining as if abed and ready for all comers.

A glint in the lens caught my attention. I fixed it in the eyepiece. 'Twas the Master of Secrets's sloop.

He had the start of me, but if I was not gaining on him, neither was he drawing away.

A matter of time, then. We would meet again on Venus. I would lay waste to his men and flesh my sword in his paunch, and I would embrace my love on the very planet that had so blessed our union.

I offered a toast to the fat man's health: he would not have it for long.

I laughed, lit my pipe, and took my ease in the snug of the cabin, my ship aswinging through the cosmos. And this I find, reader, is a pursuit that suits me right well. I recommend it to any who find themselves in anywise indisposed.

Space travel! — far more salutary than any physic or medicament!

So I drank, and smoked, and by and by, the brandy made itself felt and, reluctantly, I put the snifter aside, for I needed my wits about me.

But the intoxication grew even so. My eyelids were heavy, my head nodding.

"I am drunk." I heard myself say it aloud. And the embers in my pipe, what was the matter —?

Of a sudden, I was out of breath . . . blackness swirling . . . I was on my feet, casting about.

My eyes lit on the broken panes in the elephant's hull.

Vacuum! So many philosophers had denied its existence. Now here was proof of their error, in quantities. A starshiny seep easing through the holes in the panes, a tarry nightstuff winding about, spreading the scent of gunpowder, or surf, or hot metal . . .

In a panic, I gathered up blankets and clothes and whatnot, the vacuum stinging, wrapping about my hands as I desperately stopped the gaps with my drawers, staunched the breaches with my breeches — until at last, 'twas done . . .

Whereat I remarked a rising of the light, a rumble of thunder abaft.

It seemed that in Heaven, as on Earth, troubles did not travel singly.

The Moon was a great ivory ball, rolling and crashing towards me . . .

Oh là. What to do? I hastened to the meteorite-box, thinking to finesse my flight as a diver shapes his fall through the air.

I measured angles by scowl of brow, unscrewed bolts, tilted the box with care.

The elephant but shuddered.

I essayed a sharper angle. Another shudder, ever so slightly more emphatic.

I wrenched the box, slapped it, shouted at it.

The Moon's grip was too strong.

I saw the light that was the Master of Secrets's sloop tacking away, receding deeper into the heavens . . .

He was gone. And the Moon, here she was. Her tidal pull already lifting my brandy into little waves. So powerful, indeed, was her menstrual brunt, that I found myself stricken with symptoms of that monthly curse which, in the normal course of things, is peculiar only to women.

My temper was brittle, my abdomen bloated. My mood swung: raging, then weeping, then raging again. The Moon filled the view. A hundred thundering tundras, skullcoloured plains — hallucinatory fungal forests: stinkhorns and moulds, Jew's ears and shaggy pinkbottoms of such intimate aspect that for reasons of propriety I looked away . . .

Wracked with uterine cramps and painful breasts, I pummelled the meteorite box, — hopeless, all hopeless, as all women know at such a time — the fungal continent giving way to a mineral lake of mirrory waves; closer, the ship just a few yards up now, shaking, more windows cracking, and myself within, in the depths of feminine woe, craving sweets and bed-rest . . .

The sea ending at a shoreline: yeastscapes — now a field of giant clefty puffballs, their apertures like to urethral openings, puckering, spending themselves with sharp little bursts.

An idea! I grappled the box, wrenched it bodily to one side, succeeding in shuddering the elephant to the left, and onward, to where the puffballs were densest . . .

Into a jet of spores. *Slam!* The ship rang, was tost upwards.

Another slam, another fungal gush pushing us higher — and higher — the Moon receding . . .

Thanks be!

My symptoms eased as the lunar orb bowled westward, continuing in her eternal round.

But the damage was done. The poor elephant had suffered too much. He was rocking, swaying as his living counterparts do when distressed. I felt his anguish as a *mahout* does his mount, more so.

He pitched, set to spinning. I was tost to a wall. I became one with the chaos in the cabin; broken things, tumbling things, clothes and papers and other stuffs all smushed and torn and shattered; worse, the box of Venusian rocks — it was broken, all but one of its stones lost. My motive power was gone. The vessel slipped, staggered. A-down and down, descending through fathomless sub-ecliptical deeps, through the bitter soot of the Sun's combustion . . .

I passed into a scene such that I cannot say whether I witnessed it with my eyes or some more spiritual sensibility.

A sight full of awe. A thing made of immensity.

The titanic Engine, turning with huge Slowness of Wheel, that drives the Solar System.

In all terror and beauty, the Keplerian laws, his orbital periods, his foci, his booming ellipses of brute black iron and rust and dust and mathematical fate.

And now, the pendulum that regulated the mechanism; an immaterial chain as might serve to bind God.

And the bob at the end. A planet: dirty, discarded, its withered continents blanched, mummied, and now the pendulum swung on its upward arc, and the old planet, the Ancient Plumb Bob, careened, and its landscapes swelled into view — mighty acclivities; wet forevers — and I spied an alien sea, listless and grim —

CHAPTER THE FOURTH:

FRITILLARY

— a crash, a splash.

A bright burst of pain as my head clapped against one of the ship's beams. Tumbling confusion, a terrible chill.

I came to the realisation I was underwater. Then a panicky moment when I could not tell which way was up.

I saw light, and knew that way lay sky.

Kicking myself to the surface.

Air. Waves, gloom, wastes of water.

My head ached abominably. Paddling, I touched my skull, discovering a lump that would have killed a lesser man.

And the ship . . . Faithful elephant! His last act had been to toss me free, lest he drag me down with him. I saw a few scraps — a notebook, a *bigotelle*, a glove — then a sad sound made me turn in time to see the last of him. The glass trunk, the final few feet of it, reaching up like a drowner's hand. I flailed closer, too late; now only the tip was visible, and a moment later even that was gone.

The elephant's departure was marked by three fat bubbles like the ellipsis at the end of a sentence too sorry to conclude . . .

I leave you to imagine my grief when I understood my vessel was no more.

As a child, under the tutelage of one Father Grangier, our town priest (that town was not Bergerac, as many suppose, but a small village near Saint-Forget), I was often admonished never to grumble, this for two reasons: the first whereof, because it is a sin to be ungrateful for God's bounty; and the second, because there is always someone worse off than oneself.

Know, reader, that I took issue with the Father's first argument, especially when God's bounty, as it pertained in the schoolrooms of my childhood, seemed to consist of endless catechisms, countless whippings (the school's motto was *Væ natibus*: "woe to the buttocks!"), and thin insufficiencies of gruel.

Kindly, however, I said nothing, pitying the fellow his inferior intellect.

As for his second argument, I was unable to hold my tongue.

Surely (I said), if there be a finite number of people in Creation, one of those must be the worst off of all, just as one must be the wisest, one the most foolish, and so on.

But alas, this won me no favour with Grangier, that person of quality, who treated brightness as a fire to be beaten out, and was no slacker when it came to that important duty.

Ah, Grangier. Would that you were there with me that day, in that strange sea. With what unwonted pleasure I would have greeted you!

For here at last was proof of my argument:

There seemed no question that the honour of being the wretchedest person in existence had fallen to me, or I to it.

I searched for land, or sign of ship, or flotsam on which to buoy myself. There was none, of course, as must be for he who was the worst off of all.

For several mortal minutes I was tost about by a choppy swell. I regarded the Sun's underside, which emanated a sullen, bronze lustre orphaned of joy or warmth. I heard the calls of ærial creatures of unknown type, whose cries were expressive of an infinite melancholy. I kicked at fishish things that spooked about my legs, brushing against me in an enquiring way, and they went readily enough, but not without an air of knowing I would be theirs before long.

Overall, the experience was not as pleasant as it sounds.

When I bethought me to remove my clothes and other ballasts, I managed only to divest myself of my coat; my fingers were already too numb to work the buttons and buckles of sword and such.

Oh là, that chill water . . . Francis Bacon shewed that the essence of warmth be motion. True enough, thought I. See, Francis? Look you, even my shivering has ceased . . .

And after all (the thought came as if 'twere spoken aloud, direct in my ears), *after all*, the voice said, *is drowning such a terrible fate?*

Certainly, I allowed, it would be a pleasanter death than some . . .

And hist! — hear the music, swelling to ease me on my way. A singing, *her* singing, Roxane's lullaby hush gentling me deep down to sleep . . .

But no! I slapped my cheeks. I cursed, I swore.

I would not surrender, for her I would not! I shouted a challenge! To the Fates, to Fortune! Whatever disasters were visited on me, still I would not succumb! Là! I stormed at Fortune, and it answered in kind!

Lightning! Yellow epilepsies of it! Thunder! Cracks and cruckles and drumblings! And the rain! Hard as nails, so that air and water were one!

Ha! I had to laugh! I shouted laughter! I lost my wits. I found them again. The waves threw me hilariously about. "Is that all you have?" I boomed. "Is that the best you can do?"

I whooped and hollowed and felt the mad glee of he who knows any change, however terrible, could only be for the better.

Whereat I beheld a cloud.

It was a thunderhead like all the others. But unlike also.

It pranced handsomely on the air, flounced about as if with a will.

It descended, driving against the wind. I spied a rider atop it. Whose peculiar head (of which more later) was bent in an attitude of concentration.

The rider hauled its mount to a halt and beckoned with a knuckly, orange-furred hand identical to those of the arboreal primates the curious reader will find in Pigafetta's *Description of the Kingdom of Congo*. The manlike apes called *orang-outang*.

It beckoned again; I made to answer, was slapt in the face by a wave; I spluttered, choked, was like to spew. I was going down. Quickly, the rider brought its stormcloud close — thunderfalls of wind! — lightning to all sides! — the bolts so close they lost all magic, a dirty bluewhite as of a dull industrial process. I flailed for one of the lower billows, my hand expecting the scanty dampness of mist, or the even slighter sensation that comes of trying to touch an illusion.

The cloud was firm, pliant, shivering with life like the flank of an animal.

I grabbed with both hands. With the last of my strength I hauled myself from the water, and atop the cloud's lowest part.

I lay there gasping, supported by gnarled squalls, hard rains, stiff breezes.

Misty innards rumbled under me, a storm's internal anatomy, dimly visible.

I remember looking up, seeing the pilot reaching down for me. The feel of its hand, utterly real in mine, the fingers longer, the thumb shorter, the palm calloused but the nails neatly trimmed.

I clambered up behind the creature (apologies, friend, for referring to you thus), and onto the cloud's back.

And so away into the sky.

At first, reader, I should say my fear and wonder were lost in concentration, as the experience of cloudback riding was one that required much application. The stormcloud fully partook of the intemperate temperament native to its species. Its electrical spine bucked and arched, and more than once almost flung me from my perch as we rose — and rose — the dizzy sea far below, a distant narrative of bad weather . . .

Whereat the rider turned to me. "Now, Sir," it said, "it might be well to make our introductions. My name, if it please you, is Fritillary."

"Well met, Sir!" I gave my name in turn, and a brief account of myself, though I confess I was hesitant in my conduct, recent events having put me somewhat out of countenance.

But the essence of politeness is to put others at ease, and such was my new companion's warmth of character that the gulf that separates species — that separates men, indeed — was soon bridged, and we began to converse as equals . . .

To address the matter of this being, this kindly Fritillary, first understand that his head (I say *his*, for I had by then adjudged him male by his bearing, the manly cut of his sky-blue zouave jacket, and silver breeches and curl-toed slippers of Constantinopolitan style) — his head, as I say, was a largish lantern, greatly ornamented and handsomely formed. His words impressed themselves not upon the ear, but upon the eye: a shadow-play of cut-out letters and other figures silhouetted against his lantern's interior by the light of his intellect (no face but a typeface, no eyes but *I*s, no tongue but a lick of flame). If he resembled nothing so much as the ape previously mentioned, his conduct was ever that of a gentleman (evident in his lettering, which was excellent well wrought, especially his ampersands, being the most handsome examples of such it has been my pleasure to behold).

Indeed, although some should find his appearance fantastic or ludicrous (so that I shared with him an instant fellow-feeling), I was to find he was without equal for soberness of character and generosity of spirit.

Better still, he was a fellow *philosophe*, travelling on a specimen-gathering expedition, evidenced by the collection jars and boxes strapped to the cloud's flanks. "I had been flying by," he said, "when I chanced to see an object plummet into the sea" (this being my lamented elephant). "Approaching, I saw you in distress & came to your aid."

"For which I give you thanks, Sir," I said. "But I cannot rejoice, for 'tis not my own life that matters to me . . ."

I broke off, not wanting to burden him with my woes, but he insisted so earnestly that at last I recounted my plight, not without accompaniment of groans, and rained tears upon the cloud that usually rained them upon such as I.

"Would that my mount could bear you back whence you came," he said at last, his light dimmed with sympathy. "Still, that we cannot think of a solution at once does not mean there is not one to be had." He brightened on a sudden. "Pray, Sir. I know of an estate not far from here" — displaying a map: a coastline winding over his brow, a headland, a neck of forest. A river delta, hills, valleys, an *X* marking the location of the estate at the bottom of a valley. "Mayhap we should consult with the worthy who resides there, & with his assistance devise some way out of your predicament."

"I would not think of troubling you further, Sir," I said.

"Not a bit of it. I had intended to visit this nobleman in any case, for I have not heard from him in some time."

"Very well then!" I was lost — never has a man been more so! — deathly cold, wet to the bone; what choice had I, reader, but to accept? "And may I say, Sir," I said, "I feel confident of success already, for to judge by your example, your people must be enlightened indeed."

He shone as cordially as a grin, cracked the rains: a cruckle, a rush, and away!

Wind-swift, tumbling on thunder roll, borne forward on storm brawn!

Là! — an exhilarating means of getting about! — most sovereign for the frame of mind!

Hope was renewed. Perhaps my quest was not lost after all . . .

We continued our discussion the while, though somewhat one-sidedly, Fritillary being better suited than I to speaking over the dinning stormcloud (I mention here that we touched on several matters, among them the question of how we could communicate at all, whereat he vouchsafed me to know that the peoples of the universe employed the common tongue that prevailed before languages were thrown into confusion, as occurred on our world but not others; thus all could speak with all . . . This did not result in an atmosphere of universal peace, alas, but the opposite, as a common tongue carried insults across all races and species).

We flew on. The thunder clapped and roared and clapped and roared. My head rang like a bell. Sea gave way to shore, and an ancient landscape rank and wild, jungly and blossomsome, teeming with gleaming enamelled crocodiles, and parasitic elephants with slack gutty trunks, and herds of beasts notable for their markings, which were, as Fritillary pointed out — kindly, for I would have missed this detail — the identical colour and texture as the rest of their pelt . . . along with so many other marvels that to list them here would cast doubt on my veracity among those who have not taken this journey.

Since those who *have* travelled thus do not need to be reminded of it, let us pass on to the moment, soon after, when Fritillary spotted our destination.

"There!" he cried. "See you, in the valley ahead? The estate is nestled scenically at the base."

I saw not a valley but a tall hill, and said so.

"Oh no," he said, laughing, a delicate *ha ha ha* curling across his lantern, " 'tis an error common among those untrained in Antient Geography." On his aged world, he explained, the valleys were so clogged with detritus they had taken on the appearance of mountains, and its tired old mountains had slumped down to become valleys. "So what we see before us is not a mountain," he said, "but a valley of immense age and depth."

I went to speak, then decided to let it lie. I watched without comment as the *valley* loomed closer, its dark crags and beetling cliffs looming above us in a manner I might have found ominous had I continued in my mistaken belief that it was a mountain. I spied the villa, a grand manor-house that, before Fritillary had corrected my foolish misapprehension, I would have erroneously held to be perched on the edge of a precipice — foolish me! And when, moments later, we landed, alighted from the cloud and walked the winding cliff-path to the gates of the estate, I might have felt in constant danger of the ground giving way and us falling to our doom, were it not impossible to *fall off* a valley.

The gates were reminiscent of a birdcage in style. They were open and unattended, which gave Fritillary concern. Looking cautiously left and right, he stepped through and led me through the grounds toward the villa, at which I saw another wonder of this strange world.

For the walls, roofs, doors and windows of the manor house — and those of all the other buildings in the grounds — were not of wood or masonry, but what I recognised after a moment of incredulity as feathers, beaks and staring eyes.

CHAPTER THE FIFTH:

GYNŒCIUM PUDENDAFLORA

A madman caught in a general rising of the pigeons in a town square, say, or a riot of gulls reeling up from the seashore, might conceive some small measure of this building.

He might, in his hectic fancy, catch a glimpse of this beaked roof or that wheeling ceiling — but never the whole, never the whole intricate villa with its delicacy of ornament, its nicety of line; its finched curvets, its raptorial halls . . .

Never these pinions and bodyplans and flightpaths shaped into the very figures of bedchambers and ballrooms, doorways and window frames . . . All the blood and beauty of winged things risen up into a mad, wild, ornithological upleap of a house . . .

Fritillary but laughed to see these tokens of my amazement.

Were not birds ideal for the purposes of construction? he remarked as we wandered the building (having let ourselves in after receiving no answer at the door).

Were they not decorative? Did they not reproduce themselves with happy abandon? (We encountered several fledgling rooms in our search for the inhabitants — a juvenile bathroom, a just-hatched privy, an infant kitchen no larger than my fist . . .)

Think you, he pointed out, how they raise themselves without effort, so that often a roof was put in place before the walls . . .

I should not be amazed that his people made choice of birds to build their houses, he commented, but shocked that my people did not . . .

We passed into another great hall (as empty of inhabitants as all the rooms we had visited), where he called attention to its subtle plumage, its falconed balconies. Then up a downy staircase, while he told of fabulous avian cities festive with the bustle of lanternheaded people; and of his robinmade home, his study at where he need but reach to the wall to pluck forth a new quill . . .

Entering a salon on the second floor (I laughed aloud to see the birds of which it was made, thinking how surprised the architect Wren would have been to witness his namesakes woven to form this melodious room), he gave account of the town of his birth, the honest old childhood cottage where he grew up, surrounded by terns and turtledoves . . .

Of a sudden, he stopped.

A body was slumped in the corner.

We hurried over. She was of Fritillary's race, but by her dress and simple unadorned lantern, of humbler stock, a charwoman perhaps. Dead; her flame extinguished, her body emaciated.

Fritillary touched her lamp. "Still warm. She is not long gone."

"What befell her . . .?" I said — but he was not listening, was up, hurrying on, his worried light playing ahead of him. I followed through the shadows (no candles or lamps here — but, of course, Fritillary's people had no need of them). Signs of neglect were everywhere: dust, wing-lice, a drawing room with psittacosis, a passageway in an agony of beak-rot . . .

We found a second corpse in a small atrium in the east wing. Again female, again skeletally thin.

Another two were in the chamber beyond.

If the house was alive, its residents were not.

Tired and grieving, Fritillary paused in a corridor.

In all, we had found seven dead, some serving maids, and two who might have been young noblewomen.

He leaned against the flocked wallpaper and hung his head.

"I do not understand," I said. "All look to have starved."

He glanced at me, then turned away, light glooming . . . At which I spied the radiance of another lantern through a doorway not far distant.

As we entered the room, I became sensible of a perfume. A soft, premonitory waft. Too faint to identify.

I turned my attention to the scene before me.

A bedchamber, but it was also a waiting room. A room that was waiting.

It was made of ravens, to all sides, above and below; the black bulwarks of their wings woven to form the walls, the floor and ceiling. They stood watch with the patience of carrion-eaters, biding their time, the focus of their eyes the great bed, where lay a figure about to join the household in death.

We approached.

"Madame," Fritillary said. "Madame, are you awake?"

Dreams moved in her lantern, troubled flashes beneath the ornamental lampshade: strange flowers, a male silhouette . . .

Fritillary shook her. "Madame!"

Her light brightened, and she woke after a fashion. Sentences formed, looping and knotting: "*how could he what have they got that I havent O the dirty the flowers*" — an unpunctuated ramble, old words scritching and clicking, phrases dead and dry-worn and almost transparent from overuse — "*how could he O how could the dirty where is why does he not love me I am not so old as all that oh I starve for him where is he how could he the flowers I starve . . .*"

"Madame!" Fritillary cried again.

"*the flowers O the dirty the flowers how could he O I starve I starve the the perfume . . .*"

"Madame, please! I have oil," — lamp-oil being the staple of Fritillary's race — "I have flasks in my saddlebag! Wait, I shall get them directly . . ."

At this she turned, and seemed to address him: "*no no no nothing for to eat I must die the shame O the dirty the shame I must die with them stuck in dirt O the flowers the rooting . . .*"

If there was more, I cannot say. The perfume I had remarked on entering had returned.

It filled my nostrils. I could think of nothing else. I looked around wildly. Its source was not in this room. Fritillary glanced at me. He said something I did not bother to read.

I turned away. We could do nothing here anyway. The matron was good as dead. I stepped away from the bed, breathing deeply of the scent.

So strangely familiar. Evanescent, heaven-sent . . .

Ah. Mercy. I had it.

Roxane. It was Roxane. Her bouquet — lilies and linen and blonde skin upon which the sun has shone — and faster than it takes to read it I was gone from the room, racing without full stop, without pause, out like to the matron's rambling words into the corridor which was unlit but in no need of light, following my nose through fluttering gloom to bounce off a corner picking myself up sprinting on headlong tracking the scent, *her* scent, never wondering how she could be here, on this world (seeing her, her nakedness loose-clad in a wealth of flowers) through blizzards of feathers beaks scratching claws down a flight of stairs, shoving myself bodily through walls; the perfume stronger.

A room at the rear of the building. She was so close! I ran forward, the wall startling open, a flap of wings, ibis rising whitely, spilling me out into a garden courtyard.

The scent was almost visible — and on a sudden I wondered if it was Roxane's after all. A fœtor to it, a hint of lividity . . .

By then it was too late. The perfume pulled at me, a feminine distillation, all womanhood rendered to the most affecting aroma.

A path into the courtyard, scattered with such accessories as one sees in birdcages: a swing, a mirror, a seed-bell. A few hardy flowers growing in the soil, a scraggle of grass, some denuded trees, their leaves pecked away by the house.

The perfume reached from behind some vines, took hold and dragged me through to see them: a bevy of beauties. A dozen or so women lost in a silent, swaying dance.

I stood and gazed. I was in their spell.

In his *Memoirs for a Natural History of Animals*, the zoölogist Claude Perrault enlarges on the extraordinary particulars of the chamæleon, known for its ability to alter its colour that it blend with its surroundings.

He writes with still greater admiration of the frogs, lizards, insects and others that deign *not* to change their colours. For they have no need to do so.

These are the mimics, the cryptids: the wormlike fish, the fishlike worm, the splatty black-white spider not too proud to disguise itself as a mess of bird dung. Beasts whose impostures have reached such a peak of perfection that sometimes they are indistinguishable from the originals (as for instance the mantids: so similar to the ants they prey upon they are fooled into preying upon one another, to the ants' amusement, I am sure).

It was a phenomenon often to be seen on Earth, but more so on Fritillary's world . . . or I should say it was scarcely to be seen at all.

So exact were the impersonations, refined over so many millennia, that in many cases the originals were entirely replaced by their imitators.

This was a world of deceptions, of dreams and seemings, where nothing was as it appeared, and those that were, did not appear so . . .

When first approaching the manor, I had briefly taken my eyes from that fantastic structure to remark the trees without the building, blowing about despite a complete absence of wind (Fritillary having parked his storm at a remove) . . . A mystery that was solved when I inspected them more closely, as the "trees" were in fact aggregations of insects, like unto stick insects and leaf mantises, their 'branches' heavy with inflamed, gloss-red horrors that passed well for fruit, though not so well that I was tempted to eat of them . . .

Then the house itself, more remarkable still, and then what I found behind it . . . These ladies! At first they appeared lanternheaded, but obligingly they changed, wafted and blew until they bore somewhat the appearance not of Fritillary's race, but my own.

How thoughtful of them, how kind!

They swung and curvetted, frisked and kinked . . .

I gazed on them. These were not the skinny things some men affect to favour — as alluring as so many pairs of scissors. No, these were curvaceous, full-blossomed. Full-bosomed blooms of femininity.

They were buxom, they were lush and louche, deluxe and saucy. Casting a haze of gauzy womanhood, bewildering me with the decadence of their wanton ringlets, the incantatory fancies of their rosettes and ruffles. Their plumpscious farthingales, their chartreuse pantoufles, their leafgreen picadills and plumed barettes.

And that *scent!* — that flagrant fragrance. Articulate. Demanding I come, that I go, that I satisfy my longings repeatedly and in full measure . . .

Of course I would do no such thing. I would as soon die as betray my love.

Or such at least was my intention.

But what was this? My legs, what were they . . .? I watched, incredulous, as they took a step. Another, another . . . Almost there, a step more, to take me to the little death and the large . . . Here, ladies, here I am, arms outstretched . . .

Whereat I tripped, and fell, and was saved from a fall far worse.

I glanced up, and saw the secret these ladies had kept hidden beneath their skirts.

Woody trunks. Thorny stems. Roots, thin and writhen.

These were not ladies, but flowers; blooms akin to those orchids that deceive pollinating wasps into believing them females of their own species . . .

But — but the similitude was so close. So *detailed.* Is a perfect copy still a copy?

I wrenched my eyes away. I saw what I had tripped over.

A corpse, male this time. And others, three of them, scattered round about, smaller than the first, lanterns torn and ragged.

Was this how the lord of the manor had passed away? Had he and the other males — his sons perhaps — spent themselves here? Had they been so lost in their floral debauch they had neglected to provide for themselves or the women of the household?

These things I asked myself as I stood, as I resumed walking towards the flowers.

There was a rush of light, a thudding blow, there were orang-outang arms about me, holding on no matter how I shouted and fought. They hauled me away from doom and bliss.

CHAPTER THE SIXTH:

GALACTOGOGUE

Those arms, those monkeyhands, their unbreakable grip . . .

Grunts of exertion — *hgrph! mguhh! hwguh!* — spelled carefully in his lantern as he dragged me, struggling, through bushes, through dust, his flame turning blue for want of air (he had come after me as soon as I had fled, so I discovered later, shutting the flue of his lantern so as to exclude the flowers' scent); now a simple building, through its door, great in size, like to a barndoor, made of pigeons, flapping shut behind us, shutting out the perfume . . .

I came to myself on a feathery surface, a bench or floor.

I rose, ashamed — and compounded my shame by not offering my rescuer thanks; and so, by your leave, reader, I amend that now. Belatedly then, Fritillary, knowing you will read these words, my thanks for my life, and for my dignity.

For you should know, dear reader, that not once, then or later, did that worthy — whose *humanity* I esteem above almost all others — not once, I say, did he make mention of my misadventure.

Not even when the excited caws of the ravens began, by which we knew the matron was dead, the waiting room become a dining room — not even then, when the great carrion eaters' squabbles began, those awful grackles and mushy squawks carrying to us in the carriage house; no, not even then did he make the least mention to my actions, which had surely ruined any chance of saving her.

But instead, coolly, he offered some observations on the scientific particulars of the orchids themselves — the substance of which I shall not set down here — the main purpose being that of many such discussions, to put one at ease in a difficult circumstance.

Let us move on, then, to an inspection of the carriage house.

Though there was but little to inspect. The building was almost empty, its flapping and cooing pigeons adding to an air of abandonment.

Wandering about, I entered a separate chamber. A workshop, lit by what I took to be a large window — a curious window, difficult to look at in some manner I did not at first apprehend. It gave a view not of the garden without, but an expanse of sky.

Wait.

I froze. It was not a window.

It was a carriage.

A vehicle made of summer sky.

Mid-morning, by my guess, Italianate clouds making gestural sworls across swathes of blue.

Fritillary came up behind me. If the ravens were still feeding, I no longer heard them.

"It is impossible," I said. More impossible even than a house made of birds . . .

"Yes," he agreed, regarding the thing with admiration. "Quite. The sky is but an illusion, a blue scattering of light in the upper-airs; to make a carriage from it is therefore completely out of the question."

"So it is not real —"

"It is not real," Fritillary said, "in every respect except that it is." His flame shone. "Clearly, it was made by the race called by the name *Æolian*, whose creations be distinguished by their impossibility." Whereat he entered into a brief account of that mysterious people: "a race of impossibilitysmiths," as he had it — doers of the undoable — their bodies in keeping with their vocation, wrought, by his description, of knots and loops and plaits the very shape of their intelligence, their great, porous, whiffling skulls open to the air, that the winds may play among their thoughts. Stimulating curious notions, impossible engines, instruments of strange device, vehicles that could arise only from an intellect as whimsical as a Spring breeze . . .

But enough of them, because now, dear reader, I think you would be pleased with a description of this extraordinary piece of equipage, called by Fritillary a *Phaëton*, as I daresay you have not seen any such.

Alas, I cannot give you that description.

I can tell you its overall form, being that of a coach about the bigness of a mail-waggon . . .

But you must not be content with that, for its shape was but the least part of it.

No, its hull, that was its glory. Wrought of that especial blue, both pale and deep, to which no artifice of words or paint can do justice.

Nor could art touch the way it felt under my fingers. Though I spend many hours and much ink on the task, though I till and toil in the furrowed field of the page and raise posies of prose and poems lovely as trees, language must cough and shuffle, unequal to the high, blue thrill of laying my hand upon the sky.

Quietly, I asked Fritillary why it was here, when so many of the vehicles were gone in what seemed to have been a general flight from the house. Whereat he gave me to know that Æolian engines were notoriously difficult to operate, and that many travellers had been lost doing so.

"Look you," he said, opening a rainbow-hinged door. "How fine, how delicate . . ." Like broaching a sanctum, the bright interior, the ceiling supported by beams of sunlight, its walls made of that faint haze that fills the air on certain Summer days . . .

"Here is the engine," he said in a small font, his equivalent of a whisper.

I found it by following the arrow on his lantern. There, at the centre of the vehicle; a mechanism so finely made it required an exercise in faith to see it at all. As angels are to men, so was this engine to earthly machines . . .

"Æolian machineries are such that there can be no finer," said Fritillary.

The spaces of it, the splendours, like to vital fluids, humours, ærial workings touched by hints of salmon and crimson and other pleasances suggestive of dawn . . .

I leaned closer. A thing scarcely there. Rarer than air, its parts so dainty they were little distinct from their own images, existing as much by their beholding as of themselves, and so dwelling, in part, in the organs of my intellect . . .

"Bless me!" Fritillary cried. "What is this?" He flinched back, his lantern all exclamation marks.

Pitiable Fritillary! He leapt for the door — closed — too late in any case: the engine had awoken. Pumping, silently whirring, the Phaëton already rising.

It swept towards the ceiling, through which it eased its way, its insubstantial substance drifting through the roof as light crosses a translucent barrier.

Often have I been moved by beauty, but never so bodily.

We continued rising, and I felt as a prisoner must when tasting liberty after a long confinement.

Not so Fritillary, however. "Where are we going?" He ran to the transparent wall, appalled to see the manor house shrinking beneath us. He looked at the engine. "What set it off like this?"

I paused. "I think I know."

He whirled. The carriage was caught in a gust of wind and he stumbled. "*You* caused this?" (his italics).

"I fear so." I was glad he was without eyes, for I could not have met them then. I explained how my feelings for

Roxane, which were as beyond my control as the beating of my heart, had become tangled with the machinery, exercising their influence over the engine even as they did my limbs . . .

Quickly, Fritillary turned back to the machine and attempted to undo what I had done. Leaning into the engine, he filled his lantern with thoughts of the world we were leaving, of his home.

If you could have resisted the temptation to watch these private reminiscences, reader, you are a better man than I (and we both know that is not true).

I saw flashes of a redbreasted cottage; a feminine figure within it, his wife, light of his life . . . And what was this? — another glow growing in her belly . . .

She was with child . . .

I turned away, sick at heart.

His efforts came to nothing, and at last, he abandoned the attempt. If anything, the carriage was climbing faster than ever.

He accepted my apologies with such grace as he could muster — "You are not to blame, Sir, pray be at ease" — though I chanced to read a profanity or two on the far side of his lantern, also a few choice remarks on my character that I was pretty sure he had not meant me to see, and which I let pass without comment.

The middle-airs; the clouds; the upper-airs . . .

The Phaëton rising like the dawn, the plumb bob world visible as a whole, a mucky sphere, swinging away on its insensible chain, marking the passing of minutes, like to an hour.

We ascended towards the north celestial pole; we entered the realm of the upper worlds; we lofted like a laugh into the lacquerblack sweep of the uttermost vast.

Where was the Sun? Ah, there: achingly distant, little more than a star. My travels in the underworld had taken me beneath the outer orbits — but any objections I might have made about this inconvenience were silenced.

For there, in all majesty — and I shall never use that word again unless for this or something greater — there was Saturn.

Closer than Galileo ever dreamed, yellow, olive, scarlet, tan, crowded all about with moons, some small as rice grains, others so great they had their own moons orbiting them in turn . . .

And its *rings.*

Fritillary quite forgot his anger. He stood and stared, drinking them in.

The great, grand arc of them, a perfect circle, so a geometer would declare; in truth, in that first instant, I must report that for me (I know not why) they were the very curve described by a swift turning in pursuit of its prey.

Glinting brittly, twisting expressions of mathematical elegance.

Mirrors, lenses, prisms. Mineralised rainbows stitched, we saw now, with serpents of indigo reproduced again in the mirrored pools ashining among the flat black mangroves that wrangled upon the ringing crystal to crane their tousled heads high and thrust their roots deep below as if to stretch their toes in the cool of space . . .

Then gone, the rings swinging by, the colossal planet falling behind . . .

The stars brightening as the departing world's light dimmed. The splendours! Canis Major, Arla, Virgo . . . I was minded of those Indians of the New World whose nights were so filled with stars they used the darknesses between them for their constellations. But here were no separating darknesses.

The light was so rich, indeed, that it seemed to leave a wetness where it touched the skin. No. Soon I saw this was no illusion. For moisture was beading on the walls, gathering into runnels the colour of liquefied eyewhites, fluid scrawls puddling on the floor . . .

I cupped my hands against a wall to gather a little of the stuff, sniffed it, touched it with my tongue, found it partook of a bitter, mineral flavour, and I was not inclined to take more of it.

I recalled a book by the alchemist John French, who spake of the "white Dewe of the firmament", derived by focusing starlight into a condensing vessel. "And the Container did fill," he wrote, "with a sempiternal Liquor, being the mineral menstruüm of the Stars" — the stellar whey, passing through the sky even as it did our skyish hull . . .

As for whether that philosopher had observed this phenomenon in truth, I cannot say, never having witnessed it for myself on Earth, and only when the stars were in their lushest bloom when I was away from it. So that it may have been just a fancy, or a delusion, or else one of the codes so beloved of alchemists. For I should tell you that his description lacked a most important particular.

Fritillary noticed it first. "Look here," he said, and I joined him by the largest puddle, where he pointed out stirrings, splashes and currents, the wrigglings of fidgety squigglers.

Plankton, animalculæ of many types. I remarked extremely small and boneless toads, dabs of marmalade threaded with spittle, clocks and treble clefs of jellied glass — and a hundred other forms besides — creatures, all, who had found their nativity in the milk of the heavens as Man had found his in Eden's clay . . .

But alas, the Phaëton driving sunward, our observations were too soon cut short. Like to bearing some load of abyssal things up from ocean deeps; the sunshine growing stronger, the stars dimming, their beams resuming their familiar, dry complexion, until the puddles evaporated entirely and left the animalculæ to die in numbers.

We flew on.

I spied what I subsequently determined to be Mars. It drew close, and it was, I should say, a planet that met with my approval. An excellent handsome world, russet with the Autumn leaves of its straight-backed woods, trees fine and clean like hard-struck piano notes. Such were its charms, indeed, that I thought I should be pleased to return there some day.

Then its moons flashed by, and the red world was gone.

A period of darkness. The passing of a small comet. And by and by, a prink of blue, which swelled, and became the Earth.

And how strange it was to see my home-world again! My fat pearly world, so moist and motherly — and how strange, withal, to discover no answering warmth in my breast.

Gazing down, I felt nothing save that which a man experiences on sighting his childhood home after a long absence, a sentiment at once tender and stifling.

Yes, Earth seemed a sweet and swaddling place, a fine place to grow up in. But when that growing up was done, up and out, man! Away from that crib! It was a babyish, craven fellow who did not leap as soon as practicable into the wider world of the universe-at-large, where he could stretch his limbs and learn his measure!

The Earth twinkled wetly, and was gone, and I did not turn back but gazed forward, eager for a glimpse of Venus.

No sign yet. The Sun dead ahead. Perhaps our destination was invisible in the glare. I waited. Another comet swaggered by. The Sun's furious face grew to fill half the heavens, then: there! — a small disc off to the left, dark against the Sun's corona . . .

"Is that it?" Fritillary said, seeing it also.

"I believe so." Though by then I was not so sure.

Was this planet smaller than it should have been? And were they craters marking its surface? Venus had no craters, surely . . .

My misgivings grew as we flew closer, until at last it was clear. This was not Venus at all, but Mercury.

We spun past the little world, all incandescent, all incendiary, and flew onward, bucketing towards the Sun.

Fritillary said, "Where is our destination? Has it disappeared?"

"Perhaps it is *in opposition*, as astronomers put it." I explained the term.

"So we will round the Sun and come to it that way?"

"Indubitably," I said, dubitably.

Our path never deviated. I experienced a paradoxical chill. Great plumes leapt around us, blue zaps, orange frazzles, fierce exhalations. Complicated booms rattled my teeth in their sockets.

Closer still, the fine, granular surface visible now.

I heard it. Like surf. The crash and roar, the huge hiss and seethe. And, under it, a musical tone, as if the Sun were a great bell, knelling our doom with deep millennial chime.

We fell among the flames. A screaming conflagratory upgush.

Fires of the most unlikely colours. Cream, beige, ecru, oyster, gloss-black — every imaginable hue was here to be seen, for was not the Sun the source of all colours? — a thousand greens, a million vermilions. Flames the colour of other flames, the colour of water, the precise antique brown of the mahogany sideboard in my paternal grandfather's house on the rue des Prouvaires.

The brightness a pressure. My hand a blood-pink transparency before my face. The intricacies and hinges of the phalanges, a knot where I had broken a finger as a child.

I closed my eyes, and my eyelids were transparent. There was no escaping these sights. I looked at Fritillary, his larger organs still showing among his big simian frame. We were skeletons, flesh rotted and gone . . . Anxiously, I felt my body; it was there yet. And my heart, I saw it beneath the ribs, looking hale enough, despite all the knocks and insults it had suffered.

I noted the unhurried pulse of Fritillary's own heart, the steady in-out of his lungs, the firm stools in his bowel, and I considered that if he, who knew so much more about the Phaëton, was not afeared, then I should not be either. And almost as soon as I had given myself over to this thought, I was struck by a simple insight. The vessel was an impossibility! Fritillary himself had said so! How could one destroy an impossibility?

One could not, of course, not with all the fires of the Sun! As well speak of killing a dead man or piercing a dream with arrows . . .

Wherewith, within the father of dawns, there came the dawn of my first small understanding of the power of the impossible . . .

We men were such fools, I thought. Why had we restricted ourselves for so long to the merely achievable?

I began almost to enjoy the descent.

The light brightening, my major organs dissolving to invisibility: I farewelled my belly — empty in any case — my muscles, my heart. Now my skeleton, and Fritillary's. The frailer bones, then the heavier, load-bearing ones. Our arms and legs, our torsos clearer than gin.

I knew the moment my skull and brain were transparent when I saw through the back of my head . . . Or so I assumed. In truth, I could no longer be sure which way I was facing. Or whether I was standing or sitting — or even, as time passed, who I was . . .

Something about a nose, I seemed to recall, a sword,

a hate, a love. They seemed unlikely. I tried to hold onto them, but the light was too strong. It washed them away . . . Even "I", the very letter, was pushed over by the brilliance, italicised until it fell and was blown into the unrecoverable distance . . .

A disembodied viewpoint, another beside it; a couple of nothings ghosting through cathedraling curves of brilliance, angry tangles, orgiastic coils pulsing to the booming lubdub cadence of an immense heart.

The cadence grew louder, until all at once there it was.

The core. The Hub of the Sun where sleeps a god that sleeps even yet, and this I know, for were it otherwise you and I and all those we love and do not love would be dead, consumed in the great sundering dawn of its hatching.

Larval, laval; unborn insect lord cradled in flames, too great to be seen as a whole. Now the vast architectures of its limbs, wrapped about the Sun's golden yolk; now the abdomen, with its miraculous spiracles; now its antennæ, long, long, receiving unknowable signals . . .

And now, the ineffable head, the dreaming bijouteries of the eyes, reflecting not its surroundings but a cool, blue, indescribable place . . .

And then the Phaëton was rising once more, and somewhere, someone might have breathed a sigh of relief, had there been anyone there to sigh, and had astonishment left but room for fear.

Our ascent seemed briefer than the descent.

I will not bore you by recounting it in detail.

Monstrous flames. Detonations, cannonades. A selection of apocalypses.

Our bones returned to view, followed by our organs — we resumed our flesh; my nose waggled hello.

Firestorms churned — not so hot, I thought scornfully, after the furious core. Fie, these poor flames were only a little warmer than room temperature, if the room in question be a kiln . . .

Then up, up, and with a leap of prominences, up — into the cool and ringing silence of outer space.

Fritillary's eyes were not dazzled for the reason that he had no eyes, so it was that he spotted it first, and pointed it out to me, and after several minutes, I saw it too.

Venus, approaching swiftly.

Soon we would be upon it; the world that would be the setting of my enemy's death and the recovery of my love, and what, I was sure, would prove to be my most famous victory.

CHAPTER THE SEVENTH:

IN WHICH I DIE

Turbid, sick-room winds sucking past the hull.

The Phaëton rushing through clouds and miasmata, over livid languid forests filled with trees like pines, but which might better be called *supines*, lolling as if trapped in the mortal torpor of a relaxing disease.

This was the venereal world, infested with hallucinations and nightmares identical to those that beset the victims of two maladies, the one called the *French Pox* by the Italians, the other called the *Italian Plague* by the French — diseases identical in every respect save their names.

And as the artists of those two nations each borrow the others' styles, so those diseases shared the same palette: meaty greens, grapey purples . . . colours of a painter who has dipped his brush in corruption.

A bosky delta; a field of tumorous blooms; a ruffle of gin-blossomed hills afflicted with quakes that twitched in the rhythms of *tabes dorsalis*. Fat spirochætes, white as leprosy, flexed in mealy ammoniacal *Ürschleim*.

We flew through rain, fat swampy drops splatting against the carriage.

This sorry old trollop of a world, what were her flora and fauna but the fancies of her syphilitic mind?

We descended. Grey, boiled-looking trees reached up their limbs like penitent squid.

We wrackled through a jungly canopy, settled on a bed of underbrush.

I flung the door open. I gasped. Bath-house heat, a stink to crisp the hairs in the nose.

I bore it, leapt forth, onto plants that winced and sleazed beneath my boots.

I choked, coughed, called her name again, my voice swallowed by the foggy night.

Fritillary's lantern bobbed in the dark, an unwilling will-o'-the-wisp, his light dancing and shying, as if loath to settle upon the scene it revealed.

By his light: knuckled succulents, wormy strangles of varicose vine, conquering merkins of curling verdure shrouding a clearing ringed by trees related in a distant way to the tropical figs of Earth. Ruins slouched insolently among them, their stones held in place by the trees' grasping roots.

I made to speak, but Fritillary held up his hand. "Hist! Do you not hear it?"

I listened . . . and then, yes, there it was. A wordless song. A music to trouble the blood.

A clue, surely . . . What is that you say, reader? You find it a bit obscure, a bit thin? Should I have waited for a better? If Theseus had considered the thread that guided him through the Labyrinth a bit too thin, would he have ignored it?

No indeed. He would have grasped it as eagerly as I did the chords of that music, following it, bounding and plunging, through lianas, through fog — poor Fritillary following me in turn; the happy light of the Phaëton fading behind (our last glimpse, sad to say, of that wonderful carriage).

We arrived at the greatest of the fig trees. It was a tree of the Gothic order.

Fritillary's typeface was small with awe. "Perhaps the song is but that of a bird . . ."

I stopped reading. I circled the tree. The music's strange languors and dying falls twisted from out the maze of its ærial roots — from *here* — a gap between the buttresses, sufficiently wide to admit a man . . .

We found our way through, a bruising, airless, slimy business, and words can do little to give the measure of my joy when at last we reached the great hollow at the centre.

The shaped hollow . . . You may be aware, reader, that the strangler fig germinates in the canopies of other trees and sends down its roots to smother the host's limbs and trunk.

Here, the host had not been a tree but a building.

Windows shattered and gone, bricks and plaster crumbled to dust: nothing of the structure remained . . . but still the building was here as a ghost, its root-wrought memory, the flowing wood faithful even unto the flaws of the building; cracked walls and splintered beams retained in the kinks and wriggles of the fine hair-roots — the structure's every heavy opulence enhanced by the tree's extravagant coils — panelled walls dropsical with ornament, grotesqued cornices and parapets impressed into living timber . . .

On, into an auditorium, of a bigness such that Fritillary's lantern relieved but little of the darkness. This had been a theatre, and it was a full house, clamorous with bats, or their equivalent, their demonbaby faces startling in Fritillary's light . . .

I went a little way down the middle aisle. The song stopped.

I froze. That nape-of-the-neck dread.

"Come out!" I called.

The floor ahead of me was curled upwards by the tree's growth. I stood balanced upon a breaking wave of the baroque.

The song came from closer at hand this time. "Show yourself!" I cried.

Fritillary, at the head of the aisle, flared his lantern to attract my attention. "I saw something," he said when I turned. "A shadow across the

The attack was too swift for him to close his quotation marks.

A figure darting into his circle of radiance; the face, its grin, all the wrong muscles holding it in place; this was one of the Master of Secrets' crew. One of his actors, a Black Frantic.

Its hand snapped forward, daintily ripping a hole in the back of Fritillary's head . . .

I was running at them. It happened between one step and the next: Fritillary trying to twist away; a tool appearing in the Frantic's other hand — thin, long-handled, with an inverted cone at the end. And I knew it for a lamp snuffer.

The grinning Frantic slid the tool into Fritillary's lantern and put him out.

Darkness fell, and Fritillary. I heard him drop. I shouted his name. I heard running, a burst of song. I lunged, swinging blindly.

Something brushed the back of my neck. A bat? I whirled, my blade meeting nothing.

A laugh.

I felt breath on my brow. I lashed out with my fist. It brushed brocaded fabric. The darkness closed in. The song came from all sides. My terror threatened to overwhelm my reason so that the assault, when it came, was almost a relief.

A blow to the gut, another to the shoulder. A lusty strike to the ribs; I shut the mouth of one of them with a fist. I was thumped in the back by a club or other blunt thing. I swung my blade, it met a body, the small of the belly, I thought. I turned and ripped down to the bollix. I bore away the monster's life on the point of my blade.

A cudgel numbed my right hand. My sword dropped. My left scrabbled my dagger from my belt. I used it as a bat does its cries. But the cries were my enemies'. I withdrew, turned.

I was clouted in the back of the head, went to my knees, was up again. I stabbed out, to discover I had lost my dagger. I sustained a punch to my throat, another to the temple that set me on my rump — though whether this deprived me of my senses, I cannot say, for the night was as dark as oblivion already.

Had time passed? I seemed to be alone.

Agonies silvered the interior of my skull. Lights danced before my eyes. After considerable study, I understood they were candles.

I stood and retrieved my sword, then I went to Fritillary.

He was dead, lantern crushed and broken. I held his head in my arms. A large rip in the fabric of his skull showed a store of words. It spilt a comma or apostrophe to the floor. Weeping, I removed my jacket and bundled it under his head as a pillow.

At length, I walked to the stage, where the candles were hung. They lit a rough representation of the heavens: clouds and stars and planets of gilded wood.

The Master of Secrets's ship stood among them like a great prop. It balanced on its keel as a dancer on her toes.

I clumb upon the stage. A rope ladder depended from a hatchway in the ship's stern. I used it to let myself into the underdeck: entering a short passageway, dark and still. A thick mist. Light shining under a door. I opened it.

Inside, Roxane lay abed, peacefully sleeping.

I whispered her name as if its utterance would cause her, like silence, to disappear.

She stirred, slowly waking, turning, blinking —

— the door slammed shut.

"Poor Roxane." The Master of Secrets gave his fat chuckle. "Let us not disturb her. I fear my smoke affects her ill."

My scabbard rendered up its sword. "Strange to say," I said, "I am pleased to see you . . ." Though in truth, I could not see him right well — a bellying vagueness, a yellow crescent of grin in the thickening fumes . . .

"Why so?" said the grin.

"I am in no very good temper of mind," I said, "and am disposed to think the sight of your blood will improve my mood."

"Ah, Cyrano, your bravado knows no bounds. I think I could not have chosen a better character. Such splendid theatre."

I ran at him. The fog shewed the turbulence along my blade as I swung at — nothing.

Smoke and shadows. The Master of Secrets was not where he had been.

"You missed," he said, "and I do present a large target. This does you no credit, Sir!"

I whirled, lunged again. Again, his chuckle.

"Do you know, by attacking, you give me no choice but to defend myself," he said. "She will mourn your death, but not avenge it."

She? Did he mean Roxane? I thought not. Then who?

I essayed a swift, sure stroke that would have made my fencing instructor proud, had it but met its aim.

"Such theatre!" he said, from elsewhere. "You put me in mind of a comic show I once saw. You were portrayed by a monkey. The little brute flaunted his blade in just such a manner."

I knew the show. The owner, a Monsieur Brioché, had paid dearly for the importunity.

"How the children laughed to see the ape parade about with his toy sword and costume nose!"

How could he dance and bob so lightly? He receded down the passageway, the floor seeming to roll as I stumbled after him. I coughed, like to choking. "What are you about?" I cried. "Wherefore this enmity? Why did your creatures leave me to live?"

"Oh, she would not countenance that."

"She? Who is this you speak of with such fear?"

"Sooth, so many questions, ape!"

The passage ended at a saloon at the ship's stern, a billiard parlour, well fitted out. He was silhouetted against a broad window at the rear.

I leapt. I stabbed. At nothing, at darkness.

"Plague on you!" I cried, whirling. "Why do you not stand and fight!"

"You your sword, ape, I my trickeries," he said. "But are they trickeries after all? You fling questions into the air which is already filled with them. There are no answers. In the end the universe is but a cotton of interrogative mists . . ." The vapours coiling, convolutions, vertebral curls . . . "Do you not feel that way, Cyrano? In the light of day you think that if you but clear the obscuring haze, you will uncover the truth. But by night, by night, although it is dark, you see things as they are. You know the world is made of mysteries; a shadowing forth of seemings. You understand the veils are all there are, and not a wrack else . . ."

The floor rolled again. Lights outside the window caught my eye.

Where had been false stars, now were real.

They brightened, the constellations like foam, dashing and fuming.

"Yes, Cyrano. We are under way. We are entering the heavens. You, however, are headed elsewhere."

A knife in his fist. My own, recovered from the theatre. He beat my guard by ghosting through it, an attack against which not one of the twelve thousand, two hundred and ten combinations of the eight fencing positions was designed to defend.

He stabbed me in the heart — then laughingly dissolved, man and dagger both.

He reappeared: I cried out and swung, but not at him.

My sword smashed the great window.

A nothingy splash. Ropy currents shuddering in. Vacuum through the broken panes smacking against walls and surfaces, all but sweeping me from my feet. The Master of Secrets flailed, his pipe extinguished, and struggled for the door. I pitched myself at him; my blade damaged him only indifferently. He was gone. I tried the door. It was bolted shut.

I saw no other exit. Muscular swells of star-foaming black pressed and surged, bounding and rebounding.

I had no choice. I kicked myself towards the window, through, out into space.

A moment of vertiginous horror, the Black Absolute, stars, nothing solid . . .

My fingers smacked against the taffrail on the stern. I allowed my momentum to swing me to the rudder post. I achieved the quarter-deck. Lungs already aching; the footing treacherous on the chop-tost ship. I held a shroud line, lest I be flung overboard. I looked about, unable to blink: the water of my eyes frozen. And through those lenses I saw the ship's sail.

It was an angel's wing. Tall, so tall, and cruelly hacked from its owner's back, gory where it met the deck, with steel lines taut from bolts punched into the meat of the limb, shewing old blood dark against the chaste sparkling white — the feathers — objects of such grace and subtlety that I hesitate to describe them, for fear my lumpen words should bruise their fairy delicacy.

The sloop tacked, and the sail swung, and cast its light on a closed companionway leading belowdecks. That way lay air, that way lay Roxane.

I set off for it at a run. It opened. A shadow rose, an

eclipse of the heavens. It was a celestial phenomenon with a heavy boot. It kicked me away.

The last of my air whuffed from out my breast. I looked up, witnessing the ascension of a new nebula. *Tabula Billiardum*, north of Orion, exhibiting considerable proper motion.

He wore something over his head, like to a little brass house, a suit filled with air.

I fell back. My heart laboured. I felt the sail at my back, the great wing. My vision was a tunnel. I saw movement at my feet, tender little flowers, young vines budding from the decking where it was touched by the wing's sacramental blood; and within me, a corresponding renewal, the wing's light shining into my life, a green, inward budding infesting my limbs with strength, just a little, sufficient to raise my sword.

I stood, feinted. He was clumsy in his balloonlike coveralls. He lumbered left where he should have gone right. My sabre switched. He was startled, threw up his left hand in defence.

The sword passed through his wrist. His severed hand fell to the deck.

But I had reckoned without the other hand, and the blade in it, and it entered my breast to the hilt, and I felt the chill of it.

I remarked the handle protruding from the front of my shirt. It jumped, lubdub, lubdub, lubdub, with that cadence so familiar to us through life, the rhythm we know by heart.

My sword was gone. My legs. I was tumbling backwards, over the railing, man overboard. I glimpsed a light in one of the portholes, and wondered if it was Roxane's cabin.

The light faded as the ship sailed on . . . The dagger jerked in my breast, slowing. It beat once, lubdub, and again, then was still.

. . . its horses, or what once were — confections as lovely as anything in Louis's palace — now a single equine lump, awful, spidery, broken, a panicky grotesque, their dozen eyes rolling in madness as they lifted their muzzles and screamed.

2ND DAY

CHAPTER THE EIGHTH:

KINGDOM COME

In his *Natural Histories*, Pliny writes of the people of Æthiopia, called by the name Ylliri, notable for possessing backward turning-feet, two pupils in one eye and the figure of a horse in the other, and also for their belief that the imagination counted as an organ of the senses.

If I am not as ardent in this belief as the Yllirii, I am at least sympathetic to it. Pray, reader, think on it: without imagination, is not the world a chaos?

Without imagination, it is without mathematics, categories and stories withal. Not even the driest account of absolute fact exists without the imagination of the one who tells it.

I say *all* stories may be said to be in the first person, to a greater or lesser degree. If the *I* in my tales is as unignorable as he whom it represents, 'tis not a sign of egotism, as some have suggested, but comes of my simple devotion to the unadorned truth.

However, difficulties present themselves to those who write in the first person. One such is the element of suspense that is removed the instant the narrator uses the word *I*. At that moment, we know the hero survived all the perils he describes, else, how did he describe them?

But here again my writing proves its superiority. For the hero has perished, as you have read, and yet his story continues, as you also see.

This is that rarest of books, a posthumously written autobiography.

And rarer still: where most philosophers have been pleased to expound on the matter of death from one or other perspective, this is a book that treats on it from the benefit of experience.

As to death, then: many have likened it to the payment of a debt, Nature the creditor, Life the balance due.

If so, I say it is best to settle it at the earliest convenience, and so free yourself to get on with more important things.

For I can tell you, reader, death is no great misfortune.

The debt? A trifle. What is a man after all but a kind of nothing? His first breath is in, his last is out: in sum, even the air is unchanged by his passing.

So then, we are agreed: death is nothing . . .

But losing her (the pinkling light in the window of the sloop, drawing away forever).

Losing her, reader. *That* was terrible.

I tumbled, I wheeled, the sloop spun away, and my mind.

The tick and sizzle of the intellect dimmed belike the warmth in the hearth at the end of a sparkling evening.

Dimly, I was aware of my progressing decomposition which advanced in the customary way: a general loosening, the fibres relaxing their hold, a bodily emancipation, a fluid sigh of the flesh, my inward parts fizzing with the gases of putrefaction. Là, a zesty bubbling — ironically lively — to accompany the general ferment of my tissues.

I became drunk on the wine of my decay, a full-bodied red of modest fame but excellent nose.

Drunkenly, I looked out on the dance of the universe, a dream of stars. Time reeling past in black waves. The constellations gathering, their colours warming my bones.

Heaving volumes, spaceless space — centuries in a cymbalcrash — the stars coalescing into spiral arms, the form of the galaxy revealing itself.

A million years. A large amount of no time at all.

The galaxy receding, dimming, turning red.

It dwindled into a star, fading. Lost in the dark. The weltering black . . .

"Rouse yourself!"

Crisp linen sheets, downfilled pillows. I mumbled something that even I did not understand. I tried to rise, but sleep was a heavy thing.

"Come! Wake! Time is awasting! Will you lie there forever, you great-nosed slug-abed?"

Someone made bold to shake me. I blinked, and was met by a sight, a brightness, amazements prising open my eyes!

I sat bolt upright, squinting despite that the light, I saw now, was in fact cool — a soft, easy glow from walls and floor, the silver radiance that comes, I later learned, of marble quarried from the Moon.

'Twas not the light, but the brilliance of the artistry that had me shading my eyes. The architecture, the embellishment, the loveliness such that it stung the senses!

Dazzled, I made out a gentleman beside the bed. Pale, large eyes, strong nose, thin beard succeeding in making him look not more masculine but more feminine. He was not tall, but this was offset by his gigantic wig. His coat was brocaded with bluebells against a massy cloth of gold, from which I should have deduced his identity, for who but royalty wear gold cloth?

"Who are you, Sir?" I said stupidly.

"My name is Louis Dieudonné," he said. "Perhaps you have heard of me."

I shook my head, not in denial, but to clear it. My mind would not wake itself! Again I looked about me; this room, this chambered hollow, its froth of ornament —

frets, interlacements, stone lace finer than any cobweb! — all aglow in the lunar radiance, pale and thick and clear as albumin.

I laughed. A rare privilege, to see a Fabergé egg from within!

"Well, he is happy at least," said this M. Dieudonné.

I said to him, "Sir, I am not entirely sure if I have heard of you," and how the memory makes me wince now! "I believe I have seen you before, but I know not where."

He smiled in a manner that gave me to understand he wished I would make more of an effort. I frowned to shew I was thinking. Had I seen him depicted somewhere? If so, where? An etching, a sculpture? Perhaps. But a painting too. A portrait of some noble, some great worthy . . .

The painting's title came to me: *Louis XIV, King of France and Navarre.*

I was out of bed, on my feet, discovering as I did so I was swathed with mud, a reddish clay falling about me in clumps.

Mortified, barefoot, filthy, bowing so low that my nose touched the floor (not so *very* low, then), I cried "Your Majesty!"

"*Majesty?*" squealed the voice that had first harassed me from sleep. "You dare? You would do as well to call this personage *scullion* as *majesty*. *Majesty* be a word for mere kings!"

I noticed the terrazzo tiles, inches from my eyes, were tinily pocked with lunar craters. I hazarded a look to one side, and as some artists care to add an ugly element to their work to accentuate the beauty of the whole, so this plump little red-faced piglet of a man fit into that gorgeous room as a sort of æsthetic quip.

He glared, the very picture of small-man's rage, his eyes flashing piggy lightning under a cumulus of ringlets and curls.

"Enough, Félix," Louis said, then to me, "Pray, Sir, rise. I cherish no malice towards you. Now, be quick, you will find clothes over there."

Dazed, I went behind the screen he indicated, found soap there, a basin of warm water, a fine suit and a first-rate sabre. I stripped and washed, finding my body innocent of scars or other signs of the injuries visited upon it. When I marvelled aloud at this, the plump little fellow was scornful. "Imbécile!" he cried. "Have you not heard the phrase 'death cures all ills'? *Faugh.* We had thought you a man of wits!"

I came out from behind the screen, strapping the sword about my waist, at which I felt considerably improved.

"You look very fine, Sir," Louis said. "And pray, forgive my friend Félix. As a surgeon, he is difficult to rank among the gentles."

The man, Félix, admitted it was so with such a display of wry chagrin that my opinion of him began to change for the better.

"Now let us away," Louis said, and made for an object in the wall that would have been a masterpiece of the sculptural art, overflowing with such graces that it was more than creditable to those who had neglected no magnificence in the making thereof, and also to those visionaries under whose auspices it was made — a piece, I say, worthy of the greatest art collections were it not that art must not, by definition, have a practical purpose, and this item, alas, did.

It was a door.

It deigned to swing open. "Come along," Louis said. "Make haste, do."

"Sire," said Félix. "There is the other to be woken."

"Oh, dear me! Well, quick about it!"

The little surgeon snatched up a candle and went to a second door. It opened onto a closet larger than most apartments. Stacks of gilded chairs, candelabra, some wigstands, various unlit lanterns.

My eye was drawn to one of these last; large, handsomely formed, red in colour . . .

"Fritillary!"

I ran to him. He leaned stiffly against the wall, lifeless. His lantern was whole, repaired perfectly, even unto its imperfections.

"Hush!" Félix snapped. "This is a delicate business."

With care, the surgeon used tongs to open a small hatch in Fritillary's lantern, then insinuated the flame of a candle through the opening.

The lantern lit. Fritillary awoke. The lantern went out again.

"Blast!" Félix huffed. "These things are the very devil to light." With a silver cannula, he widened a valve in Fritillary's head. He coaxed the flame, opening the valve a little more — until suddenly it caught, blazingly bright! — Fritillary's intellect blinding us, thoughts and visions dancing, alive with all the figures of his fancy, some fantastic, some half-familiar, strangely compelling . . .

Quickly, the little surgeon turned down the flame. Fritillary stirred, stumbled, badly confused — but alive!

I embraced him. Obscure words flitted over his lantern — "*Galligaskins . . . hirr . . .*"

"Enough of that, fellows. Come along, come along," said Louis.

From somewhere or other an indefinite mass of servants appeared, and with their help the giddy Fritillary was piled into finery — a hurried ignominy that left the bows of his shoes and gloves in a tangle — whereupon the servants were gone as if they had never been; and we were off, Louis leading us from the egg-room and along a hallway filled with ravishments, with designs as cunning as ever a gentleman has had upon a lady, through an architecture in which charm and grace were ubiquities and where extravagant splendour was the medium as the ocean is that of a dolphin — and every bit as fluid, as gracile, as quiet, as riotous.

We arrived at yet a third door. It was modest, and distinguished only by a small sign over the lintel: *Petite Galerie.*

"This way, this way," Louis said. "Step lively there, Cyrano."

I paused. "You know my name, Sire?"

His laugh. "Like your nose, Sir, your reputation precedes you."

We went through the door, and into something entirely other.

It is a common observation that a great volume of space is not amenable to a proper appreciation until it is seen enclosed.

Never in my travels have I been struck by such vertigo as then, and that with my feet firmly planted on a polished walnut floor.

"Be it ever so humble." Louis led us forward.

I staggered on, gaping. *Petite Galerie!* — an irony of course, but neither would *Grande Galerie* have come close. A room beyond adjectives. Beyond such diminutives as *titanic* or *colossal.* This was an inside bigger than most outsides.

How shall I convey its size to you?

To give its breadth, I should tell you first it measured *eight-hundred-and-fifty billions of billions of leagues* from one wall to its opposite. Such architects as read this may then take up their pens and find that, if the room's form have the usual proportions for handsomeness of form, which it did, the ceiling was approximately *five-hundred-and-thirty billions of billions of leagues* above the floor . . .

There. Now you are armed with these figures, what

will you do with them?

Là. Nothing. They are mere numbers. Because it could be described mathematically does not mean that space may be encompassed by the mind. Indeed, we are merely tricked into believing those distances are amenable to our understanding, just as words like *universe* or *life* or *love* create the illusion that we may understand them also.

You cannot envision the room, your mind's eye cannot see it.

To give another clue as to its size, then, I will tell you about the chandelier that hung from its ceiling.

It was the Milky Way Galaxy.

We walked to a pavilion. It was made of silk flags.

"This is where I keep my flying vehicles," Louis announced as he hurried us within.

We passed along rows of enchanting, feminine machines, as sleek and worthy of the air as swifts or gulls, each an elegant proof that truth is beauty. We came to a large openwork sleigh, a gilded conch. There was no ceremony to it. The emperor leapt in — "All aboard!" — the rest of us scrambling after, and at once we were away, the sleigh heighing weightlessly into the sky as Félix, who as it happened had not been *quite* all aboard, fell to the craft's floor, where he was startled to find himself in the company of the conch's true owner, a gastropod violently lime-green of colour and amicable, I am glad to say, of temper, its innumerable ultramarine eyes watching in sympathy as Félix struggled, with my assistance, to get more or less upright in his seat (though the same could not be said of his wig, alas, which had slipped to expose the only thin part of his person, *viz.* his hair).

Satisfied, the gastropod returned to its chamber at the centre of the craft.

Which flung itself onward, through beauties against

which the lavishest conception of Heaven would be a poor thing — our conch announcing its advent with booming sea sounds, while Louis twisted the porcellaneous tiller at the fore of the craft, looking for more speed. "Fie! Is this the best we can do?"

Over continents of parquet, through liquid starshine that spilled like a passion in infinite jagging, curling, champagne-tallow bands and loops — through oceans of air such that if every smallest atomy of the Pacific were swole up to the size of an ocean, even that ocean of oceans would be but an atomy here.

I was overcome.

I gazed to all sides; downward, upward — upward — that chandelier . . . that exuberation of suns, pinks, yellows, whites, colours paler than white . . .

And in the middle heights? As a great sunlit hall may be sparkled with little motes, so was this place, with the difference that here, a mote was an enormity. I spied one of these motes closer to, and another. They were shaped as teardrops, and severally the colours of cloud, field, desert. I spied things belike flies zizzing to and fro about them. Or no, not flies. Galleons they were, or birds, or titanic ærial fish. Or, more correctly, a manner of creature called the *tourbillonneur*, as Félix gave me to know, when he saw where I was looking . . .

"They are colossi," he said, "originally derived from the animalculous filamentines native to the stellar whey, adapted over generations to such conditions as pertain to falling forever through the sky."

"And when they reach the floor?"

"They will be smashed to paste, what else? But you should know that these teardrops, and the lives that live upon 'em, and the *tourbillonneurs* that fly atween them — or their ancestors, or their ancestors' ancestors — or more; back a way, you know — you should know that they all,

Monsieur (these we see here are their literal descendants, if you will forgive me) — all have been falling thus for billions of leagues, with billions more to go. When their end comes, Sir, Earth's Sun will be doddering and old."

I said nothing. I turned to Fritillary, but he had not yet recovered his wits. "*Groof . . . frim,*" he said, then, "*Fnast . . . gry . . . niminy-piminy . . .*"

I knew how he felt.

I offered Félix what must have been a wan smile. "You see before you a man astounded by so many miracles," I said, "that he knows not where his amazement should begin."

He nodded with a gruff kind of compassion. "I believe you are troubled by two questions: How you came to be woken from death, and how this remarkable palace came to be. Happily, both may be satisfied with a single answer."

At which he vouchsafed to me a most extraordinary item of information.

"This news may come as a surprise to you, who did not live through the triumphs — each greater than the last, exponentiately, as the mathematicians have it — the triumphs, as I say, of state, of arms, of love and spirit, that preceded this advancement. However, I assure you very earnestly that given the trajectory of his career, it was no cause for wonder. On the contrary, anything less would have been a baffling insult."

I said nothing. But perhaps there was in my silence a note of disbelief, because Louis swivelled from where he sat at the bow, and said, "No, no, 'tis true. I must say it is rather fun too."

I had been told that on the occasion of his twenty-fifth birthday, Emperor Louis XIV, *Sacre du Roi*, had been promoted to the office of God.

That personage smiled sunnily and turned back to

the tiller, and flew on, over a kalahari of parquetry, a rug the size of Persia, fretting over the slowness of his vessel the while, which was by then travelling so speedily that his words reached me before I saw his lips move.

"May I ask where we are going, Sire?" I shouted.

"Why, to breakfast," he called. "Are you not hungry? I myself am *famished*."

At which, Félix pointed ahead. "There it is, Sire!"

"Ah yes!" Louis dipped us lower, wheeling down to bring the sleigh in by a white marble table of normal size.

No sooner were we down than he leapt out and rushed across, jumping into a chair at the head of the table. "Excellent timing! Here it comes!"

I turned to witness our meal being conveyed to us in a most curious vehicle; but as this chapter has marvels enough, reader, I shall simply tell you for now it was yet another strangeness in an adventure where strangeness had become the norm, and leave its description for the next chapter, wherein I break my fast and take steps to resuming my quest.

CHAPTER THE NINTH:

PETIT DÉJEUNER

It heaved itself across the parquet upon ringing bronze wheels, their ringing dinner-gong rims heralding this formidable thing, this rough unrelenting siege-engine of oaken beams and brass and riveted iron, its armoured hull, size of a village set on end, shewing signs of battles ancient and recent, its chimneystack guffing smoke and steam from roaring boilers, sparks and hell-glimmers visible through windows in its brute blunt prow.

Félix tucked a napkin under his chins and sat up at table.

In the kitchen/engine-room, navvies in blackened chefs' whites scurried and sweated, and cook-engineers dug into mounds of meat with pitchforks and shovels, heaving joints and haunches into the engine's furnace as the machine trumbled closer.

"Usually the meal arrives punctual," Félix aside to me, "but once or twice it has been late. I remember once when the damme thing never arrived at all. We discovered later the boilers had burst but a hundred leagues after the kitchens. Awful mess, *roux* and *périgueux*, blood, you know."

The approaching engine rewarded my inspection with a great piston hiss of steam smelling of cinnamoned-rice. "Just how far does it have to travel?"

"Oh, a goodly way." Félix shrugged. "It can be a difficult journey too. Many hazards to be met and bested."

"Hazards?"

"Giant carpet mites, dust-kitties the size of Mars. All that sort of thing."

The carriage halted and settled on its haunches as if

exhausted. A fellow of quiveringly erect bearing stepped down. His uniform blended the suit of a *maître d'hôtel* with that of a Lieutenant-Colonel of the King's Infantry. He marched forwards, stopped, and executed a salute of mathematical correctitude (grasping the front of his hat while standing precisely six royal feet from his emperor then lowering hat while placing left foot to rear and inclining the body slightly forward from waist and holding that position for a 1–2 count before returning crisply to attention).

Louis replied with an abstracted nod. "How went the journey, Chef-Lieutenant?"

"On the third night out, Sire, our middle-watch reported sighting a daddy-longlegs. There was a brief engagement; we repelled it with cannon-fire. May I recommend the stuffed fat geese?" He showed Louis a bill of fare. "They are baked Lombard style."

"I shall leave it to you with my thanks, Lieutenant Martinet."

"Very good, Sire." The Chef-Lieutenant signalled; staff leapt from the engine, bearing dishes, heaping the table with brioches and soufflés, with larded partridges, and buttered truffles chambered in heroic pies, and flights of pheasants, and herons in abundance — a roast kid, a colossal pork, and on; wonderments and condiments; a cordon blur — a veritable castle rising before us, the chefs' ingenuities proliferating with roast meat fortifications, gravy boats afloat in moats abubble with Babylonian abalones and a citadel alive with chocwork minnikins and applecheeked infants and tarty maidens and saucy wenches, and a knight astride a thoroughbread, and potatofaced peasants with their hot battered wives, and, là, an edible courthouse crammed with tortes, I shouldn't wonder, and bitter prisoners bound with foodchains in chocolate barred cells warded by butterfingered guards — or such is my memory, influenced, I will admit, by ample measures of a twinkling drink I identified at length as liquid starlight, distilled and fermented, its mineral savour made pleasant with Madeira sugar and almond liqueur: a wine to afford a gaping, dazzled, celestial kind of drunkenness, and which I would have used but sparingly had not Louis insisted on toast after toast.

Félix, for his part, was nothing loath, keeping pace easily, until his veins shone through his skin.

As for Fritillary, I was pleased to see him more or less recovered, so that soon he was contributing to the conversation, and sampling the fuel in the table-lamps the while (a variety of shale oil of which he declared himself extravagantly fond).

With time, cravats were loosened, as were morals.

Félix was coarsened by drink, and his banter came perilously close to wounding good taste, though not so Louis, who was pure in his manners, and conducted himself with modesty, being one of those hosts who puts his guests at ease by disparaging his own hospitality. Once, I remember, he complained about how difficult it was to heat the *Petite Galerie*. "And the wallpaper!" he said another time. "I assure you, Sirs, 'tis in the very latest fashion, but the walls are so distant that what you see is many centuries out of date . . ."

At last, pantingly, the meal was finished.

Louis studied me over the carnage, the shattered cadavers, the cooling wreckage . . . "I trust it was to your liking?" he said anxiously (and in truth, I find the greatest artists most fretful about their work, which others find ravishing, but they themselves find wanting in some way). "The food was quite simple, I fear," he said. "I had desired the chef to prepare some roasted phœnix, but the bird kept rising from the flames!" He laughed; indeed, he was the one who could be best counted on to laugh at his own jests. As he himself argued, who better than oneself to know what one finds amusing?

"Now, a little more for to drink?" He waved away the sommelier and filled my glass himself (it was a vintage derived from a star, as I recall, tainted with an infection akin to the sweetening noble-rot of grapes). "Oh come," he said when I tried to decline, "you may loosen your stays, Sir."

"Sire, fully do I see wherefore you are the Sun King, with your boundless warmth and largesse, and it grieves me to refuse the honour you do me, but I must. I am on a quest, as you may know. My fiancée is in peril . . ."

"You *were* on a quest," Félix broke in. "Please to use the past tense, Sir. The *very* past tense, for that was all an exceeding long time ago."

"Yes, 'twas a shame it all ended as it did," Louis said. "Though hardly surprising. That Master of Secrets." He shook his head. "A formidable opponent. Entirely too much ambition for my liking."

I remained calm. "Forgive me, Sire, my quest has not yet ended."

Louis was puzzled. "But you died. Rather a good sign of failure, surely? Nevertheless, take heart! You are here, as are we, and so let us make merry!"

"Sire, I cannot." I stood. "I must take my leave."

Louis blinked. "You must?"

"Monsieur Cyrano," Félix said, "if I might ask . . . how? Several millennia have passed since then. Are you aware of this? More than several, and more than millennia . . ."

"All the more urgency then."

"And how do you mean to overcome the impossible obstacles between you and your goal?" he said. "What is the point of pursuing a quest you know you cannot win?"

"Ah, Sir, you understand me but poorly! Better to say, 'What is the point of pursuing a quest you know you cannot *lose*!' "

"You are very bold, Sir."

"When it comes to Roxane, I am frenetic, frantic, raving mad. I've ten hearts in my breast! Here, watch me make the firmament ring, the planets shake! Though Taurus menaces me with his horns, or the Great Bear with his growls, I will fight on!"

Louis laughed. "Well spoken, that man!" He stood, swaying. "To Cyrano, tall as a coxcomb and proud as the devil!" He drained his glass, then fell back into his chair.

But Félix, who I believe was jealous that his emperor had found new favourites, was not so easily satisfied. He regarded Fritillary. "We have not heard from you, Monsieur Lampstand," he said. "Do you mean to leave us also?"

Whereat Fritillary sat up, brightened his flame, and proved himself the brightest comrade withal. He spake in the following manner:

"Monsieurs, I confess that at first I wanted nothing more than to return to my home. Recently, however, I have found myself disposed otherwise."

Félix, a slow reader, laboured to the end of the sentence. ". . . 'found myself disposed otherwise'," he murmured.

"How so?" said Louis.

"As you are doubtless aware, Sire, every race of beings has its own manner of perception. I have heard tell, for instance, of a manner of creature called the *Doloreux*, who observe the world not with light, but with gloom[1], so that a place glittering with happiness & laughter is to them impenetrably dark, unless it be lit by means of melancholy objects[2]. Elsewhere, by contrast, there dwells a more agreeable race of beings[3], who navigate the world through a keen sense of humour[4]. Then there is the

1 By which I mean sorrow.

2 A dead puppy, say, or the coffin of a child.

3 Their name, I add here, is expressed in a bark of laughter.

4 Rather, of course, than the more traditional senses; note they have no necessity of lamps or candles or suchlike, as they themselves make light of all they see.

species, called Bom asts[5], who possess cannon for eyes, & gain an impression[6] of their surroundings by monitoring the destruction that results from their barrages . . ."

"' . . . that results from their barrages.'" Félix blinked, frowned. "I declare! What is this? Is this coming to a point? 'Tis not healthful to read so much on a full stomach! And these footnotes!" He flicked a hand to the base of Fritillary's lantern. "Is he *allowed* to do footnotes? Do we have to read them as well?"

"Yes, pray, Monsieur Fritillary, what are you about?" Louis said. "I do hope you are not making mock of us."

"My apologies, gentlemen," Fritillary said. "I tend to annotate when nervous[7]. What I was coming to was the manner of perception of my own race, through the sensitive lick & flicker of our lantern flames. As the light of a candle is moved by currents of air, so our intellectual fire is blown by the subtler wash that flows through & moves all things[8]."

"' . . . and moves all things'," Félix muttered.

"In normal circumstances I am aware only of my immediate surroundings," Fritillary said, "but there are times, in sleep or in trance, when my intelligence is sensible of subtler breezes, the winds of change, faint breaths of distant storms."

"'. . . faint breaths of distant storms.'"

"When I was awoken," Fritillary said, "my flame, in its first flickers, was moved by a vision . . ."

Forms moved over his lantern.

5 A race noteworthy for the spelling of its name, for where some words are spelled with silent letters, this bears within it an invisible one: although the word is pronounced 'Bombast', the second 'b' is not evident, having been blasted from the word, philologists believe, by a misfired cannon.

6 Literally so!

7 It is a sort of hiccough over which I have little control. I will endeavour to master it.

8 So I perceive not only the surface qualities of things (ah, wait, this is another footnote, my apologies!), but also their whys & wherefores. I see not only the colours of the rainbow, I see their reason for being, and they are the more lovely for it.

Dream figures. I recognised images from when his lantern was first lit — slower, dimmer . . . What were they? Were they cords, these winding things?

A figure of knots and braids, it seemed, pulling this way and that.

And among them, another figure. A little girl.

There was, reader, in that simple little cut-out form, in the straight brave set of her head on her slender neck, such sweetness, such innocence that my heart went to her, completely and forever.

The vision was gone.

There was a little applause from Louis.

Fritillary's typeface was bold and oratory. "Despite your frivolity, gentlemen[9], I believe you restored us to life[10] for a greater purpose at which I can but —"

He was interrupted by a snore.

I looked across. Louis was sound asleep in his chair.

"Sire?" I said.

Louis started, knocking over his glass. "What! What was that? Oh, yes, bravo, bravo. Exceeding interesting, and important too, I have no doubt." He retrieved his glass and held it up for a refill. "Still, if you do not mind me saying so, Monsieur Fritillary, I think I preferred Cyrano's speech on the whole. More heat to it, more fire, despite that he is not the one with the lantern for a head!" He laughed.

"*Love*, you see, that is what counts," he said. "*Le bon motif.*" He looked at me. "You must be allowed back on your quest, Sir, no question."

My heart swelled . . .

"Sadly, however, I can do nothing to make that happen." My heart fell . . .

He drained his glass. "'Tis a ticklish business, being God. So many variables."

9 This is to inform you it will be my last footnote.

10 Oh dear, I do beg your pardon!

The *maître d'hôtel* came over bearing a ship-shaped ewer filled with scented water. Louis washed his hands. "Look, I tell you what," he said. "We shall put it before the Council." He explained the manner of governance he had established here, a Parliament of Ministers to whom various aspects of the administration of the universe had been assigned.

"Delegation, that is key. 'Tis the best thing. These fellows really are awfully clever." He dried his hands and tost the towel away. "What say you, Cyrano?"

I said it sounded well enough, and thanked him, but if one of Fritillary's Doloreux had been there to see me then, I feel sure it would have been charmed by the brilliant shadings of my sorrow that cast a bow, pretty as you please, from one side of the heavens to the other . . .

For what, reader, does a government know of love?

"Excellent!" Louis clapped his hands. "We shall leave for the Council Chamber at once." He glanced at his watch. "But what's this? Breakfast has run late."

"Should we not have a little luncheon before we depart?" said Félix.

"Splendid idea. A spot of lunch, and then we will be on our way."

With my last reserves of courage I stifled a groan as I saw more strong waiters reëmerging from the carriage bearing a fresh stream of mountainous *hors d'œuvres.*

CHAPTER THE TENTH:

MOONSTRUCK

Among the more noteworthy features of the *Petite Galerie* was its *orrery*, being the casual name given to clockwork planetary models, used to illustrate and edify on matters of eclipses and transits and the like.

So wherefore was this thing remarkable? — this the reader asks tiredly, numbed by the merely remarkable.

And in truth the orrery's construction, being only of the highest degree of excellence — the least careless detail striking one's already ravished senses with impressions more fabulous than the loftiest opium dream — made it a commonplace in Louis's palace.

No, reader, what made it extraextraordinary were its proportions.

Not that it was immense/colossal/vasty, *et* cetera — it was those things — but that, unlike most other such models, it was built on a 1:1 scale. As was only proper, it being a cartographer's duty to be as faithful as possible to whatever was depicted in a map or globe or chart.

Such as the Sun at the model's centre, which, at seven hundred and fifty one thousand, six hundred and nine nautical miles from one pole to the other, was exactly the width of its original. Its great shell was put to use as housing for the great engines that worked the polished orbits of several of the inmost worlds, and the Sun's own copper orbit withal, whereupon it traversed the *Petite Galerie* once every three-hundred million years . . .

Enough! Apologies, reader! Again, I beset you with meaningless numbers!

Instead, let us move to the surface of that great golden

sphere, as did Fritillary and I, guests of Louis (though not Félix, who had remained behind to sleep off his excesses).

For it was there, on the Northern Solar Hemisphere, that the emperor had situated his Council Cabinet, in a kind of amphitheatre, the frisk and skip of its arches and columns suggesting the Sun's flares and prominences; Louis bustling us through golden leaps of ornament, apologising the while, "You must be disappointed after seeing the genuine article. This poor copy can scarcely compete . . ." And later, while I waited for my case to be called, I considered that in a way he was in the right — how could anything compare to the terrible splendour of the Sun? — but in another he was not.

What the place lacked in heat and thunder it more than made up for in the grace of its design — in its billion bullion flames so artful that to look on them one felt their heat on one's face . . . And in its inhabitants, which the original sadly lacked . . . Là! Their vividity, their clamour! Their *life*! Rowdy, incendiary, chaotic! The air abristle and abustle with gossips and flatteries and manipulations and all the other workings of that beautiful, fiery, tiresome, tireless mechanism far more intricate and grand than any orrery, and which warrants some splendid and devilish name, but is referred to instead by the rather dry, mild term *court intrigue* . . .

The tiers rang with it, the galleries gonged and boomed with it, and with the most well-favoured ladies, who were of the type to eat the pearl and discard the oyster, and the most handsome gentlemen — political bravos in armours of sunbursts upon which it was unwise to gaze for long for one's eyes' sake — the least of their attire possessed of all the fantasticating intricacy of heathen temples.

Neither were they undeserving of such dress.

As certain worthies — Louis, King Solomon —

present themselves grandly, not from vanity but a simple desire to reflect the inward splendour of their persons (which to them was but the resting state of their heightened existence, a majesty in the blood), so the personages of that court charmed the eye even as they ornamented the race of Man.

Sitting through some criminal hearings, very brief, I discovered that crime, as it is conceived of in Europe, was all but unknown in the Empire, for the reason that many crimes were no longer considered such. Villains had to work hard to be thought of as villainous, and even when the fault was theirs, it was invariably decided it was *not their fault* it was their fault, and set free without admonishment, which, all agreed, can be more chastening than to be punished (sometimes, if it was found *absolutely* necessary, the prisoner was subjected to a quip or epigramme from one of the ladies, a remark so apposite, so brilliant, of such crystalline wit, that it shone light upon every hidden hurt that had moved the prisoner to his wrongdoings from the first, and — so it was said — cured him of his evils on the spot).

So it was. Before and around me, a spectacle beyond any conceived by the most wanton imagination . . .

And it inspired in me nothing but sorrow. I stood in gloom upon the Sun . . .

All I could think was how Roxane would have loved this place. How she would have eclipsed all, and delighted all.

What point beauty, when she was not there to see. . .

Time passed. The agenda continued apace. My application was appended to the cycle of proceedings. Fritillary and I watched the floor of the amphitheatre, which was dressed with gems representing elements forged in the furnace of the Sun, and where various of Louis's ministers presented their cases or findings before their peers and their liege.

The Minister of Beings read from a paper regarding certain newly discovered beasts and plants in the empire. An enumeration of monsters: a being that ate caterpillars and defecated butterflies, another that dwelt in geometry as fishes do in the deep, he spake too of a hot world where asbestos trees bent with soothe of breeze over streams of boiled fish and steamed clams and even hotter otters. He spake of a creature whose flesh was made of language, to whom grammatical rules formed a landscape in which . . . But no, I must not describe this last further lest it go free amogn my txet and do mischeif to it,.,,

That Minister finishing, he was replaced swiftly and without ado by the Ministress of Stars, a merry lady possessed of all the sparkle suggested by her title. She proposed the shifting of some hundred suns to create a thirteenth starsign, to be named Pantoufle after Louis's pet spaniel, which motion was seconded and passed. She spake also of a report, yet to be verified, concerning a star that cast beams not of light, but of salt pork. Then she too was gone, followed by the Minister of Anatomy, a dour nobleman calling for a rationalising of the act of coitus, which he declared messy and inefficient (a proposal that met not with the Parliament's favour — "The messier and more inefficient the better, Sir!" being the general tone of the court). The Minister of Infants came next, proposing that babies be made self-sufficient by having their thumbs produce milk (I misremember the outcome of this proposal), succeeded by the Minister of Geology, his wig fashioned into an alpine peak in appearance and size . . . replaced in turn by the Ministers of Moons, of Invertebrate Vermin, of Songbirds (wearing a gilded articulated aviary, as I recall, in which many of the subjects of his portfolio flit and twittered), of Comets and other Planetesimals, of the Colour Blue — on and on — each Minister with his or her own intelligence, avowal, declaration . . .

My head was spinning by the time my case was announced.

The Clerk of Courts banged his staff, calling for responses to the proposal that, "Monsieur Cyrano de Savinien Hercule de Bergerac (dec'd) and his companion Monsieur Fritillary Liripipe-Pipistrelle (snuff'd) be given leave to travel back in time by a period of not less than . . ."

Immediate dissent. The Clerk was drowned out. My fears were realised. The Minister of Time and Tides, among others, raised his voice in protest. He spoke so passionately on the sacred inviolability of the past that even I was almost moved to agreement. Cries of *Hear, hear!* The Minister of Love rose, and my spirits with him; then fell when he declared himself in accord with his learned colleague: "If these star-crossed lovers should so straightforwardly overcome the obstacles that separate them, what of Romance, which is by its nature Tragic? What for the poignancy of Devotion-Never-Fulfilled, the Tender Agonie of Æternal Virtue? — never to wed; a love forever pure —!"

A scream sounded through the court, and it so closely echoed my state of mind that for several moments I thought I had imagined it.

Everyone was looking up.

A girl, somebody's lady-in-waiting, on the uppermost tier. She cried out again, her words inaudible. She pointed up and to the right.

The Clerk of Courts banged his gavel in vain. Others were pointing, shouting, much exercised by something they saw over the lip of the amphitheatre.

Then all saw it. A moon, one of the orrery's jewelled satellites lofting into view.

How was it immediately clear something was wrong, you ask?

Why, reader, because its motion was not beautiful.

It had detached from the metal ring of its orbit.

All watched as it reached the apex of its flight. It began descending towards the amphitheatre.

More screams, some of the crowd beginning to scramble, to elegantly panic, to graciously push and shove. Nobly, the Minister of the Visible Spectrum jostled past me, the colour bravely drained from his cheeks. I spied a ceremonial telescope in a scabbard at his waist. I snatched it from him, silenced his noble protests with a glare, then turned and snapped the instrument open.

And a fine instrument it was. Sensitive, keen; it divined at once what I purposed to view.

The little moon, centred neatly in the lenses, was made of jet or something similar, crater-rims frosted with diamond. One of the Martian satellites, at a guess, Phobos or Deimos . . .

I lowered the telescope and looked about, spotting Fritillary. I waved him closer and together we made our way to one of the higher tiers, where I paused to search for Louis — not a long search, for he was a fellow ever at the centre of things. I saw him at the base of the amphitheatre, gazing up with a puzzled frown.

Then trumpets sounded, and a company of his royal guardsmen came to hurry him to a waiting carriage.

Satisfied, I again raised the telescope. Parts of the moon were glowing, heated to incandescence by its passage through the air.

I scanned its horizon until I found a twisted length of girder projecting from the equator, the strut that had connected it to its orbital ring.

I tried to make out the end of it . . . But the moon wobbled on its axis, and the girder was lost from view.

"Damme!" I lowered the telescope. Fritillary's fretful light looked brighter in the deepening gloom. "Would it not be wise for us to follow Louis's example and take our leave?" An arrow on his lantern indicated the nearest exit.

"It would. Be off with you." I urged him away. "Fear not. I shall be along directly."

I pushed him again, and reluctantly, he left.

I continued up to the highest tier, where the view was clearer. I felt a breeze, the moon pushing a mass of air before it.

Once more I studied it, large in the eyepiece, crags and jags melting, calving off.

I steadied the telescope on the back of a seat, stared until the girder's severed end was clearly in view.

It was a smooth cut.

So then: sabotage, as I had suspected. I snapped the telescope shut.

It was well to know whether one was facing a disaster or a deliberate attack.

But now I had that information, it was time to leave.

I bounded over the side of the amphitheatre, loped down the slope of the outer wall.

I reached the Sun's surface and ran, making for the evacuating crowds.

But there were few of them, flying away in their fantastic vessels, and the noise of the approaching moon was a constant hoarse roar, and I understood I had left it too late. I must take cover. I veered towards a golden prominence, two hundred yards distant.

The noise was mounting; the moon fat and overfull, white hot.

The ground shook with the noise. I leapt over a bundle of filaments. I felt the warmth of the moon — then sudden cool as I rounded the prominence.

I sheltered behind it: a great rococo loop as tall as Paris is wide, clockwisely coiled like that city, and wrought of handsome catenaries rising many leagues into the —

— the air shattered.

A period of —

Confusion. Chaos. I was tost and flung. Flashes, crashes.

It ended. I came to myself. My ears were ringing and my nose was bleeding (no trivial thing).

I clumb to my feet. I came out from behind the prominence.

Where the amphitheatre had been was smoke and turmoil. A jagged rift, a hole in the hull of the Sun. And to judge by the ugly broken noises coming from the crater, it had destroyed much of the orrery's machinery as well.

Fizzing zinzulations, a banging clangour.

A great screech from my right. Little Mercury jerked up over the horizon, then halted in its orbit and sat there shuddering.

Beyond it, a red point of light — I lifted the telescope: 'twas Mars, upside-down and clattering along in the wrong orbit — the orb of it wrapt in fields of fabric, I saw, admiring it even in these circumstances, immense silks to abash the grandest haberdashers, its ruched hills and classically draped valleys flapping in the wind as it flailed into the distance . . .

I lowered the telescope. The Solar System was out of order, its orbits askew.

The ground bucked. A shriek; a flywheel punched up through the ground almost under my feet. I backed away. More ratcheting bangs from below, crashes of failing machinery. The outer shell creaked and shifted. With a *crack*, a sudden gap appeared beside me. I saw darkness through it, dirty orange flickers, real flames looking vulgar next to those of Louis's artisans.

A roar sounded through the Sun.

The structure sagged, members giving way. I looked for somewhere to run. Nothing presented itself. There was a silvery noise from above; I ducked; a rogue comet came whipcracking past, precessing wildly. It slammed into the ground. Another followed, concussions of diamond and gold, opening a new fissure, zagging closer. The mechanisms of the orrery pounded and squealed. More comets came spalling down, a salvo, several in quick succession *spanging* one after another into the solar shell — but not all were hitting the surface.

Some skimmed above the ground before they lifted away again.

The gold plating swayed, moments from collapse.

I did not take the time to think. I ran. Leapt. Caught hold of a comet — fingers scrabbling through tinsel, wire struts — I hooked an arm around a cross-piece in the tail — my shoulder pulling from its socket as the comet lifted.

Further. Rising away and away — swinging out into breathless depths of air.

I saw the walnut parquet of the *Petite Galerie* an unforgivable distance below.

If I let go now, I would die of thirst before I reached the floor.

Not even my corpse would survive the descent, not even my bones. A drift of dust to scatter the parquet . . .

I looked to the rear. Parts of the Sun were dropping away. Its inner workings exposed, celestial mechanics collapsing while a flotilla of airborne carriages sailed from the chaos. I waved and shouted, but was too far away to be seen. I hoped Fritillary had found safety.

The comet quivered onward. I hung on tighter, wrapping my legs around a stanchion. Mercury reeled past, in motion again, but too fast and in a retrograde direction. I flew through air stirred into turmoil. A planetesimal lurched by, trailing thunderheads. Stormy vortices formed, tumbledown clouds, sunshowers driven aslant by whipping gales. I flew through a stinging rain, then into a region of clear air, bright and glittering, then into a second rainstorm, this one filled with moons.

There were scores of them, some banded in green enamel, others set with pearl and cut *en cabochon* from milky agate, or carved from walnut, or ivory; one bore craters in the original, Greek sense of the word, sloshing purple with wine; another, the most memorable, was wrought from what I discovered to be wreathings of living butterflies, infinite soft patternings aripple across dusty swales . . .

Gunfire began.

The unmistakable flat snap of rifleshots, the rounds hitting a moment later — three, four, five of them — nipping at the comet's flank.

I ducked and looked — saw figures on one of the nearer moons. The telescope shewed them to me. Black Frantics. I counted seven, all returning my regard. Five with rifles, simple muzzle-loaders, aiming.

I hunched my body to present a smaller target. Their weapons flashed. Then the bangs, then the bullets. Shrapnel, shards zizzing in all directions. A bit of comet cut my brow. I scrabbled over the little heavenly body to its far side.

The comet flew on, taking me away from the Frantics, a rare instance of good fortune . . .

Then, a new sound, a colossal grinding. I looked through the tattered comet to the Frantics' moon. I spied a machine they had established there. Something black, a big box, struts, a derrick that reached under the lunar surface. Tiny at this distance; even with the telescope, I might never have spotted it were it not so ugly.

They were working it, doing — what? — pulling levers, something like a tiller . . .

Mechanisms in the derrick wrenched and turned. Clearly, they were allied with the orbital workings at their moon's core.

The moon jerked. It spilled dust. It moved.

As a child, with but a poor understanding of the rules of perspective, I took pleasure in leading the Moon behind me whenever I walked about at night.

I now found that illusion made real.

The great ring upon which the Frantics' satellite rode gave plangent bassfiddle booms, musical twangs. Rain shivered from it. The moon accelerated, a month in a minute. Clouds of stuff sifted down, as of appleblossoms or snow. I guessed the surface to be wrought of the pale soft mineral called by the Dutch *meerschaum*, which answered well to the purpose of depicting a silvery lunarish place.

Further, it was light in weight, making, I supposed, for a manoeuvrable moon. I watched it dodge some small heavenly body, gaining on me.

But although the Frantics were closer, their aim, when they fired, was made poor, I believe, by the vibrations of the ground under them.

They began to reload. Their moon continued to close in on my comet.

I surveyed my surroundings. Rain, wind, clouds. Other moons clashed and clattered, some of them wrecked — half moons or less.

One was wheeling toward me, its pastel landscapes crafted from something I could not immediately identify.

The Frantics aimed. Their moon was almost upon me.

The pastel moon spun closer. I unwrapped my legs from the comet and dangled, waiting — waiting —

— I dropped. They fired. A bullet smashed through the strut where my hands had been a moment before.

The ground crunched as I hit. I punched through to a gluey layer immediately below the surface. I wrenched a knee.

I stood, testing my weight on the leg. Not broken, but sprained. I leaned against a sticky boulder and took stock.

The storm was worsening. Rain whipped around me. I could not see the Frantics, but I had to assume they had seen me come down.

I drew my sword and set off for a stand of trees.

CHAPTER THE ELEVENTH:

THE UNFATHOMABLE PUDDING

Paradise comes in divers varieties, according to taste and circumstance.

When clergymen attribute to it its various boons and distinctions, some will declare it to be a place paved with gold and gemstones and such, thereby simple-mindedly confusing monetary with spiritual worth (this is the younger priests, I find, with concerns about financial security); more senior clergy, whose outlook and eyesight have closed to the boundaries of their gardens, will hold that Paradise be a sort of parkland decked with ever-flowering plants, innocent of weeds, and so on . . .

Then there was the Paradise once portrayed to me by an uncle, a sottish old fellow who, mistaking me for one of the run of boys who find candies sweeter than truth, thought to charm me by describing Paradise as a sugary place where liquoricestick trees grew upon chocolate hills between sweet-cream streams. And so on.

That uncle had not thought through his words.

Had he considered the struggles of an ant that has found itself atop the sticky frosting of a cake, he would have known that despite the charms it presented to the palate, the landscape he envisaged for Paradise would have better suited Perdition instead.

I waded through a sweet-reeking mire, glutinous and slippery, the broad meringue plain turning to slush, dotted with albuminous pools treacherous as quicksand.

From all around came signs of the moon's dissolution, the rain softening the countryside, melting its sugars and gums. Buttery cataracts poured and gurged. A rock-candy mountain succumbed to slips, toffee fossils shewing in translucent strata. Colossal scalloped bonbons shook and fell, pink slops spilling down vanilla precipices.

Oh là là. Surely this was Louis's greatest folly.

I had heard tell of elaborate desserts presented before kings and emperors — of the pâtissier who threw himself upon his cake-knife because the sweetmeat he had constructed was too large to exit the doorway of his kitchen . . . of the christening cake made to mark the birthday of the Duke of Angoulême, animated to depict the infant duke's entry into the world via his mother's marzipan vagina . . .

But this!

This cunning combination of astronomy and gastronomy!

Confectionary had attained the literal apotheosis of its craft here . . . here, with these whipping cream seas, these dessert islands and wide brown macaroonscapes — this masterpiece, this marvellous *monde à-la-mode*!

But often a masterpiece is best appreciated from a distance.

For although this landscape offered many appealing places to settle one's gaze, the same could not be said for the feet.

After an ordeal of many minutes, I reached the woods of candy birches and elms, where the ground was a little firmer. Mint boughs and leaves fell about me in clumps. I pressed through a stand of candyapples, an orchard of glacé fruits. I spied fauna to match the flora. Chocolate frogs. A meringue orang-outang (not Fritillary, alas, though I took it for him for a moment), a little hedgehog, its mechanical armature twitching and kicking, of excellently beautiful manufacture. Such was the attention to detail that surely a magnifying glass would reveal spun-sugar microorganisms busying in the air, watchmade organelles ticking between isinglass membranes . . .

Crack, crack, crack. Gunshots! An old oak next to me shattered, nougat chunks thudding down.

Heart hammering and knee aching, I ran, ducking under boughs, pounding through gummy underbrush.

The Frantics' moon flashed between the treetops, speeding past, setting — descending. I felt the thud as it settled against the confectionary moon.

I ran in the opposite direction. The rain falling without pause, making gnarls of the trees and bushes, the ground awash with syrupy rivulets.

I burst from the forest. A clearing, a city wall. I found a gate, entered. Into a city all of sugar, minarets and battlements, a melting fairyland, bright roofs sagging, slender towers drooping mournfully.

I hesitated. Which way to turn?

A gunshot splintered a rhubarb lamp-post to my right. The Frantics had found me.

I jigged left, into a sticky maze of streets, a child's nightmare, weeping eyesocket windows, doorways leering in fantastic gummy gapes.

I heard laughter, singsong calls. The Frantics were enjoying themselves.

I entered a high street, sugarplum carriages overturned everywhere, liquefying in the rain. I was startled when a clockwork horse, still in harness, reared before me, its body cracked and bursting, mortal coils springing and clanging in its breast. The poor creature gave every appearance of agony as it kicked its taffy stumps and rolled its pastille eyes . . .

Crack! Another gunshot; the horse twisted and bled sorbet and died. I went left, right, into a street where the sagging buildings met overhead; a kind of tunnel, gloomy and tight; to one side, an open door; I was inside, a young family, father at table, the mother standing, oh là, her cherrytipped breast out for her babe, its biscuity skeleton draped with sweet flesh scraps, the parents rocking, locked in laughter, Father's lower jaw gone, Mother's *pâtes-de-fruit* eyes drizzling white before a great witchy hansel regrettal oven even as their cottage shook and splintered with a volley of gunshots and I ran with it all falling around me, a hail of shards accompanying my exit into a rear alley.

A clatter of hooves, a rattle of wheels.

I whirled. At the far end of the alley, the Frantics had mounted a carriage.

Three of them, one in the driver's seat, two capering atop the roof, laughing with the joy of the hunt.

The carriage itself the more horrible for its gay candystripe colours, semiliquid clownskull drizzling pink gobbets, lollipop wheels spinning red-and-white over gumdrop cobblestones, and worse still, its horses, or what once were — confections as lovely as anything in Louis's palace — now a single equine lump, awful, spidery, broken, a panicky grotesque, their dozen eyes rolling in madness as they lifted their muzzles and screamed.

The Frantics whipped the horses, and they came on.

I did not hesitate. I ran for them.

Startled, they had time to let off but a single shot. The horses reared. I dived under, caught hold of the harness, liquorice braids adhering to my fingers. I flung myself up and over, onto the horse-thing's complicated back, lost among a mutant disarray of horse-parts: a sudden bonbon eye, a snapping muzzle, peppermint teeth sparking blue, a rump squirting hot caramel dung . . .

I thrashed, flailed. My free hand met something solid.

Part of the carriage.

I dragged myself closer — up onto the driver's seat.

One of the Frantics right next to me, gaping in mute astonishment, a look to which I have grown accustomed over the years.

He raised his rifle too late. It had been too late all along. In a single motion I drew my sword and buried it in his ribs.

I thought it looked well there, and left it in place while I looked for the others on the roof.

The fools were peering down at the road, wondering where I had got to.

I withdrew the sword. My victim fell under the wheels to meet his just desserts. The horse-thing screamed, kicked. It thrashed and pulled the carriage smashing through the end of the alley — peanut-brittle bricks and mortar, shards and splinters — out and racing through another laneway.

Buildings cracking and tumbling, rifts, sudden subsidences, home sweet homes crashing down while I clumb up, trying to achieve the carriage roof; but alas the element of surprise was lost. They spotted me. The one tried to steady his pistol, the other affixed a knife to the muzzle of his rifle, a nasty weapon derived from the battle of Bayonne. Which he endeavoured then to demonstrate, plunging forward to stick me with his blade.

I swung. He parried, using his weapon to hook mine aside. I slid down to the edge of the driver's seat. He reversed his rifle and used the butt as a cudgel. I ducked. The butt stuck to the side of the carriage. I essayed a *flèche* at his throat. It notched the skin but cut no arteries. He wrenched his gun free and went down beside me. I backed around the side of the carriage, balancing on the running board (molten architecture flashing by: a marketplace, a palace, a fractured temple, its dome crashing in on itself, everything splitting and failing). Again, my enemy thrust; again I parried, my sword a poor match for his heavy weapon.

There was a sound like a doorslam.

I felt the round thump into my right biceps. Wetness ran down my arm, blood like strawberry sorbet.

I could not move my fingers. My sword would have dropped were it not glued to my hand. I looked up at the same moment as the Frantic atop the carriage swiftly reloaded his pistol and swung it to bear, at which a very curious thing occurred, for my nose and the end of the gun met, and as the Frantic thrust his weapon forwards, the length of my nose slipped up inside the barrel, and was entirely enveloped by the muzzle of the gun.

A moment. The two of us locked together in silent amaze. I knew not which of us was the more astonished.

My nostrils smelled the gun's oil, the bridge of my nose felt the spiralled rifling in the interior of its barrel, the metal hot against the skin.

And against my very nosetip, the ball, the bullet in its gunpowder wadding, eager to be shot.

The Frantic smiled, cocked his pistol.

The moon fell apart.

I do not, reader, hold with the notion of luck. It is a vulgar superstition indicative of a want of intelligence, as, for an instance, the Comte de Languedoc, by all accounts a Goliath in battle but a pygmy in intellect, which worthy, believing it unlucky to change the name of his steed, was obliged to ride about on a horse named Fartsome — which I would consider itself a piece of poor luck if I paid the notion any credence.

But I do not, as I have said.

Aside from its other negatives, it shews weak moral fibre, for those who esteem themselves lucky are those who esteem themselves unworthy of whatever good befalls them.

Whereas I myself am a man richly deserving of any good that should come my way. And certainly most *undeserving* of the many evils he has been obliged to suffer.

With this in mind, I think you will agree, dear reader,

that when the confectionary moon, weakened by rain, fell catastrophically apart at just the moment to save me from certain death, it was merely a small balancing of the books after all the ills visited upon me by Fate — a token of apology from a hangdog Fortune, which I accepted but reluctantly, for, by rights, I should have refused the gift, and declined to enter into any association with it thereafter.

So it was.

One Frantic began to pull the trigger, the other to lunge with his blade; there came from all around a boomy rattling roar; the moon collapsed.

Like to a stage effect. The city, the landscape, all there one second, the next, not. The scenery whipped away by ropes and pullies. All of it just . . . *gone.*

The carriage dropped from under me. The Frantics fell away. The pistol remained for a moment in place on my nose, then slid free with a *pop*.

Buildings, forests, sugar-boulders turning in the sky.

I spun through the air. Flashes of rain, rubble, distant parquetry, storm clouds roiling.

I beheld a cloud.

It was a thunderhead like all the others. But unlike also.

It pranced handsomely on the air, flounced about as if with a will.

It drove against the wind. I spied a rider atop it, steering closer . . .

Fritillary, manœuvring forward to scoop me from the air.

CHAPTER THE TWELFTH:

ARIETTE

There followed a period that presents itself but hazily to my recollection.

I remember bouncing to a halt on Fritillary's cloud; I remember lying there watching my blood spilling into its billows, and worrying that someone below might look up to see a cloud raining gore.

I remember the sensation of movement, then a firmer softness under me that I recognised for a bed.

I remember falling asleep.

Félix saw to my arm wound, and although it was an honour to be treated by the emperor's own surgeon, 'twas an honour I could have done without. The injury was deep and close to the bone, and necessitated considerable fiddling about. I bore it even so. Even as *pain* in the English tongue is our word for *bread* (and painful it is indeed to sample English cuisine), so it is the staple of many an old French soldier — and if this particular bread was not to my taste, at least Félix was a quicker worker than most.

But when the bullet was out, the strange little fellow produced from his kit something that looked like an old soup spoon for the reason that that was what it was.

He then raised a crusted bucket filled with mud and began spooning gobs of it into my open wound . . .

Me shouting, trying to pull my arm away, three burly orderlies holding me down, me seeing Fritillary, light pale with shock, never responding to my cries, while Félix continued slapping and dolloping. "Quit your struggling!" he cried. "*Alors!* Do you not feel it? Be still, Sir, be still and feel it. The vigour, the living heat . . ."

And in truth I did feel it then, the pain receding, succeeded by a new sensation, one for which there is no name. For it is a feeling we experience only in the womb. Creation, the quickening of new life.

I was still. "'Faith," Félix said, panting. He smoothed off the muck with the back of the spoon. "That you should complain so when treated by this most precious of stuffs . . ."

I stared at my arm. There are few things so fascinating to the eye as the slow bubbling of mud.

Sizzling, fomenting. Gravid little bubbles forming, swelling, popping.

No, not mud, I learned, but adamic clay. So Félix informed me. The finest possible medicament, this I learned also; not that this meant it was the finest of *all* medicaments, he said, there being many *impossible* ones to consider . . .

"I see *matter* in there," I said, staring. Threads, little spherules . . . I went to poke them with a finger. Félix smacked the hand away.

"Take care! This is a delicate stage. Soon the animalculous conglobulations will adapt and begin their ascent . . ." And yes, there, the threads dancing, winding each around each, vegetable strands, hairy roots, infinitesimal seed-fern forms.

The First Dawn's dew beaded on unfurling flesh fronds that waved and bobbed (Félix saying, "The clay is informed by its surroundings, climbing the Phylological Ladder, the Great Chain of Being . . ."), the meadow roughening now into the bark of a tree, the living woody brawn merging with my own, sturdy, staunch and steadfast, becoming then an arthropod jelly, the semiliquid flesh of an amphibian, little distinct from the stagnancy in which it swam; then stiffer reptilian tissues, the scales complicating to feathers, my proud purple and gold plumage giving way to a rough tigerish fur that ebbed as on a tide to reveal the unmarked flesh of my own arm . . .

"'Tis done."

I smiled. I grinned. I laughed.

How I laughed! O the joy of life, the lusty, hilarious, heart-deep, bone-deep gladness of it! Did I retain in me some measure of those vegetable humours? I knew the stirrings of a Springtime, a sappy uprising that sent me bounding from bed to stand before Félix and the surprised orderlies in my torn and filthy nightshirt, hands on hips, smirched with blood and mud, shouting flowering laughter!

"Where is my suit?" My hurts were gone, even those of which I had been unaware. "No, never mind that," I roared. "All I need is a sword and I will be away, to kill mine enemies and recover my love!"

"Perhaps a few clothes at least," said someone from the door, "if only for sake of modesty."

I turned, grinned. "Sire." I bowed.

"Good to have you up and about again, my friend," Louis said. "We have much to discuss. Please to join me, Sir, at your convenience."

No sooner was he gone than a flurry of menservants appeared, butling and bustling, seeing to my toilet, fitting me with outdoor suit, long breeches, scarlet cape, linen doublets, and other etceteras; in a minute they were done; they were gone.

I took a breath, let it out — then went with Félix and Fritillary to join Louis in the next room.

This chamber differed from most others of Louis's palace (each more wonderful than the last) in that it was tiny, in poor repair, and stank of cat piss.

I was too full of life to sit, but would not have in any case. The chairs were scarified, their upholstery was dank and their cushions were scratched to ribbons.

The carpets were invisible under dander and moulted fur. And where cabinets and shelves elsewhere in the palace were loaded with items so lovely as each to be worthy of its own particular religion, here they were graced with nothing, or with ordure, or chipped dishes of old cream.

I breathed shallowly to fend off the stench, and stood and listened as I was apprised of what had occurred while I was unconscious.

Louis, to whom was given the pleasure of delivering dramatic news, vouchsafed me to know that after the attack, the Council had hurriedly reconvened in an emergency court (being a room rather grander than this one, as Fritillary informed me parenthetically: a hollowed-out ruby of very great size, and so cunningly cut that the bloodred lights that had shone in its creation in geological deeps, still bounced about its facets, a thousand centuries since).

"There," Louis said, "the Captain of the King's Guards informed us that the remaining Frantics had been destroyed." And I was surprised to see tokens of sorrow in his face, sign, though I did not yet understand how it could be, that this gentlest and most extravagant of monarchs cherished above all a garniture not of the body, but the spirit; not diamonds or gold, but a sunlike compassion that shone indiscriminately even on those who deserved it least.

"It was determined that the attack on the orrery was a stratagem to turn attention from the Master of Secrets's real aim," he said, "which was to rob me of one of my most precious possessions. At this, a clamour arose among the Ministers, who understood that your quest, Cyrano, would result in the downfall of this villain who had wronged their emperor. In short, they rescinded their decision to bar you from travelling across time. Indeed, you are all but ordered to do so."

"Splendid! Let us be off then!"

"Right away?" Louis said. "Surely you will consult with my cat minder first?"

"With . . . the servant who minds your cats, Sire?" I said.

Louis nodded gravely. "She will be along directly."

A door opened at the other side of the room. It revealed an unlit hallway.

I beheld a green glow, growing brighter.

I heard the purring of many cats . . .

"Brace yourselves," Louis said — and they were upon us, squalling, mewing, screeching . . .

My hand went involuntarily to my sword.

I must tell you, reader, that cats inspire in me feelings of mild dislike, as I have honestly acknowledged to Roxane, who loves them. (Allow me to add that where I said *mild* I meant *shuddering*, and where I said *dislike*, I meant *aversion*.)

I say they are a form of rubbish; that it is no coincidence a group of kittens is called a litter.

They were like a wind whipping and suppling — a tabby gas, a moggy fog — among which there stood, suddenly, silently, like a crag above clouds, a woman.

Squat and fat, and rather older than otherwise, her eyes were alive with the same witchy green that burned in the eyes of her animals.

She bowed, or no, my mistake; 'twas no bow, but a twisted spine that had her in that position.

"Sire," she grumped, and there was some awful knitted brown woollen thing over her suit of mail, and whiskers about her chin, and her scarred hands and nocked ears seemed to bespeak a history of armed quarrels, but were more likely come of claws and catty ingratitude . . .

"Gentlemen," Louis said to Fritillary and I, "please to meet the Chevalière Biat-Chrétien, who has worked long and tirelessly in the service of my cats, seeing to their care —"

Just then, as one, the bells on the cats' collars rang. The Chevalière snapped, "A message!"

I gasped. This rudeness was unforgivable. I stepped forward, but Louis stayed me. "Do your duty, Madame," he said.

She crouched among the little brutes . . . and *listened* to them, cocking her head, heeding their purring as though it were sage counsel.

"Sire," I said, "surely you cannot —"

"*Quiet*," the Chevalière hissed. She returned to her work, frowning, making notes on a slate.

Louis leaned close to me. "Perhaps you are unaware of the phenomenon of purr-invariance," he whispered.

I confessed that indeed, I was not aware of that phenomenon.

"Oh, but it is most outstandingly fascinating," he enthused, then ducked his head, embarrassed to find himself the object of the Chevalière's angry regard.

He lowered his voice. "Very briefly, and put most simply, whenever one cat purrs somewhere — anywhere at all, you understand — then the purring of all others will be diminished by precisely that degree . . . That's as I understand it, anyway. Very simplified, as I say. Still, what counts are the practical applications, which are obvious . . ."

On the contrary, I did not think they were *altogether* obvious, and it was not until I took occasion to satisfy myself on the subject some while later that I came to understand that purring arouses into action a species of elemental fluid called the "Ailuromantick-Magnetic-Fluxion" (I hope this is of some help to you, reader), traversed by "subtile felid emanations" along such lines as connect all cats, thereby maintaining the Purr Constant: hence, with the establishment of a purr-code, should one of Louis's intelligence corps cause a cat to purr in a modulated fashion, all other purring would be decreased by precisely that amount, thereby affording the transmission of messages after the manner of the torch-semaphore of the ancients . . . Better than that indeed, for where torches are useful only at night, in clear weather, and so on, the purr-code was requiring of little equipment, instantaneous, and amenable to use wherever a cat was happy.

"We have tried other communication methods over the years, none quite as successful," Louis whispered. "Once, we used literary means, through the publication of histories and romances and such, novels, as they are called now, their *narrative shapes*, you see, suggesting the letter to be conveyed. A sinuous, winding tale, say, signified the letter *S*; an adventure in which the protagonist started at the top of his fortunes, then dipped sharply, to rise again to a happy ending, indicated —"

Again, rudely, the Chevalière cut him off. "The cats are full of news, Sire."

"Wonderful," Louis said, not at all put out. "What have our agents to say?"

"Not only our agents. There is chatter from all over. Laypeople, amateurs with only a kitten or a mangy tom to their name, all transmitting urgently." The cats' velvety rumbling rose and fell in waves, and the Chevalière spoke breathlessly, trying to keep pace with a torrent of information. "The Master of Secrets is referred to many times, as are the Monsieur de Bergerac and his fiancée . . ."

"What? What of Roxane?" I cocked an ear as if to decipher the purrs for myself.

"In the past time to which we are referring, she is unharmed. It seems the Master of Secrets is reluctant to do her injury. Curious, as he has shewn no such reluctance elsewhere. Some suggest he is keeping her as bait to trap you, Monsieur," she said. "Then there are others who believe it is because he fears the reprisal if he should do her harm . . ."

"And well he might," I said fiercely.

"Oh, he does not fear you, Sir," the woman said with a laugh. "He calls you a buffoon." (Take as a measure of my desperation, dear reader, that I let this pass.) "No, 'tis something else. Something that will come of your union with the Mademoiselle Roxane. The name 'Ariette' occurs here."

I was transfixed. *Something that would come of our union . . .* A child?

I thought of Fritillary's vision of the stage. I remembered his image of the little girl. Ariette . . .

Ariette. Our daughter.

My eyes surprised me by flooding with tears.

The meeting ended soon after, though I was scarcely aware of it.

Discovering he was late for the first of his afternoon dinners, Louis gave thanks to the Chevalière, briskly walked us from the room into the hall outside, accepted a starry wine from a waiting sommelier, urged Félix into a sedan chair, sat beside him, wished us godspeed, drained the glass, tost it away — and was gone before it had smashed on the floor.

His departure left behind it a kind of vacuum, an addlement of light and air that coalesced upon the instant into a carriage. A vehicle of such swiftness that it was speed-blurred even at rest, it set off so immediately that the effect was that we were aboard and had been travelling for many minutes before we properly understood we had started out.

The carriage spun along new corridors, queer thoroughfares — bearing us on a trip of the most rollicking, reeling, wheeling sort, such that it is not exceeding the faithful observation of this narrator in describing as the strangest journey of my adventures.

Ever and again it twisted and turned in directions difficult to name; now through a vestibule, dark and eerie of aspect;

now out a grand gateway — ever faster, down winding paths, heavenly gardens; sacred hedge mazes; a divine vineyard; celestial trees topiaried into arcades and finials and people and beasts or else topiaried with commendable realism into the forms of trees . . .

Still faster, shaking and bouncing; a shoreline visible out the windows, a rough dockyard, a pier coming into view, extending out over something not water.

Just when it seemed sure we would shiver ourselves to pieces, we careened around a corner, and the carriage began to change — passing now over a road cobbled with Philosopher's Stones, brickred or bonewhite — sending a dazzle of flashes where the wheels met the ground their rims brightening, yellowing to mark another ascent up the Chain of Being, from iron to gold, là, through the spokes, the axles, the frame, the added weight slowing us, a thousand, a hundred thousand carats, a million, our speed merely breakneck now, still slowing . . .

Until at last, the carriage slumped to a halt.

The doors flung open. We tumbled out, straight onto the gangway of a very singular ship.

Where we stood a moment, each blinking stupidly in the manner peculiar to our kind.

Then: "Come on there, lubbers!" A scruffy tar at the top of the gangway, peaked cap over a face without the decency to be pleasingly ugly. Like to an opossum's face, it was, chinless and snouty and bulge-eyed. "What ye waitin' for? Get yer carcasses aboard!"

We tottered up the ramp; were piped aboard by another old tar; the gangway was pulled up; the crew cast off.

We set sail.

And although I will not go back on my declaration above that the journey just ended was the strangest I had or would ever experience, I will add that the journey then beginning would prove to be stranger even than that.

CHAPTER THE THIRTEENTH:

THE HOURSHIP

Years passed under the hull, and decades.

A current of Summers sent up plashes of birdsong, a scent of plums and rain-warmed airs rose from the bow.

This was the Sea of Time. I knew it the moment I saw it.

How so?

Think you: the first time a man sees a tiger, so ferocious in temper, so fierce in appearance, heathenly striped and coloured, the man knows, even if he calls it by a different name, that it cannot be anything but a tiger (at least, those who take it for something else will not continue in their error for long . . .)

So it was for the Sea of Time, so much itself that it could be nothing but what it was.

Where else, after all, may one spy this pair of seabirds I saw off the bow, these broadwinged empyræans balanced on the brink of the wind, riding a rising spiral into the glittery dovegrey softness that served here as sky — creatures whose movement was so sublime I hesitate to call it flight, being as it is a word suggestive of fear, and there was nothing at all of fear in these beings native to æternity . . .?

What other sea, after all, was navigated by such ships as this, with decks of soil and giant roses especially bred to serve as sails — their stems the masts, their huge brute-beautiful blooms the spinnakers, mainsails and jibs — the conflict between their brief blossoming and the æternity in which their loveliness dwells giving rise the shivering tension that drives the vessels across the waves . . .?

Such were my reveries — until they were rudely interrupted by a mighty sneeze.

Wet matter spattered the back of my neck.

"So ye've dared show yerself here again have you?"

I whirled, and by his uniform, the man stumping towards me across the weedy deck was the Captain, though an uncommon example of the species.

"Are you addressing me, Sir?" I said. I began to introduce myself.

"Oh, I know who you are, right enough." He sneezed again.

"You have me at a disadvantage, Sir."

He begrudged me his name, which was Le Nôtre.

"Well, Captain, we seem to be moving at a pretty clip."

He sneezed insolently. "Aye," he allowed. "The sails be free of thrips and bloomin' roundly." He trumpeted into an ancient nosecloth, a vividly hideous article.

I looked away, into the living rigging, a smacking wind rattling the big stamens in their blossoms. Pollen blew down, covering the hurrying men so thickly in the butter-yellow grains it was impossible to tell officers from tars.

The ship leaned and pitched.

I asked the Captain when we could expect to reach our destination, to which he replied that I could expect it any time I pleased. "As to when it comes," he said, "that is another matter entirely."

I reined my temper. "Yes," I said, "but how *long*?"

He sneezed. The ship's three-legged cat, a ramshackle, marmalade tom, curled about his legs. "Oh, a matter of hours, I reckon." He hauled the tom into his arms, where it added its one-eyed glare to its master's.

"So soon!" I said.

"Aye." He sneezed again. "However, these hours be of an entirely different nature to those *you* are familiar with."

By his tone, the hours with which I associated were of the most detestable sort. "These be hours as might last several days each," he said, "but with those days a second long."

He sneezed. "'Else, they may be of the usual sixty-minute duration, though those minutes not be ordered in the usual way; the twelfth coming after the fortieth, say, followed by the twelfth again, though turned inside-out, or upside-down . . . By which I mean to say," he paused to blare into his nosecloth, "that time be passing strange hereabouts, and you will reach your destination when you reach it, and mayhap not even then. And let that be an end to it!"

He sneezed conclusively, snorted half-a-hundredweight of mucus up into his sinuses, and stumped away.

Voilà. There you have him, reader. Captain Le Nôtre.

In my time aboard, I discovered him to be ideal for his office in every respect save his unconquerable rudeness and his grievous allergy to flowers, though he did not allow this last to stand in the way of the proper execution of his duties. Like many salty dogs before him, whose charm was their lack of charm — their uglinesses, their peglegs, their squints so powerful they could be used (albeit for reasons this narrator cannot currently furnish) to wield a hammer — like them, as I say, he had made his indisposition into a mark of his character, which bore many marks, indeed, and was thorny as the masts of his ship.

I might have forgiven him his impudence, were it not that he seemed to reserve the worst of it for me.

'Twas as if he felt he owed me an especial enmity.

I stormed to the gunwale. Fritillary made comment about the view.

I turned away, thinking thunderous thoughts.

And the wind blew, and the ages beat at the prow, and a flight of bees rose up from somewhere or other, each as fat as my fist and jodhpured with greedy golden pollen-burdens, to shove themselves up under the petticoats of the shocked roses . . . and I was amused, I confess, to watch the men clambering up and clumsily shooing them away. By and by, the urge to revenge myself left me, for even the hottest anger must cool with time, and in the short period since the conversation above, almost a century had passed under the hull.

And I stood and breathed, and gazed out over the chop, and gave a laugh, and pointed out to Fritillary the birds I had seen before; and we watched as they banked and gave a low oboe yodel and wheeled off into the shivery distance. And the ship sailed on towards my love through the bluegreen years.

To those who use clocks to mark its passing, time is a thin thing, a ticking linearity of minutes.

Then there are those who use ships as others use clocks.

They allow time to spread itself, to stretch luxuriously out to all points of the compass. To them, time is a measureless fetch of waves possessed of all the drama and solemnity of any great body of water, subject to tempests and tides, to winds fair and foul, swift days and slow, Sargassos and Doldrums.

The Sea of Time. It is dotted with islands; paradisiacal atolls where dateless palms wave. It has its tropics, its trade routes, its oceangoing potplants communicating each to each in the language of flowers. It has its pirates, their ships rigged with carnivorous flytraps; it has its Magellans and Marco Polos who seek to circumnavigate the sea's boundless edge in their clockwood galleons, returning with tales of incurling coastlines and quicksilver cities, towering Inconstantinoples made of wind and rain and time; others telling of vast wastes of time; or of whirlpools where they encountered their past or future identities — ships returning before they set off, others doing battle with themselves, appalled to find they have killed their later incarnations . . .

It is a sea of moods, as I have said. Stirred by events in history, in the rare times of historical calm so is its weather calm, and in times of peril it is wild.

The sky darkened. The wind replied to Le Nôtre's sneezes with blusters. The sea hollowed, as sailors term it, steepening into tall crests and troughs.

The First Mate stepped up, an agreeable old tar possessed of a bottom lip so pendulous I fancied fitting a cantilever beneath it. Lustily, he rang the ship's bell, calling all hands, and shouts rose from belowdecks — a gloomy place, all roots and worms — wherefrom a score of humus-smelling men clambered, secateurs and gardener's trowels clattering in their belts.

They crowded onto the ship's flowerbeds. They set to bracing the bowlines and pruning the yardarms. They clambered up the rigging and reset the blooms.

The flowership quivered with renewed vigour, her masts shaking, her sails luffing.

The wind stiffened until Fritillary began to worry for the flame in his lantern. We repaired to the quarterdeck, finding a small rose-oil brazier burning to warm the officers standing watch, and we stood by it in companionable silence, lost in our own thoughts (unless told otherwise, you may take it as read, reader, that my thoughts went to Roxane as a compass points North).

Time dashed in billows at the bow. Hours and months foaming and churning, leaping years beneath the keel.

By and by the light failed, an ageless nighttime closed around us. Lamps burned on the weatherdeck, the navigator working in their swinging beams, the geographies of his face coming in and out of the light: an outcrop of jaw, a beardy jungle, a flashing arctic of hair up north, and at the equator, the wilds of his mouth mumbling as he marked off his charts in the manner peculiar to the Sea of Time (where navigators on Earth measure time to reckon longitude, here the opposite held).

By his manner, glancing forward then down at his map, back and forth, I guessed we were nearing our destination, so that I clumb to the forecastle; and was met by a sight that struck me to the core, so I fancy an anatomist opening my skull would be similarly struck by the image winding yet through the grey convolutions of my brains . . .

The risen moon a wheeling clockface of brass and cracked ivory, the ship's roses blowing dark against it, the hourglass clouds bright and scurrying before the spirited wind, the sea-years in a fury, rising up and up in twisting sprays made of instants, brilliantly twinkling.

There came a great crack and whip from the ship's flowers — and a cry as one of the petals tore from its bloom. The broad leathery thing turned as it fell, flung like a toy on the gale. Another followed, and at a sneeze I turned to see the Captain by the helm, shouting and laughing. I could not hear his words, but it was clear what he was saying: "*She loves me*," he shouted, hair mad in the wind, nosecloth torn and blowing like an appalling spinnaker, "*she loves me not!*"

The sea roared, the deck plunged and tipped.

I clung to a clew line. At the stern, a gang of sailors battled to remove a tarpaulin from a large blocky object, and for a moment my heart fell, for I thought it was a lifeboat.

The canvas blew aside . . . and it was not a lifeboat, but an ornate cabin such as those used by balloonists, called a gondola.

It was very large, fully enclosed, fitted with windows along its sides. A flaccid bag was strapped to its roof, the balloon, I supposed, completely deflated.

Several more tars came forward, fixing a pump to the balloon.

A sneeze behind me. I turned. "Time to be on your way!" Le Nôtre shouted over the wind. "And not a moment too soon!"

The gale whipped his spittle into my face.

"On our way? In that?" I shouted. "Surely it would take hours to inflate!"

"Inflate?" He looked at me oddly. "Aye, I suppose it would." He glanced forward, over the bow. "Make haste," he shouted to me, "we're almost upon the entry-point!" He leaned forward, bellowing into my face. "And good riddance to ye!"

Enough. My equanimity blew away on the wind. "Sir, I can tell you that whoever you believe me to be, that handsome fellow will be glad to settle the matter with you, at a time and place of your choosing, with swords or pistols —"

"*Faugh!* Be off with you!"

"Sir, I am as good as my word; when next we meet, this matter will be settled."

"Ah, Begone!" He shoved me from him, and stumped away across the foredeck.

Then the First Mate was at my shoulder. "Don't mind him, Sir," he said. "He's not been right since the sinking. The organs of the intellect, y'know. *Touched.* Come along, then, this way. Hurry now, your friend is already aboard . . ."

He urged me towards the balloon-cabin. It was fantastically carved, festooned and decorated. I saw the tars furiously working the pump: it seemed they were not inflating the balloon, but draining it further.

The Mate shouted something I could not make out over the wind. I asked him to repeat it.

"Ye shall be entering the heavens near a particular

moonlet," he shouted. "Ye will put down there first of all, there to meet with a gentleman. He's of quality, by all accounts, but queer for it. He'll be of some help when it comes to setting your course, Sir!"

"My thanks," I shouted. The ship plunged, and I almost lost my footing.

Again I looked at the tars manning the pump. No question of it; they were not filling the balloon, but emptying it, despite that it was already empty.

Before I could question the Mate, he wished me luck, and was gone — at which Fritillary reached out and pulled me inside.

The door slammed shut. I glimpsed an opulent interior, madly lavish; a crammed kitchen, paintings and statuary, rich furnishings, fine armchairs, one occupied by Fritillary . . . Then the world tipped, and I was hurled into a chair of my own.

I knew by the pit of my belly we were rising into the air.

Through the aft windows, the flowership receded swiftly. I saw its name on the stern — *Fleur Fière II* — and of a sudden I wondered what had become of *Fleur Fière I* . . .

A glimpse of Le Nôtre on the forecastle, nosecloth whipping like a vile flag, then the ship was gone, and the view was nothing but churning sea, and we flew on.

"I do not understand," I shouted over the storm. "Those men, they were deflating —"

"If they were draining the emptiness from the balloon, then it must be filled with something *less than emptiness*," he replied (my italics).

"But nothing is less than emptiness."

"Yes, and we are fortunate to have such a quantity of it. 'Tis a potent stuff too." Seeing no answering comprehension, he said, "Think you. What is more powerful than all things? Swifter than all things? Softer,

& harder, & blacker, & whiter, & bluer, & redder than all things? Nothing, nothing, nothing!"

The cabin swayed again, bouncing, ropes creaking, windows rattling. I saw a war of waves, a chaos of foam, crests like parapets, years and decades dashing and pitching.

And then a sight to freeze the blood in my veins.

A huge and violent whirlpool, a *Mælström*, swelling ahead, dark and swallowingly vast.

It happened with merciful speed.

The gale swept us closer. The *Mælström* filled the view — inhaling, sucking us down. I had time to brace myself . . . and we were in.

Silence. A long moment of darkness. Even Fritillary's lantern was gone.

I heard my own breathing.

One by one, little pricks of light appeared through the windows.

The stars. And between them, opening out like flowers, the nebulæ, blue and purple and red; and great companies of worlds; and little moons scattering all about like a spill of balls.

Fritillary's lantern appeared again, beaming happily, and I beamed back.

We had reëntered the universe; we were returned to the Seventeenth Century; we were rising towards the hub of the Galaxy, towards Roxane.

I saw a wattled dowager of a theatre, swollen with pride and clammy madness, doors unhinged, blind windows crazed; her phrensied attention, so I felt, fixed on me, standing among venereal seats as, on the stage, the neck-crêpe curtains twitched aside.

3RD DAY

CHAPTER THE NEGATIVE-FOURTEENTH:

THE MAD COUNT

The gondola bobbed, the rigging creaked, the balloon boomed.

We drifted among the stars of a nameless constellation, and for the moment at least there was peace, for which I was heartily glad.

I rose from my chair.

With the leisure to inspect it properly, the gondola presented the most splendid appearance. Too splendid indeed, as if a hundred workmen had shovelled a palaceworth of fineries into a single chamber: oriental carpets smouldering under an impenetrable thicket of furniture, a pantry standing unashamed of its lolling abundance of epic pastries, sausages and hams, their glossy pinks and reds and tans answering the colours of the blush-buttocked wantons in the paintings that crowded the walls.

Statuary stood everywhere awry and askance, the largest piece being a cupped hand lopped off some Roman colossus, which pointed heroically to the drinks cabinet, being a thing worthy of the gesture, crammed with bottles of fermented starlight of every brightness and hue . . .

Oh là. To enumerate everything in that cabin, reader, would require a particular book; it would overfill the chapter with riches even as the gondola itself.

But despite those who should contend otherwise, the reader must understand that these luxuries were not in the least luxurious, but rather *essential luxuries* — I would write *utterly* essential were it not that one should not qualify an absolute: they were as indispensable as the salt beef, waterbarrels, gunpowder and all the other desperate necessaries of the most intrepid explorer . . .

More so indeed . . . and now I wonder if there are degrees of absolute after all, for they were as vital as the very hull around us, which shielded us from the vacuum even as these opulences sheltered us from the still more dismal effect consequent upon contact with the nothingness in the balloon overhead.

Its presence, that terrible contraction of absence . . .

Buoying us even as it weighed upon our souls . . . Its existence (if the word may here be used) rendering meaningless all one loved, all one hated . . .

Even now, as I record my memory of it, I find the ink drying in my quill, and the quill itself, where once it flew according to Nature's design, slowing unto immobility — so that I find it nigh impossible to continue this sentence, and must break from writing to replenish myself with a bacon sandwich that I prepared against just this possibility — *thus* — and so fortified, return to my tale, where I find myself engaged in a discussion with Fritillary.

Who, I discovered, was quite learned on the subject of nothingness.

"I made a study of it," he said, his flame fluttering as in a bleak wind, "as a student . . ." His words trailed into an ellipsis more expressive than words of his sorrow . . .

In piteous tones, I asked how best we might stave off its effects; to which, with a stifled sob (a *boo hoo*, hastily crossed out), he said the affliction would admit of but one remedy, *viz.* a strict application of things of beauty and good cheer.

And where children are sometimes reluctant to take their medicine, we were swift and unstinting in the application of, in my instance, some gemlike fruits and sweetmeats, a reading of verse from the vessel's small but creditable library, and a half-bottle of lightly sparkling starshine collected, the label assured me, on a warm and pleasant evening; Fritillary, for his part, availed himself of, among other items, a lamp oil so well refined it resembled a type of brandywine, so that even I was tempted to drink of it.

Whereafter we turned with lighter spirits to our next care, being to master the ship's controls.

These were an assemblage of perfumed levers and dials so crafted as to delight the senses while ensuring their operation be amenable to persons who were at least half-drunk — impossible for anyone sober to understand, indeed . . . And soon, we were drunkenly moving the vessel hither and yon; it was then, reeling us about, that I spied a little moon. The one, I thought, the First Mate had mentioned.

It did not look promising: a stark arctic planetesimal growing with scraggy trees . . .

Of a sudden, Fritillary leaned forward. "I see someone," he said.

I peered around my inebriation and . . . yes, there: a tiny figure, pale against the nightside, reclining in one of the craters. I brought a telescope to bear. The figure was a man, old and raggedly dressed. I saw his face, and gasped.

"What is it?" Fritillary's words were blurred with drink.

"I know him," I slurred.

A question mark made a sceptical little *click* on his lantern.

"Well," I allowed, "I know who he is."

Again I put my eye to the glass. There was no doubt about it. He was older, certainly, but I recognised him from portraits in my friend de Colignac's château.

It was none other than the Comte Montiel de Sainte-Blandine; the Mad Count of Toulouse, the noble who had built the villa in which my adventure had begun.

Elevated by depression, we wobbled past mossy rocks,

past a dead comet, making uncertainly for the moonlet.

Into the meagre atmosphere, low winds eddying about the hull.

I studied the gauge monitoring the balloon (an instrument that took some getting used to, for where the needle stood at *Empty*, the balloon was full, and at *Full*, it was empty). I turned a wheel, venting a measure of nothingness. There came a negative noise — a silencing hiss — a hiss's exact equivalent subtracted from the general sounds around us. Ribbons of blank whipped and flourished, wafts of dejection falling in flustery drifts . . .

I vented the balloon again, again; the ground rising up to meet us; a white steppe, covered with rime; lower still, a sudden hill appearing before us; I steered us around it; lower, a little too fast; then, with an emphatic bump that rattled the crockery, we were down.

The windows were already gathering frost. It looked cold out there. Fritillary searched through an overcrowded closet, finding boots and some excellent coats, and thus dressed, we ventured out into the thin, chill air.

Rarely in my experience have the stars felt so arresting as they did at that moment; they were striking almost in the physical sense, entering the eye as the arrow did that of Harold II.

It was as if we had entered the uppermost storey of the heavens, an attic pressed up against the slung and swollen ceiling of night.

I *smelled* the cosmos, the burn of the suns, the floral scent of the nebulæ.

A starry mist blew about, a fine white rain, radiances running down the sides of cliffs and hills, cataracts eroding zodiacal canyons and trenches, congealing into a humus that crunched beneath our boots.

I found myself ducking as I walked, as if I might be

struck by one or other of the constellations that swung by.

We traversed a range of reddish dunes (which I realised with an inward thump of pure enchantment were the long wavelengths of light, frozen in place); we achieved the field I had spotted in the spyglass, craters scattered all about like ornamental ponds, brimming with starlight.

"Durst someone bring a lantern here?" The voice came from within one of the taller craters, its walls rising before us.

"It is my friend's light, Sir," I called, rather stupidly.

"Well, have him put it out! It is ruining the viewing conditions!"

"He cannot, for the light is his life."

"What care I? I told you, 'tis ruining the viewing conditions!" His bellow shattered a nearby edifice of frozen starlight.

"What care I, withal!" Fritillary grumped, and left, saying he would meet me back at the ship.

"Better," came the Mad Count's voice. "You may approach."

I did not care for the man's impudence, but neither could I turn away now.

I clambered the biscuity crater wall.

"Forgive me for not rising," he said. "Mustn't turn my head just yet — just at present focusing on an interesting formation in yon Pegasus."

The Mad Count was part of the landscape.

Crystallised radiance was wrapped about his body, a frozen ring of starlight like to a diadem about his brow.

The lower half of his face was masked with a clearish, milky, hardish stuff, and his body was submerged in a pool of starlight, with a reef of stellar-plankton gathered about him as coral about a sunken hulk. His legs and torso were lost in a brittle intricacy of spikes and whips and coralline fans . . .

"O!" he cried of a sudden. "Did you see that? Look

you! There . . ." pointing to a patch of sky, entirely blank. "A new world quickening in the gases about a star. O, the marvels!" Tears ran to freeze on his cheeks . . . This was the mask over his face: years of tears. "O, the glories . . ."

I saw nothing remarkable, and said so.

"You are blind, Sir!"

I considered that I saw well enough to know the man was mad, as advertised.

"Then again," he went on in a milder tone, "few have the eyes to see. Astronomy is a passion with me, though 'twas not always so."

Thus did we fall to discourse, and he shared with me the curious history of his life, which, by his telling, had begun long before his birth.

An esteemed and prosperous man, his wealth had given him no joy. Truly a rich man cannot enter the kingdom of heaven, he said, for the gleam of gold had blinded him to the infinitely richer bounties of Creation.

Dabbling like a duck in the littlest, most fashionable ponds of the sciences, he had one day found his pool breached and spilling into a greater body of water — this outpouring brought about by a certain Flemish alchemist and philosopher, through whom he learned of *metempsychosis*, being a process taught by, severally, Plato, Aristotle, and certain mystic traditions of the East, whereby it is believed the soul migrates from one body, at death, to the next, at birth.

"The difficulty with this doctrine," he said, "which arises when one understands that the number of living persons be greater than the number of dead, may be easily solved when we decide the soul is divisible; at death, the soul departs, and parts; a fragment to one body, another to another, and so on . . ."

There were more such ramblings, which I will not trouble to set down here . . . In fine, then, certain mystic operations were performed by his philosopher (whose qualifications I began to doubt during the telling of the tale, especially when the Count mentioned how these enlightening operations had also lightened his purse). By means of these procedures, it was determined that the Count's soul had once occupied the ocular humours of the right eye of an ancient Persian mathematician and astronomer called by the name Ibrahim ibn Sinan ("'Twas as if a great eye had opened in my own soul, Sir! — the light allowed to pour in!")

Thus inspired, the Count went on to discover divers other parts of ibn Sinan's soul — a foot, the hands, the collarbone, the *membrum virile* . . . "Never did we compose the whole Ibrahim," he said, "but together, we made for a large fraction of that man."

Wherefrom, as a natural consequence, there arose his interest in astronomy.

He slept during the day and laboured through the night; a surgeon was engaged to shave his corneas; he confined himself to the diet of the owls whose night-vision he so envied; such friends as remained drifted away, repulsed by his meals of freshly killed voles, stoats and field mice; he was nothing at all dismayed: "The Milky Way embraced me in her arms, lover enough for any man. I disciplined my eyes to stare without blinking or moving, and eschewed all lamps and candles, the better to attune my vision to the darkness. I saw the light that is emitted from warm objects, and the invisible colours that give the plainest flowers glory . . . I was not satisfied. Always more to see. Even the clearest mountain air was an abominable soup. Therefore did the group, in its genius, devise a vessel of strange device, wherein I was sent, as ibn Sinan's eye, to this little moon; and here I remain, in the most perfect bliss."

He grinned, and I saw he had blacked his teeth, presumably

to reduce reflected light. "I gorge on gorgeousness!" he said. "I sup from the cusps of the constellations!"

He laughed crazily, stirring in his bath of starlight, and I saw that the stellar-plankton had sewn themselves through his flesh — it was on them that he subsisted, I thought, not starlight — a commensal relationship such as has been observed in the seas of Earth . . .

"So much to see, for those who wish to see. Signs and patterns, sigils in the stars. It was by the stars that I knew you were coming, Monsieur de Bergerac."

I started, stared. I was a little drunk, yes, but I was sure I had not told him my name, and not once had he looked to see my face.

"Aye, Monsieur, through empyræan risings and stellar exaltations," he said, "I learned of your mission, and the grim times that lie ahead. By Camelopardalis and Aries, I see your lover. By the hypogæal descent of Scorpius, I see a strange and ruinous theatre. By the aspect of Horologium, in sextile with the horns of Taurus, I see a fat man, standing beside her . . ."

"Where? *Where are they?*"

By way of answer, the milky liquor around him stirred, and one of the creatures that dwelled with or within the Count raised its blank, brick-red snout above the surface, body segments emerging one by one until it stood a yard tall.

It swayed, as if searching, and then aimed itself at a point in the sky.

"There . . ." The Count's voice a whisper.

I looked. The constellations presented a different appearance from this vantage: the harp of Lyra unstrung, Libra out of balance, and Virgo's honour in peril from the shaft of Sagittarius . . . but it was in this last, in Sagittarius, that I saw it, the star he indicated . . .

"She is in the nighted world at the core," he said; and at once I turned to leave.

"But before you go," he said. "One thing. About the fat man . . ."

The motion of the Count's eyes was quite audible, a wet cartilaginous crunch as they turned towards me.

"He is waiting for you."

CHAPTER THE FIFTEENTH:

CHIAROSCURO

We flew for Sagittarius, the constellation at the centre of the galaxy.

Starlight lashed against the window panes, milkwhite shifting to blue; we raced through the sprawl of Scorpius, seeing there a planet all of quartz, its nights lit from below, the coming day visible as through a crystal ball. We swept through nebulæ, veils and gaseous fascinators, purpling gleams, peagreen ruffles the size of worlds. We barrelled through a solar system with a great camellia in place of a star, and through heavenly deeps alive with beasts like whales; we were moved to awe as one breached — bursting out of the vasty ocean of space, to splash back down a moment later, its boom following us as we flew on . . .

The galaxy's hub resolved its intricate structure: exploded suns in stained-glass rosettes, stars stretched into wisps and twists of brilliance.

As the Mad Count had predicted, a darkness fell.

The core was not bright, but dull. A mass clustered about it, swollen with the lumpy malignity of a tumour. There was a cancer in Sagittarius. 'Twas the antithesis of a star, radiating gloom, its shadows grained, as it were, by damp little worlds. And a larger planet at the centre, the dark world of which the Mad Count had spoken.

We approached cautiously.

Derelict boulders crowded about the ship like tenement houses, some showing signs of habitation — middens and abandoned huts, meaningless graffiti or unreadable bill posters — many orbiting so closely that washing lines were strung between them, wet unmentionables slapping against the balloon as we continued on.

The darkness thickened. The planet grew.

I remarked flickering things beyond the windows — furtive, salamanderish, visible only in glimpses, maddeningly brief! — and was deciding they were but the phantoms that dark and quiet draw from the mind, and had begun working up a simile related to how clear water draws salt across a —

Bang!

The cabin listed. A groan from the gondola. Overhead, a hawser twanged and snapped. The balloon's ropes creaked alarmingly.

We pulled to a staggering halt. "'Tis the balloon," Fritillary said, studying the instruments. "There is a leak."

"Will we fall?" And what a descent that would be, all the way to the bottom of the universe . . .

"Not at once," Fritillary said. "But the breach must be repaired without delay."

We commenced a hurried search through the cabin, and in short order, I discovered a repair kit for the balloon, while Fritillary, for his part, found a helmet, a suit designed to be proof against vacuum, finely made, with a curious mass of stuff affixed to its back, bright red and about the size of a dinner platter.

"Ah ha!"

"Ah ha? What is that on its back?" I looked more closely at it — disc-shaped, concave, furred with . . . what? Membranes, lumpy veils; the whole bulging in its harness of turnbuckles and straps, weeping a straw-coloured whey . . . Of a sudden, I experienced a belated shock of recognition, stimulated as much by the colour, I think, as its similarity to the sketches of the Dutch microscopist Jan Swammerdam.

Though I was pretty sure Swammerdam had never described blood-cells approaching anything like this in size.

Such a thing!

Gingerly, I touched its surface. Là. It squidged under my fingers. If this was the cell, what size must the blood vessel have been, and the monster the blood vessel had served?

"Since it is red," Fritillary said, "it currently bears a load of the ærial nitre essential to life & combustion alike."

The cabin listed further. Time was wasting. The helmet would never fit over Fritillary's lantern. Swiftly, I removed my sword and scabbard, donned the suit, closed the visor over my nose (not without difficulty), and trod to the front door.

I snatched it open, and thence out onto the front step. Quickly, I closed the door behind me to keep overmuch vacuum from entering the cabin.

And there I was.

Alone in space . . . The galactic hub so close it was as if I could touch it — though it did not invite touching . . .

A writhe of shadows, darknesses slumping past in flexures and slow soft twists . . .

And here again were the salamanderish things, eeling in and out of view . . .

Our vessel's hull was fitted with torches arranged that they may be all lit by means of an ingenious mechanism operated by the throw of a lever. This I did. The brilliance was overwhelming . . .

The salamanders were gone so swiftly it was as if they had never been . . .

All right then. I found a ladder appended to the hull. I hastened up to the roof; there, I clung to a joist and peered up at the balloon, the leak easy to see against its envelope of taffeta and silk, sky blue and decked with golden flourishes.

Nothingness drizzled in a stream so desolate and thin the vacuum seemed rich as butter by comparison.

I set off at once, climbing the netting of ropes from which the cabin depended.

It was difficult labour. More than once, I was obliged to cling tight to the netting as once and again the vessel dipped. By the time I reached the puncture, my hands were aching and my faceplate was steamed up. I inspected the wound: a tattered hole, emptiness fluttering from it, opening, as it were, a hole in my spirits. I might have given over to misery entirely were it not for my suit, devised to flatter the wearer's senses in every way: the tailored overalls finished with crimson damask, the helmet a pearlescent shell, the collar equipped with an ingenious nippled mechanism to bring draughts of brandy to the lips whenever necessary . . .

I swung a rose-coloured glass visor over my faceplate and got to work. This was another simple but awkward task, made the more difficult by the extravagant melancholy that draped itself over my limbs, that drooped my very nose . . . The job took longer than it should have, as is often the case with unhappy men.

When at last the patch was on, my air tasted stale. I started back down — then paused, noticing something snagged in the ropes of the balloon. I clumb over, plucked it free.

An arrow. Improvised from a billiard cue. A heavy, unsubtle thing, its head smudged with chalk.

But hold . . . I sensed a salamanderish presence, eye-corner glimpses, things moving with a nasty slyness that minded me of the prowling ways of thieves or spies.

With haste, I resumed down. By the time I reached the front step my air was foul. The stink of fear. A glance over my shoulder revealed that the blood cell was no longer red, but tinged blue. I turned the door handle — or tried.

It would not move. The door was locked.

The surprise set off a coughing fit. I stopped with an

effort of will.

My first instinct was to knock. I did not.

Fritillary would never have locked me out. Something must be badly wrong.

I sidled to one of the windows and chanced a look inside.

Dark. Fritillary half seen behind a mess of luxuries, slumped on the underside of an upturned chaise. His flame glowed dimly . . .

Then, in the shadows, a movement. And another.

The salamanders had infiltrated the cabin.

Another suppling movement. One paused by the window. Standing not a foot away, thinking itself unobserved.

About the size of a child of ten years. Damp amphibian skin falling in mottled folds about its body. Tools strapped over its back, a small bow, a quiver of arrows, their shafts adapted from billiard cues.

The creature turned in my direction, and I ducked beneath the sill.

Thoughts came slowly. I seemed to remember a hatch on the ship's starboard side, a scuttle for waste. Perhaps I could slip in that way.

I moved from the door and began making my way around the hull. I clung to ropes. I clumb along raised brightwork. I hung from window-boxes planted with vacuum-tolerant flowers.

It was an arduous journey that brought no joy at its end.

When I reached the spot where the hatch should have been, I found nothing. Thinking I must be mistaken, I went further on . . . Still nothing but hull, even when I reached the stern.

I hung there a moment, furious. What devil had stolen our hatch?

No, wait. I tried to think. Dully, I realised my error at last: the *other* side — that was starboard, this was port.

I set off, labouring around the stern, back along the length of the ship.

My air tasted of rust. My breath grew loud in my helmet. The brandy in the dispensing device smelled like rot. I resisted the urge to vomit.

I reached the scuttle. It was the humblest mechanism, but far lovelier to me than every lovely thing inside the gondola.

It was held with bolts. I unscrewed them with clumsy fingers. The hatch clapped open and something tumbled out, startling me — a mass of rubbish, dropping forevermore . . .

I looked inside the chute. It would be a tight fit. I clambered onto the lip, then with the utmost effort, heaved myself within.

I paused. What had I meant to do next? I could not concentrate. A voice sleepily complaining . . . *please, please let me sleep* . . . With a final exertion, I closed the outer hatch, opened the inner.

I clumb out with care, quiet as could be. I was inside. I slithered behind the chaise longue where Fritillary lay.

I opened my faceplate. Never has air tasted so sweet!

I breathed, breathed; then looked up. Fritillary's head was visible above the back of the longue. A fresh wound on the papery fabric of his skull. 'Twas an effort even to raise my arm. I shook him. He did not stir. I shook harder. A stray question mark drifted over his lantern, still he did not wake.

I peered around the couch. The cabin was still. The monsters had gone to ground.

I waited. The gondola swayed; a cabinet door creaked; a glass tinked against another.

On the floor, the darkness beneath a tulipwood

bureau stirred.

I froze, arrested by one of the most astonishing sights I had ever beheld.

For the shadow rippled, and splashed, and behaved in every way as if it were a pool of inky liquid — from which a salamander raised its head, surfacing from a pond . . .

It looked. Left and right. Eyes blank as warts.

I held my breath.

It sank again, to rise a moment later from the shadow of a marquetry table several feet to the right.

While, on a wall at the far side of the cabin, the darkness cast by a Roman bust ruffled, black driblets spilling down. A second salamander surfaced, an arrow nocked in its bow.

It looked about, submerged once more into the gloom, the deep shadow.

"Deep shadow". 'Twas not but a figurative term to these creatures, which clearly dwelt in darkness as the alchemical salamander dwells in fire and light.

Shadows were to them as holes in the ice of a frozen sea might be to a seal or like animal.

I felt sure this would prove to be an interesting encounter.

But first, a weapon. I spied my sabre resting between the fingers of the bronze hand at the aft of the cabin.

There were shadows all about it. A risky proposition, but no alternative presenting itself, I raised to a squat, readied, leapt —

Whisst, whisst!

— two arrows, flitting up from the shadows! — a bolt glancing from my helmet, the second flying wide, disappearing into a shadow on the floor — only to rise an instant later from another shadow, to land true, là, in my thigh — and then I had the sword and was rolling, putting the bulk of the hand between me and the rest of the room . . .

A quick inspection of my leg; the heavy suit had prevented the arrow from penetrating deeply. I yanked it out, a little blood, a trivial wound.

I looked around the side of the cabinet.

Shadows in pools over the floor, all still.

A minute passed, marked by the slow tocks of the ship's chronometer.

A single small bubble rose to the surface of a shadow not four feet from my face and burst with an almost inaudible *blip*.

A second passed. A salamander raised its head from the shadow. It looked about, rose further. It suppled across the floor, dipping under the arms and legs of furnishings.

I lifted my sword. The salamander flowed closer, leaving shadow-wet footprints. It stopped, sniffed the air.

I was afforded a nightmare glimpse of other salamanders blinking in the shadows of its underbelly.

One of them saw me . . .

It cried out; I struck; a screech; the salamander writhed around its ripped belly. It plunged backwards, into the shade cast by a bust of Gassendi . . . My blade, following it, met only carpet.

But now blood rose into the first shadow, then an adjoining one, followed by its corpse bobbing to the surface of yet a third . . .

Even so, they knew where I was. Chittering voices from all about the cabin, shadows swashing, spilling — beneath a gilt bronze sauteuse, under the frame of a painting, beneath the seat of an armchair, under a chess set . . .

Whisst! An arrow from directly overhead — a near thing, chunking a divot of flesh from the tip of my nose (plenty more where that came from) — I did not look, but flicked upwards, catching the gullet of the creature emerging from the ceiling; and one, two, three of the creatures were springing up with deadly little close-combat knives. The air hazed with black as they scuttered in — the first beating my guard — or so it thought, its knife cutting only air as I spun away, around and back, to jab my sword in its breast, and withdraw for the next. Which dodged, dived into the floor to reappear (a dark rippling sensation at my back) in my *own* shadow on the wall behind me.

And I dropped, and felt a breeze as its claws whipped by my ear, and the creature dived into a shadow cast by its fellow and rose up thinking to surprise me but met instead three feet of good French steel, my blade snagging out a loop of intestine, and a sharp high stench of dung as I turned into a blow from the third of them, its blade glancing from my shoulder as I kicked out, catching it under the jaw, causing it to crash backwards.

I cleaved it in twain.

Chittering voices. More of the creatures massing by a cupboard across the cabin, squirming in and out of the shadows of each others' bodies . . .

One parted from the group to stand before a lamp, casting shade across the floor.

Two others dived down. When they rose they would be less than a foot from me.

My eyes fell on the bronze hand, its finger pointing to the wine cabinet. A glimmer of light from the cabinet's interior was met by an answering glimmer in the mind.

When the salamanders surfaced, I was already leaping, slamming bodily against the cabinet, wrestling it over. Bottles, crashing glass, a flash flood of flashing splashes. Stellar reds and whites, vintage radiances, swilling brilliancies, flickering liquors . . .

A brightness as welcome to my sight as the air had been to my lungs a few moments before . . .

The salamanders screeched and cowered and covered their eyes.

I pounced! Là! My flashing sword led the way. Là! An angel's blade, bright as vengeance!

I pierced one quite through, and the one behind it besides, and the two were impaled like meat on a spit.

Another of them stumbled close. My blade was inconvenienced by the bodies of its brothers. I snatched up an unbroken wine bottle, swung, crushed the creature's skull.

I freed my sword and made for the remaining four, huddled by a wall. The light brightened, reflecting from my grin. I accounted for three in a stroke.

One came at me, blindly lunging, and I caught it across the snout with the flat of my blade, and it chanced to fall between the legs of a buffet table, and into the shade thereunder, and I stood and backed away, monitoring what shadows remained in the room. I thought I would be ready when it surfaced.

I was not.

I felt it first in my belly.

A busy scrabbling, sharp little fingers scratching agonies into the lining.

I bellowed, doubled over. Violation, horror! The thing *inside* me, rising into the shadows *within* me!

Next the side of my chest. I fell. I was helpless. Little claws wrote agony in my left lung, clutching for my heart. But perhaps it could not reach it. The pain receded a moment — then another blow, from within the belly. I saw it bulging there, my abdomen swelling out.

I punched it.

I hesitate to describe the little mêlée that followed for the apparently idiotical aspect in which it casts me.

Fritillary tells me he half-awoke at this time to see me gone mad, hammering my own belly, shouting abuse as if making battle with my body.

But such are my skills, reader, that even in a contest against myself, I will ever be the victor.

My punches were calculated to hurt, and that they did.

The creature flailed against my spleen, pressing out humours to heat my rage the more.

I struck it again, again. It slowed in its movements. Wanting for air, perhaps. I punched, punched, felt a crunch of bone I was pretty sure was the creature's skull and not my ribs.

I felt it retreat. The greatest relief. I spied a nearby shadow beginning to ripple; a little limb reached up, shivering.

I caught it, hauled it out. Its pelt wet with my own inner matters. I flung it into the air and let it fall on the point of my blade; and with that, 'twas done.

I was the victor. I waited for the elation to come. It did not. Perhaps the little brute had knocked the organ responsible for such feelings askew . . .

Here I pass over the next hours. Fritillary stirred, little the worse for his injury. We saw to some necessary duties; I cleaned and bound my wounds (shallow but bothersome, bits of shadow having got into the flesh); we saw to the sorry business of disposing of the salamanders' corpses (this by the expedient of dumping them into patches of shade); Fritillary tested the ship's controls, which seemed in order; at length, he steered us for the world that was our destination.

There was the soughing of wind. Fritillary gentled us down through the air. The planet rose towards us —

A *bang*! Just the same as the first . . .

My repair, or some other breach, gushing nothing!

The ship was seized by a fit of trembling!

The wind rising to a scream, throbbing and sobbing and howling and pummelling the hull with idiot fists!

I smelled smoke, saw red streamers — bits of flaming brightwork flapping up over the windows. We met the cloud-deck with a distinct *slap*; an instant of misty grey (a white crickle of lightning), out again, black landscape filling the windows.

The balloon thundering like a tympani . . . a drumroll preparatory to the crash to come . . . the landscape whirling . . . oh my love . . . a lake, a forest . . . my love never to see you . . . the tympani louder, winding up, the crescendo . . . trees bulging up in the windows . . .

The crash, when it came, was no sort of crash at all.

A feathery humph, a creak of branches, a nominal crackling from some twigs that were, frankly, embarrassed to have made any noise at all.

In all, just sufficient to let us know we were down.

I stood, shaking with unreleased tension, and looked out, and began to understand the nature of this place, and the curious reason for our light landing.

CHAPTER THE FIFTEENTH-AND-A-HALFTH:

THE EXACTITUDINAL WOODS

I have encountered in my travels so many curious prodigies of flora that I have taken it upon myself to compose a monograph treating on the subject.

The interested reader is directed to the library of the *Académie des Sciences*, where that text is to be found (de Bergerac, H-S de C, *De Prodigiis Botanicis Corporum Cælestium Mediorum atque Inferorum*). In it, you will read of a tree that secretes sticky sap onto its limbs with which to entrap flocks of birds, whose unwilling wings will bear it from place to place; or of a flower notable for being far the least likely to be included in elegant gardens, furnished as it is with cloacæ with which to produce its own manure . . .

But among the many oddities to be found in that remarkable book, the plants of this little planet were without question the oddest of all.

Though many, it should be said, were not odd but even. This being a world where, in the absence of sunlight, the vegetation had learned to draw nourishment from the one element that abounds in every part of the universe — the element that Plato felt *preceded* the universe, indeed.

The element that is boundlessly plentiful, from which one may subtract forever and never deplete, but rather enlarge; so that even this dark, frigid place was upholstered with life, rich and rank with jungle . . . and yet not jungle. And not rank, withal, but ranked. A wilderness, but fair to the eye; an unruly woodland more orderly than the most formal garden . . . Its divers fields neatly bordered, though by no farmer's hand; parterres and herbaria, beds and terraces in dizzying reciprocities, in concentricities and interrelationships, such that it was hard to credit they had been shaped only by the abstraction Aristotle called the highest form of the beautiful — and not austere — no! Lavish! A world where not even fractions were done in halves! Its greeneries lush as any music, as any painting or poem, splendid with colour, with boscage, dewy decimals, mossy square roots where adders crept and slunk . . . Ever and on, vegetable equations and formulæ boundlessly abounding: ponds scummed with algæbra; fields of sumflowers; of mathwort; beds of digitalis . . .

The mathematical world, where grew these strangest of trees, whose bellcurved canopies had broken our fall.

For as every living thing is expressive of some bit of mathematics or other, as Pythagoras attested, so these trees, with their tost coin leaves and curiously branched limbs, manifested the probability formulæ of Gerolamo Cardano and like mathematicians.

Reader, you should know that these trees attracted about themselves events of great unlikelihood.

Nor, was I surprised to learn of such, when I took the moment's thought necessary to conclude such a species must perforce exist.

A tree that attracts unlikely circumstances, and which is itself an unlikely circumstance, is, after all, by its very improbability, one hundred per-cent likely to occur in nature.

As was to our very great advantage, having brought about our safe landing (which, being so unlikely, was one hundred per-cent likely to take place), along with other barely creditable eventualities proceeding therefrom . . . For after effecting repairs to our craft and returning aloft, we chanced to spy certain bushes, certain calculations, certain vegetable logarithms — one plant leading to another — forming, it was soon clear, the very mathematical representation of my search for Roxane . . .

Proof of the doctrine that every aspect of the world corresponds to some mathematical formulation . . .

To solve the problem was to advance closer to her . . . I shall tell you only that it was a hedge maze of certain coefficients and primes, and leave the problem as an exercise for the reader, then move directly to the conclusion.

The Master of Secrets's sloop, resting upon the ground.

Fritillary lowered us to the surface a furlong away; I leapt from the gondola; at once, Fritillary and ship were gone.

A moment passed.

I crouched in the dark. A soft wind blew. I watched for signs I had been seen. There was none.

I set off for the ship at a jog, numbers crunching underfoot.

CHAPTER THE SIXTEENTH:

LE THÉÂTRE SYPHILITIQUE

Closing in, I spied something dark mounded up behind the sloop. A hill?

It moved as if shifting its weight . . .

So. Not a hill then.

The sail, the great wing, was ragged. Had the ship been caught in a storm? Feathers were missing from the edge, sacramental blood spilling down it, to the sides of the hull; the ship wrapt in life.

Skinwhite blossoms, vines, nipplecoloured buttercups . . .

Venereal deliria. Glossy bruise-blue net and snarl, gnarls and cankers of wood and splitting woody flesh under knuckled rudder . . .

I stole closer. I spied, through windows, living tissues squeegeeing against glass — organs, wobbling horribles, their colours not colours but discolours. Smutch, blotch and mottle. Dank, blear, dinge and mank . . .

Là! A footfall! A Frantic had come to stand by the gunwale on the deck overhead.

I froze, hidden among the flora as a bookkeeper hides a damning figure in his ledgers.

More footsteps, some conversation. Another Frantic there. The light swelled, the white of the angel's wing . . .

Then the scritching noise of someone writing.

Flesh began to fall from above, calligraphic lollops spilling with fatty slaps onto the hull, sliding down towards me, so that I was obliged to hasten away, glancing back to see the Frantics laughing together as with one of the angel's quill feathers they scribbled blood and tissue onto the night . . .

Fearing discovery, I went around the bow.

I saw the thing I had taken for a hill.

I could but thank Fortune for the compliment it paid me in presenting this test of my courage.

I took it all in at once: the great *gumma* at the base, one of the granulous excrescences as have been observed in the most grievous of syphilitics, so deranging the patient's flesh that they sprout with hair, toenails, lengths of gut, liver . . . Or in this case, a building. A theatre.

I thought of Augustine, who equated theatre with disease.

Writhen domes sagging like an unwelcome décolletage above a façade of toiling coils and cockled twirls, purfles and turbules, khaki and dark dungbrown, like to lines of stench broadcast on the air . . . and on the pursed doors, words of stink, unsavoury characters read with nose as much as eyes: "*PYROTECHNICON! A Lamentable Tragedy Presented in the Most Sumptuous Manner, Perfect in Ensemble and Equipment!! Mixed Full of Love, Sorrow, and Mirth, in Which the Posturing CLOWN doth Labour in Vaine to Rescue his Damsel ROXANE!!*"

I did not hesitate. I entered that definitively dreadful place. Through the resisting entrance, the sopping lobby.

Into a bony auditorium, the dark as impenetrable as that within my own skull.

But what lights burst in our skulls, reader, what nightmares glow by their own heat to illumine the brainpan's plates and sutures . . .

An inner light swelling to shew me what I would rather be blind than see . . .

The word *playhouse* is accorded the feminine gender in French, and so was this place female, in the worst sense. I saw its . . . *her* . . . curves — her bumps and folds and tender clefts — a wattled dowager of a theatre, swollen with pride and clammy madness, doors unhinged, blind windows crazed; her phrensied attention, so I felt, fixed on me, standing among venereal seats (upon which one was sure, là, to get the clap) as, on the stage, the neck-crêpe curtains twitched aside.

A simple set revealed: a table, a chair.

In keeping with a dowager's tastes, all was drenched in gems; the effect less decorative than defecatory, as if some beast had squatted overhead and miraculously shat precious stuffs . . .

A pallid, fat, green-clad form emerged from the wings, smiling mildly and puffing on his pipe.

"And so here we are," the Master of Secrets said.

"Where is she?" My sword was drawn.

"Oh, Cyrano, a sword? Again? Each time it has served only to make me stronger."

"You'll allow it pruned you well enough." I grinned to shew this was a memory fond to my recollection.

"Yes," he said. "Well, as it happened, Cyrano, that stroke of your blade proved a stroke of fortune."

He lifted his left arm, the one I had separated from its hand.

The stump was belike that of a smouldering tree, smoke rising from it. Blue fumes, well defined, cloudy fingers, a fat blue blowing palm.

'Twas like to the smoky memory of a hand, prehensile fumes, smoke rings about cloudy digits. "It comes of this new tobacco," he said. He flexed it admiringly. "It is very exclusive. I borrowed it from Louis's personal humidor, in fact."

The hand, growing, swept back and forth. "Do you not hear them, Cyrano? The levers, the gearish motions? A mechanical smoke, the ideal tool for theatre, which concerns itself with transformations . . ." The hand turned, knotting, knitting a backdrop, fingerpuppets, a shadow forest, foil foliage, cogleafed vegetation: the world, he began to explain, whence came the tobacco, a planet so small that the vegetable and mechanical kingdoms were forced to combine into —

Faugh. So much talk, so *many* explanations.

I ran, leapt. Raced over the stage, hearing an excited rustle from the auditorium.

My enemy heard it also. He whirled, quickly stiffened his will: the plants shook apart, the smoke blew down, touched me, touched off a pain in my left shoulder.

The wound spilled not blood but rubies.

"Look you, Cyrano," he said, "every fume an engine, the smoke of dreams given tools, all the horrors of my fancy afforded knives and hammers . . ."

The hand a congregation of vapours, a pungency of rust, a cogtooth halitosis rolling as again I leapt, swung — a clang! — fingerstrands met the blade, tightening.

The sword stopped dead in the grip of the stink, a strong smell indeed, its fingers fiddling minutely — the steel warming even as I tried to shift it. It was afflicted with a lapidary disease.

A fester of gemstones, jewels oozing, growing hugely.

The hand released the blade. I fell back, scarcely able to lift the great glittering thing at the end of the pommel . . . Still it grew, spikes branching, feathery spines . . .

The Master of Secrets coughed laughter. "Bethink you how I could ornament your flesh, Cyrano, or that of your fiancée."

His hand bringing forward a divan of precious stuffs, leaning and tortured, a mad saint's reliquary.

She lay upon it. Here was the beauty that countered all the ugliness in the world.

"No closer, Cyrano!" The wrist lengthened, the hand wafting above Roxane's sleeping form, a finger turning several of her hairs to blonde diamond . . .

A gasp from the auditorium.

Here was a pretty impasse, the theatre whispered to itself . . . *What will he do? What can he do?*

This: I laughed. I shrugged weightlessly. "What care I?"

"What's this?"

"You will not harm her."

The Master of Secrets studied me. "Will I call your bluff?"

"I think not. You fear the girl too much." (Do you remember, reader, the intelligence given us by Louis's mistress of cats?)

"The girl?"

"Ariette."

The name fell as a stone in the puddle of his face, shock and terror rippling out, and shame, and a nameless baize sentiment unique to billiardtables — so many expressions that a head less broad in its compass could never have accommodated them all.

Raging, he rose, he reared, he roared. The fingerish gas raked for my face.

The theatre cried out. I heaved my transformed sword, most awkward of weapons. The cords in my forearms stood out as I lumbered it around. It toppled me over.

The Master of Secrets laughed. But let him, for I had forced him away from the bed. I feinted, came back, surprised us both by landing a blow, an emerald jag burying itself in his booming belly.

He looked down. "Ah, Cyrano," he said, "you have torn the felt. In most parlours this would mean you have forfeited the game." Smoke eased from his injury, a scab of rubies.

He chuckled, swelling. "But let us play on."

He surged rhinocerosishly forward, hand swarming.

I ran, dragging the huge sword, crystal blade zagging with snowflakes, porcupines, skullbursts . . .

A finger came down to my left. The theatre shouted with terror. The fingertip scraped a chair, which chimed and spilled in a spume of agates. I plunged on, sword the size and shape of a ship's anchor; backstage now, a mess of theatrical tackle, shadows, a buttery gunge of maquillage, the dowager-theatre's makeup. The fingers again; I flung myself through cloying clouds, a slick of pomade, past props, costumes, wormy black gloom, broken nightmares slathered in lotions, lipsticks, polishes.

I rounded a false marble table dressed with a plaster banquet, painted pastries, mock foodstuffs — but I seemed to smell them nevertheless, a whiff of rot, as if they were past their best.

The smell worsened . . . The *hand*, ticcing fingers coming around from the side!

I fell the other way. A finger grazed a plaster column by my head. The theatre was in an uproar. My sword crimped, a profusion of antlers, a fantasticated hatrack. I staggered into a corridor walled with hair. Past dressing rooms, festooned lanterns. One of them formed a lowercase *i*. It winked at me —

— the hand coming for me. I swivelled, stooped, danced.

I swung, wrenching my elbows. I brought the blade into the Master of Secrets's thigh. It was a matter of indifference to him.

"Come, Cyrano," he boomed, swollen, a blowing balloon, dimpled as a Chesterfield sofa. "I tire of a game so easily won."

He swatted the blade away. It shattered against a wall. The theatre went silent with dread. The fat man advanced on me. I backed up to a door at the end of a hall. The latch was bolted with a lock of hair. The Master of Secrets raised his hand and scraped the ceiling. A slurry of gems slipped to the ground . . .

But the theatre was not quite ready for the drama to conclude, nor, I think, was she happy with the manner of the conclusion.

The door at my back clicked. It sucked open.

I fell into a large room crammed with staging gear, blind lights, broken pulleys.

The Master of Secrets bellowed and bellied forwards.

Behind him, a flickering glow.

Fritillary. He performed an action I shall not detail here. (Patience, reader.)

A flame touched a flap of old costume.

The Master of Secrets filled the doorway. Fat puckered and fluxed, blubber in spate. His hand swept out. It touched my face, once, lightly, a benediction. I cried out, staggered. There came an answering sob from the theatre. I took a breath and stood as straight as I was able, looking him in the eye.

He flabbed closer, lifted a finger — and the corridor behind him burst into flame.

He turned, surprised. Là! The flame was so playful. The friendliest of fires! How merry! Such fun, to see it prancing over the walls! It alighted, it lit. It bounced mischievously onto the Master of Secrets's coat.

He tried to slap it out. His smoke tried to smother it. In vain. This fire was too bright. It was clever. It flashed and crackled and cackled over baize and skin and blood and ivory bone.

The Master of Secrets burned. But as he did, was he so troubled by the turn of events as he might have been?

Did I see amusement in his eyes, a wink as the lids crisped away?

A smoky smirk before his lips were gone?

Fritillary tells me he accompanied me on the walk back to the stage, though I do not recall it, save for a warm glow lighting my way along the corridors, through storage rooms, into the wings.

All I saw was her.

The tip of her ear poking from her hair; the repose of her eyelids; the perfect bevel of her upper lip, its colour as if someone had given life to the pink in the sheen of a pearl.

A rising surf of applause held me upright, gave me strength to take her in my arms.

Her body was soft and warm from sleep. She rested her head against my chest.

Then she was awake, staring at me.

And exhausted, in pain, and sick unto death, it was in a heavenly reverie that I fainted dead away.

The applause swelled. The scene was done.

CHAPTER THE EIGHTEENTH:

ROXANE

Now, dearest reader, in the lull that must needs take place while I lay insensible — in the queer, hushed, between-moment when the curtains are closed and the stage hands are scuffling about changing scenes — let us take occasion to address Fritillary's doings that took place during the events above, his escapades which surpass any ten elsewhere in this account . . .

So, at least, began the chapter you may no longer read.

Fritillary himself has entreated me to remove the episode from this history, save for the briefest outline — and such was my gratitude that I removed the chapter at once (this is still reflected, the attentive reader will already have noted, in the numbering of the Table of Contents), despite that the writing therein was every bit as worthy as that which it described.

The finest in this account indeed. A prose to loft you, reader, to the aching peak of the art — to send you *diving*, sentences banking, dipping, descriptions coming in a buffeting rush: telling of the inspired way Fritillary escaped detection when landing beside the theatre; of his infiltration within disguised as a stage-lamp; of his hiding backstage, where he awaited the opportunity to come to my aid; and lastly, the rescue itself . . .

Although removing that chapter gave me no less hurt than it did the canon of literature, I destroyed it as soon as I understood that to do otherwise would have given more hurt still to Fritillary — whose flame accords with what the philosopher Jakob Böhme calls the male's "fiery essence", designed by Nature to commingle in lawful and chaste congress with the female "tincture of light" to bring about new life in the candlery of her womb . . . Hence, those who should allow their flame to quiver forth in circumstances other than lawful and chaste congress (backstage, say, in a theatre made of syphilis), are committing the equivalent of the solitary vice that Clergymen deplore in public every bit as vigorously as they commit in private . . . (But with that said, let us also ask this: is the act a sin because it prevents the creation of life? Wherefore I say in Fritillary's case, the sin was no sin at all, for if it did not create a life, it saved one, *viz.* my own.)

There, done.

Having spared my friend's blushes, let us move on, touching but lightly on the events hard after: the moment when Roxane awoke to see me unawake; when she glanced up and understood that the lantern illuminating the scene was a living creature; when she saw very quickly through Fritillary's fantastic appearance (as once she had done for me) to perceive him as a kindly being.

When she proved, if proof were needed, that she was a woman far above the common run.

They bore me back to the ship. Fritillary took the controls and we rose away from the planet.

I came to myself for a short while, and saw her there looking down at me; and although in agony, I was made powerful by joy.

I understood no mortal hurt could pierce the armour of my amour.

I awoke a second time to see her wringing out a cloth with which she had been mopping my brow.

She smiled to see me conscious. I returned her smile, though it was torture.

The facial wound. Every breath was an anguish that referred to other parts of my body, and further, even into the couch under me, cushions weeping, wooden legs buckling in anguish . . .

Fritillary came forward. Some words on his lantern. I could not focus on them . . .

He had a small pail. He said — I managed to read it — he said something about finding it in a cabinet in the stern of the ship.

He scooped up a measure of adamic clay — just the sight was a relief — and ladled it onto my face . . .

A slow warmth, an easing . . . Shivery sizzles, a delicious livingness, a sparkling of the flesh, I knew how it was to be champagne, a firework!

I sat up, I stood! I burst, I crackled! I faced Roxane and Fritillary! I grinned, I laughed!

Which they answered not with awe or joy, but dismay (not so easy to read on Roxane's face as it was on Fritillary's, until he thought to remove the word from his lantern . . .)

Something was amiss. I touched my face.

"Pray," I said, and heard a difference in my voice, a chiming tone, "bring a mirror." Fritillary did so; I held it before me and stared at the result of the Master of Secrets's touch, the side of the bridge of my nose, the upper part of the cheek, the join between flesh and crystal healed, but the crystal, the crystal still there, some an olive green, some a bluish mineral the name of which I knew not, but which would have been quite handsome, I supposed, in another setting . . .

I lowered the mirror. I turned away and hung my head, and if I let fall a tear I can but hope the reader will give me some allowance . . .

Roxane, for her part, gave me none whatever. "What is this? Come, is this the tempestuous Captain Satan? Fie!"— along with more such.

She turned me around and looked at me sternly. "In truth, these new features are a truer expression of your character. Always have you been a man of many facets, brilliant, adamant . . . The man I love is not changed," she said, "his qualities have merely been made more obvious to the eye."

Here she is, reader, presented for your worship.

She said, "To me, Cyrano, you could not be more precious were you made entirely of diamonds."

We kissed.

I trust the reader holds in fresh remembrance my claim, made in an earlier chapter, that I do not hold with the notion of luck.

Let it be known that I retract that claim.

We kissed; and so the adventure ended.

The enemy destroyed, the lovers reunited and on their way home, to live out their lives in peace . . .

What is that, reader? It is *not* over, you say?

Well, remember I had not your advantage of seeing how many pages are left in this history.

I believe Roxane might have had some idea our tale was not yet done — though 'twas possible she was thinking wishfully, for she gave me to know she considered it most unfair that she had missed all the excitement. I apologised, and assured her she would be fully conscious of every horror we faced in times to come, which jest she met with whatever one should call the opposite of amusement, and wrapped herself in a cloak, detailed after the Persian fashion with yellow moons and stars, and swished away to a window, and looked without, into darkness amended by some thoughtful race of creatures with flotillas of lantern-moons.

I went to her.

"My love," I said, "even after a quest is won, an adventurer's spirit sometimes continues uneasy, as a ship will continue to roll after the storm is past."

"It is not that."

"You will see," I said. "When we are safe in France, we will —"

"Wait," she said. "The lanterns. Look you."

"What?" I saw a clutch of pale purple lamps swinging by, their corners pranked with silver bells. There seemed nothing odd.

"*Look*. There, another went out! And another!"

Ah. Yes. I saw it. One by one, the drifting lanterns were being extinguished.

At the helm, Fritillary's own lantern was pale with horror. "The planet is changing," he said . . .

I snatched up my spyglass, turned it on the world we had recently left, its mathematical flora calculating its orbit through the night . . .

The surface was gone, lost under ridges and troughs of cloud, fingerprint whorls, the planet a child's toy smudged by greasy hands, the whorls massing and rising to form a hand, cirrus wrist, a cumulus arm reaching up, mechanical anatomy of atmospheric bones, fogshaped body, head of steam, cue-ball bald, gasmachine billiardmoon grinning with teeth of stink.

When I glanced at Roxane, I was appalled to see she was smiling.

We fled.

The hand coming after us, snuffing the lanterns it passed, the darkness closing in even as we built up speed, shouldering through shoals of lanterns — scores, hundreds, every shape and colour — yellow crescents, green roundels, navyblue spheres scraping and slamming and bumping over the hull. The hand a shadow behind us. I looked to the fore, a huge lantern ahead, looming; Fritillary never turning but crashing through it — clearly he shared no fellow feeling with these objects — masses of lacquered paper, japanned wood, torches tumbling over, everything burning as we boomed through the great drumming interior, on through the other side, out . . .

The great hand swinging up now, the sky a palmist's chart of abridged life lines.

Fritillary dived. The fingers razing and shearing. Smoke-flesh slathering, the hand raking through lamps, turning them to gemstone, a slurried dazzle, mineral lights raining down.

A dreadful din. The balloon wracked and thundered.

Fritillary increased our speed and angle of descent, a desperate plummet, engines at their shuddering utmost. We entered the state called by Galileo *free-fall.* Pastries began to float, lighter than air; carpets flew as if charmed by Aladdin's genie. Our own weight dwindled.

I turned at a laugh from Roxane, afraid lest fear had made her lose her reason. "Oh, Cyrano!" she cried. "It is so exciting!"

She spun *en point* on nothing. I reached for her. She laughed and playfully whirled away . . .

There was a shivering bang. Behind her, a wall opened.

It makes me sick to remember it: the vacuum swirling in, splashing and resplashing, the sucking wind taking her towards the breach.

No! I would not have it!

I leapt, reaching, reaching — caught her — her hand in mine, my other hand grabbing something solid . . . She hung on, eyes wide, grinning wildly!

A steady crunching noise as more of the hull chunked away. Detritus falling through the gap.

The din softened, not because the danger was easing, but the opposite. The air was becoming thin. I felt something wet against my face — water — astonishingly, it was rain, little stormclouds forming in low pressure zones near the ceiling, lightning snickering down to set a rug alight.

A shout from Roxane, hanging beside me. "What is wrong with Fritillary?"

I peered through the weatherfronts. His lantern was dull, his light burning strangely.

And not only his lantern; all the lamps in the cabin were turning blue, their flames wobbling into soft spheres.

"Fritillary!" I called. He regarded me woozily. "What ails you?" I said. "Is the lack of air causing you some impairment?"

"Not at all," he said, his words blurred. " 'Tis but the weightlessness . . ." There was a pause, so long that I thought he must have passed out. "But!" he said suddenly. "*But!* — it is not such an unpleasant, you know. In fact I feel better . . . than I did for some time . . . The weigthlessnessess, you see . . . & resultant lack of convection . . . do you not find it affects yor combushton . . . in teh most delicious, delictious, way?"

An uneven *teeheehee*. "I wonder if I should, should increase the speed of desent, if it enheances the effect . . . I could detach the balloon entirely. It is just sl, slowing us down . . ."

I gave him to understand that that might not be the wisest idea at that particular juncture, whereat he held up a finger and sagely replied, "*Hipshot . . . hoggerel.*" Then, rounding out the argument: "*Pawky . . . zenzizenzizenzic . . .*"

At which he fell, or rather *rose* into sleep, turning head over heels into the air.

The released tiller jinked and pivoted. The ship spun. We were out of control.

I began forwards.

I swam through tempestuous air. I dodged busts and paintings, wineglasses, a stormfilled teacup. Through little tempests, rain and miniature lightning bolts the size of fish forks. My hair on end, my nose burning with St Elmo's fire.

I learned to resent the term "soft furnishing" when a whirling armchair banged cruelly into my ribs . . .

And always, the great hand outside, closing in . . .

I turned at a shout from Roxane, in time to see a sloshing chamberpot come winging towards me — a case where the pessimist saw the vessel as half-full. Or more than.

Dazed, gasping, I cleared my eyes of ordure, to glimpse something worse outside, above and to the rear, like moons at first, then they moved, and were not moons at all, but the crescents of fingernails.

The hand had caught up. The fingers reached down. They touched the balloon.

The envelope brittled, shattered, calved away. A crashing chime. The oblivion within the balloon spilled forth.

The gondola began to drop.

And because nothing descends more swiftly than an object descending freely through vacuum, the absence caught up with the falling gondola almost at once.

Weightless tons of it roaring silently down, through the holes in the hull.

We were submerged in nothingness.

CHAPTER THE NOTHINGTH:

AN IMAGINARY MÉNAGERIE

Often, I confess, my tales are such that, if they were not true, they could not possibly *be* true.

Indeed, my detractors, of whom I boast a considerable number, have made so impudent as to claim my histories are but fantastic fictions.

Some I find to be among my most devoted followers, buying up my publications to search out niggling inconsistencies, logical infelicities and like flaws.

And how delighted they are when they find one, as if with it they have shewn the whole thing to be a deception!

To which I can say without fear of contradiction (not that I will not be contradicted, you understand, but that I have no fear of it) that if my histories were false, would I not have removed any flaws in fear of being exposed?

That I have left my tales intact, complete with imperfections, serves not as proof of my dishonesty, but the opposite! Any blame lies not with the poor author who writes with the strictest regard to honesty, but with the events themselves.

Whereof I now offer this testimony. You may read on, reader, greeting every shortcoming as sign of my integrity. You may remain happy in the knowledge that I have maintained the same relationship with the truth that I have enjoyed since my first day as an author, when I sat down to recount my adventures in a ship wrought from magnetic iron, drawn on its inexorable journey to the North Pole . . .

Nevertheless, that said, I am obliged to add that for the

next few pages at least, nothing of what I describe took place.

I hasten to add, however, that my account of it is entirely true.

Nothing happened.

It happened violently, welteringly. Velvetly enveloping us, blustering uttermosts of blank.

It swallowed us, and for a long while I saw nothing.

As was to be expected: what was not was that this *nothing* partook of great variation and richness . . .

Là.

Consider, reader, how many things *are not* — so very many more than *are* — the very existence of one thing engenders a dizzying profusion of others that do not . . .

Think you, also, of the difference between a missing tooth and a missing child — between a heart stilled by expertly wielded words, or by an expertly wielded sword.

Some zeroes are large, some small, they are rarely equal. One absence is not the same as another.

As I can attest, for I found myself surrounded by them.

A wealth of them, *tons* of them.

Overhead, for instance, was a vaulting expanse that was nothing at all, but was *most specifically not* a cloudless Summer sky, and beneath my boots was a nothing that was *especially not* a green grassy meadow . . . and so a countryside of absences came to my eyes, clearly seen, for although there was no light, neither was there darkness to obscure my vision . . .

A nonattendance of trees, a rolling lack of hills, a swarm of unbees dumbly buzzing over unrisen roses that would have, had they existed, breathed forth the finest of perfumes. Seeing Roxane no distance away at all, I joined her and we sat beneath a leafy spreading oblivion, where we embraced and were free from care. For where before the nothingness had inspired such dread, I now discovered there had been nothing to fear all along (is it not ever thus, like to a reverse of the laws of perspective, our fear diminishing when that which we fear is close and we see it for what it truly is?)

I answered Roxane's unasked questions about our circumstances, silently telling her much of what you have read in the preceding pages, reader: of Louis and his palace, his purr-code, of the flowership, and the other curious particulars of my adventure . . . but alas, just as I was about to touch on the subject of Ariette, we were interrupted by what might have been the sound of footsteps had there been any sound whatever.

Seeing Fritillary approaching, we stood and joined him, and we strolled to nowhere in particular, at which destination we very soon arrived, finding there a nothingness that might as well have been a town as anything else, with streets that would have been lined with pretty cottages — had there been streets, and had they been lined with anything at all — which would have put me in mind of the cabins and lodges of Québec or other rustic New French settlement (consider that 'Canada' derives from the Spanish "*cá nada*": "here is nothing").

Wherefrom a group of townspeople might have emerged, and invited us with marks of pleasure (or no displeasure) to accept such comforts as they had to offer, being none whatever; upon which we would have found them to be the most genial race, and the happiest withal — happiness being more associated with absence than presence: a want of troubles, a shortage of shortages, a dearth of death . . .

No time at all passed before some personages of quality, or of no qualities at all, would have arrived to extend an official welcome had they spoken, inviting us to an audience with he who would have been the Governor of that town had he or town existed; whereat, agreeing gladly, we took our leave of the villagers, or would have done, and would have been conducted by horseless carriage to what I am sure would have been a very grand Town Hall, where we would have been granted immediate audience with the Governor, who would have proved, to be a rotund, orotund, zero-shaped personage. In keeping with which, he would have welcomed us very roundly, and with great cheer, had he taken the least notice of us, and would have been pleased to grant us every largesse and munificence at his disposal (none at all).

To which we replied that to our regret we could not tarry, for we had business elsewhere, and purposed to leave the nothingness and be on our way.

Whereat the Governor might have paused between the pauses of which his speech was composed, and made comment that his Advisor might have had some ideas on the matter, were there any to have and were the Advisor in any way extant.

Which he was not, as we saw the moment he did not enter. Not at all a personage of stately bearing and august presence, he would have led us to a flawless sitting room lined with priceless artworks and a shelfless library empty of a great many books, where, I am sure, we would have taken our ease and fallen to discourse. He would have launched into a disquisition on the unscience of nullness, treating of the nonextant sextant, used in naughtical navigation, and the antiattributes of negative zero, the geometric form called the *nonagon*, and the excellence of an arithmetic based entirely on zero, which, had it existed, would have found great favour among schoolchildren for its ease of use.

In short, he said nothing whatever, and we might have given over to despair when we were interrupted by a noiseless commotion in a hall that was not outside the chamber — a ringing silence of alarum bells, soundless shouts and cries.

Upon which a door might then have flown open and, one assumes, a breathless functionary burst in to announce that the animals of the Governor's Ménagerie had escaped — a not-uncommon occurrence, one imagined, in a zoo without walls or cages.

There would have been no time for terror to cross the faces of the Advisor and functionary before the creatures, had they existed, would have been upon us.

Nonbeings, a countless number of them, they would have spilt into the unwalled room — members of the set of animals characterised by nonexistence — things that would have been doubly freakish — and how they would have aroused the passionate interest of de Colignac, these monsters without monstrous attributes: a hornless unicorn; a two-headed calf remarkable for having but one head; a five-legged lion missing a leg — all silently hooting and roaring and capering around us in what would have been a most terrifying manner.

The danger multiplying, the moveless turmoil redoubling, we managed to escape being trampled in the stampede only by virtue of the fact that there was no stampede whatever.

The Advisor would have been nowhere to be seen, and worse, the Governor's palace would have collapsed had it ever stood — worse still, the town also would have been gone if it had existed in the first place, destroyed as utterly as if it had never been.

Such was our distress and confusion that it seemed that, had we been anywhere at all, we would have been somewhere else entirely.

Were it anything, it might have been a beach — ungulled, *sans* sands.

But not *entirely* nonexistent . . . I became aware of waves, becoming realer, like to a rising tide, rolling in.

Waves of time, amplitudes of a second or less, larger choppy minutes, big bombora hours crashing and breaking . . .

But my amazement did not end there.

For with the Sea of Time came a light I had seen before, heralding a flowership not far offshore, its sails a chuckle of buttercups.

I sighted a figure at the bow of the boat, the source of the radiance.

I heard Roxane gasp.

This was Ariette. Our daughter.

I would have recognised her ten leagues away with my eyes closed.

She was small, blonde, round-faced. She wore a party frock. Her hair was in a ponytail.

Innocent as a piglet. Pure as a new ukulele.

She waved and laughed, then turned to address what appeared to be a mass of rigging at the rear of the boat: knotted, a tangle of cords shaped not unlike a man, I thought then, if a man were obliged by force of circumstance to build his body out of ropes.

I noticed the head, balanced loosely at the top: loosely knitted, whiffling, the yarned skull open to the winds, the breezes free to play among the thready thoughts.

It was Fritillary's turn for astonishment. His letters quivered. "An Æolian . . ."

The girl laughed again, snatched up an orange kitten from the deck and cuddled it roughly while the Æolian spun the tiller and the little tittuppy ship turned about, tripping and skipping, away and away over the sea that swilled and pitched, time piling in, the yacht receding over the days and months and years, and for all the time that swirled about us, Roxane and I never lost that moment, that first glimpse, beginning of a love that would not end.

Still the years churned, events piling on events.

The next being the sight of a jollyboat heaving towards us from another direction.

"Ahoy! Ahoy there!"

I recognised the First Mate from the *Fleur Fière II* . . . But *was* it he? He looked slimmer. Then I heard a sneeze, and saw a fellow at the stern who might have been Le Nôtre, the Captain of the *Fleur Fière II*, were he not so fit and unlined, and stranger still, *smiling* . . .

The jollyboat beached its prow. Roxane was helped aboard by the bo'sun, then Fritillary, and then — "Come along there, Sir!" — the Mate reached for me, his pendulous underlip waggling, and I took his hand, and the Captain sneezed a welcome, and I was hauled up and over the gunwale.

The waves rose higher; the tars pulled at their oars.

Roxane returned my gaze with kindling eyes. I realised that, all along, there had never been any need to tell her about Ariette.

A mother does not need to be told such things.

Another flowership came into view soon after, larger than Ariette's but very charming, sitting at anchor. We docked. Ropes were lowered to the jollyboat. We boarded. We weighed anchor; we set sail.

The waves plashed. The masts creaked. Reality fell about our ears — a crowding rush — sights, sounds, smells . . .

Overhead, sailroses blew and cracked in the wind. I glanced up at them: a mistake. I was all but blinded by their molten crimson vividities . . . their pursed and opulent mouths bruising the air with dusky tonnages of scent . . . their colours, clumsy and eager as puppies, bumbling into the backs of my eyes . . .

The Captain steadied me. "You may be disoriented

for a while," he said. "No need to be ashamed. Perfectly understandable."

I nodded but could not speak. I squinted at Fritillary, whose lantern was filled with disordered images: the nothingness, the girl's boat, the Æolian . . .

And Roxane. I felt her gladness as a warmth against the side of my face. I turned to her.

She looked at me and said but two words, "Our daughter."

The beauty of the moment all but killed me.

CHAPTER THE NINETEENTH:

BRIDGE OF SIGHS

Sneezing, Captain Le Nôtre trotted ahead of us down the companionway.

"You slipt out a nothingness atween one moment and the next." He begged our pardon and blew his nose. "'Twas impossible — without precedent — despite that it's been done several times previously . . . Ah, here we are!"

So saying, he led us into his stateroom. Lined with alternating panels of clockwood and a honeycoloured prehistoric timber, it was fitted with portholes of bevelled timepiece face-covers, and furnished with rose-roots, polished and espaliered into the forms of living tables and chairs.

He chose a fresh handkerchief from a scented pile on a dresser. "Now then," he said, dabbing his nose. "How may I see to your comfort? 'Tis chilly, is it not? We have some mammoth-wool jackets somewhere about, I reckon. Where's that steward of mine? Tremendous stuff, mammoth-wool, almost frighteningly warm. No?" He sniffed, making a miserable bubbling noise in his sinuses. "Something for to eat then? Some oil, mayhap, for your lantern, Sir? Some wine, Monsieur?"

"I should like none of your wine, Captain Le Nôtre," I said, and Roxane turned, surprised by my tone.

The Captain squinted his watery eyes. "You have me at an advantage, Sir."

My reply was forestalled by an uncouth yowl from the door. "Ah! Here's old Guimauve to welcome our passengers aboard!" Le Nôtre cried. A marmalade cat bustled importantly into the cabin, sat and began nibbling at a tick.

I regarded the animal sourly. Though in an improved condition, it was clearly the brute from the *Fleur Fière II* — a three-legged piratical rascal of early middle years, its waxed whiskers rakishly curled either side of its broad and comprehensively scarred head.

Tossing the beast a tidbit, Le Nôtre informed us it was traditional for flowerships to carry felines, "for the rats, y'understand, and the communications, o'course, and 'cause the sailors reckon they help speed the journey, being as cat-years are shorter than human ones . . . 'Twas Guimauve here who picked up your distress signal, y'know," he said.

The creature groomed itself proudly.

"Distress signal?" Fritillary said. "We sent no signals."

"No? Are ye sure? 'Twas right powerful, outpurring everything on the lines."

"Of course I am sure," I said. "We have no cat, as you see."

"The little girl had one." Roxane's eyes were bright, almost feverish. "A ginger kitten," she said, then, to Le Nôtre: "Did you see another yacht when you found us?"

He sneezed. "My lookout did spot another vessel, aye, on a heading most unusual, yawing against a quartering sea — taking her *sidewise*, y'understand, sailin' quite against the normal flow."

Roxane turned to a porthole, as if hoping for a glimpse of buttercup sails. I took her hand. "Be patient, my dear," I said. "We *will* see her again."

She smiled bravely, nodded and said, "Well, then — it would be the height of rudeness not to thank old Guimauve for his assistance."

"Take care, milady!" the Captain cried when she went to stroke the cat. "Pray, he makes a habit of greeting newcomers with teeth and claws!"

But far from attacking her, the cat accepted her caresses with heavy purrs, and by this, and other marks of affection, gave every appearance of reuniting with an old friend.

I turned to Le Nôtre. "Captain," I said, "you and I have some business to which we must attend."

"We do? Sir, I —"

"Beg pardon, Cap'n." A steward arrived with soap, warm water and other items for our comfort, so that there was a general fussing about, and the moment was lost, although I did not allow the Captain to depart without a warning glare (the reader will recall the reason for my sour feelings against the fellow, for all that the man himself did not: he replied to my glare with a blank gape).

After seeing to our toilet, we returned abovedecks, where I found myself feeling much improved, and better able to gain an impression of the ship, which was a younger, brisker vessel than the *Fleur Fière II*, her lines girlish, her brightwork jolly, the cakey loam of her decks rich enough to eat. Her men were well-disciplined, and magnificently ugly, as befits a sailor, such that it would have required several degrees of flattery to call them gargoyles.

As for her roses, they were indecently lovely, fat pompous bosomy blossoms blooming with rude exuberance (a rumour, told us by one of the ship's hands, had it that an Admiral in a passing barque had once sent word offering marriage to the mizzen sail, and although I cannot attest to the truth of the tale, I can at least assure you the sail was an eminently marriageable entity).

The wind was light.

We skipped across the waves.

The flowers frisked and flirted, pouring their perfume down over the decks in a delectable wash — as to which, Le Nôtre was indisposed to a full appreciation.

A sneeze announced his advent. "Just seein' you all been properly attended to. All's well is it?" Another sneeze. "I must say I envy you your nose, Monsieur," he said. "Aye, crystal membranes, most sensible. The astronomer Tycho Brahe had one similar, y'know, though 'twas of silver. Lost the original in a duel . . . I contracted an acquaintance with him on a tour through the 1500s. Interesting fellow. He owned a tame elk, y'know, until it drank too deeply of its beer and a-fell down the stairs. Also kept a dwarf what claimed to be a seer, but the little charlatan could scarce see over a table!"

He went on in this wise for some while, laughing and jesting, so guileless, so eager, that I could scarcely credit him to be the same bitter wretch who had conducted himself so impudently on the *Fleur Fière II*.

But it was he, no question, and would pay.

"By your leave, Sir!" The ship's signalman came forward, Guimauve trotting beside him, and offered a soft salute — typical cat-lover — unmanly, with the plush, plump, overgroomed look of a puffin. "Word from the palace, Sir."

Le Nôtre took the proffered page and read it in a few moments.

"'Tis a communication about your enemy," he said, addressing the three of us. "Now enemy of us all. It seems he is expanding unchecked, growing, like to a gas, to fill the available space . . ."

Being, of course, all the space there is . . .

Sneezing grimly, the Captain indicated a passage of purrs. "Worse, it says even space will not do, and the monster is expanding through time withal. It says he poses a threat to the palace itself."

Of a sudden, he grinned. "But be of good cheer! We are sailing with the current, an' so we'll stay ahead of the beast. And some solution will present itself, sure! No matter how bleak things seem, they will always change for the better!"

Before leaving with the signalman to compose a reply,

he took me aside. "Now, Sir, I apologise we've not had that chat ye wanted, but on my word, soon as this is done, I will join you."

He left. Roxane and Fritillary wiled the time by observing the curious beasts of that curious sea, which, I am sure, were very wonderful to any who has not seen their like. Fritillary was much taken with sinuous creatures, I think called *clepsydra eels*, native to the streams in water-clocks — and Roxane cried out to see splashes marking where they were being preyed upon by larger fish, like to marlin: blue, princely brutes powering along their long migratory routes from the distant future to millions of years past, where their young basked in the warm dawn of Creation . . .

More time passed — the minutes dashing and gushing, summing to an hour; and I confess that my resentment lightened, as it had in my first journey with Le Nôtre — the load easing, no matter how I held onto it, so that at length, I decided I should wait no longer, lest I lose my anger entirely.

I took my leave of the others, which earned me a hard, curious stare from Roxane. I betook myself first to the signal deck, where he was not, then elsewhere, here and there about the boat, until I found him at last on the port flowerbeds.

"Ah, Monsieur!" he called. "My apologies again. When the message were done, this thing with the soil cropped up. But now we can talk."

"Captain," I said, "as you have many pressing calls on your time, I shall put this briefly. I will accept an apology. Otherwise, we may —"

"Skipper!" A hideous deckhand. "Bit of difficulty, Sir! A report from the bow-watch."

Le Nôtre went to answer. I stayed him. "Sir, you will hear me!"

He shrugged my hand off him. "You realise, do ye not, that a Captain ain't on the ship for the sole convenience of his passengers?"

"Sir, I —"

"Skipper!" This from a navvy at the bow.

"Sir!" I drew my sabre. His eyes widened. "At our last meeting, which was my first, but your second . . ."

"Cap'n!" A cry from the lookout, a bumbling bee-striped fellow high in the sailflowers. "Cap'n, if you please —"

"Sir, you did me a dishonour, which I mean to —"

"Cap'n, Cap'n!"

— an appalling crunch from the region of the bow.

The deck tipped.

A shout, a sneeze, a scream.

Pollen showered from above. Soil tipped over the sides . . .

"*What is it?*" the Captain bellowed.

"Venice, Cap'n! Venice ahoy!" the Mate called.

"*Venice?* Why did ye nae tell me before this, y'scut!"

"I was *trying* to, Cap'n." The Mate looked at me meaningly. Understanding, Le Nôtre favoured me with a glare: a hint of the bitter man I had known on my first voyage with him (and it was then, reader, it was then I understood, as I am sure you did long before, that this was a previous incarnation of Captain Le Nôtre, and that he had done me nothing but good . . .)

The Captain stumped away, shouting orders.

"*Reeve in the parbuckles! Ease off! Prune the spankers!*" He sneezed. "*Brace abox and passaree the stun'sail!*"

A hive of activity, lines hauled, petals trimmed while the crushing, crunching, splintering noises continued from the port bow.

I staggered to the gunwales, where Roxane and Fritillary were peering over the side, aghast.

I looked down. And saw Venice.

The movements of the Sea of Time are born not of tides but tidings: currents of the current — pasts, futures — events coming in waves informed by hundreds of wonderful underflows thundering through secret trenches of deep millennia — everything arushing, afoaming, turning . . .

Or so it seems to such as we, whose manner of perception, so I am told, depends on a sort of combustion, like to Fritillary's flame; our flickering thoughts, moving through time, affording us the illusion that 'tis time that is moving — like to the scenery flying by a racing carriage, whereas it is we who are moving, the scenery that is still.

As is the Sea of Time.

In a larger sense at which we can only guess, it is moveless.

Think you, reader, of the waves across a windblown field. The stalks do not advance across the ground; the forward progress of the waves is but a misapprehension . . .

So it was with these waves. Every moment fixed, every instant immutable . . .

But what of it? What does it matter?

If our every deed was determined at the Start of All Things, it counts for nothing if they are exactly the deeds we would have performed anyway (or so it was determined from the Start of All Things I would say).

That day, however, as the *Fleur Fière* met her end, I was no longer so sure. I began to wonder if it might sometimes be better to try to behave in ways other than those which it seemed had been determined by fate . . .

The ship gave an agonised shiver, impaled on a corner of the Palazzo Contarini Minelli dal Bovolo, one of the smaller palaces on the left bank of a canal near the Campo Manin.

I saw the façade below. Its spiral stairs, a great aquatic snail of gothic arches.

I heard Le Nôtre sneezing orders at the helmsman,

who twitched the wheel this way, then that. Coralline masonry gouged the timbers, and it was as if they gouged my heart.

Soundings were called by the navigator, a bony, humourless, sandcoloured man, a historian, who had done a worthy job of steering us through the known hazards thus far.

But there were dangers at which his library (of a size that it doubled as ballast) could only hint. Drifting obstacles for which the crew must always be vigilant.

I learned that our current peril had come of a disagreement between calendars, specifically, the discrepancy that arose in 1582, when the Julian Calendar had been replaced by the Gregorian.

The Vatican had solved a divergence between them by removing ten days from October of that year.

So those days were cast adrift. Lost, dangerous flotsam. Bits of time jettisoned into the waters, with Venice most often to be seen, being as she was a timeless city to begin with . . .

The hull screeched. Le Nôtre called orders. The helmsman gave the wheel another tweak, another — small increments easing us away, a little more, a little more.

Part of the façade crumbled, its stones splitting to ooze mineral juices, and the ship gave a low note, like to a cello, and the decks jumped, and by the shout of joy from the sailors I knew we were free.

Their joy was short-lived. Several timbers were punctured; the sea was flooding in, weeks and months swamping the bilge. "*Shore up that breach!*" Carpenters hurried below with planks of clockwood.

We continued on, steering a careful path between parapets and palisades . . .

Another cry from the crow's nest. "Church of Sant'

Eustachio, Cap'n!"

"Where-away?" was the Captain's reply.

"Three month off larboard bow!"

"Hard a-port!" Le Nôtre cried.

We avoided the church's rising campanile, the roof and outer walls coming visible, its statuary yellow and carious as decayed teeth.

Suddenly, Fritillary pointed forward. "There! Off to port!"

"Aye," said the Mate, close enough to read his words. "Well spotted, Sir. Looks to be the Palazzo Querini. Look sharp there, helmsman, ten seconds to starboard!"

We turned, and turned again.

Roxane looked at me, and said quietly, "Do you see, Cyrano, what your magnificent fierceness has brought about?" Then she turned back and silently watched the city ghosting below . . . A city in which at that moment I thought I might feel at home . . .

Phantom gondolas easing through darkness, melancholy revellers in ancient masks . . . The Doge's Palace, province of crabs, walls and columns soft and pallid, the entire edifice an egg-sac pulsing with the movements of a great curled spermshape within, flexing its vague masonry tail in slimes of wet dust . . . Now the Bridge of Sighs, and never had that name seemed so apt . . .

Then: *doom, doom, doom!* — the ship's bell was tolling.

She sat heavy in the water. Ropes and hawsers creaked, booms swung, tars ran and swore.

Hearing a rasping moan, I looked up to see the mainmast writhing weirdly — *growing*, I realised, the soil of the middle deck humping up around it.

Its delicate scent coarsened, faded. Its petals browned, ageing with the rush of years gushing in below . . .

Something bulged in the centre of its flower; a rosehip, heavy and ugly. It too began to age, waning as swiftly as it had grown.

Limping onward, we left the outskirts of Venice. But the damage was done.

Roses swayed, their leaves leathering. The decks listed crazily. I heard the crackle of breaking timbers. A thunder of barrels rolling free of their stays. Shouts, more cries. An officer stumbled on deck, coughing blood, nursing a shirtful of broken ribs.

Still the bell rang and rang, until it was silenced by a falling yardarm, and I remembered the superstition that the bell is the soul of a ship, and knew her end was near.

I do not care to give a minute account of the period that followed.

In brief: the ship listed further, the topgallant-mast collapsed, it crashed through the galley. A fire started; it spread to the powder magazine; an explosion blew out the hull; several men were lost, others were horribly wounded.

We put to sea in lifeboats; the ship lifted her stern; her roses fell with visible *whoofs* of perfume . . . their petals were a wreath cast upon the sea for the *Fleur Fière*.

She was no more.

Night fell. The stars flowed with smooth Swiss movements.

At the rear of our lifeboat, the signalman communed with Guimauve, Roxane paying close attention to the procedure. The cat had been injured in the sinking, one of his eyes closed and bloody, but in Roxane's presence his purrs were strong; and when, after a while, she suddenly looked up, blinked, and said, "Someone has responded," I realised she had come to some measure of understanding of the cats' code.

Sure enough, rescue came. An old vagabond of a

fishing wherry, guided closer by further signals from Guimauve and the light of Fritillary's lantern.

It hove to. The *Fleur Fière's* crew crowded aboard. The wounded were led to beds and improvised stretchers, at which I caught sight of the Captain, stunned by a blow to the head. He whimpered and muttered as he was borne past, face twisted in sleepy rage. He spake my name as he might have a curse . . .

The uninjured were sent belowdecks, where we shared the hold with the fishermen's haul; bristlemouthed grotesques trawled from the deeps of time, spidery fins and scales patterned like the mosaics of Herculanæum.

Time flowed slowly under the boat's rude bow.

The palace harbour rose into view, the docks.

Nor was any solace to be found there.

For on disembarking, Roxane, Fritillary and I were met by royal guardsmen, who informed us that, for the first time in its history, the empire was bracing for war.

We avoided the church's rising campanile, the roof and outer walls coming visible, its statuary yellow and carious as decayed teeth.

4TH DAY

CHAPTER THE TWENTIETH:

A MASSIVELY WELLKITTENED FORTRESS

War was in the offing, yes, but I should say we saw but few preparations for it on our giddy golden ride back through the heavenly gardens and within Louis's palace . . . through mazy halls and colossal lobbies, under domes and vaults as would circumference Jupiter. And those preparations we did encounter along the way were so merry in tone, so bright and colourful in appearance, that the palace seemed more to be making ready for revel than for battle.

And at last, when we passed into the *Petite Galerie* — which sight Roxane met with astonished laughter — my grim humour began to lift.

I began to delight in her delight.

We boarded another vessel, more art than craft, its motive power derived from elegance. We went aloft, laughingly, over vastitudes, through spills of hallelujatic starlight with the aplomb of a moon turning about its world . . .

Past a landscape painting larger than landscapes, a set of continental shelves displaying pieces of china larger than China — then the orrery, wrecked, but still appallingly grand in form and ornament, Fritillary pointing out the confectionary moon on which I had engaged with the Frantics; it was falling yet, having plummeted but a small fraction of the distance to the far, far floor . . .

And under a brittle, clamorous Saturn, fashioned by millions of little nesting birds from shredded bark and spiderwebs; curlews and curlicues and spinning crashing rings of an iridescent material about which our pilot, a chasteningly handsome captain of the king's guards, took occasion to satisfy Fritillary, who had expressed a keen interest in the stuff.

The material was, we learned, "what it is and nothing else . . ."

Any who would discover the very finest threads from which they were woven, the pilot said, always discovered threads finer still . . . "Finer and finer," he said, "finer and finer. All the way down to — well, all the way down."

At which Fritillary's light burned especially bright. He turned forward to remark something far ahead, hanging in midair.

A lonely building. Vanishingly small in this vast Room: a fortress, we saw, approaching, of father of pearl and frothed marble and overwrought iron . . .

The building was suspended in midair, as I have said, from a great cable tied in a bow.

As to this cable, our pilot thought fit to apprise us of one unusual particular; an item of information I thought I could have done well enough without.

He told us the cable from which the building hung had snapped near its upper end soon after it had been put in place.

It had not been repaired since.

We were entering a fortress hanging from a broken cable.

But although, after going within, we advanced through the place in a state of nervousness, there was no call for fear.

Indeed, the engineers responsible for the construction of the fortress, centuries before, had considered the breakage a happy event (as you may read for yourself in the archives of Louis's *Académie des Sciences*). Indeed, they had been greatly affronted to find themselves being called before a council of concerned Ministers, where they were accused of incompetence.

"Incompetence?" they had cried. "Do you mean to suggest we did not know what we were doing? *Faugh!* We knew to great mathematical exactitude how weak the cable was. We knew precisely when and where it would snap."

In fact, they said, *any* cable so improbably long, stretching into the near-infinite heights of the *Petite Galerie*, would have been unable to support its own weight, let alone that of this massive building.

The breakage, had been almost inevitable. "But we *made sure* it would snap," they had said, "by weaving it from a metal that was manifestly not sufficient for the job."

The Ministers had expressed their shock on hearing such a frank confession of sabotage.

Whereat the engineers (better able to reckon the tolerance of materials than of their fellow men) had chuckled condescendingly. "If there has been sabotage, where is the damage? As you see, the fortress has shifted not an inch."

This the Ministers could not deny. And to be sure, in the centuries since, the fortress had remained in place.

It had not swayed — it had not shivered.

It was as if the cable had never parted . . .

It seemed inexplicable, but in fact the reason was simple: Since the cable had parted near its upper end, the *effect* would not be felt down at the base until it had first travelled down the cable in a wave of finite speed.

And because the cable was all-but-infinite in length, that journey would take a very, *very* long time.

Barring other disasters, the fortress would hang in place longer than the sturdiest bridge. It would abide after the noblest cathedral had collapsed. After the stoutest mountain had crumbled to rubble and that rubble crumbled to dust.

In practical terms, the engineers had assured the Ministers, the fortress would *never* fall.

We advanced through chambers and climbed stairs of marble so sensitively carved they were supple underfoot, others of living parquetry, or of adamic clay, or of the stuff but recently mentioned, of which the orrery's rings were made, and in which Fritillary had taken a particular interest . . .

We achieved the top of the fortress. We entered an audience chamber.

"Welcome!" — a hearty cry! — and glad I was to see Louis, in a fantastic costume, laughing and clapping his hands, Félix beside him, making their way towards us.

We met, embraced. There were introductions and greetings; there was some discussion about how I had come by my crystal wound; compliments were exchanged; Fritillary was commended for his light, which Louis observed was burning more richly than ever; I was pleased to present Roxane, and she was praised for her beauty, which the emperor made bold to remark was clearly lit from within, like to Fritillary's lantern, by a worthy heart and a formidable intellect — along with more such, not requiring of being set down here, and to which I paid little attention in any case, for despite Louis's apparent high spirits, I saw that (risking my vision in the glare of his medals and buckles) his eyes looked tired, perhaps sad, his face drawn.

I noticed Félix was also keeping a concerned eye on his emperor . . .

"Pray, sit, do," Louis said. "Let us not stand on formality."

He himself sat heavily, the chair creaking under the

weight of man and costume, which I might have called a uniform were it not that the word suggests there were others like it, and this thing, a work as much of architect as tailor, could never be matched, if only because its construction must have expended the last of the world's medal-ribbon and epaulet-gold.

He clapped his hands again. "Is it not exciting!" he cried, rather too heartily. "Battle is in the offing! Brass and leather, spit and polish! Cannon ready to shout flames from brazen throats!"

"Are you so pleased by the prospect of war, Sire?" Fritillary said.

"Why, no." Louis was shocked. "No, of course not. But the *preparation* for war! Ah, that is where the fun is! The parades, the pomp, the costumes!"

He straightened his cuffs, twin acreages of woollen twill sufficient to furnish the sails of a windmill.

"But there *will* be a war?"

"Oh, I suppose so," he allowed. "Though let it be known I am against the idea. And I have no doubt we shall be very thoroughly trounced."

A shocked silence. "Do all these preparations count for nothing, then?" Roxane said.

"Not at all, Mademoiselle. They are very important. We spend a deal of time and effort on them, as you see. But as for war itself, ha! We are not ready for that at all!" He laughed lightly. "Still, I am sure there will be a way to put everything to rights in the end."

"May I ask how, Sire?" Fritillary said.

"Well," he said after some thought, "we have been chasing around one or two ideas. I was playing with the notion of adjusting everything, you know, just a little, to give the moral virtues the imperative of physical laws. Something of that nature. Would put an end to this mess nicely, I should think . . ." He paused again. "Or else —

I believe some of the fellows at the *Académie* have been working on a scheme to convert the entire universe into a ship, or some such, with which to speed us all away from the approaching danger. As for how they mean to go about this, I cannot tell you. I mean, as I said to them, if you are moving the *universe*, which I have always understood to mean *everything that exists everywhere*, what is it moving *through* . . .?"

He lapsed into silence, then laughed suddenly. "But let us not be downcast! Undim thy light, bright Sir! Let us amuse ourselves while we may!" He stood. "Now come. I wish you to see something."

We followed him into an adjoining hall of great size, more of the ring-stuff, recognisable for its iridescence, never one colour or another, the inconstancy also borne out in its other characteristics, sometimes sagging in wattles and flews, sometimes massive, sometimes diaphanous, as in this hall, and rippling at the merest breath — and now leaping and jolting at a shout from the far end of the hall.

"Ho there, hold! Halt in the Emperor's name!" An officer ran in, chasing a marmalade kitten.

The animal skittered near, hissing and spitting.

I dived, missed. Fritillary essayed to catch it, as did Félix.

Laughing, Roxane kneeled, waited for it to run towards her, and gently scooped it into her arms.

"Oh, thanks be," the officer said, panting. "I thought I had lost him for good."

"Greetings, Admiral," Louis said.

The man turned, started, then bowed deeply. "A thousand pardons, Sire! I did not see —"

Louis smiled and bade him rise, and presented to us Admiral Anne Hilarion de Contentin, le Comte de Tourville, chief officer in the fortress's communications room, called the *Chambre de Ronronnement.*

"The kitten is giving you difficulties, Admiral?" Louis said, when the introductions were finished.

"The little devil! He is one of our finest purrers, but does nothing but scratch and bite!"

Louis glanced pointedly at Roxane, where the kitten was settling into her bosom and purring loudly — as well he might, thought I.

She beamed. "Oh, Guimauve would never harm me."

"*Guimauve*?" I said. "Do you mean to suggest this is the cat from the *Fleur Fière*?"

Fritillary came forward, and the kitten basked in the warmth of his regard. "The animal is younger, certainly, but it does seem to be Guimauve," he said. "Doubtless, another vicissitude of the Sea of Time."

"It is not unknown for our cats to graduate to the Sea of Time," the Admiral offered. "If you will allow me, Mademoiselle."

When he went to take the kitten, it bit his hand, leapt to the ground and bounced away. Roxane laughingly recovered it.

"There seems but one course open to you, Admiral," Louis said.

De Tourville nodded ruefully; and bowed to Roxane, and asked if she would be so kind; to which she replied it would be her very great pleasure, if I had no objection, whereat I replied in easy tones — here, reader, I confess to a lie — I replied that I did not mind at all; and so we went our separate ways, she and the Admiral with Guimauve to the *Chambre de Ronronnement*, and I with the others, crossing the great hall in silence.

My thoughts turned to the literary code Louis had referred to some while before, in which (the reader will recall) the shapes taken by certain narratives denoted letters in secret messages; I began to wonder which letter would be signified by my own journey.

Once, I might have supposed it would be an *I*, not for reasons of what some have been pleased to call my arrogance, but simply because it was the direction I had set for myself.

The trajectory of a rocket. A firm undeviating upstroke, rising surely towards glory.

It was not to be.

Was my course more diagonal then? Was it italicised? Was it a *W*, a *Q*? Was it one of Fritillary's more ornate ampersands?

Or a lowercase *n*? Rockets do not rise forever, after all. Would I soon find myself on the curving downstroke of my fate?

Whatever it was, I knew I desired but one thing. That it should end with us wed, with Ariette waiting pertly for us upon the final serif . . .

What I did not know was that Louis wanted precisely the same thing.

We arrived at a door. The emperor paused to rest.

"Are you quite sure you are well, Sire?" Félix said.

Louis sighed. "Ah, Félix," he said, "I wonder if I am getting too old for all this . . . Perhaps it is time I moved on."

"Moved on?"

"The crown weighs heavily. The job has lost its savour."

Fritillary's light flashed with shock, nor could I hide my own surprise. "Sire! You are not thinking of *retiring*?"

He laughed. "Well, for the evening, at the least." The door opened. "But before I do, there is one thing I should like you to try, Cyrano."

CHAPTER THE TWENTY-FIRST:

LA CHAMBRE DE RONRONNEMENT

"King Neptune's bedchamber and all that," Louis said apologetically.

The royal apartment was possessed of the utmost degree of loveliness-per-square-inch possible within physical limits imposed by certain fundamental constraints of the universe. Adapted from the interior of a giant oyster shell beautiful beyond consonance, its burnished furbishments were created after the manner of pearls — except where most pearls were engendered by grains of sand or other irritants, these had been brought about by furnishings: a gleaming bed, a nacreous secretaire, an exquisite longue . . .

Upon which Louis now sat with gratitude.

"Make haste, will you, Félix? Am I to wait forever?"

The surgeon rang a bell, and a door shivered open at the other end of the room — the *operculum* with which the oyster had guarded its shell — admitting a servant, a scrivener, who handed Félix a velvet-lined case.

He opened it with reverence.

Within was a tailor's measuring-tape. It was scuffed, frayed, sordidly grimy.

Fritillary was transfixed.

"Who is to be measured, Sire?" said Félix.

Louis looked at me. "I thought you might find it diverting, Cyrano. It is an instrument made, I believe, by a curious race of people called the — what is it, Félix?"

"The Æolians, Sire."

"I knew it!" Fritillary's eager light played over the tape. "It has all the hallmarks. How absurd it is, how unthinkable[11]," he said, annotating excitedly. "How *impossible*![12]"

There followed some discussion about the tape: I learned that its cloth was of moral fibres, that its markings were set out not in quantitative, but qualitative units, that it was "an instrument that determine neither height nor breadth, but *depth*," as Félix had it. "A device to take a man's measure. The procedure is objective and infallible, and the results are frequently surprising — dwarfs who are moral giants, heroes who turn out to be emotional infants." Whereat I believe I was favoured with the briefest glance . . .

"Come," Louis called, "are we to wait forever?"

Félix bade me lie on a couch. I did so, not without foreboding, and there suffered myself to be measured — Félix dancing around, whipping the tape this way and that, calling out strange, codified readings to the scrivener the while: "Forty-five left, twenty right! Nineteen! East! Spots! June 28th! Ætiolated!"

Though fully dressed, never had I felt so naked.

I wondered if Louis, in his mercy, had engineered it that Roxane would not be here to see me so exposed. "May I ask what this is for?" I said.

"Be still! No talking," Félix barked. He continued: "C-Minor! Thirty! Vanilla! Twelve point six! Eleemosynary! Thirty-seventy-fourtyfiveteen!"

Even when the measuring came to an end, the ordeal did not.

I watched Félix and his assistant convening at a table, Fritillary looking over their shoulders as they processed the measurements.

They laid bare my soul, now chuckling over some detail in the readings, now scowling, now tutting.

---

11 Except to those to whom the only *thinkable* is the *un*!

12 Every bit as much as the ring-stuff! A trove of impossibles! What more is to come?

A report was produced. Félix handed it to Louis. I craned, trying to make out the results — inscrutable — Louis flicking through abstruse diagrams, tables, charts.

"Ah yes," he said at last, "it is as I thought. You are in many ways the very finest of men."

I braced myself for the *but* . . .

"But," he said, "like most men, you are a study in contradictions. Which is no bad thing, do not misunderstand. It gives the best of us our fire — the hot friction of opposites." He turned the pages. "You are temperate and intemperate; a cynical idealist; a righteous sinner; a hopeful pessimist."

He pored over an intricate figure. "Here: you love peace."

"I do."

"And yet you have slain so many." Of a sudden, I found myself fixed on the gimlet of his gaze. The King, the Judge.

I looked away.

He laughed suddenly, to my very great relief. "Fie!" He tost the report away. He stood, stretched, yawned. "What does it matter if you are not suited to the work?"

The work?

"Really, it is a ticklish business, this job, finicky, not much of interest in it for a man of action."

I was speechless. Had he been thinking I might *replace* him? The floor seemed to sway, and I was keenly aware of the broken cable on which the building depended.

"Well," he said, "that is that, is it not? Be off with you, then, all of you! A fellow needs his rest."

Still speechless, I followed the others into the hall, where Fritillary took his leave, departing with Félix and his assistant to further investigate the Æolian tape . . .

I stood there for a minute in no small state of perplexity.

Then I went to find Roxane.

Descending from higher floors to lower, following the directions of troopers along the way, I met with a happenstance which I relate for the close bearing it has later in this tale.

I was passing through a doorway, when I stopped dead. Là! The door led outside into a pastoral scene . . . Buildings, temples, other noble edifices, a forest dressed with bayed arcades; and people ranged about in elegant groupings — such people! — their bearing so noble! — their faces of the most solemn character . . .

"Mind yourself there, *Mijnheer!*"

An artisan was hurrying towards me.

"Mind yourself, if you please, *Mijnheer!*" His clogs clattered on scaffolding I had not previously noticed. "Please to use the walkway!" He was tall, bald, and skeletally thin, his smock spattered white and yellow and blue.

"It is the oils I am worried about," he said, stopping before me. "Not to smear them, yes? It takes *zeer* long to dry!"

At last I understood my error. This was but a painting, a *trompe-l'œil*, a masterly trick of the eye.

More than masterly, dazzling . . . Even as I saw the other painters and plasterers scattered about the scaffolding, my eyes persisted in seeing them as less real than their art.

I felt painted breezes, smelled painted flowers . . .

"And the handrail, yes, if you please, *Mijnheer*," the painter was saying. "Lest you will be falling into the forest, and may becoming lost."

Which I took for a jest or an unfamiliar idiom, I knew not whether; but I took to the walkway as advised when crossing, and kept firm hold of the railing the while.

"Cyrano!" Roxane came running, carrying a happy

Guimauve. "Oh, my dear, is this not the most delightful place?"

I kept my own counsel on the matter.

We were in the fortress's rank catty heart, the *Chambre de Ronronnement.* A great grand room wanting for nothing for the health and good cheer of the feline race . . . A cat paradise with hot mountains of duvets for burrowing, baskets of fresh, warm laundry for sleeping, important papers to sit upon, ponds of fat, slow fish, small living things that moved quickly in random directions, high vantage points, low hideaways, furniture for clawing, priceless carpets for defecation . . .

It was the kind of place a virtuous Siamese or Russian blue might hope to end up in the hereafter — whether there has ever been such a thing as a virtuous cat is a question I leave for other philosophers.

All around me, moggy currents of slink and hiss — purrily furling and furrily purling.

I was lost, adrift in an ocean of cats . . .

"Cyrano, you are pale," Roxane said. "Are you unwell?"

"No, my dear, forgive me. I am come from an audience with our emperor." I told her about my encounter with Louis and Félix and the measuring tape.

"*Mon dieu!*" She gave a horrified little laugh. "Are you terribly disappointed to be turned down?"

I thought about it. "I believe the feeling is more one of reprieve."

"Well, if anything, I say you are overqualified for the job."

"Ah, yes, well, when a higher position becomes available then."

We laughed. She bade me sit with her. We repaired to a brocaded loveseat which a fat Burmese deigned to share with us.

"Cyrano," Roxane said. "I have received a message."

"A message?"

"It came not long after I arrived here." With a curious smile, she handed me a page of vellum:

> *Be it known that He who is State, and Creation, and Stars and the Spaces Between, sends his Respects and Invites the Mademoiselle Magdelaine Robineau de Neuvillette, known as Roxane, and Monsieur Cyrano de Savinien Hercule de Bergerac, dec'd, to their Own Wedding, to be held this Day.*
>
> *And so on, and expecting them not to fail in the Fulfilling thereof, and hurry up about it too, I subscribe this with my Hand etc.*
>
> *L.*

I looked up, blinking. "But how can this be? It is — it . . ."

"It is absurd," she said, "and the height of impudence. Even if the fate of the world depended on it I would pay it not the least heed, except . . ."

"Except?"

"Except, Cyrano, he is in the right. You are ready."

In her face I saw how distressed and baffled my own must have appeared. "My poor dear," she said. "It has been such a journey."

We embraced, and I closed my eyes, and saw the old appletrees in the orchards outside Saint-Forget, bordering the woods in the Vallée de l'Yvette.

The trees were so ugly in the cold months, gnarled and leafless, serving as crabbed old enemies in my childhood adventures.

But all along they had kept a secret that Spring, in its gentleness, had known how to urge forth.

My smile was one I had seen on others, on happy fools.

I had never known before how it felt, what it meant, an appleblossom of a smile.

CHAPTER THE TWENTY-FIRST-AND-A-HALFTH:

DUSK

In the perils that followed, reader, I must tell you the Cyrano who bore them was not the Cyrano you met at the outset of this tale.

When the fortress suddenly shook — when the signals officers about the *Chambre* stood as one, and stared at their cats — Roxane with them, Guimauve purring oddly in her arms — when she said, "It is starting . . ." — and I understood the war was beginning, not days from now, but now — even then my hand did not go to my sword, but remained in hers.

Even as I followed her gaze to the great chandelier in the *Petite Galerie*, dimming, the Milky Way's numberless lights darking — as night fell, heavily, in dim balklines, in folds and crumples and greasy pleats of billiardtable baize — even as I saw fleets of syphilitic ships come arolling across the fields of night — and even as Louis's forces replied in their own peculiar fashion — not with artillery, but with fireworks, with bunting and bouquets, and musics to which the drum and thunder of battle formed a jolly counterpoint — even when I saw we were not returning fire, but decorating the *Galerie's* spaces with blossoms and uptost stars and red and green and pale blue gaseous streamers arching through the spreading gloom — when I saw these were preparations for the wedding, for the ceremony to come . . . and yes, even when more fleets arrived, crewed, it was discovered, by the creatures called *Bom asts*, referred to earlier by Fritillary, their cannon-eyes firing so arbitrarily they blasted more letters from their name, and more, and so are now more properly referred to as *om a ts* — even then, reader, my gaze scarcely left her, her eyes, the avian sweep of her collarbone . . .

And yes, before long, we heard someone calling us over the noise.

The Admiral, standing by a doorway. We went to join him; he led us into another chamber, this one notable for its gilding . . . everything richly coated in gold leaf, every surface, even things made of gold were gilded — even the air, reader, was freighted with glittering dust, making visible with shivery ripples the great echoing reports from without, the strains of wedding music, the crashes of cymbals or armaments, percussions or concussions . . .

Et voilà! Here were Félix and Fritillary, and Louis, comical in nightshirt and slippers, a sleeping cap flopping over one ear. Laughing: "Is it not wonderful to see things going so prettily to plan?" — and laughing the harder when the war chose that moment to reach into the chamber with a stubby limb and flail it about.

The fortress swung. There was another blast, and another. Louis's smile became a trifle uncertain. "Sire," the Admiral said, "your carriage awaits."

A still greater explosion, a noise so loud it was nothing but loudness. Chaos, smoke. When it cleared, I saw Roxane scrabbling through the rubble — I went to her as, weeping, she found Guimauve, one of his legs crushed beneath a toppled gold table.

But although I was sore grieved to see him hurt, I remained calm, knowing he would live on to become a ship's cat by and by (and sure enough, when a junior officer ran forward to take him, it was the puffin-like signalman of the *Fleur Fière*, though several years younger).

The Admiral made bold to remind his emperor that a carriage awaited him.

Louis scoffed: "There is a more scenic way . . ."

At which he strode off, and there was another blast, a nasty crisp sound to it, commotion, buffeting flames, the air soupy with gold dust, a bullion bouillon, I was inhaling thirty carats with every breath, I spied a golden statue of Louis, toppled against a fallen ceiling beam.

Odd. And Félix, why was he pressing a bandage to its forehead?

Then I understood it was no statue, but Louis himself, covered in flaked gold, blood from a wound on his brow like thick enamel.

"He is badly hurt," Félix said when we hurried over. "I have no tools. If he is not treated at once I fear —"

Louis coughed, gilt flakes simmering on his ragged breath. He murmured something. I strained to hear. It sounded like nonsense. He said it again, two words.

"Gerrit Dow?" Félix repeated. "What is it? A name?"

"What's that?" The Admiral's eyes bulged. "Dow? Oh, well now, Gerrit Dow! The virtuoso!"

"Virtuoso *what*?" Félix cried.

"Why, he is a painter, of course. Though the word scarce does him justice . . ."

I remembered the artisan I had encountered on my way to the *Chambre de Ronronnement*.

I stood. I felt a tickle on my cheeks. I put a hand to my face. Airborne gold had settled in the lines of my skin. When I pulled my hand away, a facial tracery came with it, set in an expression of calm resolve.

I let it drift away. "I know what Louis means us to do," I said.

I led us, Fritillary lighting our way, back through the hall; through the burning *Chambre*, its Ring-stuff walls ringing, warping and dancing; on into the salon with its extraordinary *trompe l'œil* . . .

There he was, the artisan, Gerrit Dow, abandoned

by his assistants, desperately sweeping dust and rubble from his painting, touching up damaged areas with his innumerable paints and brushes.

"It *is* him!" The Admiral clapped his hands like a boy. "The master himself! Look at the work! Miraculous!"

He hastened along the walkway, the rest of us close behind. Hearing us, the artisan looked up.

"No!" he called. "The scaffolding is not good. It is broked. It will not take more —"

And the night deepened, and the fortress quivered, and the walkway collapsed sidewise . . . first the section under Louis, who was being carried by Félix and Fritillary, then the timbers under Dow himself, and then Roxane, falling with a smile and a wave to me.

The boards under the Admiral gave way, then the ones under me.

I half-fell, half-dived, laughing into the false depths of a painted day.

CHAPTER THE TWENTY-SECOND:

ESCAPIST ART

I spun through alternating light and shade, rushing turpentined air.

The textured sky whirling, riotous rich deep cobalt blue, eggshell clouds, a fatly spinning yellow-orange-red Sun churning out gouache blazons of oily radiance.

I landed with a thump upon a daisied meadow, rendered in dabs of green and yellow-green.

Hearing mirthful shouts, I looked up. 'Twas the Admiral, a splendid likeness, climbing to his feet, brushing himself down and preening his mustachios — done with long confident brushstrokes belike those of an Oriental calligraphist. "Extraordinary," he cried, "simply extraordinary!" He turned his attention to one of his sleeves, then to me. He came closer. "Truly," he breathed, "Dow renders even the ugly beautiful!"

"Have a care what you say, Sir."

He started, unaccustomed to art that talked back. "Pray, Sir, be not offended," he said, "but take my words as the compliment for which they were intended."

I told him to be at ease, that I was but amused, and he chuckled, and we looked about, discovering we had come down by a silvery lake, bordered by forest and temples.

The salon we had left was invisible, as were our companions.

We moved away from the lake, deeper into the painting; we hiked about for a considerable time but, still seeing nothing of the others, made bold to approach a pair of Dow's painted figures, godlings in the classical style; so expertly rendered! — their every detail — the hairs on the forearms, the puckered knuckles of their hands, in clever little squirls of ochre and mauve . . .

We enquired of them whether they had seen Roxane and the others, whereat they made reply that was entirely pictorial, but intelligible even so: with inclinations of the head, with eye-shimmers, frowns and smiles, with nuances, infinitely subtle, in the set of the shoulder, the arch of a brow, the *contrapposto* placement, just so, of a foot, a finger, a toe, they conveyed that our party had indeed left the banks of the lake and moved over there, just beyond the cypresses to the right; and moreover, that we had best make haste, one of our number having sustained a serious wound which, in their opinion, though they were no experts, looked quite grave, possibly an impacted fracture . . .

Quickly, we moved away along the green towards the cypresses, through trees and dancing blossoms, greens and golds shivering underfoot as we passed through the copse . . .

A scene before us: an old public square.

An ancient willow leaning its shaggy head against the wall of a picturesque ruin. In its green shade, Fritillary's lantern casting a dramatic gamboge wash — dark light, luminous shadows . . .

Everything, the character of the light, the spatial arrangements, the poses of the figures, all were disposed to guide the viewer's eye to the patient on the ground, Félix kneeling by him, a discarded bandage a livid scribble on the cobbles to one side of Louis, his wound making for a striking red note against the sombre hues.

"Oh heavens," the Admiral said, recognising the style of the scene. " 'Tis a *pietà*!"

We became part of the composition . . . Roxane glanced at me, her face touched with the faintest suggestion of a smile.

A master's touch, that, accentuating loss as bright colours accentuate dark.

I looked at Félix, meaning to ask how Louis fared. There was no need. The surgeon's shoulders were slumped, the picture of heartbroken futility . . .

Then: "Excuse my lateness! Excuse!"

Clogs clattering on the flagstones, Gerrit Dow bustled forward, briskly mixing colours on his palette. "Excuse for the delay. This pigment is very delicate in the making, yes — *couleur chair*, mine own recipe — blue, *zeer* translucent, olive, a cerise, a touch of bonemeal to match the facial pallor . . ."

He drew something from a pocket and held it pinched between his fingers.

Seeing my interest, he raised it for me to observe. "One of my roundheaded brushes," he said. "The bristles they are made from the down from the cheeks of a baby animalcule."

"Ah, yes," I said, nodding, though in fact I saw nothing. The brush was invisibly small.

"It does not bad for the coarser strokes." The painter turned to Fritillary. "Please to come closer, *Mijnheer Lantaarn*. This light is too dim for me to be doing my work."

Whereupon he bent over Louis and, remaining faithful to the high-keyed, flat-coloured Dutch style, began painting over the wound.

He laid down the first undercoat of tissues, the minute fibres and other structures of the flesh . . .

After a moment, Roxane looked up. "What is that sound?"

I looked also, hearing a dry rustling.

I turned to see the lake glinting between the trees. Its waters were moving strangely . . . Not rippling, but ripping . . .

Tears and cracks forming in the glaze . . .

The sounds worsened, but Dow never hurried — as well-composed as his art . . .

Coolly exchanging his invisible brush for another still more invisible, he began mending Louis's ruptured circulatory vessels — the blood ceasing to spill — then he started on the small muscles and nerves, the flesh twitching and wincing . . .

The lake crumbled and cracked, showing the original sketches underneath the paint . . .

Beside me the Admiral, with eyes only for Dow, said quietly, " 'Tis an honour to see the master at work."

The crashes and crackles coming louder, I said I wished it did not take so long for a *trompe l'œil* to be done . . .

"*Trompe l'œil*?" The Admiral's whiskers shivered. "Sir, *trompe l'œils* are poor childish things. They only appear to increase the size of a room, while in fact *decreasing* it by the thickness of the paint. No, Sir, to hang one of Dow's flower studies is to bulge the air with perfumes; his skill is such that he can depict blue objects with yellow paint. His works fool not just the eye, Sir. They are *trompe réalités*!"

Dow worked on: now the scalp, the manifolded dermis, the tiny organs and glands . . .

I looked back to the lakeside, scarcely recognisable. Fading, crumbling away.

Dow painted the follicles, picked out pores in hallucinatory detail, realer than real, one by one, one by one . . .

The crumbling radiated outward, a rumble growing louder.

Dow finished the last hairs with swift, curling brushstrokes, and signed his name in a ringlet on Louis's forehead.

He stood and wiped his hands. The job was done.

We waited.

I felt the ground shake under me. The landscape shifted and moved. Louis did not.

"Has it worked?" Félix whispered.

Still Louis shewed no sign of life.

"I do not understand," Dow said. "It is my masterwork, every particular exact. Why does he not move?"

"Because I am waiting," Louis said where he lay, "for you to do something about the lines in my brow as well."

He sat up, grinning, and as one we let out a laugh and a sigh of relief; and standing, he gave a bow, thanked us for our concern, and said to Dow that he owed him a debt of gratitude.

" 'Twas my honour, Lord," Dow said. "But now, by your leave, we are retiring to another part of the painting. One that is more agreeable, yes?"

As we left the square, I looked back to see a bed of elderberry flowers blanching, turning from pink to *pank*, the past tense of pink. I saw some of the godlings beating a sluggish retreat, their movements slowed by their lead-based paints; I saw degrading colours rising up in a craquelure tide to catch one of them, who screamed silently — pictorially: a flung arm, an arched neck, a desperate eye glimpsed through a sweep of hair . . .

And he was gone, lacquers falling to reveal the underlying studies, pencil and charcoal, the gesso, the bare plaster . . .

We arrived, led by Dow, at a lone tower, its depiction precise if uninspired, Dow being one of those artists to whom architecture was more *context* than *subject.*

We passed inside, clumb a simple staircase, entered onto a rooftop.

The prospect was broad and offered wonders: strange forms hazily visible ahead, new horizons, untamed lands for the venturesome artist to explore. Africas of wild figuration. Outlandish but compelling means to depict the forms of nature . . .

Back the way we had come, the degradation continued. The lake was gone, even the plaster had fallen away, revealing the laths underneath.

Cracks forked over the fields, reaching the tower. The rooftop shuddered under us.

"Why are we up here?" Félix said. You have heard the term 'distressed' used to refer to a technique in painting, reader; I now saw it for myself in Félix's face.

He turned on Dow. "You have trapped us, Sir! You have doomed us!"

Dow said nothing, nor glanced up from his palette, again mixing colours. Several shades of yellow, some browns: fleshtones, so true to life the paint throbbed . . . But he was not satisfied. "*Vloek*! Not right, not right. It wants for red . . ." He hummed in Dutch a moment, then — an idea — he reached into his smock, brought out a brush just visible to the naked eye, charged it with a dob of off-white, and began slashing at the air before him.

With extraordinary economy of line, with dash and splash, with motions that recalled the finest sort of swordplay, he painted a squarish form. He afforded it depth and volume: a cylinder, depicted in broad strokes, not large, about the size of a man's fist.

It acquired further detail, and texture — rough, as of a ceramic jar — and all at once it was a canister, such as contain artists' paints . . . Dow taking it in his left hand, scrawling a label on it — *ROOD, Beste Kwalteit* — prising it open.

It was brimming with sumptuous oil paint. It was of the colour called 'Dutch red'. He dipped in a knife, added the smallest driblet to his palette, blending furiously.

Not far away, there was a loud bang. Louis shouted in surprise. We saw him staring at something that had fallen to the rooftop but three feet from where he stood.

It was roughly triangular, its edges ragged. He picked it up, turned it over. The other side was bright blue.

"A piece of the sky," Fritillary said.

The heavens were giving way.

More slabs fell, raining down over the landscape, pelting down around us, chunks shining like reflecting pools where they landed.

I went to Roxane and we huddled together. I shielded her as best I could.

I looked across at Dow, who stood, unprotected, precariously on the lip of the wall.

He leaned out, and out. Stretching so far that it seemed sure he would fall.

But still further he went, out over a neighbouring palace . . . then the villa next to it, his shadow falling over a far meadow.

Away and away. Over forests and plains, flouting perspective, effortlessly stretching, his body never foreshortening and so giving the impression of immensity as it receded: a god above the world of his making, uncaring of the sky fragments, the heavens powdering his smock, scalp, the backs of his hands as he waved away an obscuring cloud and reached with his brush and touched it to the side of a distant wooded hill.

There came a terrible hissing *crump* to the west. A piece of the Sun, dusky red where it had fallen.

I looked back at Dow. He had painted the beginnings of human figures on the hill; three, four, five of them — no, wait, the last was not human. It stood in an orang-outang crouch. Its head round, and glowing.

Dow afforded one of the men a piglettish shape and small stature, another a nightshirt and sleeping cap, the third an Admiral's uniform.

He added some gold to his palette, then began plying his brush with affectionate kissing dabs.

I stared, recognising Roxane, even at such a distance, a miraculous depiction, all her wit, her character implied in tiny pinkling points. Beside me, the painting's original gasped. "My!" she said. "What a curious feeling!"

"*Mijnheer* Dow!" Louis was wading through fallen sky to where the painter stood. "*Mijnheer*, if you don't mind a little suggestion . . ."

I saw Dow lean back, and Louis speak softly to him; the artisan listened, considered a moment, and looked at me, and Roxane, and chuckled. "Why, *natuurlijk*, Lord. 'Twould be my pleasure."

He leaned out once more. He resumed painting. I looked a question to Louis, who pretended not to notice.

The artisan was reworking Roxane's portrait. Her dress was changing, taking on new colours, brilliant whites and clear greys, shining against the growing dark.

A chunk of Sun landed in a nearby forest. Soon the woods were blazing, the oils burning briskly. Fauns and nymphs and other such creatures stampeded. Painterly smoke blew dramatically across the landscape.

Finished with Roxane, the artisan began composing my likeness. I made out a fine moustache, a proud carriage; the noble shine of a part-crystal nose.

Then I noticed the differences, the most obvious being the suit. Green and deep red, with glints of silver, and rather formal.

As the depiction took on detail, I experienced a most curious split in my perception.

Conscious of myself, here, on this rooftop, trapped —

And also I was on that hillside, coming awake.

When my new eyes were finished, I looked back at my first self regarding me from the doomed tower, far away.

From both vantages, I saw the rising dark, the painting flaking to pieces.

From both vantages, I watched the artisan, towering over all, his vast hand moving more quickly as he worked on the fifth figure on the hilltop.

It was male, painfully skinny; I saw the beginnings of a smock, clogs . . .

He was still working on it when the tower gave way at last.

The stones fell, the lacquers chipped and melted. The tower collapsed, and was gone.

One of me felt it, an awareness of my own death, and worse, of Roxane's.

I felt the dark, the great erasure. I heard distant cries. Dow shouted out something more expressive of frustration than pain or fear. The brush fell from his hand. It spun hugely, end over end, splashing down into a harbour. The bristles came to rest on the shore, the handle crushed three ships in the bay, and crashing waves reduced a nearby dockyard to kindling.

Watercolour trees, wildflowers, pastel foliage sparkling, romantically dewy.

All was softened with the translucent *sfumato* layers of pale lavender and gold that painters use to depict distance.

"Well!" Félix said. You have heard 'relief' used to refer to a technique in the arts, reader, and I saw it for myself now in his face. "This *is* more agreeable!"

A light shone to my right. I turned; it was Roxane.

I gazed, struck dumb by her astonishing gown. She smiled through her veils.

The Admiral clapped his hands, startling a gemlike bluejay from its nest. "It was beyond belief! Did you see? All done with implication! The mastery! And your wedding gown, Mademoiselle . . . Words fail me . . ."

As was proper, I thought, for they should be timorous in their description who enter upon the merits of anything sacred.

The gown; its long train trailing as a pearlescent fog, dewing the grass, strumming the harps of spiders' webs . . .

A wonder of another order.

At best, reader, I can advise you to leave off reading, and if it be a fine day, step outside and see the bright clouds above you, the robes with which the Earth guards her modesty, and imagine them given the most comely and womanly figure, fashioned into a garment which, in keeping with the best wedding gowns, was at once chaste and designed to whet the amatory appetite to the highest degree.

"The bravura execution!" the Admiral said. "The details not set down one by one, but *alluded* to. Reality? — it pales in shame. Actuality? — hang your ragged head!" He laughed giddily, teeth coated with mad impasto glints. "*Mijnheer* Dow, you have . . . *Mijnheer*?"

We heard a noise, a sloppy noise, a wet Dutch grunt.

A pink-brown-white thing flopped on the ground. At one end a pair of smudges — clogs — at the other, in the unformed head, a blotch that opened and groaned, the lips working. There came a dribble of painter's alcohol and linseed oil.

"My friends," Louis said, "I fear *Mijnheer* Dow is still a work in progress."

And he would never be finished. Gallantly, he had left his own portrait to the last, and had died before completing it.

The Admiral tried to hold the head, fleshcolours drizzling between his fingers. The thing flumped and luffed. It shuddered painfully.

"The chest is not properly depicted," Félix observed. "The lungs cannot draw air."

A blue smutch opened, a desperate eye; the nose ran, and the face. The figure groaned again, convulsed, limbs flailed; and then, mercifully, was still.

There was no time to mourn him.

The Sun was little more than a few bright flecks in the remains of the sky. Fields and forests were crumbling to nothing.

Fritillary flashed. "See," he said, "he is pointing . . ."

One of Dow's half-formed fingers was winding between the grass blades to point to the crest of the hill on which we stood.

With sorrow we left the corpse, upwards, through darkling woods, past uncertain greenery, the trees becoming splotchy as we moved into the background, trunks and canopies done in quick palette knife daubs, the perspective shifting weirdly as we reached the top. Which was the horizon.

At our feet, the sky met the ground. Beyond was

a pale bluewhite suggestion of distance, the boundary marked with a carved wooden bar that I recognised as the lower edge of a picture frame.

Together, as one, we stepped over it.

I felt fresh and glossy. I was leaving something of myself behind, an unregretted loss. An old chapter was over, a new one beginning.

CHAPTER THE TWENTY-THIRD:

A CURE FOR BILLIARD TABLES

"Dearly beloved," Louis began, "we are gathered here to join this man and this woman in holy matrimony . . ."

That light is not so swift as its opposite, will be obvious to any who consider that darkness is ever the first to be wherever light is still scrambling to get to.

So that I was not so surprised to find that, when we entered the *Petite Galerie* once more, it was more by darkness than light that we perceived the Master of Secrets at the far end of the Room.

Movements of black on black.

"If anyone may shew just cause why they may not be joined together, let them speak now or forever hold their peace . . ."

Our journey had taken us from one painting to another — a small and minor masterpiece hung low on the wall in an obscure corner of the *Galerie*. It was more or less directly opposite where the fortress hung — the building itself was invisible at this distance, but the monster moving about it was not, its thoughts so titanic they were easily read . . .

"Matrimony is commended to be honourable among all men," Louis said, "and must be entered into reverently and solemnly."

We saw the moment the Master of Secrets realised we were no longer in the fortress . . .

Then: the twang of tendons, the creak of vertebræ, the head revolving in a manner to dwarf any sort of armed political revolution.

The monster's gaze, when it found us, was a physical impact.

"Cyrano de Savinien Hercule de Bergerac: wilt thou have this woman to be thy wedded wife, to live together in the holy estate of matrimony?"

I believe I have been remiss, reader, in describing my own apparel, which was very flattering and convincing in its depiction; a fine set of breeches, a waistcoat, a fresh coat of paint; for painters take pride, I know, in their portrayal of folds of cloth.

I should tell you also that he depicted me without a sword. And no matter how it might excite incredulity in you who have followed the career of the terrible Cyrano de Bergerac — to whom death was a way of life and who was so ferocious he was called Captain Satan by his fellows and worse by his enemies — I must tell you that despite one or two setbacks and a persistent sensation at my waist as of the phantom limbs that afflict amputees, I have never worn a weapon since.

Dow had not drawn a sword, and neither would I ever again.

"Wilt thou love her, honour and keep her; and forsaking all others, keep thee only unto her, so long as ye both shall live?"

I said I would.

A distant footfall, another, each an event worthy of an account from Pliny the Younger, who recorded the destruction of Pompeii.

The Master of Secrets tore through the empire's wedding decorations — bunting longer than lines of latitude, colossal bonbons flying, the monster picking up pace . . .

Square miles of parquetry flaring and turning to dust with every step; a Leviathan like to that imagined by Hobbes, man as commonwealth, city lights flickering behind smoky ribs, empires of organs, throttling metropoli, living pistons pumping with the rise and fall of civilisations, blood vessels coursing with jellied galleons, trains of intention conveyed along nerveways in the literature and oral traditions of proud nomadic races, the paired continents of the thighs resounding, the wobbling backcountries of the rump shaking and clapping, so that I could scarcely hear when Louis asked Roxane if she would have me, and she said that she would.

It was time for me to give a ring, which I did not have, and there was a moment of panic, until Louis found one on his person; 'twas a band of unfamiliar braided design; a gift, he informed us, from his Minister of Planets, who had found it encircling a world belike Saturn except for its small size.

It sat warmly in my palm. I spied three tiny moons rotating about its plane. I took Roxane's hand and placed it on her finger. It fit prettily.

The monster was desperate. He sprinted towards us . . .

Louis said I could kiss my bride. Her veils parted.

The Master of Secrets diving, plunging, a billiardtable night falling . . .

Time slowed, as it will in moments of peril.

Seconds took on the stately measure of hours and days. Our kiss lasted a long while.

In the timelessness, our daughter stood, smiling.

The others were gone. We were three.

We occupied a soft patch of happy radiance (poets and balladeers have observed that sunshine is brighter, colours richer in happy times, which principle the scholars of Louis's *Académie des Sciences* have put to practical purpose by reversing the process so that lamps were powered by degrees of elation or bliss).

"I am sorry to leave things until the last moment," Ariette said. She looked eight or nine. She wore a party frock and pink dancing slippers. "I thought it was all right to appear to you in the Sea of Time. But here . . . well, more proper that I wait until you were married . . ."

"Good girl," Roxane said, and I commended her propriety, and observed that it was a quality she must have got from her mother.

There came from the shadows behind the girl a sound; a voice, or a creaking of ropes. "Oh," she said, turning, "this is my friend. He is a bit shy. He wants to give you a wedding present."

A hand made of twine reached into the light. In the knotty palm was a box such as is used to contain snuff.

"For you, Father," Ariette said. "He made it specially."

The box, when I took it, was finely made, and fashioned from a metal that is to gold as gold is to dung.

I thanked the unseen friend and said it was very pretty.

"No, silly!" Ariette said. "The present is inside. It is a medicine."

"But I am not ill."

She laughed and made comment that it was more usual for the parent to urge the child to take its medicine than the other way around. I began to suspect that as I had met my match for wits in Roxane, so it would be with her daughter.

"Still, I do not understand, dear," Roxane said. "Why does your father need this?"

"I knew there would be lots of questions," Ariette said. "That's why I brought the book."

She reached into a pocket of her party frock and brought out a copy of the book you are now reading.

"I like it, Father," she said. "I like the bird houses best, and Fritillary . . . Now, where is it?" She flipped through the pages. "Ah, here, top of page 240."

She held it up for us to see, and we leaned forward and read these very words, this very sentence, this full stop.

We read this sentence, which served as a specific reminder of Sister Marie Jakob-Lôrber's writings from the Mad Count's library, which had referred to the Master of Secrets, or his race, as an illness in need of remedy (a detail I confess I had until then forgotten) . . .

We read this paragraph, which treated of treatments (I believe I would have found a more felicitous phrase), by which was meant physicks and their medicaments; it offered the insight that *health*, as we use the word, is a relative term signifying a greater or lesser *diminution of ill-health* (with which I agreed). By contrast, the paragraph said, the wellbeing afforded by the Panacæa was absolute — but then it trailed off in a manner to suggest there was something it was reluctant to say . . .

The next paragraph had no such qualms, briskly pointing out that according to the Paracelsian doctrine that all medicines be poisons to some degree, the Panacæa, being the greatest of medicines, must also be the deadliest of poisons.

Not to all, however, the following paragraph countered. For the Panacæa was a type of snuff (come, I thought. Are we expected to credit this? I was sure I would have contrived something far more suitable) — yes, a type of snuff, the paragraph insisted, lethal to all save one whose nose was infused with crystal (really, this was too much).

There followed a descriptive passage, telling of my dismay, my amusement, my disbelief; of how I thought to simply toss the box away, but did not, caught in the grip of the words telling of my actions; how I opened the box to find the contents were indeed a type of snuff; of my slight clumsiness when I scooped up a generous measure of it, being unfamiliar with that vice; of when I sniffed it into my nostrils; of when I felt nothing, but Ariette explained it might be a moment before it took effect . . .

Of when she called a merry goodbye, and broke our hearts by skipping away, to her little yacht, her radiance touching the Æolian so that we glimpsed the weave of it, its windblown intellections, its body winding out a leave-taking in a ropy script.

Of how, with a waft of buttercups, with a "Farewell, Mother! Farewell, Father!", the little tittuppy ship lifted on inrolling waves of time . . .

"The next time we meet will be our first!"

The seconds and minutes flowed, resuming their customary rate; the Master of Secrets was overhead, his face a flabby sky bearing down, dousing us in his furious weepage, in snow from the high peaks of his teeth . . .

I began to feel it. The snuff taking effect, though 'twas nothing much: a tingle, a sniff, a snort, a grimace, a little crystal sneeze.

Well then. Although I do not favour snuff, many enthusiasts, such as the Baron de Colignac, declare it to be the most salutary improver of mood, affording the user a sense of general wellbeing, that all was right with the world.

The difference with the Panacæa was the feeling was no illusion.

The easing of ill-health, except the illness 'twas not in my body, but in my life.

We heard a fat man's scream. An eightball clattering into a corner pocket. A rumble of thunder.

And that was that.

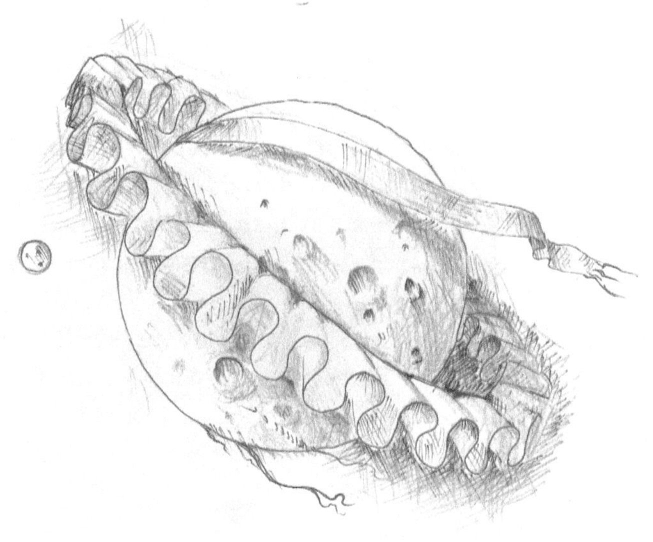

After a difficult labour, the book is born. I will leave the manuscript here, on Mars, knowing it will be recovered eventually.

THE HAPPY DAY

CHAPTER THE TWENTY-FOURTH:

IN WHICH, THE KNOT BEING TIED, SO TOO ARE THE LOOSE ENDS

"Excellently well played, Sir," Louis said to me, reclining on a twelve-measure rest graced with musical ornaments.

It was somewhat less than an hour later. We were in flight, lofting one last time through the still dark skies of the *Galerie* in a vessel wrought of wedding music, an unbridled waltz that had caught us up where we stood, the five of us borne into the air, soaring through the night . . .

"I scarcely feel I can take credit, Sire," I said.

"Ha! Cyrano de Bergerac, so modest? You *have* changed!"

The second movement began, pitch rising and falling, notes swelling in battering erumpments from a pipe-organ far below, a Baroque cliff but dimly visible in the gloom — bronze and spruce and jet, its worldsized interior filled with windstorms . . . cyclones twisting in pipes and bellows . . . wheeling terns . . . lightning in deeps of fippled valves . . .

"If I may ask, Sire, what of your plans?" Fritillary said.

"If you are enquiring whether I still intend to retire, then yes," Louis said. "In truth, I have derived the finest pleasure from this period of my career, but there is nevertheless a joy more delicate, more refined, to be gained, I find, when a pleasure is afforded to another." A bow to Roxane. "Your daughter, Madame. An excellent little girl."

Roxane tried to speak, could not — and there was a trembling chord, an emotional quiver in the music — and I thanked the emperor in her stead.

"It will be a controversial appointment, Sire," said Félix.

"Ha! I am glad. I care not a cucumber. Why should it be some bearded old gent who takes it on? Why not a little girl? Why not innocence, why not cheerfulness? Why not a universe ruled by sweetness?" He inhaled deeply. "Even now, I feel her influence touching the *Galerie*."

And sure enough, at that moment, over the music, there came the sputtering sound of a fuse being lit.

All looked up, seeing a spark, far, far above, hissing and fizzing, curling this way and that, giving off slow smoke — running through clouds, behind interstellar webs and tangles, around and around, approaching the centre.

A pause.

A whooshing *bang*!

It lit! — the Milky Way! — that endless firework!

Catherine wheel spume and flash!

The ferment of the firmament! — the stars abursting! — shining, freshly washed! — celebrations like a thousand hosannas: living greens, incredible reds, bright spiralling swoons of blue, a scarlet so categorical that even if it were another colour it would *still* be scarlet . . .

Spilling over the *Petite Galerie*, its vastitudes returning to view, the parquetry far below, strewn with the leavings of the war belike the floor of a hall after a grand ball.

The battle was done, the cannon spent, the om a ts had returned to whence they came (having sustained still further injury to their name, its letters blasted away so the spelling was at last "   " — without forgetting to capitalise the space once occupied by the first *B*).

A funereal theme insinuated itself into the music as we flew over the remains of the Master of Secrets, a sad relic, broken, a dawn-dispelled nightmare, his Frantics tost and crumbled, mere papier-mâché and paint, props and words, thin descriptions, fading.

The Panacæa's work was done. All ills were remedied, all sorrows reversed.

Even you have been touched by its broad effect, reader, to the extent that you have had the great good fortune of reading this book.

And although it is nearly at an end, alas, you may look forward to reading it once more, that you derive further benefit from its wisdom, to which I feel certain you paid insufficient attention the first time through.

The music resuming its merry tone, we were conducted in sonata form into the orrery; flying once more through its worlds, the inner worlds, Earth's tintinnabulatory Moon whirling by on its polished orbit, craters and rilles chiming, adding a new depth to the music, as were the other planets besides, an immeasurable carillon, bell-worlds and angelus-moons; Jupiter booming, Saturn ringing, distant Neptuneful chimes singing out trills and runs and tremolandi to mark our descent to the representation of the Earth — an emerald ocean, a silver Argentina, a damascene Damascus; the Black Sea with its knelling waves, then France, jewel of Europe, and northward, still descending, arriving into the city of Versailles, a low note bringing us just a foot or so above the ground, through pealing streets lined by all the Ministers and Nobles of the realm — billowy Contessas, countless Counts; Baronesses, mad and grand, pigeons riding pillion on the great gibbous spinnakers of their gowns as they showered their emperor with shouts and tears and farewells . . .

"There it is!" Félix cried. "How strange it is to see the old place again!"

I saw a representation of Louis's original palace.

A minuet took us through a hall, a gallery, the chambers of the *Grand Appartement du Roi*, fraught with perfection.

The music slowed, pausing at a door. The key of C

turning in the lock . . .

"*La Galerie des Glaces*," Louis announced. The door opened.

Beyond was a room far greater in size than the *Petite Galerie*.

Space bounced and rebounced in arcaded mirrors that were themselves reflections, infinities piled on infinities stretching forever beyond the doorway, every image a world, a new eternity.

Louis turned to us, silhouetted in the light from the chamber behind him.

"Empire as *objet d'art*, that was my goal," he said. "The courts, the parliament, the etiquette, the fashion of dress — all elements in the structure of the work." The light played in his wig, shone through his ears and fingertips. "I own it could be an unwieldy medium in which to work," he said, "though it offered freedoms not given to other forms. Perhaps I fixed on the details, to the detriment of the larger scale. Still, I flatter myself that I met with some moments of æsthetic interest." The brilliance shone through the film of his clothes, his body a silhouette, softly veiled.

"The empire will be an ornament to history, Sire," the Admiral said. "It observed the measure and form necessary in any art. In inventing this new medium, you have created what will be the exemplar for all such pieces to come. "

"My thanks, Admiral." The light seemed to shine through Louis's eyes. "And to you all, most especially to you, Cyrano, for your contribution of the *thema*, the binding thread, without which it would have all meant nothing. Love. *La corde d'amour*," he said, enveloped in glorioles . . .

"But what are we waiting for?" he cried. He glared at Félix. "Quit your gawping, man! Are you coming or not? Away, away!" He entered the mirrored gallery, Félix scrambling after, and on a paroxysm of brilliance, the door closed.

An appoggiatura took us further through the château, on through more apartments, the music picking up pace — the next movement, a lively measure, its notes rolling, rich pitch pitching, shaking marble from the walls.

Faster still — *con moto*, *con brio* — faster — *prestissimo* — a scriptorium, a salon, a kitchen, a shivering privy — faster, *molto agitato* — into a larger gallery, and the crescendo!

Orchestral bump thump smash, yelp and howl! The whole musical assemblage happily collapsing!

We were dumped in an undignified heap upon the floor.

Recovering, I looked about, seeing paintings. Hundreds of them, some overlapping, hung several deep.

Fritillary's light flashed with surprise, and Roxane clapped her hands. "They are Dow's!"

"They are, Madame," the Admiral said. "His back-catalogue. Now, where is it? I am sure it was — ah, here we are . . ." — lifting a modest canvas in a tortoiseshell cassetta frame, a portrait done in a High Gothic mode, the sitter a young, gangling, red-haired man.

It was Dow himself, in gouache and silverpoint and black chalk. The Artist as Young Man, standing at an easel in an atelier.

"Greetings, Admiral," he said, his words, in keeping with the medieval style of the painting, depicted in a "banderole" threading out of his mouth on a linen ribbon. "And visitors also. Welcome!" This early portrait seemed not to recognise us, but greeted us warmly nevertheless. "I am always glad to be receiving visitors."

"*Mijnheer* Dow," the Admiral said, "I believe your guests might be interested in that ship of yours."

The artist said it would be an honour, whereupon the Admiral thanked him, and led us through the chamber (Dow's eyes following us the while) — such a profusion of paintings! — I could not understand how one man could possibly . . .

Then I realised. Dow was not one man, but many — everywhere were his self-portraits, all working away . . .

We arrived at a large piece. It was painted with a field of stars, the planets of the Solar System, and — "Ariette's yacht!" Roxane cried.

Or rather, as the Admiral informed us, not hers but ours. Doubtless, we would pass it on to our daughter when she was of age.

The music struck up again, an encore, lifting the Admiral into the air, and he bid us a fond farewell, and was gone; and with that, we turned, and stepped into the painting. Fritillary lighting the way — onto the yacht's extended gangway — a sudden vacuum stirring around us — the room behind us lost in a constellated swirl — our laughter freezing in our wake as we hurried aboard and belowdecks . . .

A cabin, small but well appointed, with couches and tables of chaste and admirable design, and, in place of a galley, a gallery, stocked with paintings of meals for our pleasure and sustenance, as well as paintings depicting paintings, in which many objects of utility were efficiently stored.

A pastoral landscape hung aft, a watercolour meadow blown by a Spring wind, serving to keep the air sweet, and adding its soft daylight to Fritillary's glow.

On the for'ard bulkhead was a portrait of Galileo Galelei, who proved helpful in navigational and astronomical matters. He informed us that by entering the painting, we had returned to our own time. The familiar worlds turned by, scruffy and soiled in appearance after their depictions in the orrery, but as welcome as old slippers at the end of a long, hard slog of a day.

We dipped beneath the boundary that divides the upper worlds from the lower.

The pendulum-world came into view.

And Fritillary's homeland. His lantern filled with such a mist of tears I feared his flame would be extinguished.

"There!" he cried at last. "On that mountain ahead. My village perches by that lonely crag!"

"Mountain?" Roxane said, peering. "Is it not a valley?" At which I allowed myself a chuckle at her geographical naïvety.

We set down by a simple but lovely cottage of robins. A tender scene followed: the cottage door flapping open; Fritillary's wife, Amaranth, rushing out; their embrace; the flashes of joy; the sweet beams.

Inside the house, Amaranth, shy with her husband's strange new friends, brought their newborn from the dovecote nursery; a boy, a little desklamp of the handsomest design; the new parents shining with pride.

Later, when it was time to leave, Fritillary walked us to the ship.

By the companionway, I asked for his forgiveness, at which he laughed, and told me to entertain no further apprehensions on that score, and that he felt indebted indeed, for while there had been some pretty scrapes, it had never been disagreeable to him to witness the wonders presented one after another belike floats in a parade; whereat we embraced and I boarded, and departed for the upper worlds, and Earth; although we did not hurry about it, but rather began our honeymoon proper, or improper, among the moons of Saturn, repairing from the cabin out into one of Dow's painted meadows, or a moonlit desert, or other more exotic landscape, where our actions gave the works a theme suitable only for gentlemen's drawing rooms, although I believe there were classical elements that saved them from mere salacity.

Then Earth, night, Toulouse, the estate of the Baron de

Peyrescous de Colignac.

We found him slumped asleep in a deep armchair, a fire crackling in the hearth, among the trophies of his collection. I saw a new acquisition: a unicorn's horn with authenticating notes, a magnifying glass beside it. Various others of his prodigies were ranged about us: a basilisk's spherical egg, a petrified book of Noah from before the Flood, a green waistcoat woven from the wool of the vegetable lamb of Tartary . . .

I stood in the shadows, another wonder for the collection. I remembered how affronted I had been, to think that de Colignac should find me bizarre or outlandish, whereas now I was glad of it. How strange, that we should take offence at being called strange. After all, as the reader has discovered, there is infinitely more in the world that is strange than is not.

"De Colignac," I said gently.

He coughed, woke. He winced as he sat straighter in his chair. I noticed he was still strapped up against the injuries done him in the Animalcule House.

I smiled to see him.

He blinked. "Who is there?"

"Well met, my friend." I remained in the shadows.

"Cyrano?" he said. "Is that you?"

"Monsieur de Colignac," Roxane said.

"Mademoiselle Roxane?"

"Mademoiselle no longer."

"What is this?" He struggled out of his seat. "Can it be? This is a dream."

I said, "I may be a figment of your imagination, I am not qualified to judge. But I daresay even you, with your marvels, could never devise a fancy so lovely as my bride."

"Your bride!" Of a sudden, his expression changed. He roared laughter and stood, then fell back into the chair, grimacing with the pain. And laughed again.

"My friends, my friends! If it is a dream, it matters not. You are married! And here we are, together again!"

"For but a short time, alas," I said.

"Ah!" A gallant wink. "Of course I understand. Well, then, I am grateful even for this brief visit."

"Not at all," I said. "My friend, I am here to express my gratitude to you, and to fulfil my promise to replace your snuffbox, ruined by the Master of Secrets."

I set the empty Æolian box on a table. "I hope this will suffice."

It sat there, filling the room with grace.

For a long moment, De Colignac was at a loss for words.

"It will take pride of place in my collection," he whispered at length. "But I must confess the real gift would be to see you, my friend. Will you not come into the light?"

I did so, concerned that he would greet the sight of my crystal wound with shock and fall back in alarm — and to be sure, when he saw me, he paused, and his eyes widened, and he cried, "You are so different!"

Was it my nose after all? Or my newfound happiness? My fine clothes; my fresh coat of paint? Was it the faint shine in my skin acquired from a recent tipple of stellar wine?

"Your sword!" His tone was of utter astonishment. "It is gone!"

There was a little more: he drank to our health; we drank to his; we laughed; we took our fond leave of him, and like to dreams, left to board our flowership — and thence for Mars, chosen as setting for the shared solitude we now desired.

CHAPTER THE LASTH:

THE READ PLANET

Eight months and a half have passed.

The trees native to this world would have made a worthy addition to my volume on the floral prodigies of the universe, were it not that it is almost certainly unnecessary to do so, for likely there is already such a description here, scattered somewhere among the leaves . . .

The tallness of the trees. It is this that one first remarks on seeing them. Their canopies are risen to such heights that in the evenings we hear the rustling and breaking of branches as one of the moons passes by in its orbit, shouldering through the upper leaves.

But it is not their height that makes them so worthy of note.

They are a vegetation so improbable as to prove, in and of themselves, that the universe is boundless in extent; for as Cicero spells out in his *De Natura Deorum*, only in an infinite set of random events can an infinitely unlikely eventuality take place; only with an infinite variety of worlds and manners of life, could these trees have come about.

I wonder if Cicero's writings are here also, scattered among the forest litter.

It has been my custom to take a constitutional in the mornings, strolling through the woods and collecting such leaves as catch my eye, then returning with them, after some hours, to Roxane, in the little cabin we found in one of the paintings aboard the ship.

Her time is near, and she is happily weary, often resting on a broad couch, sipping tea, or abed, reading.

It is always Autumn here, the world red with it, and the leaves I offer her are rotted away to their skeletons, their veins letters, words, sentences. Sometimes they make for brief tales; sometimes little poems of poignant beauty — these last Roxane especially prizes, pressing them in an album, along with any lullabies and nursery rhymes she saves for when Ariette is born. When the spirit moves her, she will hold one of her favourites before the window, their verses cast by the sunlight upon the walls.

After lunch, she sleeps again, and I retire to a clearing behind the house where I keep my desk and writing utensils. I work, the trees that rise to all sides throwing shadow-letters and words on the ground, so it is as if my writing is spilling from my page. Oftentimes, when I am lost for a phrase, a chance arrangement in the litter provides inspiration. Several handsome or grand combinations have come about this way — and it is ever thus for the artist who can but hope to catch such ideas that fall from on high and in all humbleness pass them on.

Sometimes, when I tire of being still, I take a turn among the flowerbeds, their whitish petals patterned with letters. I take pleasure in their literary scent, and pluck a posy — an *anthology*, the word derived from 'a collection of flowers' — which I take to Roxane in the afternoons, when she eats lightly, and retires again to the couch to read, or knit, or perhaps to bed again. It is my habit to kiss her on the forehead and steal from the house, and take another walk, or write a little more, revising the day's work.

Then dinner, and afterwards, in the evenings, we will sit before a fire burning with wordwood, sentences and paragraphs crackling merrily. Sometimes, Ariette will kick, her foot causing Roxane's belly to bulge a little, and I will try to catch it, and laugh, and it is less the hearth than my joy that warms me, this luxurious uxoriousness, this quiet bliss.

It is done.

After a difficult labour, the book is born. I will leave the manuscript here, on Mars, knowing it will be recovered eventually — a far more agreeable process than soliciting publishers, agents, fees, all the rest of it.

I have striven to include such things as a girl needs for a rounded education.

Various philosophies; moral principles; mathematics; botany and zoölogy; astronomy; cookery; music and discussions of the Liberal Arts and the Humanities, especially where they concern inhuman creatures. Matters of an adult nature are touched on, together with some intimate facts about lanterns that may shock some; but I believe half an education is no education at all, and so have laboured to be comprehensive and judicious at once.

Because most children are keen to know the tale of how their parents came together, and how they themselves came to be, that has been the main burden of my tale.

Later, my reader, my daughter, when *you* are born, we will travel again. Travel also is an excellent education. We will revisit de Colignac, and Fritillary and his family, and then set course for the most curious worlds, for oceans of the strangest water, for adventures of the most wonderful stripe.

And later still, daughter, you will come by this book. You will read it, and Fritillary will be your favourite character. At last, you will arrive at this final page, and this line, the final one, in which you will learn that I love you and am devoted to you, and am pleased to inform you that the tale ends as all little girls' tales must, with the solemn assurance that we all lived happily ever after.

Signed,

Your Father

ACKNOWLEDGEMENTS

Thanks to the Serapeum Novel Workshop: Matthew Chrulew, Brendan Duffy, Paul Haines, Keith Stevenson (thanks, too, Keith, for your patience as editor and publisher); the Soggy Parrots Writers' Group: Josie Gibson, Matthew Lovering, Andrew McAliece, Sue McAlister, Erina Reddan, Felicity Turner, Julie Turner; the SuperNova Writers' Group for their crits of the early chapters; Jack Dann and Clare Forster, whose best efforts were greatly appreciated; Dr Miranda Siemienowicz for her crits; Jeremy Shaw for his wisdom; Lee Battersby for his copyedits and enthusiasm; Wendy Waring for her translations of French websites and her many corrections of my French, German and Latin (all errors are mine, not hers); Stephen Higgins for his generous encouragement early on; the excellent Wikipedians (Clio, Sluzzelin, Hydnjo, Jack of Oz, et al) at the Reference Desks for their tireless assistance (all errors are mine, not theirs); Donald Webb, for his guidance in Renaissance science and philosophy (all errors are mine, not his), and his online translation of Cyrano's trip to the Moon; Chris Barnes for his advice on Seventeenth Century weapons (all errors are mine, not his); John Dixon (aka Harrison Bergeron), most excellent friend, for his encouragement and notes; Sam Sejavka, for his mentorship early on; my family, Rose, Alan, Chris, Julie, Julian, Judy, Tom and Harriet, for their unflagging support; Katerina, for her belief. And Harriet, light of my life.

In memory of Paul Haines.

Adam Browne

ALSO FROM

COEUR DE LION PUBLISHING

ANYWHERE BUT EARTH

Award winning independent Australian press coeur de lion publishing presents *Anywhere but Earth* — twenty-nine all new science fiction stories of humanity's adventures out there, anywhere but Earth, featuring original works by Margo Lanagan, Sean McMullen, Richard Harland, and Kim Westwood among a galaxy of new and established Australian and overseas speculative fiction authors.

'Sit down, buckle up, you're heading off world now — trust me, it's going to hurt, but you won't regret it.'
Trent Jamieson — award-winning author of the Death Works and Nightbound Land series.

to buy online or to see our list of stockists go to
www.coeurdelion.com.au

Paperback ISBN 9780987158703
Ebook ISBN 9780987158710

X^6 — a novellanthology

Journey beyond the borders of the real with six all new novellas from the most exciting speculative fiction authors working in Australia today –

Margo Lanagan, Terry Dowling, Paul Haines,
Louise Katz, Trent Jamieson and Cat Sparks.

A Locus Magazine 'Recommended Read' of 2009

'in the race for the "Best Anthology of The Year" title'
Gardner Dozois — *Locus Magazine*
'a resounding six of the best for anyone who still doubts the novella is the ideal length for speculative fiction'
Sean Williams — #1 New York Times bestselling author of *The Grand Conjunction*

Winner - World Fantasy Award for best novella —
'Sea-Hearts' by Margo Lanagan

Winner - Aurealis Award for Horror Short Fiction
Winner - Sir Julius Vogel Award for Best Novella
Winner - Ditmar Award for Best Novella —
'Wives' by Paul Haines

to buy online or to see our list of stockists go to
www.coeurdelion.com.au

ISBN 9780646510354

Blue Tyson, Tom O'Bedlam, Tom Rynosseros; the man from the Madhouse who won Blue and a fine sandship from the tribes. The Coloured Captain who roams the interior, searching out a hidden purpose, the secret knowledge which affects not only Nation but the Dreamtime itself.

In eleven linked stories Tom will uncover his origins, discover what truly happened in the Madhouse and learn the meaning of the three signs that have haunted his life. In Rynemonn, the Blue Captain will come home.

'At once epic and intimate, sweepingly romantic and stirringly adventurous, the Tom Tyson stories stand amongst the very best work that science fiction has to offer. A book to be treasured.'
— Jonathan Strahan

'The only contemporary writer who comes close to that wondrous talespinner, Cordwainer Smith.'
— Locus

ISBN 9780646477879

A decidedly original collection of new Australian speculative fiction

Just what does it mean to be a man now, in the future, the past, other realities?

Find the answer in eleven all new stories by Lucy Sussex, Richard Harland, Geoffrey Maloney, Stephen Dedman, Chris Lawson, Cat Sparks, Robert Hood, Adam Browne and John Dixon, Jacinta Butterworth, and Paul Haines.

'This slim volume features eleven disturbing, humiliating, gratifying,annoying and mind-blasting stories … A brilliant debut collection.'
— Orb Magazine

'The first title from a new Australian small press is an exploration of masculinity through the speculative fiction short story. There is some impressive work here. This is the kind of project which can only be done by the small press, and which makes the small press essential.'
— Aurealis

Featuring the 2006 Ditmar winning novella by Paul Haines 'The Devil in Mr Pussy'

to buy online or to see our list of stockists go to www.coeurdelion.com.au

ISBN 9780646462066

www.ingramcontent.com/pod-product-compliance
Lightning Source LLC
Chambersburg PA
CBHW020930310726
48980CB00007B/704/J

* 9 7 8 0 9 8 7 1 5 8 7 2 7 *